Celebration at Christmas Cove

Celebration at Christmas Cove

CARRIE JANSEN

JOVE

New York

A JOVE BOOK
Published by Berkley
An imprint of Penguin Random House LLC
penguinrandomhouse.com

Library of Congress Cataloging-in-Publication Data

Names: Jansen, Carrie, author.
Title: Celebration at Christmas cove / Carrie Jansen.
Description: First edition. | New York: Jove, 2021. |
Series: A Sea Spray Island romance
Identifiers: LCCN 2021020470 (print) | LCCN 2021020471 (ebook) |
ISBN 9780593438954 (trade paperback) | ISBN 9780593438978 (ebook)
Subjects: GSAFD: Love stories.
Classification: LCC PS3612.I34475 C45 2021 (print) |
LCC PS3612.I34475 (ebook) | DDC 813/.6—dc23
LC record available at https://lccn.loc.gov/2021020470
LC ebook record available at https://lccn.loc.gov/2021020471

First Edition: October 2021

Printed in the United States of America
1st Printing

Book design by George Towne

For those who love the ocean and each other in every season

Chapter 1

MONDAY—DECEMBER 19

"YOU'RE *BUMPING* ME?" AS A WRITER FOR AN ELITE TRAVEL magazine, Celeste Bell had flown around the world over the course of the past seven years and she'd never been bumped from a flight. She knew it was bound to happen sooner or later; she just didn't want it happening *now*.

"We paged you three times, but since you weren't at the gate for initial boarding, we assigned the seat to another passenger," the agent explained.

Celeste wasn't at the gate because she'd had to bring her luggage to the ticket counter after changing out of the ugly sweater she'd worn to her office holiday party earlier that day. This season, she'd been avoiding Christmas festivities like the flu, but since participation was mandatory, she reluctantly donned the most hideous apparel she could find: a fluffy white sweater with a cartoonish fir tree emblazoned across the front. The tree was crowned with a blinking LED-powered star, and a dozen miniature, multicolored sleigh bells were strung from its boughs with silver tinsel. The sweater bore an uncanny resemblance to a yuletide craft Celeste had made in first grade from a paper plate, cotton balls, glitter and various geometric shapes cut from red, green and yellow felt. Oh, the things she did for the sake of her career.

"I get it. Symbolism," Brad, the college intern, remarked. Holding a plastic cup of eggnog in one hand and a chocolate mint brownie in the other, he gestured toward her midsection with his chin. "You chose that sweater because your last name's Bell, right?"

The bells were actually Celeste's least favorite part of the sweater, which was saying a lot. Whenever she walked from her cubicle to her boss's office or to the break room and back again, their jingling made her feel like a Clydesdale—it didn't help that she'd gathered her long, thick blond hair into a high ponytail—and drew increasingly annoyed looks from her coworkers over the course of the day.

She intended to switch wardrobes before a colleague drove her to Logan International Airport, but at the last minute, the magazine's editor in chief, Philip Carrington, tasked Celeste with proofreading Brad's post about the Boston Harbor Holiday Cruise. And by *proofreading* Philip meant *rewriting*. Brad's draft was so poorly structured, it took Celeste half an hour to reword it, and by that time her coworker was threatening to leave without her.

When she arrived at the airport, Celeste wheeled her luggage into the restroom so she could change. She removed her heavy winter coat, scarf and gloves, and she stuffed them into her suitcase, along with her socks and shoes. Then, she opened her smaller carry-on and checked to make sure she had a travel blanket with her before adroitly exchanging her slacks and ugly sweater for a casual slate-blue swing dress and crochet cardigan. Finally, she slid her feet into a pair of canvas sneakers. Celeste intended to be ready for the tropical Caribbean temps the moment she stepped off the plane.

But first she'd have to step *onto* the plane.

———

"ARE YOU SURE THERE AREN'T ANY SEATS LEFT?" IT WAS AN inane question, and Celeste could hear the whine of desperation in her own voice.

"I can book you on the eleven thirty-six flight tomorrow morning. Of course, we'll compensate you for the inconvenience, as well."

Tomorrow was December 20. Technically, Celeste didn't need to be in the Caribbean until first light on December 23. That's when the Christmas carnival—or simply *carnival*, as it was called—for the particular island she was visiting kicked off a daybreak street party known as *j'ouvert*. The trip was a mix of business and pleasure; after taking a couple days to enjoy a much-needed break, Celeste would spend December 23, 24 and 25 attending carnival and describing its highlights in a Christmas Day post on the magazine's blog. That meant if she didn't leave Boston until almost noon tomorrow, she'd squander nearly a full day of vacation. Even so, Celeste cared less about that than she did about the weather forecast, which warned that a nor'easter was brewing. If it followed its projected course, the storm could pack a wallop in terms of snow accumulation, and who knew how that might affect air travel for the next few days. She couldn't risk it.

"Would you check for flights on other airlines, please?"

The agent's fingernails clicked against the keyboard, her expression impassive. After what felt like an eon, she said, "If we hurry, I can book a seat for you on a flight with our partner airline, Island-Sky. There would be a brief layover on Sea Spray Island—"

"I'll take it," Celeste said as the woman continued to speak.

"—then you'd continue to New York City and from there you'd fly nonstop—"

"Yes, thank you, that's what I want to do." Celeste didn't care about the small print; she just needed to get on that flight.

A few more minutes of keyboard clicking and then Celeste was off and running, dodging fellow travelers and circumventing airport vendors as she darted toward Terminal C with her carry-on bag in tow, the sweater inside it jingling all the way. As she ran, she recognized it wasn't really the need for an extra day of relaxation that spurred her on. Nor was it solely that she'd made a professional commitment to cover the carnival. No, what really urged Celeste forward was the fear that if she didn't leave now, *right now*, it would be too late and then there'd be no escaping for Christmas.

And escaping was her primary purpose in volunteering to immerse herself in a Caribbean carnival while all of her coworkers were celebrating Christmas with their families. From the rollicking parades and music to the lively dancing, vibrant costumes and mouthwatering food, the carnival wasn't likely to evoke memories of the calm and cozy but joyful Christmases that Celeste used to celebrate. On the contrary, going to the Caribbean would keep her from thinking about how it had been just over a year since her mother passed away. And it would take her mind off the fact that she was still lonely. Still alone.

Just thinking about not thinking about it made her lungs contract.

Or maybe it was the exertion of tearing through an overly dry, hot and crowded airport trailing an unwieldy piece of luggage in her wake. As fit as she was, by the time Celeste arrived at her gate she was gasping. Light-headed, she hardly registered that the descending ramp the agent directed her to follow led outside to ground level where the plane awaited her on the tarmac.

Celeste skidded to a standstill. The realization hit her like a gelid gust of air: *it's a* prop *plane*. When it came to prop planes or Christmas festivities, it was almost a toss-up as to which distressed her more. Almost but not quite. Pressing her dress flat against her legs so it wouldn't fly up in the wind, Celeste numbly soldiered forward, the end of her ponytail lashing sideways at her face.

She climbed the four ladder-like steps and entered the dimly lit interior where a flight attendant—or was he the copilot?—reached to take her carry-on for stowing while simultaneously issuing safety instructions. Overcome with either regret or relief, Celeste plunked herself into the seat closest to the door, fastened the buckle around her waist and closed her eyes. She was finally on her way.

NATHAN WHITE STOLE A QUICK GLANCE AT THE ONLY OTHER passenger on the plane as she collapsed into the seat across the very narrow aisle from him. Then he took a second, longer look. Considering her short dress and delicate sweater, he assumed she was traveling from somewhere warmer. California, maybe? Slender but athletic—yes, he'd glimpsed her strong, shapely calves—she appeared younger than his thirty-six years, although it could have been her ponytail giving him that impression. Her long nose, slightly pointed chin and the generous spray of eyelashes curving toward her brow created an elegant silhouette.

Ordinarily, Nathan would have at least said hello, since they were literally bumping elbows, but as soon as the woman snapped the metal halves of her seat belt together, she snapped her eyelids shut, too. Fine by him. He had too much on his mind to give her another thought.

As the plane taxied onto the runway and began its arduous ascent into the choppy air, Nathan stared out the window and ruminated on his trip to Boston, where he'd just received good news and bad news, and even the good news was bad news. A continuation of bad news, that is.

Massaging his right temple, he thought back to September. That's when the community center, where he was the executive director, lost the majority of its funding for both its lease and operational expenses. The primary benefactor, a billionaire who owned a summer mansion on Sea Spray Island—or "the island," as the locals referred to it—passed away unexpectedly. Due to several omitted pieces of information, her will—including the legacy gift she'd intended to leave to the center—was deemed invalid. Long story short, her children indicated their intention to withdraw all financial support effective January 1, when the center's five-year lease was scheduled for renewal.

Nathan teamed with the board of directors in a mad scramble to solicit donations, but the major philanthropists in their network either already contributed to other needs at the center or they dedicated their resources to projects elsewhere. The center's last hope was the grant Nathan had applied for earlier in the year from a foundation in Boston. That's why he'd gone to the city this morning.

And that's why he had a headache now.

"As you're aware, the community center's proposal was one of two finalists under consideration. Because both projects were so strong, we had an extremely difficult time choosing between them," the foundation rep had begun by saying, and Nathan held his breath. "We always regret when we have to decline supporting such a worthy cause as yours."

Nathan exhaled, speechless.

"It's unlikely, but if the winning organization forfeits the award for some unforeseen reason, it will be offered to the community center," the rep continued, but Nathan knew the chances of that happening were somewhere between zilch and zip. "So, we'll wait until we've crossed all our Ts with the other finalist before we send you an official written notification of our decision. It should be by December 26. Or December 27, at the latest, since we're required to award the first installment of monies before midnight on December 31. Regardless, we hope you'll apply again next year."

Next year there won't be any need to apply, he thought.

Because the community center was located on Main Street's

prime real estate, in order to secure the five-year lease, the proprietor required a down payment of a full year's rent on January 1. Without their previous benefactor's funding, their organization simply didn't have that kind of liquid assets. They'd be forced to vacate the premises by February 1, and since they had nowhere else to go and virtually no operational budget, Nathan would be out of a job.

He winced. That's where the so-called good news came in. His other purpose for being in the city today was to follow up on an interview for a position as the director of an exclusive community center—more like a club, really—in a wealthy Boston suburb. Even though he'd informed his current employer that he was job searching as a contingency plan, Nathan had felt disloyal when he half-heartedly submitted his résumé last month. But he really hadn't expected it to turn into anything. More accurately, he hadn't *wanted* it to turn into anything; he loved his current position.

He knew he should have felt elated, or at least grateful, when he was offered the position, which came with a salary that was 35 percent more than he was earning now. But he had his eight-year-old daughter to consider. Almost three years after her mother's death, Abigail had finally come out of her shell. In fact, she was thriving. Nathan was concerned that if he uprooted her from their community, she'd withdraw again, as skittish as a hermit crab.

But jobs on the island were scarce and he had a mortgage to pay. He supposed he could sell the house, and he and Abigail could stay at his sister and brother-in-law's inn through the off-season, but then what would happen come spring, when all the rooms were booked? No, living at the inn temporarily wasn't prudent, especially since a better option had all but been presented to him on a platter. Opportunities like this one didn't come around often. He'd have to accept it.

What else can I do? he agonized. If there was another solution, he was going to have to figure it out fast. He had agreed he'd let the

Boston community center know whether he was going to accept their offer by December 26, since they needed the new director to begin in late January. *Some Christmas season this is turning out to be—*

"Ugh," the woman next to Nathan uttered as the plane jounced several times in succession.

He swiveled his head to see her pressing her stomach and almost imperceptibly rocking her shoulders, the way Abigail did when she felt carsick. Nathan reached into the pocket of his suit jacket and produced a mint.

"Thanks."

As she unwrapped it and slid it into her mouth, he took note of her ring finger; it was bare. Not that it mattered—Nathan had given up on having a romantic relationship, much to his sister's disappointment. For two years after his wife died, he wouldn't even consider dating again. However, last spring his sister had made a mission of setting him up with every unmarried woman who lived on the island year-round—all seven of them—but other than geographic location, they shared absolutely nothing in common.

Then, in July, he met a teacher from upstate New York who summered on the island, and the two of them actually hit it off pretty well. But when he brought her home so she could get to know Abigail, his daughter went into high-stress mode. She bit her fingernails down to the quick, started having nightmares and even wet her bed a couple of times. The pediatrician said it wasn't unusual for a child whose parent had died to experience anxiety when the other parent began dating again. Nathan figured since Abbey was old enough to remember her mom, she might have felt like her mother was being replaced. Or, she might have been afraid she'd "lose" her father to a relationship, just as she'd lost her mother to death. Maybe she was simply overwhelmed by the possibility of another change occurring within their family dynamic.

In any case, he decided no relationship with a woman was worth distressing Abbey, who had already been through so much in her young life. His daughter's best interests were his first priority, closely followed by his responsibility to the community. *I can control whether or not I date anyone, but unfortunately, I can't control whether or not the center stays open,* he brooded.

The plane evened out again, and the woman heaved a sigh. Figuring small talk might distract them from their worries, he cleared his throat. "Let me guess, you're headed to the island to take the polar plunge."

She turned to face him. Nathan's vision had adjusted to the lighting enough to notice she had freckles across the bridge of her nose. He couldn't make out her eye color, but she was arching her brow. "Excuse me?"

"Not many people would wear a dress like that to the island in December. I thought maybe you're acclimating to the cold so you'll be ready for our polar bear plunge."

Of course, he didn't really think that, and once he'd said it aloud he realized "a dress like that" might have come across as an insult. Or as a lead-in to a comment about her legs. This day just kept getting worse.

"Is the polar bear plunge a New Year's Day tradition?" the woman asked.

"Yeah, but in Christmas Cove we don't actually jump into the ocean. As a token gesture, we toss a bucket of ice into the heated outdoor pool at the Mayflower Resort, swim a couple laps and then hit the hot tubs. No one wants to kick off the new year with hypothermia."

"Oh," she said flatly without explaining why she was dressed for summer. "You really live in a town called Christmas Cove?"

"Only during the month of December, when our mayor temporarily renames it. The rest of the year it's known as Quahog Cove, which is decidedly less festive," he said. "This must be your first time visiting the island?"

Her lips twitched with a hint of amusement—or was it condescension? "I'm not visiting—I'm on my way to the Caribbean. You know, where the *other* islands are."

"Never heard of them," he deadpanned.

Her mouth fell open, and she tilted her head in apparent disbelief before a smile dawned across her face. Dimples; he knew it.

Another pocket of turbulence vigorously jostled the plane. Nathan leaned forward and lifted the air-sickness bag from the seat pocket in case the woman needed it, but she shook her head.

"I'm not nauseated, just nervous."

"No need to be. Tim and Gary have us covered."

"Who?"

He pointed to the cockpit. "Captain and first officer."

"You know them by name?"

"Sure do."

"Wow, the island is smaller than I realized."

"No, the *plane* is smaller than you realized. They're not local. They introduced themselves when I boarded. When you boarded, too."

Nathan's gibe had an edge to it. It irked him when people didn't pay attention to other people's names, a tendency he associated with urbanites. One more reason he didn't want to move to the city.

"Did they? Ugh. I'm sorry. I guess I was too frantic about catching the flight to remember," she apologized sheepishly. Maybe he'd misjudged her.

"That's all right. I flew with them last month, too, so their names probably stuck with me. I'm Nathan, by the way."

"Celeste." She twisted, reaching her right arm across her body to shake his hand.

Just as their palms touched, the plane dropped precipitously as if it were a toy model that had been knocked off a shelf. Celeste clamped Nathan's fingers in hers like a vise and held on until the fuselage stopped shaking. When it did, he wiggled his arm and wisecracked, "If I say uncle, will you let go?"

FLUSTERED, CELESTE RELEASED NATHAN'S HAND AND ANGLED her torso so she was facing forward again as the plane regained altitude. She hadn't meant to grab him like that, and she was torn between worrying she'd hurt him and hoping he hadn't interpreted her death grip as an attempt at flirting. Not that she would have minded a little flirtation under different circumstances. Just not when the plane was practically in the middle of a barrel roll, and not with someone like Nathan. Sure, his wit was moderately charming, but Celeste didn't even know if he was single. And judging by the enamored tone of his voice and the way he kept saying "we" and "our" when he talked about Christmas Cove, she figured he was a lifelong islander. Small-town guys weren't her type.

Actually, big-city guys weren't her type, either. Celeste didn't date enough to *have* a type. That's because she traveled so often she couldn't keep a plant alive during her absences, much less sustain a romantic relationship. But that was okay. She didn't need or want one, thanks to her father.

Celeste's parents had married against their parents' wishes while her mother was in college and her father was a law school student. Celeste's mother had then dropped out to support her husband while he earned his JD. The plan was for her to go back to school when he was finished, but the day he passed the bar, he left her for a classmate. A week later, Celeste's mother learned she was pregnant, but Celeste's father wanted nothing to do with either of them. His child support payments were spotty at best, and then he died in a snowmobile accident when Celeste was a toddler. Her mother had to work two, sometimes three jobs cleaning other people's homes, watching other people's children and answering other people's phones in order to make ends meet and, eventually, to send her daughter to college.

"Having a degree can open doors and give you more career options than you'd have without an education," her mother had said when Celeste balked at the expense of tuition. "I never want you to feel stuck."

Although she hadn't added "Like I did," Celeste understood that to be the implication. Because she appreciated how hard her mother had worked to ensure Celeste didn't wind up in a similar situation, she poured herself into her studies and graduated summa cum laude. After almost three years of writing for smaller publications, she landed a role with the publisher of the prestigious magazine *Peregrinate*. She had to start over in an entry-level position, but she was grateful to get her foot in the door and immediately began working her way up the ladder.

During one of their very last conversations before her mother died, Celeste assured her she intended to keep earning promotions until she was awarded a coveted senior writer position—and the hefty pay increase that went with it.

"If that's your dream, I'm behind you all the way," her mom had replied, cupping her daughter's chin.

"Thanks, Mom. I'm going to make you proud of me," Celeste promised.

"Oh, honey, don't you know how proud of you I already am? You're *my* dream come true."

Motivated by a desire to honor the sacrifices her mother had made for her, as well as by her own ambition, Celeste traveled so often that even her closest friends had given up trying to schedule time with her. Lately, she chatted with her dry cleaner more often than with any of them. The way Celeste saw it, she was more or less married to her career. Or at least in a committed relationship with it. So, no, she definitely hadn't been flirting with Nathan. Still, since she'd nearly fractured his fingers, she owed him an apology.

"I'm really sorry about that. I travel all the time, but prop planes give me the jitters." Major understatement.

"Where else do you travel, besides to the *other* islands?" He pushed a shock of dark hair off his forehead and then rested his hand on the overcoat folded across his lap. No wedding band.

"Almost everywhere. I'm a writer for *Peregrinate*. It's a travel magazine featuring national and international dream-vacation destinations."

Unsurprisingly, most people thought *Peregrinate* was a publication for birders, so Celeste tried to preempt their confusion by using the magazine's tagline whenever she talked about it.

"That sounds exciting."

It *was* exciting—at first. But after seven years, certain aspects of Celeste's job had begun to lose their shine. Although it was still a thrill to experience new places and cultures, she sometimes found herself longing for the familiarity of a steady routine.

But she worried if she turned down even a single assignment, she'd be relegated to intern status. Then she'd be back to creating content about local attractions for the publication's social media accounts instead of writing about international destinations for its official blog, the way she did now. She'd seen writers demoted before; Philip could be ruthless. But he also rewarded hard work, and recently he'd begun assigning Celeste brief articles for the magazine's print and digital issues, which were considered a big step up from the blog. However, she was still a long way from becoming a senior writer, and even further away from writing about a destination featured on the magazine's cover. So Celeste made it a practice to never refuse an assignment; as a result, she'd occasionally begun to experience symptoms of burnout. Nothing major, but enough to smudge her rose-colored glasses.

Nathan coughed, and she realized he was waiting for an answer even though he hadn't really asked a question. "You're right, it's definitely not your typical desk job. Most of the places I visit are absolutely incredible, and I love learning about different cultures. I love being a writer, too."

"But?"

Oops, her ambivalence was showing. She'd better weigh her words carefully. "But I think people sometimes have a misconception about what it's like to travel for a living. It's not the same as going on vacation and then coming home."

"Yeah, people sometimes make assumptions about what it's like to live on the island year-round based on their summer vacations, too."

"And it's not as wonderful as they think it is?"

As Nathan leaned toward her, she noticed his nose was mildly crooked, as if he'd once broken it. She found asymmetry attractive. "In some ways, it's better. Tourism is the island's bread and butter, which means we work really hard in the summer and play really hard in the winter. But don't tell anyone I said that, okay?"

"Only if you don't tell my editor I implied traveling isn't always what it's cracked up to be."

"What happens in the sky stays in the sky."

As Nathan sat straight in his seat again, Celeste gave him a surreptitious once-over. Although he wore a well-tailored suit, he'd unbuttoned his collar and loosened his tie as if he weren't accustomed to them. Or maybe it was that his shoulders were so broad the shirt felt constrictive.

"Do you commute to Boston for work?"

"No, I work on the island. I'm the director of the community center. We recently lost a major donor, so I was in Boston to, uh, discuss funding." A frown crinkled his forehead and Celeste could guess why.

"How did the discussion go?" she asked softly.

Nathan paused. "It's too early to say."

That was the kind of vague response Celeste gave when she didn't want to talk about something. She wouldn't press it. "Well, I wish you all the best, and I hope you find out soon. Waiting can be agony."

"Thanks." He rubbed his jaw, drawing attention to the cleft in his chin. "Speaking of luck, you're lucky to have a layover on the island. You'll get to see Christmas Cove's Main Street decked out for the holidays. It's the quintessential New England coastline."

"Oh, I'm only stopping long enough to switch planes. I'm catching an incoming connecting flight to New York."

"It's pretty windy," Nathan said, as if she hadn't noticed. "If this keeps up, they'll probably cancel your flight. You'd better count on spending at least a night on the island."

"That is *not* an option." Celeste would swim to New York if she had to.

Just then a gust from below lifted the plane, and for a moment, it felt as if they were suspended, weightless, before the aircraft righted itself, then dropped abruptly and thudded into a bank of low clouds. The ensuing vibration was so relentless Celeste could feel her elastic band slipping down her ponytail. Another gust struck and again they were yo-yoed up and back down. The sudden motion lifted Celeste's feet right off the floor. After that, she and Nathan both clutched their stomachs until the shimmying subsided.

"We're beginning our descent, folks," the pilot announced a moment later. "The ride might get a little bumpy, so hold tight. We'll be on the ground in a few minutes."

Get a little bumpy? It had *been* bumpy, and not a little. Celeste dug her fingernails into her palms, folded her arms across her chest and tucked her fists beneath them, hugging herself to keep from quivering.

"Look, there's Santa's Sailboat in the marina, and Main Street, all lit up!" Nathan was tapping his windowpane like a little boy. He shifted so Celeste could see around him, but she only caught a passing glimpse.

A short distance later Nathan pointed to another line of lights. "We're circling the airport. The captain must want to land from the other direction. That's the runway, see?"

"The runway? It's the size of a postage stamp!"

Nathan cracked up. "Not to worry. Presidents have been coming here on their summer vacations for years. If the runway is big enough for Air Force One, it's big enough for us."

Celeste wasn't convinced. She pinched her eyes shut and blindly tightened her seat belt until her hips hurt. The wings seesawed once, twice, three times before the wheels bumped against the runway and the plane bounced upward. Another bump and they were airborne again, scudding like a rock skipped across water. Two more bumps and they finally touched down for good. As the aircraft careened along the tarmac, it occurred to Celeste that her luggage was going to make it to the Caribbean a day before she did because whether or not her next flight was canceled, there was no way she was getting back on a prop plane tonight.

Chapter 2

WHEN THE PLANE FINALLY ROLLED TO A STOP AND THE CABIN lights came on, Nathan noticed Celeste was trembling. She'd been so sympathetic when he'd mentioned his meeting with the foundation, he wanted to reciprocate her kindness.

"You're going to need this." He handed her his overcoat, half expecting her to refuse it, but she nodded compliantly and put it on.

As if in a daze, she disembarked the plane before Gary had a chance to retrieve her carry-on from stowage. Nathan waited to take it and then had to jog to catch up. As she trudged toward the terminal, she kept her chin tucked to her chest, her ponytail flailing wildly above her head. Nathan's coat hit her legs just below her knees and her hands disappeared within its sleeves. She looked so downcast he had a fleeting urge to wrap his arm around her. Instead, he opened the door and the wind pushed her inside.

Almost immediately they were greeted by one of the five Island-Sky employees who lived on the island. "Hi, Nathan. How was your meeting?"

"Hey, Patty. It was all right, thanks. They said our proposal was strong, and they'll let us know the final outcome sometime after Christmas."

Although Nathan's statement was technically true, he felt a twinge of guilt for misleading her. Not just because he was putting a falsely positive spin on his meeting, but also because Patty, along with all the other residents on Sea Spray Island, had no idea how much was really at stake.

They shouldn't have even known he was meeting with the foundation rep to discuss the grant application in the first place. However, the community center's receptionist, Samantha, had a bad habit of sharing the information she gleaned when screening Nathan's calls, and rumors on the island spread faster than the common cold. So, thirty minutes after the rep phoned last week to invite him to a meeting, virtually everyone on the island, including his daughter, knew he was going to Boston today. Ironically, since Nathan had been at the garage having his tires rotated when the call had come in, he'd been the last person to find out about the meeting—his mechanic told him.

At least Nathan and the board of directors had been able to keep the center's financial crisis under wraps after the death of their major benefactor. The staff and islanders knew he'd applied for a grant, but they had no idea how big or how crucial the monetary award was. And Nathan had no intention of telling anyone else, including his staff, about the outcome of the meeting until he'd called the board president, Mark Gilchrist, tomorrow. In turn, together the two of them would tell the rest of the board members the outcome. *If I'm lucky,* they'll *break the news to the public so I won't have to,* he thought.

Patty squinted at him and puckered her lips to one side, as if she wasn't quite buying his answer, but fortunately, she moved on to question his traveling companion, who still appeared a little peaked.

"You must be Celeste Bell, the passenger scheduled to continue on to New York," Patty deduced. "Sorry, hon, but there aren't going to be any more flights in or out tonight, unless Santa himself shows up with a sleigh and eight flying reindeer."

Once again, Nathan anticipated an expression of dismay, but Celeste merely nodded and asked where the rental car agency was located.

"It's in that direction." Patty jabbed her thumb toward the opposite side of the terminal lounge, which was just a large rectangular area with two vending machines standing back-to-back in the middle of it and a row of blue plastic chairs around the periphery.

Celeste scanned the room. "I'm sorry, where?"

"That way. About two miles up the road."

Nathan winced. Patty could be . . . imperceptive at times. Way too literal. He trusted her intentions were good and she earnestly meant to be helpful by providing Celeste the information for which she asked, even if it wasn't the information she needed to know.

"So then, how would someone rent a car from *here*?" Her tone indicated she'd snapped out of her stupor.

"They'd call Buddy—he's the rental car manager—and he'd pick them up and take them over to the agency. Simple as pie."

"Okaaay." Celeste drew the syllable out as if struggling to keep her patience. "Would you happen to know how I can get Buddy's number?"

"It's taped on the wall above the courtesy phone over there, but he's off-island for the holidays, so if you call him, you'll get a recording telling you to call Beatriz. But since Beatriz has three little ones, she's probably getting ready for bed. You'll have to wait until

her husband comes home from the restaurant before she can drive
over to get you—"

Celeste's complexion was going pink, and she looked as if she
was on the brink of either screaming or sobbing, so Nathan cut in.
"Listen, my sister will be here in a sec to pick me up. She'll be glad
to give you a ride to the nearest inn, okay?"

Before Celeste had a chance to reply, Patty threw in her two
cents. "That's a great idea. I already logged off the computer so I
can bring it home with me, and I've got a few bins to empty before
I lock this place up. How about if we wait until tomorrow morning
to reschedule your itinerary? Whether another plane arrives early
tomorrow or the one you just took continues on to New York, it
wouldn't leave until nine thirty, even under the best of conditions.
I'm an early riser because of my grandbaby, so give me a ring anytime after five thirty and I'll get you squared away. Here's my contact info." She fished a card from her pocket and pressed it into
Celeste's hand. With a wave over her shoulder to Nathan, she tot-
tered toward the office.

"Unbelievable. Absolutely unbelievable," Celeste muttered.

Nathan understood her frustration, but he hoped Patty was out
of earshot. "Welcome to Christmas Cove," was all he could think
to say.

Celeste stared at him as if she was trying to determine whether
he was being sarcastic or sincere. Blue. Her eyes were steel blue,
the color of the ocean on a cloudy winter's day.

She must have decided he was being sincere because she
blinked and asked, "You don't think your sister will mind giving a
stranger a ride? I don't want to inconvenience her."

"For one thing, on an island this size, no one's a stranger for
long." Nathan was being corny on purpose, to lighten the mood.
Celeste rolled her eyes, but a teeny smile flickered across her lips,

and he could tell she was calming down. Either that or she realized she didn't have any other transportation options and decided she'd better be cordial to him. "And I doubt she'll mind since she and her husband are the proprietors of the inn."

"Of course they are," Celeste said wryly. "I suppose when you grow up on a tiny island, you're related to half the population."

"Nah, just to my daughter, sister and brother-in-law. But I didn't grow up on the island—I moved here from Connecticut two years ago."

When the community center's former director had retired, Nathan's sister urged Nathan to apply for the position and relocate to Quahog Cove from a Hartford suburb. She claimed the change would be good for Abigail. Turned out, it had proved every bit as helpful for Nathan.

"Really? You talk about the island as if you've lived here your entire life."

"I *feel* like I've lived here my entire life. You will, too."

"After one night?" Celeste challenged. She was clearly still under the delusion the wind would die down and she'd be able to fly out the next day.

"I wouldn't be surprised. It's a pretty special place, especially at Christmastime." Then, struck by the possibility this might be his last holiday on the island, he added ruefully, "You might just discover you like it here so much you never want to leave."

NOT IN A MILLION YEARS, CELESTE THOUGHT, BUT SHE DIDN'T say it.

As they crossed the terminal, if you could call it that, she caught a glimpse of her reflection in the window. Nathan's coat was ridiculously long on her—he was even taller standing up than he'd appeared sitting—but it was still too short to conceal her unseasonably bare legs and sneakers. She couldn't determine the state of her makeup from that distance, but her hair gave new meaning to "messy ponytail." Maybe she had time to brush it before—

"My carry-on! I left my—"

"I've got it right here." Nathan turned to show it was strapped over his shoulder.

"Oh, thanks. I don't know what I would have done if I'd left my laptop and camera behind." Although, come to think of it, the plane wasn't going anywhere overnight, so she probably could have just asked Patty to ask Gary or Tim to set her bag aside for her until morning. There had to be *some* advantage to flying on such a small plane to such a small airport in such a small town. "Here, let me take it, and I'll give you your coat."

He shook his head; somehow *his* natural waves looked even better windblown than they had on the plane. No fair. "Nah, you keep the coat, and I'll hang on to this until you get your land legs back."

"Land legs?"

"Yeah. You seem a little . . . disoriented."

Celeste laughed and tried to smooth her hair into place. "I think the word you're looking for is disheveled."

Nathan came to a halt and turned to face her. A frown disturbed his forehead with lines and narrowed his deep-set, hickory-brown eyes. He swallowed. Shook his head. "I-I didn't mean it like that. I meant it was a rough flight and you seem kind of shaky."

Touched by his sentiment, she *felt* kind of shaky. Or maybe it was the pronounced dip above his upper lip that was making her legs wobble. How had she missed it? It was even cuter than the cleft in his chin. *Stop staring at him. Three. Two. One. Now.*

"I appreciate your concern, but I'm fine," she managed to say and they continued walking again. "So, how old is your daughter?"

"Abigail's eight. You'll get to meet her. She stays with my sister when I'm away, since it's just the two of us in the house—yup, here they come now." A dark green hybrid SUV pulled parallel to the sidewalk in front of the airport.

They stepped outside and Nathan opened the front passenger-side door so Celeste could climb in. She had to give it to him; he had better manners than most guys she encountered in the city.

"Hi, I'm Nathan's sister, Carol. It's great to meet you," the be-spectacled, smiling, curly-haired driver greeted her, as if Celeste were a long-awaited visitor instead of a total stranger half-dressed in her brother's clothing.

"Hi. I'm Celeste."

"I'm Abigail, but you can call me Abbey. Merry almost-Christmas," Nathan's daughter chirped from the back seat. Was everyone on the island this friendly or was it just his family?

By the time she shook hands with Carol and turned to smile at Abigail, Nathan had put Celeste's bag in the back, slid into the seat behind her and closed the door.

"Hi, Dad," Abigail said, and Celeste heard the rustling of her jacket as she hugged her father.

"Hi, Abbey. Hi, Carol. You've met Celeste? Her connecting flight was canceled so she needs a ride to the inn."

"Wonderful. You'll have your choice of rooms. We only have one other guest, Mr. Williams, staying with us right now. The inn is surprisingly quiet at this time of year. I guess people are too caught up with their Christmas preparations to visit the island, which is a shame because Christmas Cove is positively magical during the holiday season."

"That's what Nathan has been telling me."

Celeste peered out her window, but without streetlights or the moon shining, it was too dark to see anything except for a few stubby trees—probably pitch pine, like on Cape Cod—moving in the wind.

"How was your meeting?" Carol asked her brother as she turned left onto what appeared to be the main roadway, although it was only one lane in each direction.

"It was all right. Nothing definitive yet."

Celeste noticed that Nathan took his avoidance tactics up a notch by quickly switching subjects, asking his daughter about her day at school.

"It was okay, except we had to practice this old-fashioned handwriting that's kind of hard. It's called *cursive*," she said, eliciting laughter from all three adults.

"Where were you headed before your flight was canceled, Celeste?" Carol asked.

"To the Caribbean."

"Nice. Are you getting away for vacation or do you have family there?"

It was a reasonable question to ask, but Celeste bristled. *I don't have any family anywhere,* she thought. "No. I'm primarily going for a work assignment."

"What is it you do for work?"

"I'm a writer for *Peregrinate*. It's a travel magazine."

Carol whistled. "It sure is. It's one of the best. Most people in the hospitality industry would give their right arms to be featured in it. I've heard there's an eighteen-month wait period just to buy space for an ad."

"That sounds about right. It can be a long wait, and ad space is pricey." *If it weren't, I wouldn't be compensated as well as I am.*

As Philip liked to remind the writers, the vast quantity of advertisement and subscription sales, and the high quality of sponsored travel were what separated freelancers from *Peregrinate* staff.

Which was another way of warning his staff that if they quit in order to become independent travel bloggers, they'd never have it as good as they had it at the magazine. His threat was thinly veiled but effective; no one ever resigned. Although, on occasion they did get fired.

"My husband, Josh, travels for work, too. Just domestically though. He's an IT business consultant. Right now he's in North Dakota until the twenty-fourth. His client is a real Scrooge. I hope your employer is letting you get back home in time to enjoy Christmas."

"Mm," Celeste murmured, but otherwise she let the remark hang in the air. If Carol thought her husband's client was a Scrooge, what would she think of Celeste if she knew she'd deliberately planned a trip to avoid celebrating Christmas altogether?

NATHAN WONDERED HOW TO INTERPRET CELESTE'S LACK OF response to his sister's question. Was it that she hadn't heard it, or that she had to work through Christmas but didn't want to insinuate her employer was a Scrooge, too? She was a tough one to figure out.

Abigail filled in the silence. "December is so much fun. It's tied for being my favorite month."

"What's your other favorite month?" Carol asked.

"July. Actually, I love all of the summer months, but in June there's school at the beginning of the month, and in August, we have to go back to school at the end of the month. But in July, there's no school at all, and I get to go bodyboarding almost every day."

After Holly died, Abbey hardly spoke a word to anyone—not even to Nathan—for more than a year, so it both reassured and

amused him to hear her prattling away. Celeste seemed enter-
tained, too, because she asked Abigail why she liked December as
much as July.

"That's easy. First, because of Christmas Countdown. Second,
in December we get a week off school for winter break and some
half days, too. And there's usually at least one snow day."

"Gee, Ab, if you keep talking about school like that, Celeste
won't know how much you love it," Nathan said.

He was proud of his daughter's interest in learning; she didn't
always get the best grades, but she was an avid reader, and she approached her assignments with diligence and an irrepressible curiosity. To him, that was more important than getting straight As.

"I *do* love school most of the year, Dad. I just love bodyboarding
and Christmas Countdown more."

"What's Christmas Countdown?" Celeste questioned.

Abbey leaned as close to the front seat as her seat belt would
allow her to get. "It's this really awesome thing the community center does every day from December 1 to New Year's Day. Everyone
in Christmas Cove gets to go and it's free. There's always a theme
and mostly it's related to Christmas, but we do some things for
Hannukah and just some plain winter things, too." She was talking
so fast that when she paused to take a breath, it sounded like a
gasp. "Samantha—that's the receptionist—she gives the events
these really cute rhyme-y names. So, like, on December 1, it's Smit-
ten Mitten Knittin' Day. That's when the group of ladies—and one
of their husbands—at the center who love to knit teach kids how to
make mittens. Or else they just make the mittens themselves and
give them to the kids, because knitting is hard and a lot of boys
don't want to try it."

Carol and Celeste chuckled, and Nathan would have laughed,
too, but Abigail's gleeful description of the Christmas Countdown

events underscored how important the center was to the community and to his daughter. How was he going to tell the board president what the foundation rep had told him? And how could he tell Abigail they were going to have to move? He hated letting everyone down like this.

Abbey rambled on. "Tomorrow is Make-a-Flake Day. That's when we make snowflakes to decorate the activities room for Souper Supper and the Ugly Sweater Contest. See? Every day it's a fun new thing we get to do together. And sometimes it's outdoors. Like, we go sledding or ice skating. Oh! And there's the Snow Slash Sand Sculpture Challenge. The slash just means one or the other. Because if it doesn't snow by then, we go down to the beach and make sand sculptures instead."

"Wow, that does sound like a ton of fun," Celeste agreed. "You know what? People in the Caribbean are having a big celebration right now, too. They call it carnival. The one I'm going to is on a small island and it only lasts for three days, but on one of the bigger islands, carnival lasts from November to January."

As she explained the cultural significance of carnival and described some of its festivities to his daughter, Nathan was struck by how naturally Celeste was connecting with Abigail. It made him wonder if she had children—although it seemed she would have mentioned that, especially since she'd be away from them at Christmas. Maybe that's why she didn't answer when Carol asked if the magazine was allowing her to get home in time for Christmas. Maybe it was a sore subject because she resented being away from her kids and other family members. Or from her boyfriend. If Celeste had been anyone else, Nathan probably would have asked about her family outright, but she seemed more guarded than most people. He'd have to circle around the subject to satisfy his curiosity.

"Carnival must be amazing, but it's too bad you have to work right up until Christmas morning."

From behind he watched her shoulders lift and drop in a shrug. "I get a couple days of vacation before it starts and the assignment will feel more like pleasure than business, anyway. Besides, it gives me a professional edge. No one else wanted to work over Christmas, so my editor was very grateful I volunteered."

So that's it. She's trying to advance her career. Nathan should have guessed. Celeste was clearly a very bright person, and she was undoubtedly a talented writer, too. But if *Peregrinate* magazine was as renowned as his sister indicated, he suspected promotions didn't come easily. He understood Celeste's ambition, even if working through Christmas wasn't a choice he would have made for himself.

"I wish you could stay another day and write about the countdown. I could give you a tour of the community center and introduce you to everyone," Abigail proposed.

Nathan's chest swelled with pride at his daughter's hospitality. He hoped she wouldn't lose her friendliness if they moved to the city. Although she'd probably have to, as a matter of safety.

"Thanks, Abbey. That's a very nice offer. I don't think it'll work out for me this trip though. Maybe I'll come back in the summer and write about the island then."

Somehow, I doubt it. And even if you do return next summer, Abbey and I won't be here. Neither will the community center, Nathan thought.

"Everyone writes about the island in the summer. This place is crawling with critters," Abigail complained.

Hoping she wasn't referring to the vacationers as "critters," Nathan asked what she meant.

"You know, all the people who write about us. Like the theater critters and the resort critters. Or the food critter who only gave

Mr. Almeda's restaurant three stars even though the *pastéis de bacalhau* he makes should get, like, twelve stars."

Nathan guffawed with relief. "Oh, you mean *critics*."

"What*ever*," Abigail scoffed.

That girl could transform from cheerful child to sullen teenager in a split second, and she wasn't even nine yet. Nathan didn't know how he'd manage to raise her without daily help from Carol, who'd been like a second mother. He shook his head and glanced over at his daughter. She was slumped low in her seat with her arms folded across her chest and a scowl pasted on her face. In that moment, Nathan felt every bit as miserable as Abigail looked.

CELESTE FELT SORRY FOR ABIGAIL AND WISHED NATHAN hadn't laughed like that. She'd clearly been trying to impress Celeste, which probably made her even more embarrassed about using the wrong word. Celeste would know; Philip had ridiculed her word choice more than once.

"I love salt cod fritters, too, Abigail. And your Portuguese pronunciation is a lot better than mine. That's why I just call them salt cod fritters, otherwise no one would know what I was talking about . . . Does Mr. Almeda's restaurant serve caramel custard for dessert?"

"Yeah, but I always order angel wings." Abigail's monotone indicated she hadn't yet recovered from her father's reproach.

"There's a terrific Portuguese bakery on Main," Carol interjected. Celeste got the feeling she was the peacemaker in the family.

The road they'd been traveling was dark and uninhabited except for more trees and clusters of dense shrubbery on one side. Carol said there were dunes leading to bluffs descending to the ocean on the other side, but Celeste couldn't see the water until they crested a hill and Carol stopped to point out the marina below. Presumably because it was winter, only a single, very large boat was still docked in the cove; it must have been the one Nathan had referred to as Santa's Sailboat.

Lights of every color were hung from its riggings, strung across its mast and twisted around its taffrails. From bow to stern, the boat was covered with prismatic designs in every hue imaginable. The vessel was rocked by the wind and waves, and its radiant reflections on the water had a dizzying effect on Celeste. Or maybe it was giddiness she felt. "That's amazing."

"It is, isn't it?" Nathan seemed almost sad.

Abigail didn't. Not anymore. "You should see Sandy Claws in front of the community center, Celeste. He's hilarious!"

It sounded as if Abigail said *Sandy Claws* instead of Santa Claus, and Celeste silently willed Nathan not to correct her pronunciation. "What does he do that's so funny?"

"It's not what he does. It's what he *is*. He's a lobster. Get it? 'Sandy Claws' instead of 'Santa Claus'?"

Celeste laughed appreciatively. "Good one."

"See, Dad? I told you it was funny."

"Yeah, yeah."

According to Nathan, after the island was hit by a severe tropical storm last autumn, he told the kids at the center if they helped the elderly villagers clean debris from their yards, they could choose the community center's Christmas lawn display. To his consternation, the kids' vote was unanimous: they demanded an oversized inflatable lobster, Sandy Claws.

"Not everyone on Main Street is a fan. It's not quite up to the standards for décor, if you know what I mean."

"Dad says it looks like something a Brobdingnagian would use for a floatie in the cove," Abbey grumbled. The *Gulliver's Travels* reference made Celeste burst out laughing again. She was really starting to like this family. "Can we take the long way through Main Street so Celeste can see him?"

"No, not tonight."

"But, Dad, it won't even take five minutes. Please?"

"No, Abbey. Celeste wants to get to the inn so she can unwind from her trip."

Celeste appreciated Nathan's suggestion because she could hardly wait to take a shower and then hurl herself into bed, but she could hear how much this meant to Abigail. When she was a kid, Celeste loved Christmas lawn displays, too. The tackier and brighter, the better.

She surprised herself by saying, "That's okay. We can take the long way through Main Street since I've never been to Christmas Cove before."

She didn't add, *And I'll probably never be here again.*

"Are you sure? You don't have to."

Celeste wavered. Maybe she'd spoken too soon. She glanced back at Abbey. It was too dark to see her expression but her stiff, still posture was a giveaway; she was holding her breath. Celeste couldn't change her mind now.

"Sure, I'm sure."

"Yes!" the word whooshed from Abigail's mouth. "It'll be worth it, I promise."

Celeste had her doubts, but in the face of the young girl's elation, what was five more minutes?

Chapter 3

"THAT'S THE PORTUGUESE BAKERY I TOLD YOU ABOUT, CE-leste. Their egg tarts are out of this world."

As they drove along the town's one-sided brick-paved Main Street, Carol also pointed out a bookstore, two coffeehouses, three art galleries and numerous boutiques, bars, restaurants and specialty shops. Originally houses, the buildings stood shoulder to shoulder in a cozy mismatch of heights, widths and designs, all facing the cove. Aglow with white Christmas lights, the storefronts were tastefully garnished with garland, ribbons and wreaths—a quiet contrast to the sailboat's explosion of color in the water opposite them. Except for a few stray boughs and a sign that had come unhinged in the wind, Main Street was postcard perfect, the definition of quaint.

No matter where else Celeste traveled, there was something about coastal Massachusetts that held a special place in her heart. Probably because every summer from the time she was eight until the year she'd graduated college, Celeste and her mother spent a week on Cape Cod, beachcombing, bike riding, sunbathing and swimming. And browsing in shops that looked a lot like Christmas Cove's.

I can only imagine what Mom must have given up having or doing for herself in order to afford to give me a vacation every year . . . Celeste furtively dabbed an unexpected tear from her cheek with the sleeve of Nathan's coat. How much longer was this trip down Main Street going to take, anyway?

As if reading her mind, Abigail announced, "The community center's right down there, at the very end of the stre— Hey, Sandy tipped over! He must have come untied. We've got to fix him, Dad, or he'll blow away. Quick! He's going to get impaled on something! He's going to p-p-pop!" Abigail whined.

"Could you pull over here, Carol?" Nathan calmly requested. "You can take Celeste up to the inn. Abbey and I will batten down the lobster and walk home from here."

Carol stopped the car but argued, "The two of you can't handle this on your own. Let me get Celeste settled in, and I'll be back in a jiff."

Is this really happening?

Aside from boarding another prop plane, the last thing Celeste wanted to do in this weather was wrestle with a gigantic inflatable lobster, while wearing a summer dress, in public. But with Abigail so distraught and no one else in sight, of course Celeste insisted she wanted to help, too.

Because the lobster took up most of the space on the narrow strip of lawn in front of the center, Celeste stood on the sidewalk, marching in place to keep the wind from making icicles of her legs. A few feet away, Abigail burrowed her face into Carol's coat while Nathan surveyed the damage. Apparently, two of the tether lines had come loose, so the colossal crustacean was sprawled on its side, bobbing up and down against the ground with the wind. It was only a matter of time until it pulled completely free of its fetters.

"The dirt's frozen. I can't pound the tether spikes in tonight. I'll unplug it so we can take it inside."

"But, Dad, if you unplug him, he'll deflate. Can't you at least *try* to put the pegs back in?"

To Celeste's relief, Nathan reasoned, "We can always inflate him again, Abbey. It takes three minutes. But if I don't secure him well enough tonight and the wind—"

"You're right," Abigail interrupted, as if she couldn't bear to hear her father describe Sandy's demise. "We've got to get him inside."

Nathan unhooked the intact tether lines at their bases before going to unplug the decoration. Meanwhile, the women held on to the slack lines dangling from the sides of the shellfish in order to prevent the entire creature from taking off after Nathan loosened the other ropes.

As she struggled to keep her side of its carapace pinned down, Celeste studied the lobster. Sandy was probably twelve feet in length from head to tail fin, and his claws and antennae extended another four feet beyond that. Equipped with internal lighting, the decoration changed colors—from red to yellow to green to blue to purple—and blinked off and on at varying intervals. No wonder Abbey liked him. And no wonder the Main Street business owners didn't.

When Sandy's light blinked off and didn't blink on again, Celeste knew Nathan had pulled the plug. The lobster promptly collapsed into a limp heap, and Nathan unzipped the base and removed a couple of sandbags, which he picked up to take inside. Celeste and Carol loosely folded the plastic in half and then in half again, like a sheet. It was heavier than it looked, so they each took a side and lugged it up the walkway.

"Fa-la-la-la-la-la-la-la-*lob-ster*," sang Abigail, happy again as she held the door open for them to pass through.

Her humor and manners were just like her father's, and now that it was bright enough to see her better, Celeste realized Abigail had her dad's big brown eyes, too. But her hair was straighter and two shades lighter than his, and her nose was small and upturned, probably more like her mom's. Celeste assumed Nathan and Abbey's mother were divorced, since he'd mentioned it was only him and Abbey in their house. It made Celeste wonder where his ex was. Nathan had said the only people he was related to in Christmas Cove were his daughter and sister. Did that mean he didn't consider himself related to his ex-wife or that she didn't live on the island?

"Let's put this stuff in the events room so no one trips over it in the morning," Nathan said and led them through the lobby.

The inside of the community center was bigger than its exterior suggested. There was a window facing the cove that was two stories tall and ran the width of the entire wall. The lobby had an open floor plan that included a centrally located reception area, numerous oversize leather couches and chairs, a large gas fireplace, restrooms and a staircase leading to the second-floor interior balcony. Because Nathan hadn't turned on all the lights, Celeste couldn't see down the hall, but she figured there was a kitchen close by.

"Something smells good."

"The teen cooking class made meat loaf today. They passed out samples. It smelled better than it tasted, trust me," Abigail tattled. She skipped ahead of them into the events room, which was also bordered with large windows and contained dozens of round tables and stacks of chairs all pushed to one half of the room because, as Nathan explained, the preschoolers had a dance class in the other half in the morning.

"We should set this in the corner, where it'll be out of the way," Carol suggested.

She released her side before Celeste let go of hers, causing the lobster to partially unfold as it spilled from Celeste's arms. Splayed

open on the floor, its pincer and crusher claws each clasped deflated white rectangles, which Celeste had mistaken for snowballs
when he'd been lying facedown outdoors.

"What's Sandy got in his claws?" she asked.

"Two lists—you know, to keep track of who's been good or bad.
Except Dad made us cover the word "naughty" with white paint and
then write "nice" over it with black duct tape," Abigail told Celeste
when she asked.

That sounded like Nathan, from what Celeste had observed so
far. Celeste could just hear him claiming there were only nice people in Christmas Cove, so there was no need for a naughty list, not
even a pretend one. She tried to suppress a snicker.

She must have failed because Nathan defended himself. "That's
because I was worried it might scare the little kids to have a giant
lobster waving a naughty list at them whenever they came to the
center. I have to answer to their parents, you know."

"Oh. I guess I can see how that might make some children
afraid to come inside."

"Or make them afraid of lobsters," Abbey added. "And then they
wouldn't want to go to the beach."

"Or to half the restaurants on the island," Carol chimed in, and
they all cracked up. Especially Celeste.

*This has been one of the most bizarre layovers I've ever experi-
enced,* she mused. But it wasn't the worst. Not even close.

ALTHOUGH CELESTE HAD SEEMED PRETTY EASYGOING ABOUT
it, Nathan felt guilty she'd had to help them wrangle the lobster
into the center. So as they crisscrossed their way up the hill behind
Main Street, Nathan told Carol not to bother dropping Abigail and
him off at his house—they'd walk from the inn.

"Good idea. You can come in, and I'll heat up leftover lasagna for you and Celeste since I'm sure you didn't have supper."

"How far away do you live?" Celeste asked Nathan.

"Right around the corner."

"That's convenient."

He cringed. For some reason, Nathan didn't want Celeste to think he was completely incompetent in the kitchen, even though he was. If it wasn't for Carol, he and Abbey would subsist on nothing but scrambled eggs, pizza and whatever he could toss on the grill, which he used year-round.

"Here we are. The Inn at the Cove. Also known as home sweet home," Carol announced as they turned into the driveway.

Nathan was glad to see the garland he'd draped on the picket fence was still intact, and so were the lights he'd fastened to the doorframe and awning of the large, white, classic colonial inn, as well as those he'd wrapped around the railings of the widow's walk.

"Ooh, how beautiful," Celeste gushed. "I've always loved how colonial-revival-style homes like these are so classic and stately. Especially yours. It's very inviting. I can't wait to go inside."

"Thank you. That's exactly how I want our guests to feel."

Nathan could tell Carol was pleased; she poured herself into creating an elegant, warm and welcoming setting for her guests. As they got out of the car and ambled under the trellis and up the walkway, she explained the turn-of-the-twentieth-century inn was originally a sea captain's home. Although it had undergone several external and internal renovations, Carol and each of the previous proprietors made sure the changes were aesthetically consistent with the house's history and blended in with the neighborhood.

Inside, Nathan handed Celeste's bags to her, and she followed Carol upstairs to choose a room before supper. Abigail charged off to set the table, so Nathan retreated to the living room to stoke the

fire in one of the first floor's two fireplaces. When Abigail still believed in Santa, Nathan used to hang stockings from all four
mantelpieces—two upstairs, and two down—at the inn, as well as
from the one in their own house. Returning the poker to its stand,
Nathan wondered how many memories of Abigail's childhood would
fade once they moved away from Christmas Cove. A spate of de-
pressing thoughts flooded his mind.

"Did you hear me, Nathan?" Carol seemed to appear out of the
blue. "Celeste is changing. When she comes down, why don't you
keep her company while I prepare supper?"

He couldn't be quite sure, but Nathan suspected his sister might
be playing matchmaker. It wouldn't have been the first time. But if
he moved to Boston, it might be the last . . .

"Okay."

He popped his head into the annex built onto the far end of the
room to check if Arthur Williams was lounging in his favorite chair
with a book in hand, as usual. Nope, he must have turned in early.
Nathan ambled back toward the fireplace and sank into an oversize love seat so he could check the weather on his phone. As he
suspected, the winds were nearing gale force and the airport would
officially remain closed until further notice. Next, he texted his
friend Clint, who worked at the ferry dock. Same story, different
mode of transportation.

Pocketing his phone, Nathan caught sight of Celeste in the
doorway. She'd changed into black leggings and a black cotton top,
which didn't appear any thicker than the dress she'd had on earlier,
but at least the leggings reached her ankles. Loose and smooth, her
locks reminded Nathan of the color of dried dune grass in autumn,
and her lips were rosy with fresh lipstick. *Dazzling,* he might have
called her, but her expression was more glower than glowing. As she
surveyed the Christmas tree just inside the room, she held her arms

stiffly at her sides, her hands balled into fists. What was wrong? Did she prefer monochromatic lights? Was she allergic to Fraser fir? Nathan had no idea.

"C'mon in and warm up."

She crossed the room but didn't take a seat. "I almost forgot you need your coat back. I hung it on the rack in the hall."

"Thanks. I'm sure Carol has a jacket you can wear tomorrow that will fit you better than mine does."

"That's okay. I made it from the terminal to the plane without getting frostbite today. I can do it again tomorrow."

She honestly believes there's going to be a flight out tomorrow? Either she was really naïve or she really, really wanted to get off the island. Probably both.

"Yeah, about your flight . . ." He couldn't bring himself to say the words, but she read between the lines.

"What? You don't think it will be canceled, do you?" She looked like a six-year-old who had just been told there was no such person as Santa Claus.

"Sorry, but yeah, I do. The airport's closed until further notice."

She paced a couple of feet in each direction, drumming her chin with her fingers. "Okay then, can I borrow your phone? Mine died so it's charging. I should schedule a cab for the morning before it gets too late."

"A cab? This is an *island,* you know. You can't leave by car." It was a feeble joke, but her anxiety was throwing Nathan off. Kind of like when he'd first met her on the plane.

She huffed exactly the same way Abigail did when she was exasperated. "I *know* it's an island. I'm going to take a cab to catch a ferry first thing tomorrow morning so I can fly out of Boston in the afternoon. I'm sure a 737 can handle a little turbulence better than that puddle jumper we flew in tonight."

Maybe it was because his headache hadn't fully subsided, but Celeste's statements irked Nathan on so many levels he was momentarily dumbfounded.

First of all, the *little* bit of turbulence had made her so nervous she'd practically crushed his fingers to dust—and the wind speeds were forecasted to increase overnight.

Second, there was something about the way she'd said *puddle jumper* that made him want to tell her to get off her haughty high horse.

Third, a cab? Not here. Not in winter.

Fourth, a ferry? In a *nor'easter*?

Okay. Those last two were unfair. Nathan would have come up with the same cab-and-ferry solution when he'd lived off-island. He knew better now. Anticipating how disappointed Celeste was going to be—and knowing he'd have Carol's fury to face if he was impolite to a guest—he decided to break the bad news to her gently.

"Okay, so here's the thing. Cabs don't run on the island during the off-season. There's not enough demand. And most of the people who work as independent drivers during the summer have different jobs in the winter. However, I'm more than happy to take you to the ferry dock . . ." He paused, gathering courage to add, "when it opens again."

He didn't get the chance.

"Great, thanks! I really appreciate it."

Having put such a brilliant smile on Celeste's face, Nathan regretted having to wipe it off again. "Unfortunately, I just texted a pal who works at the dock, and he said the ferry is out of service until the wind advisory warning expires. And the wind is going to pick up overnight, so . . ."

"Seriously?" Celeste shoved her hands against her hips. "Why do you people do that?"

You people? What does she mean by you people? This time Nathan wasn't cutting her any slack. "Do what? Schedule a nor'easter to ruin your Caribbean travel plans? I don't know. I guess we're just rude." *Like you're being right now.*

She threw her arms in the air and flicked her fingers apart as if *she* were the one who'd been insulted. "I wasn't referring to the storm. I was referring to the way Patty told me all about the car rental place and it was closed. And the way you just said you'll take me to the dock, but the ferry it isn't even running. Why get my hopes up like that? Why set me up to believe you're going to help me get off this island and then pull the rug out from under me? Doesn't anyone around here ever give a straight answer?"

The words shot out of Nathan's mouth so fast he couldn't stop them if he tried, which he didn't. "All right, you want a straight answer? Here's a straight answer. There is absolutely and positively no way you're getting off *this island* tomorrow, unless the Coast Guard shows up in a three-hundred-and-seventy-eight-foot cutter to rescue you. And even *that's* iffy." He crossed his arms and pushed back against the cushion in smug satisfaction.

"Thank you. Thank you very much. That wasn't so difficult, was it?" Celeste asked sarcastically, but her voice wavered and she quickly dipped her chin so her hair obscured her face.

Whoa. He hadn't expected *that*. Was she near tears because she wasn't going to be able to leave the next day or because Nathan had clearly taken so much pleasure in *telling* her she wasn't going to be able to leave the next day? Either way, he felt like a jerk. After all, she had a point. Both he and Patty could have spared her some disappointment if they had cut to the chase.

"Listen, I understand it's upsetting that you can't leave, and I didn't mean to add to your frustration. What I was going to say was I'll be happy to take you to the ferry or to the airport as soon as they're back in service."

For a moment, Celeste didn't say anything. Then she sniffed and sat down on the edge of the love seat. Instead of meeting Nathan's eyes, she stared into the fire. "I'm sorry. But I really don't want to be stuck here during—never mind. I just need to get to the Caribbean as soon as I can."

Mentally telling himself not to get offended by her use of the phrase *stuck here*, Nathan asked, "When is it you said the carnival starts? The twenty-third?"

"Daybreak on the twenty-third, yes. Which means I need to arrive by the evening of the twenty-second, at the latest."

"That's good. Today's only the nineteenth. Maybe by tomorrow night, the ferry will be running again. And even if you don't leave until the day after that, you'll get to the Caribbean in plenty of time."

"I guess." Celeste stretched her legs out so her toes were closer to the fire. "I was looking forward to enjoying a few days of vacation before carnival, that's all."

Nathan could sympathize. It seemed like whenever he tried to schedule time off, some urgent problem at the community center interfered with his plans. The last vacation he'd taken was in late June, when he and Abigail went camping in New Hampshire, but they had to cut their trip short by three days because the community center's storage annex flooded. Even though Nathan tried to make it up to her by pitching a tent in the backyard for the duration of the week, Abbey was inconsolable. But maybe Celeste would be open to the idea of a sort of Sea Spray Island staycation.

"There's no reason you can't relax while you're here, is there? Our weather isn't exactly tropical, but most people consider Christmas Cove to be a 'dream vacation destination,' worthy of *Peregrinate's* pages. You should see how many people flock here in the summer."

"But it's *not* summer. It's almost Christmas." Celeste emphatically gestured toward the tree with one hand and the fireplace with the other, her lower lip trembling. "And Christmas is when people spend time together with their loved ones. That's why it's so important for me to get—" She again stopped short and shook her head, but it wasn't necessary for her to finish her sentence.

Nathan finally understood. How could he have been so dense? She urgently needed to get to the Caribbean because she wanted to spend Christmas with someone there. Her boyfriend. It had to be, since she already told Carol that that wasn't where her family lived. The realization should *not* have bothered Nathan as much as it did.

From the doorway, Carol announced supper was on the table.

Rising, Celeste turned toward her. "Thanks for going to the trouble, but I'm afraid I need to call it a night. I'm beat."

Nathan felt pretty worn out himself. After he, Carol and Abbey bid Celeste good night, he shoveled down his meal, walked home with his daughter and tucked her into bed. She claimed she was getting too old to be tucked in, but that was one ritual he wasn't going to give up. Not yet.

As he paused at the door to switch off her light, Abigail said if the airport remained closed all day, she was going to invite Celeste to the Make-a-Flake activity the next afternoon. Nathan tried to think of a diplomatic way to say that it didn't seem like a good idea, since Celeste seemed so aggravated. "She might want to just relax tomorrow."

"Christmas Countdown *is* relaxing. And after she goes to an event in person, she'll want to write about it for her magazine." Abbey yawned and pulled the blankets up to her chin. In a drowsy voice, she added, "Then we'll be famous and all the rich people who read about Christmas Cove will make donations to the community center. And you won't get so many headaches anymore, Dad . . ."

Too choked up to utter "sweet dreams," Nathan stood in the threshold a long while, listening to his daughter breathe and racking his brain for a way to keep the community center open.

Chapter 4

CELESTE ROLLED OVER IN BED AND REACHED FOR HER PHONE to check the time. Six forty-eight. Patty would have been up for more than an hour. Sinking her head into the pillow again, she couldn't decide whether to call her for an update or check the airport website and weather online.

Rubbing her eyes, she remembered a meteorologist she'd dated briefly who'd told her the media was encouraged to create the most dramatic weather headlines possible. *Millions in the path of catastrophic triple-threat storm.* Or, *One-fourth of country under siege by historic heat wave.* Even, *Gorgeous summer conditions expected to give way to stunning sunsets.* According to him, forecasts were more about ratings than reality. As a writer, Celeste could appreciate the use of hyperbole, but this morning she needed a report that erred on the side of understatement. Figuring Patty was a better choice for that, she slid Patty's business card off the nightstand and entered the number into her phone.

"Good morning, sunshine," Patty answered before Celeste identified herself. She wondered if the airline employee was expecting someone else or if that was her standard phone greeting when anyone called her at this hour. An infant was babbling in the background. "Did you get a good night's rest? Most guests say the inn's mattresses are the most comfortable they've ever slept on."

"I can believe that." The bedding was so comfy that even though her mind was awhirl with anxiety about the approaching nor'easter, Celeste had dozed off within three minutes of lying down the previous evening. The only thing that had disturbed her otherwise perfect slumber was a vivid, recurring dream of being visited by Christmas carolers whose singing caused her to retreat into her bedroom, hide under the covers and block her ears with her hands. "I slept like a baby."

Patty chuckled. "Usually people who say they slept like a baby have never had one. Isn't that right, my little dumpling? It is, isn't it? Isn't it?"

Celeste was taken aback until she realized Patty's questions were intended for her grandchild, who giggled in response. "Nathan told me the airport was closed until further notice, but I thought I'd check in with you personally since you must have the most recent information on its status."

"Well, judging from the sound of the locust tree branches banging against my rooftop, I'd say the wind speed has increased a good ten to fifteen knots, so my best guess is that the airport's still closed to all incoming and outgoing flights."

Her best guess? Celeste was expecting a more definitive answer. "Is there a way you could confirm that for certain?"

"Sure, once Jerome calls me."

After her exchange with Patty the evening before, Celeste should have anticipated she'd need to ask follow-up questions. And now that she wasn't exhausted, she found the older woman's circuitous communication style marginally amusing, but she still wished she'd had a shot of caffeine before engaging in this conversation. "Who's Jerome?"

"He's the IslandSky employee who updates our system and gives me the verdict after he receives word from Port Authority. Since he hasn't called me, I assume he hasn't heard from the commissioner." Patty made a loud raspberry noise, presumably to her grandchild, before adding, "Then again, Jerome's a late riser, so it's doubtful he's checked the airport's e-mail or voice mail yet. I can give you his number if you'd like to speak to him yourself."

"No, that's okay. I don't want to wake him." *Or to waste my time.* Unfortunately, Celeste could hear the wind howling, and she deduced Patty was right; the wind had intensified overnight. "I'll keep checking the website."

"Okay, but feel free to call me back anytime. And now that I've got your number, I'll let you know the minute I find out we can put you on an outgoing flight."

It won't be a minute too soon. Celeste sighed as she phoned her original airline, navigating through so many automated phone menus that they made Patty seem straightforward by comparison. After discussing her options for rebooking her flight to the Caribbean once she was able to either return to Boston or continue to New York, she got up and crossed the room to lift the window shade.

The sun had risen, but the sky was tarnished with clouds. From this vantage point—higher than the roof of the smaller house across the street—she had a clear view of the wind-whipped whitecaps peaking throughout the silvery-gray waters in the cove. Given how tempestuous the seascape appeared, the outlook was bleak that she'd be able to leave the island any time today. So what was she going to do to pass the time?

She shook her head as she recalled Nathan asking "There's no reason you can't relax while you're here, is there?"

It was a perfectly reasonable suggestion, and Celeste was chagrined by what must have seemed like her whiny response. Actually, she was embarrassed by her entire interaction with Nathan in the living room, including going off on him about the way he and Patty communicated and sniveling about being "stuck" on the island. On the surface, her behavior seemed petulant, even to herself.

But she knew it wasn't the delay in her travel plans that had set her off. And it wasn't really anything Nathan had said in particular, either. It was that as she'd walked into the living room and glanced at the tree, she'd spotted an aqua-colored, blown-glass starfish, speckled with flecks of gold. It looked almost exactly like the one her mom had purchased from a Cape Cod artist the summer Celeste graduated from college.

It was her mother's tradition to buy an ornament every year and present it to Celeste when they decorated their tree. She'd always enclose a short, unsigned note of advice or endearment with the gift. That Christmas—no doubt in response to Celeste's concern about whether or not she'd succeed in her career—her mother had written, "You're already a star!"

When she noticed a similar starfish on the tree yesterday evening, it struck Celeste that she'd never receive another word of encouragement from her mom again. She'd never ever be able to offer one to her, either. Celeste had learned to cope with countless thoughts like that during the past year, with varying levels of success. But last night it had taken every ounce of her willpower to hold back her tears and try to converse with Nathan like a semireasonable adult.

The similarity between the ornaments was a peculiar coincidence. A one-off that wouldn't happen again. But the fact was that Celeste could have just as easily dissolved into tears if she had smelled gingerbread baking or heard "What Child Is This" playing in the background. *So yes, there* is *a reason I can't relax while I'm here,* she silently answered Nathan's question again. *It's because I'm afraid every time I turn a corner, I'll be reminded of how much I miss Christmas with my mom.*

And for that very reason, Celeste decided she might go for a walk to the beach, but other than that, she'd spend the day stowed away in her room. However, right now her stomach was growling. When Carol brought her upstairs last evening, she'd mentioned she was going to make waffles in the morning. Certainly Celeste could keep it together long enough to enjoy her favorite breakfast food, couldn't she?

FOR THE FIRST TIME IN HIS HISTORY AS THE DIRECTOR OF THE community center, Nathan dreaded going to work. He didn't want to call Mark Gilchrist, schedule a board meeting or face the staff and villagers knowing what he knew. Nor did he particularly want to deal with the limp oversized lobster laying in the activities room. *But at least I won't be letting Sandy Claws down—he's already deflated,* he thought wryly.

Of all the mornings *not* to have a headache, it had to be today, so he couldn't even legitimately call in sick. He sat up in bed, powered on his laptop and for the umpteenth time reviewed the center's financial reports, hoping to find money hidden somewhere or an accounting error in their favor. Nada. *That's what we get for electing such a competent treasurer.*

Then he conducted yet another online search for last-minute donors. There were always at least a few corporations or individuals

who wanted to make sizable end-of-the-year donations for tax purposes, if for no other reason. He had no expectation that he'd ever
be able to secure the amount of funding the center had received
from their previous benefactor. But if he could pool a half dozen
substantial contributions, it might be enough for the down payment
on the lease, which would buy them more time to apply for additional grants and to appeal to donors in the new year.

He came up with a handful of prospects he hadn't appealed to
yet, so his efforts weren't a complete waste of time. But Nathan
wasn't a natural fundraiser—he was more used to doing things for
other people than asking other people to do something for him—
and he was concerned about "making the ask" on his own. Especially since there wasn't enough time to set up in-person meetings
and he'd have to request donations over the phone, a huge no-no for
gifts this size.

He knew he really should involve the board president, Mark Gilchrist, in the solicitation process, but that would have meant he'd
first have to tell him the center hadn't received the grant. And Nathan hoped he could counterbalance that bad news with an announcement about a few sizable, last-minute donations that would
keep their lease afloat. It was a long shot, but what else could he do?

He put his laptop on the nightstand and lay back down in bed. It
was only seven-fifteen. He could steal another half hour of sleep.
Maybe when he woke up again, he'd realize he'd been having a nightmare and the community center would actually be rolling in money.

But before he even closed his eyes, Abigail came bounding into
his room, moaning that she'd left her backpack at the inn. "I totally
forgot to do my math homework."

"You *forgot* to do it?" He propped himself up on his elbows. "Or
did you neglect to do it on purpose since you were anticipating a
snow day because of the nor'easter?"

"No, Dad. I forgot to do it accidentally, I promise. I'm not going to skip doing my homework because of a snow day until tonight." She clapped her hand over her mouth. Busted.

"Don't count your flakes before they fall," he warned. He supposed he could allow Abigail to go to his sister's alone, but he didn't want her dawdling at the inn. "Go get dressed and we'll jog over there."

As she disappeared down the hall, Nathan threw the blankets to the side and shifted his legs to the floor. It was a start. He rubbed his eyes with the palms of his hands and then got up and pulled on a pair of jeans and a flannel shirt. Good enough. Should he shave? Nah. He didn't intend to go inside the inn and it wasn't as if he'd cross paths with anyone on the sidewalk this early in the morning.

When he entered the kitchen, Abbey was zipping her jacket. Nathan did a double take. She had brushed her hair into an off-centered ponytail, high on her head. Apparently, she lacked the dexterity to gather it all because strands were randomly sprouting out around her face and trailing down her neck. She looked as if she'd changed her mind halfway through the styling process.

People often told Nathan that Abbey bore a resemblance to him, but he couldn't look at her wide mouth and upturned nose without seeing Holly. Naturally, he thought their daughter was beautiful, inside and out. But he didn't want the other kids making remarks about her messy appearance that would upset her. Maybe she'd accept Carol's help with her ponytail.

He tested the waters with an objective remark. "I see you're doing something new with your hair."

She grinned at him. Sometimes he felt like she was growing up too fast, but when she gave him a gap-toothed smile like she was doing now, he realized just how young she still was. "It's like Celeste's. I think her hair is really pretty, don't you?"

Nathan dodged the question, answering, "Oh, yeah, now that you mention it, I can see you've got the same style going on." He smiled and pressed the button on the coffeemaker, hoping Abbey wouldn't ask him again what he thought of Celeste's appearance. Of *course* he thought she was physically attractive, but that wasn't something he wanted to discuss with his daughter. The sixty seconds it took to brew a cup felt more like an hour.

"Can you take that with you?" Abigail asked when it was done.

"Sure." As Nathan lifted his overcoat from the rack to get his shorter peacoat that was hanging beneath it, he noticed a faint whiff of perfume. It smelled like . . . lilies? Gardenias? It smelled like *Celeste*.

Abbey tapped her foot. "You ready?"

"You're sure in a hurry. How much homework did the teacher give you, anyway?"

"Only two pages of comparing fractions. But Aunt Carol told me she's making poached eggs and waffles with sautéed apples for breakfast, so I need to get there before they're all gone."

She was out the door before Nathan could tell her they were only going to grab her things and come right back. It would have been a futile warning, anyway; when Carol and Abigail teamed up against him, Nathan didn't stand a chance.

Technically, the inn was a bed-and-breakfast, so his sister didn't need to offer any meals except breakfast. However, as Carol often explained, she loved to cook as much as she loved to eat. And while she loved to *cook* alone, she didn't love to *eat* alone, which she had to do frequently, since her husband traveled for work. So she always invited the guests—as well as Abigail and Nathan—to join her for as many meals as they wanted to. And Abigail *always* wanted to, since Carol was a much better chef than Nathan was.

When they let themselves into the inn's kitchen through the

back door two minutes later, Carol sent Abigail to the dining room table to do her math, saying she wasn't ready to start the waffles yet. Arthur didn't usually come downstairs until almost eight, and she had no idea when Celeste would rise.

We'd better get out of here before she does, Nathan thought. Judging from the sky and the wind as they walked over, there wouldn't be any flights or ferries out for the next twenty-four to thirty-six hours. Maybe not even for forty-eight, depending on how much snow they got. He didn't want to be around Celeste when she found that out. Nor did he want to be around Celeste if she *had* found that out already.

His sister fixed herself a cup of coffee, refreshed Nathan's and then sat down at the table and patted the surface, indicating he should join her. "So, what's on your agenda for today?"

First I'm going to dodge my coworkers' questions about what the foundation told me yesterday. Next, I'll call the board president to schedule a meeting that will effectively shut down the center, which will devastate everyone on the island. Oh, yeah, this afternoon I'm also going to tell a whole bunch of school kids that I had to take down their lawn ornament indefinitely.

Nathan took a long pull of coffee. "Not much, why?"

"You should invite Celeste to the center. Give her a tour. Treat her to lunch."

Skipping the part of the conversation where he pretended not to notice his sister was trying to set him up, Nathan bluntly replied, "I'm pretty sure she has a boyfriend in the Caribbean."

"No, she doesn't. She's single. No kids, never been married. Completely unattached."

"How do you know all that?"

"She told me when I was showing her the room last night."

That was a new record. Carol had only been upstairs with Celeste for three minutes. His sister had a knack for prying private information out of people in the most conversational of ways, so they never knew it was happening. She said it was necessary to get a sense of what kind of people she was hosting, since Josh was frequently away and she was in the inn alone. But Nathan knew her personal safety was the last thing on Carol's mind when she wheedled Celeste's marital and relationship status out of her. He only hoped his sister didn't try to push *him* on Celeste as aggressively as she was pushing Celeste on him right now.

"Still. Not interested." It was the first of many white lies he imagined he'd tell today. Nathan may not have been interested in giving Celeste a tour of the center, but he was admittedly curious about why she was so bent on getting to the Caribbean for Christmas if she wasn't meeting her boyfriend there.

"Why not? You're always saying you're not going to meet a woman on the island unless she drops from the sky. Celeste has literally fallen from the sky."

"And she's literally going back up into the sky by tomorrow at the latest."

"That's why you've got to act fast."

His sister sounded like a nineties infomercial. Nathan *did* have to act fast, just not about Celeste. About *donors*. "I've got to shave and get to work, that's what I've got to do. Do you mind walking Abigail to the bus stop?"

"You're not staying for waffles?"

"Thanks, but I've got a lobster to deal with before the preschoolers' Dancers & Prancers class begins." Nathan went into the dining room and said goodbye to Abigail. He was rounding the corner on his way to the front door just as Celeste stepped off the staircase and directly into his path. He stopped short at the last second, close enough to catch a whiff of her fragrance again.

"Oops, sorry 'bout that," she apologized, stepping back. "And good morning."

She was wearing the same black leggings and top she'd put on last night, but something about her was different. Was it that her hair was . . . What did women call those kinds of braids? Dutch? No—French. French braids.

"Good morning. How was your sleep?"

"Terrific, thanks." She looked up at him, and Nathan couldn't help but notice her hairstyle elongated her neck and emphasized the sharp angles of her features. "Except I kept dreaming I was visited by carolers."

"Were they singing 'The Twelve Days of Christmas'?"

"Yes—how did you know?"

"That wasn't a dream. It's the clock on the town hall tower. Instead of chiming, it announces each of the twelve gifts. On the hour, every hour. But only for the month of December."

"Don't tell me, the mayor changes it back on January first." She pressed her lips together, either forcing a smile or fighting one; he couldn't tell.

"Yep. Funny, though, it's only at night when everything else is quiet that you can hear it. Or maybe most of us are so used to it in the background, kind of like the sound of the ocean, that we don't notice it." Talking about island life was only a few sentences away from talking about the weather, and Nathan didn't want to stir up a tempest in a teapot, so to speak. He edged toward the door. "I've got to run. Carol's just starting breakfast now. She'll come looking for you in a couple of minutes. Most of the guests like to relax in the living room while they're waiting. If she didn't mention it, there's coffee in there, too." Carol deliberately set the coffee in the living room to keep the guests out of the dining room because it was too close to the kitchen; she hated being interrupted or having people hover around her while she was cooking.

"Okay, thanks." Celeste moved aside so he could pass. "Have a good one."

Not likely. "You, too." Nathan flung open the door and lumbered home against the biting wind. His headache was back already, and his day had barely begun.

HE COULDN'T GET AWAY FROM ME FAST ENOUGH, CELESTE thought as she approached the coffee station in the living room, keeping her back to the Christmas tree.

Nathan's presence had stopped her cold; he'd looked so rugged with his morning scruff and wearing a red, gray and black flannel shirt beneath his navy peacoat. Kind of like a cross between a lumberjack and a sailor. But he'd appeared to be brooding. There was something on his mind, she could tell.

Or maybe he just wasn't a morning person.

Celeste popped a holiday-blend pod into the coffee maker and inhaled the delicious aroma—was it apple pie?—wafting from the kitchen. Whatever Carol was making, Celeste couldn't wait to try it. When her coffee was ready, she added a splash of milk, and as she was mulling over whether she should sit near the fire or take her drink upstairs, a tall, thin, elderly man came into the room. He had a salt-and-pepper mustache and a short beard, a horseshoe ring of hair and he wore glasses and a bow tie. *Arthur Williams*, she silently guessed, and he confirmed it as they exchanged introductions.

After fixing a cup of decaf cinnamon tea, he gestured toward the opposite end of the living room. "Would you like to join me while we wait for breakfast?"

So Celeste followed him to the annex and took a seat in one of the two tall armchairs facing the windows.

"I suppose it's warmer in front of the fire, but I like to admire the view and watch passersby," he explained, adjusting his silver-framed glasses behind his ears. "Not that I'm sitting very long. The events at the community center have kept me busy for most of my stay on the island. I'm here for the month, you see."

"Did you come here specifically for Christmas Countdown?" Celeste thought that seemed a bit extreme. Then again, she figured Arthur was a retiree. He wasn't wearing a wedding band, so maybe, like her, he didn't have any family. This might have been something he'd been looking forward to doing all year.

"In part, yes. I'd heard good things about the island, and I wanted to see for myself if they were true. I'd hoped my son and his family might join me at some point, but . . . they have other plans for the holidays." He lifted his mug to his lips.

Because she'd become hypersensitive to even the most benevolent questions about her family since her mother's death, Celeste tried to be careful not to intrude on other people's privacy. So when she sensed she'd trespassed—or at least, that Arthur didn't want to talk about being alone at Christmas—she quickly switched topics. "So you don't have to be a Sea Spray Island resident in order to participate at the community center?"

"No. Anyone who goes there is automatically considered a member, but in actuality, there are no membership requirements or dues. All are welcome."

That was *so* Nathan. Nice gesture, but no wonder the place needed funding. "Year-round or just during Christmas Countdown?"

"Both. We're always happy to have more people join us, if you're interested."

Wow, Arthur was only a visitor to the island, and he was already using the collective "we."

"I'd like to, but I've got to stick close to the inn so I'm ready to go the moment the airport opens again."

Celeste explained about her job and then Abigail bounced into the room. Nathan must have done her hair for her; either that, or it was even windier outside than it looked.

"Good morning, Mr. Williams. Aunt Carol says breakfast will be on the table in two minutes."

"Two whole minutes? I'm not sure I can wait that much longer," he joked.

"Yeah, I know. I had to do math homework on an empty stomach. And it was fractions, so the whole worksheet is filled with pictures of pies sliced into different portions, like thirds or fifths. It was *torture* to look at them."

Celeste realized her chair was angled in such a way that the girl hadn't immediately noticed she was there, so she interjected, "Good morning, Abbey."

"Oh, hi, Celeste! I didn't know you were awake." Her face fell. "You changed your hair."

Celeste reflexively lifted a hand to her head. Suddenly she understood Abigail's windblown look: the girl had tried to copy her hairstyle from yesterday. That was maybe the sweetest compliment she'd ever received from a child. She suddenly understood why people said imitation was the highest form of flattery—until now, she'd just considered it a poor excuse for plagiarism. "I had to braid it because it's so windy outside. Last night the ends kept whipping into my eyes."

"I was going to braid mine, too, but I didn't have time," Abigail claimed.

"If you'd like, I can help you with it."

"Sure, but not until after breakfast. I'm starving."

The waffles with sautéed apples and cinnamon Carol made tasted even more delicious than they smelled, and the foursome chatted cordially as they devoured the hearty breakfast.

"Celeste, do you want to come to the community center this afternoon?" Abigail asked toward the end of their meal. "It's Make-a-Flake Day. We make snowflakes to decorate the activities room."

"Um . . ." Celeste hesitated. She enjoyed hanging out with Abigail at the inn, but venturing into the community center was another story. "Thanks for inviting me—Mr. Williams asked me to come, too. But I'm afraid I can't, just in case there's a break in the weather and I need to leave quickly."

"There's not going to be—" Abigail started to say, but Carol cut her off.

"It's almost time to catch the bus. You should go grab your things."

"Wait. First Celeste is going to re-do my hair for me. I'll get a brush."

Celeste finished the final bite of her waffle and then joined Abigail in the living room, where she quickly braided her hair.

"How does it look?" Abigail asked. "Is it the same as yours?"

"No, it's much prettier than mine. It almost looks like a crown." Actually, the guileless expression on Abbey's face was so pure that her hair looked more like a halo. Celeste channeled her inner mom, adding, "The only bad thing about this hairstyle is that your ears can get really cold, so don't forget to wear a hat."

Within a few minutes, the young girl was on the bus, Arthur was reading the newspaper in the annex and Carol was joining Celeste for a second cup of coffee in the dining room. "Thank you for helping Abbey with her hair," she said. "She won't let me touch it, and I have no experience with braids since mine's so curly I gave up trying to do anything with it a long time ago. Abigail's mom used to wish her daughter had inherited the Whites' waves, as she referred to our family's hair, but I think she's lucky hers is stick-straight. It's easier to manage."

Celeste noticed that Carol had used the past tense about Abbey's mother; it seemed as if Carol hadn't spoken to her in a long time. Did that mean Abigail's mother wasn't involved with the young girl, either? "I was glad to do it. She looks darling."

"She has really taken a liking to you, unlike the other woman Nathan dated this past year," Carol said. Then she quickly clarified, "Not that Nathan's dating you, obviously. I just meant that usually Abigail isn't so quick to bond with women her mom's age."

It was too late; her little slip of the tongue was more evidence that Carol was sizing Celeste up as a potential girlfriend for Nathan. She'd suspected it from the way Carol was fishing for information about her relationship status when she'd shown her to her room last evening. But Celeste had quickly dismissed her hunch, figuring Carol was aware she wouldn't be sticking around the island long enough to go on a date, much less have a relationship with Nathan. So she'd told Carol she wasn't married, didn't have children and traveled too often to be in a relationship. Now she realized maybe she should have emphasized that last part.

Aloud, Celeste agreed. "Abbey's been very welcoming. She probably gets her sense of hospitality from you."

"I don't know about that. Nathan's pretty friendly, too. He might not be at his best right now because it's such a busy time at the center, but he's an incredibly warm, caring person."

That lacked subtlety, but Celeste let it slide. "Speaking of being warm . . . Do you suppose I could borrow a coat? I plan to stay in for most of the day, but I might take a walk later."

"Of course! I should have asked you last night if you had paja-mas or a nightgown. Is there anything else you need?"

"No, thanks. I've got spares of all the essentials in my carry-on bag. It's a trick of the trade."

But Carol insisted on loaning her a sweater, too, and since the only sweater Celeste had in her carry-on bag was the one with the Christmas tree on it, she accepted her offer. She led Celeste down the hall to her bedroom, opened her closet door and lifted a stack of shoe boxes off the top of a mahogany storage chest. She chatted away as she flipped its lid open and unzipped the garment bag inside.

Pulling out a white turtleneck with a blue-and-red anchor print, she frowned. "Why am I keeping this? I went on a cleaning spree recently and laundered all of my clothes, but the only reason this could have ended up back in here was because I thought it was too ugly to donate."

"It's not ugly. It's just sort of . . . vintage," Celeste replied diplo-matically. She touched a dark green, cable-knit fisherman's sweater. Not exactly her taste, but it looked warm. She also noticed a thick, black thermal shirt. "Can I borrow these?"

"Sure. Take a couple more. Just in case you're here for a few days." Carol held up a classic heather-gray crewneck in one hand and a maroon wool pullover with leather elbow patches in her other hand.

I'd rather freeze, Celeste thought as she surveyed the maroon sweater. But since she didn't want to offend Carol, and she'd be leaving the island before she had to wear a second sweater anyway, she took both of them. She also accepted a pair of gloves and a green and lavender knit beanie ski hat that Carol claimed "went perfectly" with the purple down jacket she let her use. *This is obvi-ously from the same fashion phase as the elbow-patch sweater*, Celeste thought, smiling to herself.

Once she returned to her room, she deliberated about whether or not to text Philip to tell him she'd been rerouted to Sea Spray Island. He had a tendency to get all worked up when his staff's travel plans changed unexpectedly, especially when their assignments involved posting blog content. That was partly because subscribers to the site were promised that *Peregrinate* would vicariously whisk them away to "a new dream vacation destination" each week. More importantly, sponsors were guaranteed their events, locales and accommodations would receive sole coverage from the publication on specific dates. So there was no wiggle room with blog content deadlines. Although Celeste would be covering three days of carnival, she'd only be posting once—on Christmas afternoon, one of the more expensive sponsorship slots—which raised the stakes even higher.

The higher the stakes, the higher Philip's blood pressure, she thought. And since December 23 was still three days away, she decided she'd spare him the anxiety and wait until she was in the Caribbean to mention she'd been delayed getting there. *Besides, technically, I'm not traveling for work—I'm traveling for vacation,* she rationalized.

And because she was on vacation—and she had nothing better to do, anyway—she reclined on the bed and snuggled beneath the quilt for a long winter's nap.

Chapter 5

NATHAN GLANCED AT THE CLOCK. WAS IT REALLY ALMOST TEN? Time flew when you were hiding out in your office. He started to call another prospective donor from the list he'd made earlier that morning when Samantha, the receptionist, rapped on the door and then rolled into his second-floor office in her wheelchair.

Perfect timing, he thought, grateful for an excuse to disconnect before entering the last digit. Each time he picked up the phone to try to schedule an appointment with one of the philanthropists, his stomach cramped and his forehead broke out in a sweat.

So far, his last-minute efforts had yielded nothing but embarrassment, with three of the four people he'd called telling him they might have been able to help if he'd contacted them sooner—which was even more discouraging than the donor who'd given him a flat-out *not interested.* And even though Nathan knew he didn't have any control over the extenuating circumstances that resulted in these eleventh-hour calls, he felt like a failure.

"Hey, Nathan. I didn't see you come in this morning." Samantha snapped her gum as she pulled the spare set of keys from the hook by the light switch. "Kanesha asked me to open up the events room for the Dancers & Prancers class, since Lee's not in yet. He must still be getting crowned."

Nathan was befuddled. "Crowned?"

"His tooth, not his head. Don't you remember?"

Nathan had completely forgotten that the custodian and groundskeeper had scheduled the morning off. He'd also forgotten until just now that Sandy was still lying on the activities-room floor, and the preschoolers and their parents or babysitters would arrive any minute. The children were adorable, but Nathan recalled the day last summer when Lee had left several shipping boxes in the corner of the room so he could break them down and recycle their contents later. Unfortunately, the kids had discovered them and created a "blizzard in July" with the foam peanuts and a large floor fan.

While the parents applauded their children's imaginations, they weren't as quick to give a hand with cleaning up the mess afterward. Suffice it to say, Kanesha, the program director, made it known she was not pleased with Lee, the parents, their kids, Nathan, the inventors of foam peanuts and anyone else who happened to cross paths with her that day. The characteristically unflappable woman later apologized for losing her cool, confiding she'd just found out that morning that her husband had needed open-heart surgery.

She's had several really difficult months, Nathan thought, keenly aware that her stress was going to double when she lost her position at the community center.

He figured he owed it to his staff—especially to Kanesha—to prevent whatever aggravation he could in their workplace. Other than using the plastic lobster as a tumbling mat, he couldn't imagine the children could do much harm to it, the room or themselves, but he wasn't going to give them the chance to prove him wrong.

"I'll go downstairs with you," he told Samantha, jogging into the hall after her.

"What did you find out when you were in Boston yesterday?" she asked as the elevator doors closed. Fortunately, they were the only ones in it. "Did we get the grant?"

"Nothing's finalized yet."

"They invited you to come all the way to Boston just so they could tell you nothing's been finalized?"

Yeah, that did sound fishy now that Nathan thought of it. "My sentiments exactly," he hedged.

A big grin broke across Samantha's face. "We got it, didn't we? But you aren't allowed to say until you officially tell the board, right?"

"No!" Nathan was vehement. The last thing he wanted was for her to spread a rumor that would raise everyone's hopes even higher. "Seriously, Samantha. Don't tell anyone that. It will make things even more difficult when we don't—*if* we don't get it."

She mimed zipping her lip and tossing the key over her shoulder. "Your secret's safe with me." Right before the doors parted, she said, "For the record, I never had any doubt. I was sure your proposal was great, just like all the work you do here. And I'm not just saying that because I'm hoping for an extra-large bonus in my stocking this year."

Inwardly, Nathan groaned. It so happened that the board *had* voted to increase everyone's year-end bonus this Christmas. *Little consolation that's going to be compared to losing our jobs,* he lamented.

"Morning, Nathan," Kanesha greeted him as Samantha handed her the key and then headed back toward the reception area. Nathan explained to Kanesha why he needed to access the events room, too, even though he wasn't sure what he'd do with the shrunken lawn ornament once he moved it into the hall.

"That's fine—I'm glad I bumped into you," she said. "I need you to sign off on a check to pay for the chowder and bisque for tomorrow night's supper. Salty's Restaurant gave it to us at a steep dis-count, but I still may have gone a little over budget. We had fifteen more guests sign up this year than last. And I wanted to order extra in case there are any last-minute attendees. Times are tough."

"It's not a problem," he assured her, knowing that for some fami-lies on the island, Souper Supper wasn't just a holiday celebration; it was a much-needed free meal. If he had to, Nathan could reallocate funds from another area of their budget since they probably wouldn't have to worry about their long-term expenditures now, anyway.

"Thanks. You know, I never say this kind of thing because I don't like to make comparisons, but I think this has been one of our best Christmas Countdowns ever. It will be hard to top it next year."

"I wouldn't worry about that," Nathan replied sadly, before he real-ized he'd spoken aloud. "I mean, you always do such a fantastic job."

"Thanks. Back atcha!" Kanesha started to cross the room when she stopped, pivoting around to face him. "Hey, I forgot to ask how the meeting went yesterday."

Nathan squatted down and lifted a corner of the heavy folded plastic so he wouldn't have to make eye contact. "It was fine, mostly a formality. They wanted to thank us in person for applying before finalizing their decision."

Like the clouds on the horizon, Nathan's little white lie was grow-ing bigger and grayer. If he kept this up, pretty soon it would block out the sun. He walked backward toward the door, slid Sandy across the threshold and into the lobby, where Lee strolled up to him.

"Hey, boss," he said, his speech slurry as he pointed to Nathan's shirt. "I thought the ugly sweater competition wasn't until tomorrow."

Nathan chuckled at his own expense. "How's your mouth? Was getting a crown painful?"

"Only the part when I had to pay the bill. My wallet's seven hundred bucks lighter—and that was *with* insurance. Imagine how broke I'd be without it?" he asked, and Nathan frowned, realizing that after they were laid off, the staff would have to pay higher premiums to keep their insurance coverage. Lee pointed to the lobster. "I know I said that thing was a vandalization victim in the making, but I swear I wasn't the one who put him out of his misery."

Nathan had helped Lee set up the ornament on the front lawn on the first day of December. The weather had been unseasonably cold, and just like last night, it was difficult trying to drive Sandy's tether spikes into the hard, frozen ground. Surrounded by impatient school kids offering unsolicited advice, Lee had bellyached the entire time. Nathan suspected he'd been exaggerating for their benefit—his grumpiness made it even more meaningful to them when the lobster was finally anchored in an upright position.

On occasion, Lee would threaten that next year he was going to buy a lawn ornament that looked like a gigantic pot of boiling water and stick Sandy in it. Although he meant it as a joke, unsurprisingly, the students didn't find this funny. They were convinced he was plotting to do the lobster harm.

"Nah, I know you didn't do it. I had to take it in because of the wind, which I doubt will decrease enough for us to put Sandy back out there before the snow falls. But don't worry, I'll break the bad news to the kids." *It'll give me practice for breaking the bad news to the adults,* Nathan thought.

Rubbing his cheek, Lee slurped. "Don't tell them I'm the one who suggested this, but I could set it up right here in the lobby."

Nathan looked up at the ceiling above the second-floor interior balcony. "I suppose it would fit over there by the staircase, but I don't know how we'd keep it upright without tethers. I wouldn't want it to fall on anyone."

As he was speaking, Ray Forman and Vince Motta, two of the seniors who played partners in the morning cribbage tournament, came up to them.

"We just heard the center received a grant," Ray remarked loud enough for everyone in the lobby to hear. "How much moola are we talking about?"

Already? Samantha told everyone already?! Nathan silently fumed, glaring at the receptionist across the room. She ducked her head and began rummaging through a drawer. The only thing worse than a blabbermouth was an *inaccurate* blabbermouth. If it turned out the community center didn't close down after all, Nathan was going to have to call her on the carpet for disclosing confidential information. *Again.*

"I hope another pool table is at the top of the list of what you plan to purchase," Vince suggested. "Ever since Kanesha had that bright idea that the senior citizens should teach the high schoolers to play, they've been monopolizing the tables in the afternoon."

Ordinarily, Nathan would have had more patience, but his head was throbbing and Vince's remark sounded like three complaints rolled into one; he was disgruntled about the number of pool tables, the program director's decision and the high schoolers' behavior. "There are at least two bars on Main Street that have pool tables and people under twenty-one aren't allowed inside. So if you're dissatisfied here, you might be more comfortable spending the afternoon there, because we *didn't* get a grant," he snapped. Then, realizing he shouldn't have said that, he added, "The grant hasn't been awarded to anyone yet."

His tone was lost on Vince, who tapped the side of his nose and said, "Gotcha. No grant . . . yet."

Before Nathan could reiterate that they weren't awarded any funding, Ray cut in. "What's up with the pile of plastic?"

"It's the lobster from outside. I was just telling the boss that I could rig it up over there, but he's worried it'll tip over and land on someone, and we'll get sued," said Lee.

Until this moment, Nathan's only concern was that someone might get hurt; he hadn't thought about the center being sued. In general, the islanders didn't tend to be a litigious group, but considering the way the past couple of months had gone, Nathan couldn't rule out the possibility. "Yeah. Help me roll it up so we can put it in storage."

"No, no, no," Vince protested, waving his hands. "The kids worked really hard last fall for the right to put Sandy Claws on display. It's like a trophy to them. Ray and I are sailors. We know a thing or two about tying knots. We'll help Lee secure it nice and tight."

Despite sometimes being a pain in the neck, Vince could be a real softie. And very helpful, too—virtually all of the members were. That's why the center had always been able to function with such a small staff; there were so many faithful volunteers who kept everything running smoothly. To them, the community center was an extension of their homes and its members were an extension of their families. The older islanders in particular commented that pitching in gave them a sense of purpose. Knowing the center might close soon, how could Nathan deny Vince and Ray one more opportunity to do something that would have a positive effect on the local school kids?

"Okay. It's worth a try," he agreed.

Once the four men had successfully situated and secured the lobster into place, and Nathan was back in his office again, he mentally repeated the phrase, *It's worth a try.* Then, with new determination, he picked up his phone and dialed another prospective donor.

CELESTE RAISED THE LID TO HER LAPTOP AND CHECKED THE airport status and weather report for what must have been the twenty-fifth time. It remained the same: the wind speeds were increasing and eight to ten inches of snow were expected to fall overnight, tapering off by sunrise. She resigned herself to the fact that she wouldn't be leaving the island until the following morning.

After secluding herself in her room for several hours—napping, streaming her favorite TV shows and conducting additional research for her assignment in the Caribbean—Celeste was beginning to feel a little stir crazy. A little hungry, too, which surprised her. Even though it was after two o'clock, she'd eaten so much at breakfast she didn't think she'd have an appetite until suppertime. So she decided she might as well go for a walk and then grab a bite to eat.

She'd already put on the gray pullover Carol had let her borrow. With the jacket over that, she was confident the top half of her body would be warm enough. However, she pulled a second pair of leggings on over the pair she was already wearing. That's when she realized she didn't have any socks. She supposed she could have asked Carol for a pair, but she'd mentioned she was going grocery shopping this afternoon. So Celeste opted to go barefoot beneath her sneakers. *It's not as if I'll be tromping through snow,* she reasoned.

Buttoning the jacket to her chin, she caught a glimpse of herself in the antique floor mirror across the room. She looked like an eggplant, but it was better than going cold. She zipped her phone into her pocket, slid on her gloves and hustled downstairs and out the door.

On the front step, she paused, struck by the fact that almost every house on the street had its outdoor holiday lights on, although it was only the middle of the afternoon. Tiny white bulbs twinkled from the trees and shrubbery, the awnings and trellises dripped with icicle lights, and in almost every window, a candle glowed. Even on one of the dreariest days of the year, the neighborhood was the epitome of warmth and light. But as she imagined the families inside these homes decorating their trees, wrapping gifts and baking cookies, Celeste felt as if she'd emerged onto the set of a play— rather, of a Christmas pageant—in which she no longer had any role.

The thought was almost enough to make her retreat to her room again, but instead she scurried off the steps, along the sidewalk and down the hill. At the bottom, she located the gravelly side road she'd read about online and hiked toward the public parking lot at the end. From there, she took a narrow, well-trampled path over a dune to the beach. She turned left, aware that if she headed right, she'd eventually be walking parallel to Main Street's busy block of shops and eateries, as well as the community center. With the wind at her back, she ambled along an uninhabited stretch of coastline.

She'd barely gone a hundred yards when she spied a "Private Property—No Trespassing" sign, so she twirled around and back-tracked. The soft, uneven terrain was difficult to navigate in her flimsy shoes, especially against the stiff wind. However, the tide was still fairly low and the water had receded far enough that there were long, flat areas of hard, damp sand interspersed between rows of tidal pools. Because the packed ground would be easier to traverse than the loose sand, Celeste strolled out onto the exposed floor of the bay.

Head down, she wound her way around the deepening puddles. As she walked, she remembered that when she was young she was too afraid of crabs to wade through the tidal pools at the bay on the Cape. So she and her mother used to make a game of meandering around them, as if in a maze. Whenever they hit a "dead end" where two pools converged, and they couldn't continue without getting their feet wet, they'd reverse their course and try another path.

That was the same strategy Celeste employed now, stopping every once in a while to admire the starkness of the sky and the wild swells of the incoming tide. *Mom would have loved walking on the beach during the winter as much as she did in the summer,* she imagined. Her mother, who had lived in upstate New York, had never been to the New England coast later than September. Celeste had always wanted to take her back to the Cape in February or March, but it never worked out.

At least I got to take Mom to some amazing places during the warmer months. Every summer, she'd treat her mother to a two-week vacation somewhere neither of them had traveled before, including Maui, Sweden and Greece, to name a few.

A year ago last April, when Celeste started making plans for them to go to Belize in July, her mother had protested. "Honey, I appreciate how generous you are, but you can't keep spending all that money on me."

"Why not? You've given *me* the world, Mom—it's my turn now."

"You're my daughter. I'd do anything for you."

"Good, then come to Belize with me," Celeste had cajoled. "Or to some other place you've always wanted to see."

Her mother had eventually given in, but by the time their trip rolled around, she'd been diagnosed with cancer and was in the hospital recovering from surgery. Celeste spent two weeks at her side instead, which was the only place she wanted to be.

As she trekked along, Celeste's eyes teared up, from the wind or from loneliness, she couldn't say. Every now and then an especially strong gust would nearly push her backward, so she'd pause and wait for it to diminish before trudging onward. She walked for a good twenty minutes, so lost in thought that she nearly plodded right into a tidal pool.

At the last second, she halted and looked up. Slightly to her left, a bank of low clouds darkened the horizon. To her far right, Main Street's storefronts looked like dollhouses; she was almost exactly even with the community center at the end of the row of buildings. She hadn't realized she'd walked that far. *This is a good time to turn around anyway,* she told herself, changing direction. *I can't feel my toes anymore.*

Since the wind was at her back again, she was able to straighten her posture and pick up her pace. But when she reached the opposite end of the long sandbar, Celeste discovered an incoming current was coursing over it, which meant the expanse of sand she'd been traveling on was encircled by water. *Terrific. I'm marooned on an island while being marooned on an island*, she thought drolly.

She surveyed the broad stream. It couldn't have been more than two inches deep, but it wasn't the depth that concerned her; it was the width. And the temperature; her feet were already freezing. She had no choice but to jump over the current and to do it quickly, before it widened any further. As she backed up to get a running start, it occurred to Celeste that although she was too far away to see into the community center's wall of windows, anyone who happened to be looking out would spot her bright purple jacket against the otherwise gray horizon. *So much for being inconspicuous.*

She took a deep breath and then sprinted as fast as she could, her stride long and her legs limber, the wind pushing her forward. She felt so agile—almost weightless—she was sure she'd sail straight over the rivulet. But she mistimed the puddle and leaped too early, her right foot touching down in squishy muck, her left clearing the stream entirely. Propelled by her momentum, she ran a few more paces before she could stop. Her right foot was so cold it burned, but at least she hadn't taken a pratfall into the frigid water.

She traipsed another five or six steps before the tingling in her toes was so intense she had to stop again. Glancing down, she realized she'd run right out of her shoe. She whirled around, limping on her tiptoes to retrieve it. But the windblown current had carried the canvas sneaker a couple yards downstream and into the second, deeper pool, just beyond Celeste's fingertips. She removed one of her gloves with her teeth as she repositioned herself at the edge of the water. Then she bent forward and thrust her bare hand beneath the surface. Leaning on her palm for balance, one leg stretched out behind her, she reached as far as she could with her other arm. She almost had it . . .

———————

IT WAS NEARLY THREE O'CLOCK AND NONE OF THE PROSPECTS
Nathan had uncovered this morning had panned out. He had absolutely nothing hopeful to offer that would offset the foundation's decision. There was no getting around it; he was going to have to call the
board president. Actually, he was kind of surprised Mark hadn't called
him yet. The president knew how vital the grant was to the center's
future, so it seemed he would have been waiting with bated breath to
hear the foundation's decision. *Maybe in the holiday rush, he forgot
yesterday was the day I met the rep in Boston,* Nathan surmised.

Regardless, he had told Mark he'd call him today, so he picked
up his phone and stared at the dial pad. Nope, he couldn't do it.
Not without some liquid courage; coffee, in this case. It would keep
him awake half the night, but he'd be awake, anyway. Because as
awful as it was going to be to tell the president, the board and the
islanders about the center shutting down, it was going to be even
more agonizing to tell Abbey they had to move.

Nathan exited his office and headed toward the stairs. Several
women—the mitten knitters—were clustered on the indoor balcony, facing the window. In warmer weather, this viewpoint sometimes afforded a glimpse of breaching whales, so Kanesha kept two
pairs of binoculars on a peg in the hall for just that purpose. But
today, Nathan assumed their curiosity was weather related.

"What's going on? Did Santa's Sailboat tip over?" he asked.

"No. Marty and Joe took it out of the water already. There's
someone out on the tidal flats," Vivian Liu reported, squinting into
the binoculars. "She's acting strangely."

"I think she's doing yoga," Brent Wilcox chimed in. He was holding up a camera, apparently recording the person. "That's the triangle position."

"No, the triangle pose is like this," Sally Archer corrected him, demonstrating. At seventy-two, she was more flexible than most people half her age, and she wasn't shy about letting them know it. "She's doing the half-moon pose. She's pretty good at it, too. She's been holding it a long time."

"I think it's Carol," Alice Wright said. She was using the second pair of binoculars. "I recognize her coat from a few years ago. It was in the lost-and-found bin, but after no one claimed it for three months, it went up for grabs. Carol was delighted to take it."

"What's that in her mouth?"

"It's a glove," Vivian reported, lowering the lenses.

Nathan agreed it looked like Carol's old coat, but it definitely wasn't Carol's shape. He held out his hand to Vivian. "Can I see those a sec?"

He swept the seascape until he honed in on the woman and adjusted the focus. He was right—it wasn't Carol. It was Celeste. And from what Nathan could tell, one of her feet was bare. He zoomed in, following the direction of her hand; her shoe was floating in the tidal pool. The wind was so strong she appeared to be teetering. If she wasn't careful, she was going to—

"Ohhh!" Sally, Brent, Alice and Vivian chorused, just as Celeste toppled sideways, splashing into the water and landing on her rump.

Nathan pressed the binoculars into Vivian's hands, grabbed his jacket from his office and flew downstairs and out the door. Charging across the street, he scampered down the rocky retaining wall and then slogged through the tidal pools toward Celeste. By then, she'd stood up and was clearly trying to navigate the driest way around the tidal pools, but if she kept zigzagging on that course, she was going to end up farther from shore. She was clutching her sneaker to her chest like a baby. Or maybe she was trying to keep herself warm.

"Stop!" he shouted. "Stay where you are. I'll come get you."

She lifted her head, apparently surprised. Her face was dripping. She held out a hand, like a cop stopping traffic. "It-it's mucky. Your f-f-feet are going to get c-cold."

"Waterpoof boots," he called back, splashing through the puddles straight toward her. When he reached her, he took off his jacket and wrapped it around her shoulders, exchanging it for her shoe. Then he turned and squatted down so he could give her a piggyback ride to shore.

"No, I can't," she protested. "I-I-I'll be embarrassed if someone from the c-c-community center happens to look out and see us."

"It's a little late for that. How do you think I knew to come out here in the first place? C'mon. Hop up before the tide comes all the way in."

He waited as she gingerly wrapped her arms around his neck. He grabbed on to the backs of her knees, stood up straight and began marching back toward the community center. She was so quiet he twisted his head to the side and asked, "What were you doing out there, anyway?"

"Testing your theory."

"What theory?"

"The one about whether the Coast Guard would be able to get me off this island," she said over his other shoulder. "But they never showed up."

Nathan chuckled. "You would have had better luck if you'd waited until high tide before you stranded yourself."

When she giggled, he could feel her warm breath on his ear, and he was so distracted his grip on her leg slipped. He had to stop in the middle of the tidal pool, sort of bouncing her upward so he could adjust his grasp.

"Hey!" she yelped. "You just made your jacket fall off of me."

"No problem." Nathan turned around to fetch it from the water.

But as he started to bend forward, Celeste pulled on his shoulders, begging, "Wait. Please put me down first. One swim is enough for today."

So he set her on the drier sand and sloshed back into the tidal pool. Electrifyingly cold, the water lapped over the tops of his boots, stinging his lower legs and ankles. Realizing how uncomfortable Celeste must have been, he wrung out his jacket and rolled it into a ball. "Here, hold this," he instructed. "I'm carrying you the rest of the way. It'll be a lot quicker."

Before she could argue, he swept her up and hoofed it back to the community center as quickly as he could. When they reached the building, Kanesha stepped out, holding the door open so he could carry Celeste inside. As soon as they entered, Nathan realized there were twenty or thirty people gathered in a semicircle, facing them. Concerned that Celeste would be mortified by the attention, he immediately set her on her feet, and when he did, everyone burst into applause.

"That was some great entertainment, you two!" Vince called out and whistled between his finger and thumb.

"If you enjoyed the matinee, wait until you see the evening show," Celeste shot back, making everyone laugh and charming Nathan so thoroughly he forgot about how cold he was and how much his head hurt and that he still needed to call the board president and tell him they hadn't gotten the grant.

Chapter 6

BY THE TIME NATHAN HAD CARRIED CELESTE ACROSS THE threshold like some kind of soggy, purple bride, she was too chilled to care that almost everyone in the community center had witnessed her klutzy dunking in the cove. Besides, she figured after Nathan came to her rescue the way he had, the least she could do was have a sense of humor about her graceless escapade.

"Stop giving this girl a hard time and move out of the way, Vince." A trim woman with white hair pushed past the man who had whistled. She handed a pair of pink socks with navy toes and heels to Celeste. "I just finished knitting these. They'll warm your tootsies right up."

She had barely put the first one on—it was the softest sock she'd ever worn—when several women flocked around her and escorted her to the women's locker room to outfit her in an assortment of workout clothes from the lost-and-found bin.

"You can choose anything you want. It's all been laundered," a woman who introduced herself as Alice told her. "I'm a germaphobe, so I take everything home and wash it. Which reminds me, I've got to talk to Nathan about getting a washer and dryer installed here, now that we won all that grant money."

Celeste grabbed a pair of navy running pants and a navy sweat-shirt and went into a changing room. She peeled off her wet clothes and draped them over the side of the stall.

"I'll hang these up for you so they dry," someone said and snatched them away before she could say it really wasn't necessary.

When she came out, all of the women had dispersed except Alice, who was talking on her cell phone. She stopped and covered the mic to whisper, "You feel warmer now?"

"Yes. Thanks so much," Celeste whispered back. "I'll ask Carol to wash and return these clothes for me tomorrow."

"Don't worry about it. Finders, keepers," Alice said and then resumed her phone conversation.

Celeste went into the lobby, where she caught sight of her wet garments draped over a folding chair in front of the fireplace. Even though her underwear was damp from landing on her backside, she was relieved she'd kept it on; otherwise, it might have been dan-gling from the mantelpiece for everyone to see. On a second chair, Nathan's pants, socks and jacket were also on display. But no one was sitting in the area—everyone else seemed to have resumed what-ever activities had brought them to the center in the first place—so Celeste hurried over to warm herself near the fire.

She'd just sat down when Nathan came out of the men's locker room. Although he was wearing his own sweater, he had donned the bottoms of a black-nylon track suit. His socks were identical to Celeste's: navy with pink toes and heels.

"We're twinsies," she said, lifting her feet as he dropped into the leather sofa beside her.

"It was either I wear these or a used pair of knee-high tube socks from the eighties," Nathan sheepishly replied. "At least they smelled like they were from the eighties. I think someone mistook the lost-and-found bin for a hamper and chucked them in there."

Celeste giggled. "Fortunately, all the clothes in the women's bin were clean."

"Yeah. Alice washes them. But she refuses to touch the men's clothes—she says if she makes it too easy for us, I'll never invest in a washer and dryer for the center."

"That's funny. She just mentioned she wanted to talk to you about that, now that you've received a grant. Congratulations, by the way—I hope the money solves some of those funding issues you mentioned."

Nathan's eyes went wide, and his Adam's apple bobbed discernibly as he swallowed. "Uh, we, uh . . . Thanks."

He must be really intimidated by Alice to stammer like that. Maybe I shouldn't have repeated her comment? Celeste thought, as a young woman with highlights almost the same shade of purple as Carol's jacket rolled up to them in a wheelchair. She was balancing two mugs on a tray on her lap.

"Nathan told us to give you some space, but I made you a cup of cocoa. I used almond milk in case you're lactose intolerant. I'm Samantha, by the way."

"Ooh, thanks, Samantha. I'm Celeste." She accepted the mug and took a sip. It brought her back to the days when her mother used to make the sweet, steamy beverage after Celeste went sledding. "Mm, I haven't had hot cocoa with big fat marshmallows like this in it since I was a kid."

"Yeah. It's the only way to drink it." Instead of giving the other cup to Nathan as Celeste expected her to do, Samantha lifted it to her own lips. "That hits the spot. There's more in the kitchen if you want it, Nathan. Sorry, I could only carry two."

It almost seemed as if she was trying to get rid of him. But Nathan shook his head. "I'm good, thanks."

Samantha took another sip before asking, "So, how did you two meet? Nathan doesn't tell us anything about his personal life. I always thought it was because he didn't really have one, but—"

"Thanks for bringing Celeste the cocoa, but I think your phone's ringing, Samantha," Nathan interrupted.

The young woman cocked her head and put her hand behind her ear. "I don't hear it, and I can hear that thing even when there are fifty people in the lobby and I'm clear on the other side of the room. Sort of like how a mother can identify her child's cry on a playground full of kids."

"But I'm sure you have work to do. If not, Kanesha mentioned she's backlogged with expense reports."

"All right, all right. I can take a hint," Samantha claimed ironically, since she clearly couldn't. She spun around and wheeled toward the reception desk.

Nathan's discomfort was as plain as the grooves across his forehead. "Sorry—she has a history of coming to some awfully far-fetched conclusions."

"It's not *that* far-fetched." Celeste only meant to shrug off Samantha's comment because Nathan was so concerned about it. But then she realized it sounded as if she might be hinting she wanted him to ask her out or something, so she quickly clarified, "I mean, it's not that far-fetched someone would make an assumption like that. You should hear the wild rumors that fly around my office. Totally baseless stuff. I've learned to tune it out."

"Yeah, most of the time that's what I do, too." Nathan visibly relaxed his posture.

"I appreciate everyone giving me dry clothes to wear. I know I said I'd be embarrassed if someone saw me being carried across the cove, but now that the damage has been done, you really didn't need to chase everyone away."

"I didn't want them crowding you, that's all."

Celeste set her cup on the coffee table and held his gaze so he'd know how earnestly she meant it when she said, "I appreciate your coming to my rescue, too."

"I was glad to do it." The way he smiled made Celeste feel shiveringly flushed, if there was such a sensation.

"Sorry about your jacket."

Nathan waved his hand. "It's almost dry already. Unlike your shoe."

"That's okay. I'm in no hurry to go out in the elements again. But you probably have work to do. Don't feel like you need to stay here with me. I'm fine hanging out on my own."

"Okay." He slapped his hands against his thighs and stood up, before offering, "I could give you a tour if you're interested in seeing what kinds of things we do here."

"Won't that interfere with whatever you've got planned for the rest of the afternoon?"

Nathan vigorously shook his head. "Nope. There's nothing I have to do that can't wait a little longer."

So as they carefully made their way through the community center in their stocking feet, Nathan pointed out the pool lounge, classrooms, kitchen, small gymnasium and workout room. Along the way, he introduced her to other staff members and the numerous villagers who approached to ask if she and Nathan were both sufficiently warm now. Nathan also showed her his office and the view of the cove from the second-floor indoor balcony. Then they circled back downstairs, where two women were directing a parade of elementary school children into the activities room.

"Kanesha's conducting the Make-a-Flake project today. Once the younger kids have completed their decorations, the middle and high schoolers will come in and set up more tables and chairs for our event tomorrow. We partner with the after-school program in the public education system to provide engaging activities for the students. Since there are so many working parents on the island and not enough childcare, they appreciate that their kids have a safe, stimulating environment to socialize in."

"I wish my mother had had a place like this when she was raising me. It's such a great resource for single moms," Celeste said wistfully.

"For single dads, too." Nathan stroked his chin as he peered into the activities room. "After Holly—that was my wife's name—after Holly died three years ago, I was a mess. I don't know what I would have done without this community. Or without Carol and Josh, of course."

Oh, he's not divorced. He's a widower. The realization was sobering to Celeste. His family seemed so . . . so *merry* that she wouldn't have guessed he'd suffered that kind of loss. That *Abigail* had suffered that kind of loss. Moved, she confided, "My mother died a year ago. It's been rough, but it's not the same as losing a spouse, and it's certainly not the same as losing your mom when you're as young as Abbey was."

"Your mother died only a year ago? I'm sorry to hear that." The grooves in Nathan's forehead reappeared as he scrunched his brows together. "Do you have brothers or sisters to help you through it?"

"No. I was an only child. I mean, I *am* an only child. Well, I'm not a child, but I am an only." She'd meant that she was alone, without any other family. But now that she'd called herself "an only," it seemed the perfect way to describe how she felt.

SO THAT'S WHY SHE DIDN'T WANT TO ANSWER WHEN CAROL asked about her family last night, Nathan realized. "So, this is your first Christmas without your mother?"

Celeste shook her head. "No. She passed away early last December. But I was so . . . I was so out of it until almost February that I hardly remember any of the holiday season last year."

Nathan understood: technically, it wasn't her first Christmas after her mother's death, but it *felt* like it was. Celeste's lashes beaded with tears, and she quickly excused herself to go to the restroom. Nathan almost wished he'd gone upstairs to call the board president after all. Upsetting Mark would have been preferable to talking about something that made Celeste so sad. He tried to think of something comforting to say when she got back from the restroom, but everything that came to mind was a cliché, even if it was true.

A tug on his sleeve pulled him from his thoughts. "Hi, Dad."

He did a double take; Abigail's sloppy locks had been arranged into an intricate pattern of braids. "Hi, Ab. Your hair looks so pretty. Did your teacher do it for you?"

"No. Celeste braided it before school. Why are you dressed like that?"

"My clothes got wet. It's a long story, but Celeste fell into the cove and I had to help her out. She's okay, but do *not* tease her about it, understand?"

"I won't." Abbey huffed, as if he should have known she'd never do something so insensitive. However, the next second she gave him an impish grin. "But can I tease you about those funny pants?"

He pretended to be insulted. "What's so funny about them? I think they're great. Listen to the sound they make when I walk." Nathan paced back and forth in front of her, the nylon fabric swishing when his legs rubbed together.

"Dad! Stop it," his daughter begged, but he exaggerated his strutting.

"I like this tracksuit so much I think I might ask Samantha to cancel the ugly sweater contest and hold a 'fancy pants contest' instead."

Abigail covered her face with her hands, but she was giggling. He loved her giggle—it reminded him of Holly's. He was taking such pleasure in making her laugh that he didn't notice Celeste had come out of the restroom.

"Hi, Abigail," she said.

Nathan came to a dead stop, and Abigail dropped her hands from her eyes. "Hi, Celeste."

"How was your day?" Celeste asked cheerfully, even though her nose and eyes were red-rimmed.

"It was okay until I came here and found out Sandy is inside instead of outside," Abigail grumbled, pointing to the towering shellfish. "Why didn't Mr. Lee put him back on the lawn, Dad?"

As a sign of respect, all of the school kids referred to Lee and Kanesha as Mr. Lee and Ms. Kanesha, but Samantha insisted on being called Samantha, since she said the title *Ms.* made her feel old. By which she meant over thirty.

"You know why—it's too windy out there. And we spent a long time rigging Sandy up this morning, so no complaining."

"But whoever heard of an indoor lawn ornament?"

"He's not an indoor lawn ornament," Celeste said, winking at Nathan. "He's a lobby-ster."

"Hey, that's funny," Abigail said, giggling when she caught on to the pun. "Do you want to come and help us make snowflakes, Celeste? It's not just for kids. Anyone can help. I told my friends about you, that you're a writer. You can sit at our table. Dad might come down later, too—*if* he changes his pants first."

As touched as he was by his daughter's admiration for Celeste, Nathan didn't want Abbey putting her on the spot. "Honey, Celeste might be ready to go back to the inn."

"Oh, there's no hurry," Celeste told him. "I'd love to make a few flakes with you if I can, Abbey. But let me get my cell phone out of your aunt's jacket. I need to check my messages to make sure I didn't miss any important calls."

"Okay. I'll be at the table near the back." As Abigail galloped into the events room, a phone sounded from the direction of the fireplace.

"That's mine." With one hand, Celeste reached for the purple jacket. With the other, she gave Nathan a small wave. "See you later."

I hope so. As he climbed the stairs to his office, he schemed. *After the Make-a-Flake event is over, I could give her a ride back up the hill and maybe Abbey and I will eat at the inn tonight.*

When he reached his office, Nathan dropped into his chair and clasped his hands behind his head, staring at the cove and basking in the pleasure of what he'd learned about Celeste this afternoon. Namely that she had a surprisingly good sense of humor. That she'd braided his daughter's hair for her. And, most importantly, that she wasn't aloof; she was grieving.

The more he thought about her, the more he found himself wishing he could get to know her even better. *Maybe we could meet up sometime after the holidays,* he daydreamed, *since she only lives in Boston.*

The word *Boston* snapped him out of his reverie. He still had to call the board president to tell him about yesterday's meeting. Make that plural: yesterday's *meetings.* Nathan was going to have to discuss his job offer deadline as well as the foundation's decision.

However, earlier in the afternoon, he'd decided he would ask Mark if they could wait until they'd received written notice from the foundation before telling the rest of the board—and certainly before telling the public—about the grant. That way, Nathan would have a few more days to try to pull a rabbit out of the hat, metaphorically speaking.

Plus, he didn't want to spoil the other board members' holiday preparations. Like Mark, who lived in Westchester County, none of the directors was a year-round resident; they were all wealthy summer homeowners from Connecticut, New York and New Jersey. Of course, there was a world of difference between summering on the island and *being* an islander. But considering all the time, talent and resources the directors had invested into the community center, Nathan knew they'd be as devastated as anyone else in Quahog Cove if it closed down. Why not allow them the same blissful ignorance until December 26?

He tapped out the president's number and waited as the phone rang repeatedly. The voice mail didn't pick up, so he disconnected and tried again. When he couldn't get through the third time, he deduced the phone service must have begun experiencing disruptions because of the increasingly blustery weather. Nathan considered e-mailing instead, but this was hardly the kind of news he could deliver in writing.

He realized if he had called Mark an hour ago, he probably would have reached him. But now he had the perfect excuse for putting off the troublesome conversation until tomorrow. Maybe in the meantime he'd uncover another prospective benefactor.

I guess it was serendipitous that Celeste fell in the water, he mused. *She might not be happy she's had to stay on the island an extra day, but I sure am.*

CELESTE HAD LANDED ON HER LEFT SIDE WHEN SHE'D LOST HER balance in the cove, and her phone had been in her right pocket, so she was fairly confident it hadn't gotten wet. But she was still pleased to hear it ring. Even more pleased when she saw the number—it was Patty's. That could only mean one thing: she could book her flight out of here.

"Hi, Patty," she greeted in a singsong voice.

"Hi, hon. I just heard you were doing yoga in the marina, and you threw out your back doing the half-moon pose. Are you okay?"

Celeste chuckled at Patty's version of events. "That's not exactly what happened. My shoe came off in a puddle, and I got wet trying to fish it out. But yes, I'm okay, thanks."

"Glad to hear it." Patty released a big sigh. "All right, well, you be careful out there, and I'll talk to you soon."

"Wait!" Celeste exclaimed so Patty wouldn't hang up on her. "Weren't you calling to reschedule my flight?"

"No. I just wanted to make sure you were okay."

"Oh. That was nice of you." *Sort of,* Celeste thought, wishing the woman hadn't gotten her hopes up again. "So you haven't heard anything else about the weather?"

"Only that it's going to start snowing tonight, but it should end by noon tomorrow."

"*Noon?* I heard it would end by sunrise."

"Well, sometime in the morning, give or take a few hours."

Celeste took a deep breath and slowly exhaled as she processed this information. *There's no need to panic,* she told herself. Tomorrow was only December 21. Even if the snow didn't stop until noon, the roads would be cleared by midday. And even if the airport's runway wasn't plowed for some reason, the dock would undoubtedly be open again. If Celeste took a ferry back to the mainland late tomorrow afternoon, she could still catch a late-night flight from Boston and arrive at her destination in the early hours of December 22. She'd probably spend the entire day—all that would be left of her vacation—jet-lagged or sleeping. *But I'll have a full twenty-four hours before my assignment begins, and that's the most important thing,* she silently reasoned before saying goodbye to Patty.

When she disconnected the call, she noticed she had a text notification. Uh-oh. It was from Philip. How's the Caribbean? Boston has high winds with snow on the way. You sure picked the right time to vaca in the tropics. Everyone's envious, the message read.

I didn't pick *this time to go on a vacation*—he *needed someone to cover carnival, so I volunteered because it was the* wrong *time for me to stay home,* Celeste thought. As for her colleagues being envious, what a joke. They'd practically dove under the conference room table last April when Philip had asked who'd be willing to work on a Christmas Day assignment.

As annoyed as she was by his phoniness, Celeste knew now that Philip had texted her, she was going to have to tell him about her delay. She slipped down the corridor—literally, since her socks had no traction on the wood floors—and into a vacant classroom. Speaking softly, she dictated into her phone, "I got bumped from my flight and then I was rerouted to Sea Spray Island. It's too windy to leave. The airport and ferry dock are closed, but they'll reopen tomorrow. I expect to arrive in the Caribbean late evening on the twenty-first or early morning on the twenty-second. Either way, I'll be there in plenty of time for *j'ouvert* on the twenty-third."

Her phone immediately rang. When she answered it, Philip didn't bother to say hello before delving into a tirade. His voice was so loud Celeste held the phone away from her ear. "Doesn't the airline realize how much business we give them? How many loyalty points we've earned? I can't believe they bumped you."

"It's not really their fault. I missed their page because—"

"You missed their page? How did that happen?" Philip interrupted her explanation to *ask* for an explanation, which was typical of his communication style.

If you really need to know, I was changing out of the abominable sweater you required *me to wear to the work party.* "I didn't hear it. I must have been in the restroom," Celeste answered.

"Why didn't you give yourself more time to get to the airport in the first place?"

The question—and his tone—made her feel as if she were a

tardy high school student requesting a hall pass, and she resented it. Yet somehow she managed to refrain from retorting that she *had* given herself plenty of time, but *he'd* assigned her the dubious honor of editing Brad's work, even though *she* wasn't an editor; she was a writer. *Philip* was the editor.

"I thought I did, but I guess it wasn't as much time as I needed. I'm sorry." Celeste figured if she assumed responsibility, Philip would let the matter drop, but she was wrong.

"Why didn't you tell me sooner that you were rerouted?"

Because I was concerned you'd react exactly the way you're reacting now. "I guess I thought since I'm technically on vacation, I shouldn't bother you with the minutiae of my travel itinerary," she fudged. "Especially because you're so busy with more important things."

Fortunately, Philip was a sucker for flattery and he accepted her excuse, which was actually a fraction of the truth. "Yeah, all right. But if there's another delay, call me immediately. I wouldn't want you to jeopardize your exemplary reputation. You're one of the few junior writers who has never let me down."

That was exactly why Celeste thought he should cut her some slack. But she recognized that he wasn't complimenting her; he was *warning* her and she needed to respond carefully. "I'm not going to miss *j'ouvert*. I'll be there in plenty of time," she assured him again. "But if anything changes, I'll let you know right away."

After she said goodbye, Celeste's stomach was seized with cramps. In the entire seven years she'd worked for the magazine, she'd never been late for a flight, a deadline or even an editorial meeting. She had worked *so hard* to get where she was. What's more, her *mother* had worked so hard to *get* her where she was. Which still wasn't where she wanted to be—she wanted to be a senior writer. And since Philip was the person responsible for staff promotions, Celeste was filled with self-recrimination for getting bumped from her flight. *I shouldn't have spent so much time rewriting Brad's article. And I shouldn't have stopped to change in the bathroom at the airport, either,* she thought. How could she have been so careless as to risk losing Philip's trust in her?

Feeling woozy, she returned to the lobby, gathered her clothes and tried to put on her sneakers. But they wouldn't fit over her thick socks, so she had to wear them over her bare feet. Her right shoe was still so wet that water squirted out the sides when she took her first steps. The way her day was going, she was worried someone would slip in the wet trail and break a leg, so she bent down and used her dry leggings to soak up the excess water.

"Hi, Celeste." Carol was standing over her. "I wondered where you went this afternoon. I slid a note under your door to ask if you wanted to join Arthur and me for supper. I'm going to spend about an hour here helping set up for tomorrow night and then I'll head back to the house. We'll eat around six thirty. It's nothing fancy. Fresh haddock and roasted potatoes with a side salad."

Maybe she stood up too quickly or maybe it was because her sneakers smelled like the ocean, but when Carol said "haddock," Celeste's stomach lurched. While backing away, she covered her mouth and mumbled through her fingers, "Thanks, but I don't feel so great. Could you tell Abbey I'm sorry, but I couldn't stay to help her?"

Carol tipped her head. "You want a ride back up the hill?"

"No, thanks." She was almost at the door. "I'll be fine as soon as I get some fresh air." *As long as the fresh air is in the Caribbean.*

WHEN NATHAN CAME DOWNSTAIRS AND INTO THE LOBBY AT FIVE thirty, he found his socks and slacks neatly folded—Carol must have done that for him—on the table where Abigail was reading.

She had undone her braids, and her hair hung down in long waves, obscuring her face.

"Hi, Abbey. What are you reading?" Nathan asked, and she showed him the cover without answering. It was a book about wolves. "So, how many flakes did you make this afternoon? A flurry, a squall or a blizzard?"

She shrugged. "I don't know. Not that many."

Nathan was surprised by her lack of enthusiasm. Ever since she'd gotten her hands on the calendar of events for this year's Christmas Countdown, Abbey had been jabbering on and on about how the girls at her table were going to make double the amount of snowflakes any of the kids at the other tables made. Nathan had to remind her repeatedly that the activity was meant to be a collaboration not a competition, but now he wondered if his lecturing had been in vain.

Is she upset because another group of students made more snowflakes than she and her friends did? Knowing his daughter usually needed time to work through her emotions before she was ready to discuss them, he didn't press the issue.

"You ready to go? I thought we'd give Celeste a ride to the inn and then maybe we'll stay for supper."

Abbey closed her book, slid it into her book bag and stood up to put her jacket on. "Celeste left a long time ago."

"Really? How many snowflakes did she make before she went?"

"None. She just, like, left. Aunt Carol said she felt queasy."

Ah, now he understood Abbey's indifferent attitude *and* why she'd taken the braid out of her hair: she was upset because Celeste had ditched her. And apparently, she hadn't even told Abbey directly that she was leaving. It made Nathan wonder if she was truly sick. She'd seemed fine when he'd gone upstairs to his office. He didn't want to be the kind of parent who excessively coddled his child and tried to make other adults coddle her, too, but at the same time, he was annoyed Celeste had disappointed Abbey. He would have preferred she'd let *him* down rather than hurt his daughter's feelings.

"Oh, that's too bad she's sick," he said to disguise his irritation. "Do you want to go to Aunt Carol's for supper, anyway?"

"Nah. Let's go home. We can have scrambled eggs on toast or something."

"Sure. Just let me change into my own pants so you're not too embarrassed to walk with me."

"It's okay, you don't have to. It's dark out."

He pulled his boots on over the navy and pink socks, donned his jacket and they plodded up the hill. It was so windy they couldn't pause to admire their neighborhood's lights the way they usually did, but Abbey seemed too dejected to care.

Despite his attraction to Celeste—or maybe because of it—Nathan felt disenchanted, too. *Sing we joyless all together,* he sang to himself, satirically changing the words to the carol as he followed his daughter home in unmerry measure.

'Twas the season.

Chapter 7

AFTER A LONG, LUXURIOUS SOAK IN THE CLAW-FOOT TUB IN her bathroom, Celeste's nausea and stomach cramps subsided considerably, and she actually felt her hunger returning. She figured she'd borrow a pair of boots from Carol and walk back into town to get a bagel or something light and bland. She got dressed and tentatively opened her bedroom door, wary that the smell of fish might make her squeamish again. She didn't smell anything cooking. Wasn't Carol home yet?

As she crept down the stairs, she could hear voices coming from the dining room. Arthur and Carol were seated across from each other at the table, and when they spied her, they immediately stopped eating and asked her how she felt.

"Much better, thanks." A faint aroma tickled her nose. "Is that soup you're having?"

"It's chicken broth, yes. Does the smell bother you?"

"Not at all. But I thought you were making haddock tonight."

"I was going to, but I know how awful it feels if someone cooks something like that when you're already qualmish. So I kept the meal really simple—it's broth and bread."

"Not just any bread—Portuguese rolls from the bakery," Arthur added, dipping a piece of crust into the broth and then popping it into his mouth.

"Would you like a bowl?"

"I'd love it." When Carol got up and went into the kitchen, Celeste said to Arthur, "That was really considerate of her to change the menu. But I feel guilty that you only get broth and bread for supper."

"Don't feel guilty on my account. I grew up in a family of seven children. We were very poor, so we often had broth and bread for supper," Arthur replied. "Those were hard times—but they were happy times. Sometimes having less is far more satisfying than having a lot."

"I know what you mean. When I was a girl, my mother used to take me to Cape Cod for a week each summer, and we stayed in a tiny one-bedroom cottage. After I started working as an adult, I was able to take my mother on vacations. And because of my professional connections, we were able to stay at some pretty extravagant places. But none of those trips ever quite measured up to the time we spent at Cape Cod when we were living on a shoestring."

Celeste surprised herself by confiding in Arthur like that, but he'd been so open about his background just now that sharing details about her own life came naturally. To her relief, he nodded knowingly, but he didn't comment or ask further questions as Carol reentered the room.

She set a steaming bowl in front of Celeste and asked, "Is it true you lost your wallet in the cove today and fell in the water trying to fish it out?"

"Her wallet?" Arthur paused with his spoon halfway to his

mouth. "I heard she'd lost the keys to the inn. And that Nathan ran out to the flats to help her look for them because you were furious."

"What?" Carol was incredulous. "That's so untrue. I never gave Celeste any keys to the inn. As you know, I leave the door unlocked for our guests between seven A.M. and midnight."

Arthur clarified. "In the story I heard, you'd left your only set in the pocket of the coat she borrowed."

Chuckling, Celeste interrupted to tell them what had really happened down at the cove. Then Carol regaled her and Arthur with other absurd rumors she'd heard over the years at Christmas Cove. By the time she'd finished her broth and two Portuguese rolls, Celeste's stomach was aching again, but this time it was from laughing so hard.

"Let me help you do the dishes," she offered to Carol after Arthur had excused himself to go read in the annex.

"No, don't be silly," Carol protested. "It only takes a sec to pop these things in the dishwasher. I don't have plans for the evening anyway, except dropping by my brother's house. It's supposed to start snowing tonight, and I think he has my windshield brush."

"Do you mind if I go with you? In case I don't get to talk to Abigail before I leave tomorrow, I want to tell her how sorry I am I had to duck out of the Make-a-Flake event."

"Sure. Just give me two minutes to tidy up, and I'll meet you by the front door."

Celeste ran upstairs to brush her teeth. Then she hastily applied a coat of lipstick and carried her sneakers with her downstairs. The right one was still damp, but Nathan had said his house was just around the corner so she figured she could tough it out. However, when Carol saw her, she balked at the idea and insisted Celeste borrow a pair of boots. She brought her extra socks and a different jacket as well. Even so, as soon as they stepped out the door, a gust of wind made her hunch up her shoulders.

Noticing Carol's jacket was unbuttoned, she shrieked, "Aren't you freezing?"

"Nah. Not with this built-in furnace in my belly," Carol griped, patting her stomach. Celeste would have just assumed she was using a figure of speech if Carol hadn't stopped walking and smacked her forehead. "Oops. I didn't mean to say that out loud."

Then it dawned on Celeste what Carol had inadvertently disclosed. "You're pregnant?"

"Yes, but no one knows yet," Carol replied in a hushed tone, looking around as if anyone else would have been foolish enough to venture outdoors on a night like this. "Not even my husband. I'm going to tell him on Christmas Day."

"I promise I won't say a word to anyone." Celeste felt the same brief stitch of wistfulness she experienced whenever one of her friends from college or coworkers announced she was pregnant. But the feeling passed as quickly as it had come, and she smiled, exclaiming, "Congratulations—that's really wonderful."

"Thank you. I'm so excited I can hardly wait."

The pair continued toward Nathan's house, and as they approached, Carol suggested, "Instead of knocking, let's sing Christmas carols until he opens the door."

"No way. I've got a terrible voice." Celeste's voice wasn't all that bad, but she couldn't take the chance that she'd start out singing and wind up sobbing. Christmas music had a way of doing that to her.

"Just one song, please?"

"Oh, all right. But let's sing something easy and quick, like 'We Wish You a Merry Christmas.'"

The wind must have drowned out their voices because Nathan

hadn't answered/? the door by the time they finished the first verse and refrain.

Undeterred, Carol continued. "'Oh, bring us some figgy pudding. Oh, bring us some figgy pudding—'"

"Have you ever even *tried* figgy pudding?" Celeste interrupted. "The traditional kind that's made with real suet?"

Carol ignored her and increased her volume. "'We won't stop until we get some. We won't stop until—'"

"Because I tried it in the UK once and I have to say, in my opinion, it's not worth singing about."

Carol laughed, scolding, "Cut it out. You're ruining my concentration."

"I thought you said you wouldn't stop singing until you got some figgy pudding," Celeste retorted.

Carol laughed harder, picking up where she'd left off. "'We won't stop until we get some. So bring it RIGHT HEEERE!'"

The door opened and the floodlight came on. "Carol? Celeste! What are you two doing?" Nathan asked.

His sister put her hands on her hips. "I'm *carol*ing you, obviously."

"And I'm *Celeste*-ing you."

Nathan didn't even crack a smile. "When the neighbors complain tomorrow, I'm going to tell them to take it up with you guys."

Abigail pushed her way around her father. "Hi, Aunt Carol. Hi, Celeste. Come on in." As the two women eased past Nathan and into the living room, Abbey said, "I don't know what figgy pudding is, but I can make popcorn for everyone."

"No, you can't. Celeste is nauseated. It'll upset her stomach," Nathan countered, an edge to his voice. Was he annoyed at her for some reason?

"Actually, I feel a lot better now. But you don't have to make popcorn, Abbey. I just came by to tell you I was sorry I couldn't help you and your friends this afternoon."

"That's okay. I'm glad you feel okay now." Abigail had the cutest jack-o'-lantern smile. "I wanted to make popcorn anyway because Dad and I are going to watch A *Christmas Carol*. Do you want to watch it with us?"

"Sure," her aunt said.

Celeste hesitated. She and her mother used to watch the Dickens film adaptation every year in the evening on December 25. They'd get into their pajamas, fill their plates with leftovers and snuggle under blankets at the opposite ends of the sofa to view it.

Last year when her mother was in the hospice, Celeste pulled out their copy of the movie so they could watch it together, even though it was only December 4 at the time. Her mother had no appetite, and she'd fallen asleep five minutes into the film, so Celeste ended up turning it off and sitting in the dark, just holding on to her mother's hand. After standing Abigail up once already today, she didn't want to turn her down now, but she couldn't shake the mournful associations she had with that movie ever since her mother died.

"Well, that story makes me pretty sad, and I'm not sure I want you guys to see me cry. Especially since I've already embarrassed myself once today by falling in the water," she said lightly, even though she was serious.

"That's okay. I cry during movies sometimes, too," Abbey replied.

As much as she appreciated the young girl's empathy, Celeste knew there was no way she could stick around for the film. She tried to think of another excuse to leave without hurting Abigail's feelings or telling a lie, but nothing came to mind. Mercifully, Nathan spoke up.

"We could play a game instead. How about charades?" he asked. His suggestion was such a relief it made Celeste want to wrap her arms around him even tighter than when he'd given her a piggyback ride that afternoon.

"Sounds great," she said.

NATHAN HAD SENSED CELESTE'S DISCOMFORT WHEN ABBEY HAD invited her to stay for the movie, but he was pleased that she compromised about staying for a game. She even agreed with his daughter's request to make the charades Christmas-themed. They all covertly scribbled the names of Christmas characters or scenes on slips of paper and mixed them in a basket so they could take turns acting them out.

Before the game began, Abbey made popcorn, but Carol said she was craving something sweet to go with it. Since Nathan didn't have any baked goods in the house, his sister melted chocolate chips and drizzled them over the popcorn, along with slivers of a candy cane she took from the Christmas tree and crushed with a rolling pin. He noticed Celeste hungrily munched on the snack throughout the evening, but he decided to give her the benefit of the doubt; there was no reason she would have lied about feeling sick earlier. Besides, if Abigail forgave her for not helping make snowflakes after saying she would, who was he to hold a grudge?

His sister insisted they pair up in teams, with Carol and Abbey competing against Nathan and Celeste. The game took well over an hour and the four of them spent more time laughing than miming. Finally, they were down to the final slip of paper in the basket. The game was tied, and it was Celeste's turn to act and Nathan's turn to guess.

"Don't worry," Carol told Abigail. "I know which charade it is—it's one of the suggestions I wrote. Your dad will *never* get it."

But as it turned out, Celeste did a dead-on impression of Mrs. Cratchit reluctantly toasting Mr. Scrooge, and Nathan guessed it right away. He and Celeste cheered, but Carol had the last laugh, hinting, "You two must have a lot in common—you were on exactly the same page just now."

Trying to downplay his sister's overt matchmaking, Nathan boasted, "Yeah. We're on the page that says, 'We won.'"

"It's not all about winning, Dad. It's about having fun with your friends," Abigail had chided, waving her finger as she echoed his advice to *her* about the Make-a-Flake event. Was that really what he sounded like? She turned to address Celeste. "Are you coming to Souper Supper and the Ugly Sweater Contest tomorrow?"

"I'll probably be on my way back to Boston or on to New York by then. The storm's supposed to move out quickly."

"But if it doesn't, will you come?" Abbey pleaded. "It's really fun and there's more to eat than just soup. The desserts are *epic*."

"Don't badger Celeste. She knows she's welcome to join us if she's here and if she wants to, but if she doesn't, that's okay. We just appreciate it that she came over tonight, don't we?" Nathan prompted.

Carol harrumphed. "And don't forget about how much you appreciate Aunt Carol, the one who pulled a dessert together out of thin air."

"Yeah, it was really good. Thanks, Aunt Carol," Abbey said. "And thanks for coming over, Celeste."

"I had a blast, and I'm glad I got to see you again. I didn't know if you were going to stop by the inn for breakfast before you went to school tomorrow morning."

"There's not going to be any school tomorrow. It's going to be a snow day," Abbey said.

Celeste's eyes widened. "School's been called off already?"

"No. But it will be. You'll see."

Later, as Nathan lay in bed watching the eleven o'clock news, he concluded that Abbey was undoubtedly right; he expected to wake up to eight to ten inches of snow on the ground and school would be canceled. However, Celeste was probably right, too; the roads would be cleared by midday, and she'd be on a flight by early evening, if not before. Clicking off the TV, he sighed and rested his head against his pillow. He couldn't recall the last time he'd laughed as much as he had that evening. His sister and daughter had really clicked with Celeste, too; it was as if they'd all known her for years.

Nathan found himself wishing she could stay for Souper Supper and the Ugly Sweater Contest as much as Abigail did. *But this doesn't necessarily have to be the last time we see her,* he thought. Once again, he allowed himself to entertain the idea of calling Celeste after the holidays were over and she was back from the Caribbean. Whether he actually would or not, he wasn't sure but the possibility put a smile on his lips as he drifted off to sleep.

Sometime later, he was woken by the clattering of a snowplow rumbling down the road, followed by a scream. His heart thundering, he raced to Abigail's room even before he was fully aware of what he was doing. He flicked on the light to find her sitting upright in bed, hugging herself as she rocked forward and back. Nathan rushed to her side and drew her to his chest.

"What's wrong, sweetheart? Did you have a nightmare?"

"Yes. A really bad one," she sobbed.

Nathan knew from experience she'd tell him about it once she caught her breath, so he held on to her until she quieted.

"You and I were sitting on the sofa in the living room, and

Celeste was sitting in the middle of us and it snowed so much our roof collapsed," she said. "But the snow only fell on top of me, not on you or Celeste. It was like an avalanche, and I was buried so deep you gave up looking for me."

"That's a terrible dream," he acknowledged. "I think what must have happened is that while you were sleeping, your ears heard the snowplow go by and your brain was still sleepy so it made up a dream to go with it. The avalanche you dreamed about was really just the racket of the plow scraping the pavement."

"Why would my brain make up such a terrible dream to go with the noise instead of a good one?"

Unfortunately, it's probably because of my *behavior,* Nathan thought guiltily. He didn't know much about dream interpretation, but his daughter's nightmare was too symbolic for his comfort. *She's afraid Celeste is going to come between her and me,* he thought. Abigail was very perceptive; she must have picked up on his attraction to Celeste. And as fond as *she* was of the woman, Abbey was probably worried Nathan would forget all about his little girl if he got involved in a romantic relationship. Clearly, his daughter's anxiety was manifesting itself in her dreams.

Then again, maybe her nightmare was caused by eating too much popcorn right before bedtime. Or by reading a book about wolves, for that matter.

"I don't know," he admitted. "Sometimes our brains do odd things when we're asleep. But our roof is very, very sturdy, so there's no way it will collapse from the snowfall. And there aren't any mountains on the island, so it's impossible for us to have an avalanche."

"But if there was one, or if I fell into a really deep snowbank, you'd keep digging until you found me, right, Dad?"

His daughter's question pierced Nathan's heart. "Of course I would. If you and I ever got separated for any reason, I'd never stop searching for you until you were safe in my arms again."

"I know that when I'm awake. But in the dream it seemed so real, like you didn't even notice I was gone. I wish I could get that dream out of my head."

"Maybe if you lie down and tell me some of the good things you're happy about, they'll seep into your dreams."

Abbey flopped back against the pillow, and Nathan switched off the light and perched on the end of her bed. Tomorrow, she'd be embarrassed for crying about a nightmare, but he could tell she still needed him with her. "So, what are you happy about?" he asked again.

"I'm happy that there's enough snow on the ground for the plow to come, even though it made me have a bad dream. Because that means I was right about there not being school tomorrow."

Yeah. It's a good thing school will be canceled because she's going to need to sleep in an extra hour. "What else?"

"I'm happy about the Ugly Sweater Contest. I can't wait for you to see what I'm wearing. I think I'm going to win."

This year, Abigail wouldn't allow Nathan to see what she was wearing ahead of time, and he'd kept his sweater a secret from her as well. "I wouldn't be too sure of that. Mine's awfully ugly, too."

Actually, it was more ridiculous than ugly. He'd worn the same sweater for the previous two contests: a red-wool pullover with white cuffs and a black belt depicted across the front, a la Kris Kringle. He'd paired it with a Santa hat. Understated, but enough of a nod to the occasion that he could participate without completely sacrificing his dignity.

This year, however, Abigail had challenged both of them to *make* their sweaters. So, he'd saved the cuttings from the Christmas tree and used his staple gun to secure them to a green, hooded sweatshirt in a roughly treelike pattern. He'd wound tinsel around the torso and decorated the whole thing with red, silver and gold ornaments he'd bought at the thrift store. His creation's crowning glory was the twelve-inch, battery-operated, digital star he affixed to the tip of the hood; it flashed a variety of patterns in orange, pink, blue and purple.

"You know what else I'm happy about?" Abbey asked. "I'm happy that even though Christmas Countdown is almost over, it will only be six more months until my other favorite holiday—summer."

Honey, summer isn't a holiday. It's a season, Nathan thought, but he knew what she meant. Abigail loved summer in Quahog Cove so much that every day felt like a celebration. Unfortunately, the following year they might not be there to enjoy it.

Nathan shuddered. He only had a few more days to find a major donor. Every minute counted, so as long as he was awake he might as well resume his online research. Come morning, he'd squirrel himself away in his office and eliminate anything and everything that distracted him from his goal—including daydreaming about seeing Celeste again in the future.

Chapter 8

EVEN AS SHE LANGUIDLY NESTLED BENEATH HER QUILT, CE-leste knew it must have snowed a lot because twice during the night the plows had woken her. *Good. The sooner it falls, the sooner it gets cleared away and the sooner I'm on my way to the Caribbean.* Then she wouldn't have to worry that she'd irreparably "jeopardized her exemplary reputation" with Philip any longer. Or that he'd do something punitive in response.

Punitive. The word was both fitting and belittling. She wasn't a child; she was an employee. A high-performing one at that. "I wish I had him here. I'd give him a piece of my mind to feast upon," Celeste spoke aloud, quoting Mrs. Cratchit's toast of Scrooge from *A Christmas Carol.*

Then she chuckled as she reflected on her evening of charades with Carol, Abigail and Nathan. Despite its focus on Christmas characters, the game had been a welcome distraction from her earlier conversation with Philip yesterday. Especially Nathan's hilarious miming of Elvis singing "Blue Christmas." Celeste had known who he was pretending to be the second he'd snarled his lip and pushed his hair back into a rough likeness of a pompadour. But she'd kept claiming she had no idea what he was trying to convey so he was forced to act out other clues. By the time the buzzer rang, she, Carol and Abbey were gasping with laughter over his "Shake, Rattle and Roll" imitation.

And although it was obvious that Carol had been pushing her toward Nathan, Celeste hadn't particularly minded. Carol was right; the two of them really *had* seemed to be on the same page last night, once he got over whatever was bugging him when they first arrived. She'd felt so comfortable with him and his family that it was easy to let her guard down around them. *If he didn't live on Sea Spray Island and I didn't travel so often, he'd be the kind of guy I'd want to date,* Celeste thought. But since those were two insurmountable *ifs*, she dismissed the idea and got out of bed.

Raising the window shade, she expected to see up to a foot of snow on the ground, which was what the last report she'd listened to before she'd gone to bed indicated. Instead, there were only about six to eight inches, although it was hard to tell for certain; the wind was blowing so fiercely the flakes blurred her range of vision.

If the storm is petering out already, I might be able to leave sooner than I expected, she thought as she opened the mahogany armoire. She removed the lost-and-found running pants from a hanger and layered them over a pair of leggings in case she had time for a walk this morning. As she considered her sweater options, she felt like Goldilocks choosing a bowl of porridge. The green cable knit was too bulky to wear under the jacket from Carol. The maroon sweater looked itchy *and* it had elbow patches. She'd already worn the gray pullover the day before, but only for a few hours, so it wasn't as if it was dirty. "Just right," she decided.

Once she was dressed, she hurried downstairs into the dining room. She was glad to see Nathan seated at the table with Arthur. As she greeted them and took a seat, Abigail shuffled into the room. Her nose was pink and her hair was damp; some of the ends were so stiff they appeared frozen.

"Hi, Abigail. Were you out making a snowman already?" Celeste asked. "Or were you sledding?"

"Nope, nothing fun like that. The start cord on my dad's snow-blower snapped, so I had to help him clear the sidewalk," she complained exaggeratedly. "What good is a snow day when your father makes you spend it doing backbreaking manual labor?"

"Backbreaking manual labor?" Nathan scoffed. "You've been throwing down rock salt and doing a little sweeping. It's a big help, but it's hardly backbreaking. When I was your age, your aunt Carol and I had to help your grandpa shovel after every single storm—we didn't have a snowblower."

"Why? Weren't they invented yet?" Abbey asked.

"Very funny." Nathan seemed less than amused, but Celeste figured maybe he was tired from the exertion of clearing the sidewalk.

"When I was a boy, *snow days* weren't invented yet," Arthur claimed. "It didn't matter if it snowed up to our waists, school was never canceled. Not once."

"Really?" Abigail's eyes went wide.

"Really. Why do you think we called it the Ice Age?"

Everyone chuckled, and a moment later Carol entered the room carrying a tray of covered dishes. As they passed around the eggs, oatmeal and fruit, Nathan explained that usually he cleared Carol's sidewalk and driveway, as well as his own and a couple of other neighbors' sidewalks, too.

"Most of the houses on our street are owned by elderly couples or they're only summer residences, and we're one of the few families with a snowblower."

"Mr. Lee has a snowblower at the center," Abigail hinted.

"He has enough work to do clearing the accessible parking lot, sidewalks and walkway at the community center. We're not going to ask him to come up here and do our work for us."

"I didn't say he should come up here. I just said he has a snowblower. *You* could bring it up here. Then Aunt Carol and I could use it. We'd get done a lot quicker." Abigail lowered her eyes and pushed a spoon through her oatmeal.

Carol must have noticed the tension between her niece and brother, too, because she diplomatically changed the subject. "Don't you want any scrambled eggs, Abbey? The protein will help keep your strength up as we're laboring away."

"No, thanks. We had scrambled eggs for supper last night, and we'll probably have them again this week," Abigail reported, and her father's face went red. "How long do I have to help Aunt Carol before I can go to the community center, Dad?"

"You just have to help finish the Johnstons' sidewalk and Aunt Carol's driveway. There's not that much more left," he answered. "What is it you're so eager to do at the center, anyway? No one will show up for a while unless they walk, since the visibility is so bad. It's not as if you're missing out on anything."

"Never mind." She seemed uncharacteristically sulky.

"Doesn't the center close because of inclement weather?" Celeste asked.

"No. During storms, it's more crowded there than ever. In part, it's because it's a great opportunity to socialize in general. Also, it's because we have a generator. So if residents lose their power, we always have heat or air-conditioning, as well as a kitchen for making sandwiches and reheating food people bring from home."

Abigail perked up again. "You could come there with me when I'm done shoveling, Celeste."

"Well . . . I plan to stick around the inn again today, so I can leave at a moment's notice, but if you have a spare shovel, I'll help you clear the Johnstons' sidewalk and your aunt's driveway."

"Yes!" Abigail pumped her fist.

"I couldn't let you do that," Carol protested. "You're a guest here."

"Yeah, you can't do that," Nathan agreed. "I'd stay and finish the last bit myself, but I've got some really important calls to make."

"It's okay. I want to help, and I've got nothing else to do," Celeste insisted. "Besides, I should help make sure the driveway's clear, since Carol said she'd be so kind as to give me a ride to the ferry." *Not to mention, she's pregnant and I don't know if she's under any activity restrictions, so it makes sense to give her a hand.*

"All right then. Thanks," Nathan conceded and stood up. "I'd better get going. See you all later."

After all the fun they'd had together the evening before, Celeste was a little surprised by how offhandedly he'd said goodbye. She kind of thought he'd at least wish her a good trip or say he'd enjoyed getting to know her or something, but maybe he hadn't enjoyed their time together as much as she had. Or was he including her with the others when he said he'd see them later? *Maybe he figures it's going to snow so much, I'll still be here this evening,* she thought, panic jangling her nerves.

Arthur pushed back his chair and rose to leave the room, too. "I wish I could help you women shovel, but the doctor says I shouldn't. I have a heart condition," he explained apologetically.

"Thank you for the thought, Arthur, but we definitely don't want you to put your health at risk. As Nathan said, there's hardly anything left to do," Carol assured him. She collected the dirty dishes and took them into the kitchen.

Alone with Abbey, who was drinking the last of her juice, Celeste offered, "If you want, I can braid your hair before we go out, so you don't get icicles on the ends of it."

"No . . . that's okay. I'd better not. My ears will show when I go to the community center."

"Why does that matter?"

Abigail bit the corner of her mouth and looked down into her juice glass. "Because Bobby Riley might be there, and he said . . . he said I had ears like an elf."

Call it maternal protectiveness, but Celeste had the fiercest urge to track down this little Bobby Riley and dump a shovelful of snow over his head. She took a deep breath and tried to think of a constructive response. She supposed she could tell Abigail that even though it was unfair, sometimes if a boy liked a girl, he made the mistake of teasing her instead of showing affection. But was that theory age appropriate for eight-year-olds? She decided it would be better to address Abigail's body image. "Like an elf? I didn't notice anything green about your ears."

"No, he meant they're pointy. See?" She lifted her hair back and showed Celeste her ears. The top ridge of cartilage was partially "unfurled," but it was hardly pointy.

"That doesn't look pointy to me. Not one bit."

Abigail shrugged nonchalantly. "They *definitely* look pointy to me, but I don't care. My dad says my ears are just like my mom's, and he loved whispering secrets into them."

Celeste's breath hitched, so she faked a cough. She'd often imagined what it would have been like if her father had loved her mother and her enough to say something like that. *Nathan might be a small-island type, but he's a* good, good *man,* she thought.

Abigail was looking intently at her, so she asked, "If it doesn't hurt your feelings or embarrass you when Bobby says you have ears like an elf, why don't you want him to see them?"

"Because if he says it in front of my dad, he might feel sad or lonely," she explained. Again, Celeste had an almost visceral response to the child's thoughtfulness and had to swallow a gasp. In the next sentence, Abigail showed her age by adding, "And I don't want my dad to feel like that, especially not at Christmastime, even if he makes *me* sad by forcing me to do manual labor."

Celeste chuckled. "The quicker we get started, the quicker we'll finish."

"Yeah, but I hope the time doesn't go by *too* fast because then you'll have to leave, and I really like having you here."

Strangely enough, I'm beginning to feel that way myself, Celeste thought as she went upstairs to put on another pair of socks.

NATHAN STARED OUT THE WINDOW, HIS THOUGHTS SWIRLING like the snowflakes in the wind. He understood that Abigail was excited about the school cancellation, and she probably couldn't wait to build a snowman in front of the community center with her friends. But it wasn't like his daughter to put up a fight about helping her aunt. Abbey hadn't really done that much work this morning—she'd spent most of her time making a fort, which had been fine with him. He'd even helped her build one of the walls, but he hadn't had much time to spare since he'd needed to get to the office early. Was that why Abbey was pouty? Nathan supposed she could have just been tired from waking up in the middle of the night. *He* certainly was.

Or maybe it was his dread of calling the board president that was draining his energy. Deciding he'd only feel worse the longer he procrastinated, Nathan picked up the phone to try Mark again. This time the call went through, but it was Donna, Mark's wife, who answered.

"Hello, Nathan," she greeted him in a hushed voice after he identified himself. "Mark actually just dropped off to sleep. I don't want to wake him because he threw his back out yesterday and he's been up all night."

"Oh, no, that's awful," Nathan empathized. "Was he shoveling?"

"No, it was before the snow started. Our children had just arrived for the holidays, and he bent down to put our youngest grandchild on his shoulders. But he must have pulled a muscle or wrenched his spine wrong. Anyway, he's going to be out of commission for a while, so would you like me to give him a message?"

"Just that I hope he feels better soon. The issue I was calling about can wait until he's back on his feet again."

Donna clucked her tongue. "I'm afraid that might not happen for a while."

"That's okay. No hurry. Even if it's not until after the holiday, that's fine, since it sounds like you'll be busy hosting your family," Nathan suggested, feeling guilty when Donna expressed how much she appreciated his patience. They wished each other a merry Christmas before disconnecting.

Nathan opened the bottle of extra-strength acetaminophen he kept in his desk and popped two of them into his mouth, chasing them down with a big swig of coffee. Ever since he'd spoken to the foundation rep, he'd been dreading telling Mark they didn't get the grant, but now that he *couldn't* actually tell him, Nathan felt let down. Not only would he continue dreading their discussion, but he'd have to continue carrying the burden alone.

He wished Josh, his sister's husband, wasn't out of town. Other than Mark or Carol, he was the only person Nathan trusted implicitly to keep the news a secret. However, if he told his sister, she'd fall to pieces about him and Abbey moving, whereas Josh would be disappointed, but he'd be a rock-solid source of support. He'd help Nathan through all of the logistics of moving, just like he'd done after Holly died. The two men had been buddies since college; in fact, Nathan was the one who'd introduced Carol and Josh. That was how his sister justified trying to set up Nathan—she was returning the favor, she'd say.

His thoughts circled around to Celeste again. He recalled how empathetic she'd been during their flight when he'd told her he was coming home after a meeting in Boston to discuss funding. How unpretentious she'd been after falling in the cove. And how graciously she'd intervened this morning by offering to help Abbey shovel snow. He closed his eyes and imagined her dimples when she'd laughed last night at his imitation of Elvis during charades . . . *Focus, Nathan. Focus,* he ordered himself.

He silently deliberated whether he should call the foundation to ask if the other organization had accepted the grant yet. After several minutes, he decided not to because it smacked of desperation. Nathan *was* desperate, but his time was better spent soliciting new donors than harassing the one who'd already promised him an official answer after Christmas. Sighing, he picked up his phone and found a text from a number he didn't recognize. *Is it a donor?* he wondered hopefully.

When he tapped on it, he saw there was a video attached. It was shot outdoors and at first it was difficult to distinguish who was in it because the wind was kicking up so much snow. Then he recognized the blur of Abbey's bright red jacket. She was shoveling with her back to the camera, oblivious.

"Hi, Nathan. I thought you'd want to see how hard Abbey's working. She's the one who insisted we shovel the Bensons' driveway after

we finished the Johnstons' sidewalk. You should be proud of her—
she's very considerate," Celeste narrated as she filmed. "Anyway, I
also wanted to say how much fun it's been getting to know you and
your family. So, um, Merry Christmas and best wishes."

Beaming, Nathan replayed the video four times before dictating
his reply. "Thanks for the video and for your compliment about my
daughter, Celeste. We enjoyed getting to know you, too. Hope you
have a smooth flight and a refreshing time on the *other* islands."

He considered adding, *I hope we can see each other again.* Or,
Maybe I'll call you after Christmas. But he reminded himself he'd
resolved to stay focused on the present problem of keeping the community center open, and not get distracted by some fantasy of getting together with Celeste in the future. So he hit "send" and dialed
the next prospective donor on his list.

IT WAS FOUR-CALLING-BIRDS-O'CLOCK ACCORDING TO THE
timekeeper atop town hall, and the snow had let up, but it hadn't
completely stopped. The weather reports Celeste had been obses-
sively checking throughout the afternoon indicated the nor'easter
was stalled over New England and the surrounding waters. Although all the major roads on the island had been plowed, the
winds were still howling, the surf was still roiling and the visibility
was less than one-quarter mile.

Celeste knew the answer to her question before she phoned, but
she called Patty anyway, pacing in front of the living room fireplace.
She was growing more accustomed to the Christmas tree, and it no
longer packed a sentimental punch whenever she walked past it. Especially since she'd covertly moved the starfish ornament to a back
branch when they'd returned from Nathan's house yesterday evening.
If Carol noticed anything was out of place, she didn't comment.

"What are the chances there are any flights or ferries out tonight?" she asked after Patty picked up and they exchanged pleasantries.

"About half as good as a snowball's chance in the Sahara," Patty said.

The Sahara. Next Christmas, *that's* where Celeste was going. At least if she got stranded there, she could hop on the nearest camel and ride out of the desert. That had to be a lot easier than trying to get off Sea Spray Island.

Aware that if she wanted additional information from Patty, she was going to have to draw it out of her, Celeste asked if she had any updates about the ferry dock or airport opening the following day.

"Nothing official yet, but the forecast calls for calmer skies, although the seas might be choppy for a while. Jerome says the runway has been plowed, so as soon as Port Authority gives us the green light, we'll be good to go."

"Okay, I'll call you in the morning."

"Anytime after five thirty," Patty cheerfully reminded her.

Carol ambled into the room wearing a coat and wiggling her fingers into a glove just as Celeste hung up. "No flight?"

"Nope. No ferry, either."

"Oh, I'm sorry to hear that—although I have to admit, I'm glad you'll be staying with us another night. And whenever you need a ride tomorrow, just let me know."

"Thanks, I appreciate that."

"You want to come to the community center? I'm going early to help with a few things, but the event doesn't begin until five o'clock. You don't have to wear an ugly sweater—you can just come for the supper. As Abigail said, the desserts alone are worth the trip."

"I would but I've got . . . I've got work stuff to do this evening." Namely, she had to work up her courage to call Philip, and that might take hours.

Carol offered to whip something together for her to eat before she left, but Celeste insisted she was still full from the spinach quesadillas they'd had for lunch. After Carol closed the front door behind her, Celeste flopped down on the couch in front of the fireplace, contemplating what she'd say to Philip. He undoubtedly was aware she couldn't leave the island yet; virtually every flight out of New England was canceled or indefinitely delayed. But since she'd agreed to touch base with him if there were any additional delays, she couldn't get out of making the call. Apparently, he'd forgotten all about her promise.

"You didn't tell me when your initial flight was rerouted, but now that every runway in New England is shut down, you find it necessary to let me know you're still on Sea Spray Island? What purpose does that serve except to put me on edge?"

You think you're *on edge?* "We agreed I'd call as a courtesy," Celeste reminded him. Not that Philip knew the meaning of the word. "And I wanted to assure you I'll be on my way tomorrow."

"When have I heard that before?" Philip muttered sarcastically. Then he instructed, "I expect you to text me your flight confirmation number tomorrow morning by nine o'clock sharp. Otherwise, I'm sending someone else. Got it?"

Her stomach dropped. Would Philip really pull the assignment right out from under her? Not only would that be unfair to Celeste, but the colleague he sent in her place would be *furious* with her for making them miss their Christmas celebrations. "Got it," she agreed. "But I promise it won't be neces—"

He didn't let her finish her sentence before he disconnected. Celeste's legs felt wobbly, and she plopped onto the love seat. Staring at the phone in her hand, she railed, "What a despotic, micromanaging control freak! That's the last time I ever volunteer for an assignment no one else wants!"

Celeste heard a cough followed by rustling nearby. *Oh, no—*

Arthur's in the next room. She got up, shuffled over to the annex and took a seat in the armchair beside him, abashed.

"Sorry I went off like that. I didn't know you were here," she apologized. "I talk to myself a lot."

"They say that talking to oneself is a sign of high intelligence." Arthur folded his newspaper and set it on his lap. "Although in this case, it sounds as if it might be smarter if you expressed some of your frustration directly to your employer—except you might want to find a more tactful synonym for 'despotic, micromanaging control freak.'"

Celeste smiled, in spite of herself. "I could never express my frustration to Philip, no matter how carefully I worded it. He's the editor in chief. He holds all the power at the magazine where I work because the CEO and president back him up 100 percent. Everyone knows he's a . . ." She tried to come up with what Arthur had referred to as a tactful synonym to describe Philip but she couldn't. "Everyone knows what's he's like and that he's not going to change. So I've got to grin and bear it if I want to be promoted to senior writer."

"And that's what you want—a promotion?"

Celeste wasn't sure why Arthur was asking her that—she thought the answer was implied in what she'd just said—but she confirmed it, emphasizing, "Yes, more than anything."

"*Any*thing? If you could receive *any* gift you wanted this Christmas, you'd want it to be a promotion?" His eyes were kind as he peered over the rim of his glasses, and Celeste got the feeling he wasn't asking the question again for his sake; he was asking it for hers.

"No," she confided honestly this time. "What I'd want more than anything is to spend Christmas with my mother, but since she's no longer alive . . ." Her voice cracked, and she couldn't finish her sentence.

"Ah. I see." Arthur nodded slowly. There was something so accepting and compassionate about his quiet demeanor that Celeste wasn't even embarrassed when a few tears rolled down her cheeks. They sat in silence for several moments before he suggested, "If you don't mind me saying so, in my experience, loneliness isn't something a person should suffer alone."

Celeste wasn't following him. "What do you mean?"

"I mean I wish you'd join the party this evening. I think it would benefit you, and I *know* it would benefit others to have you among us. And it would get your mind off that joy-thief boss of yours . . . What's his name again? Ebenezer?" he asked facetiously, making her smile.

"I don't know if I'm in the mood for a party right now, but I appreciate the invitation."

"Okay, but there's always room at the table in case you change your mind."

After he left, Celeste went upstairs to steep in a nice, long bath. The hot water seemed to steam the tension from her mind, as well as from her aching muscles, and she began to vacillate about whether to go to the community center or not.

On one hand, Arthur was right: getting out among others would be more beneficial than staying in by herself and worrying about whether she'd blown her chance at a promotion. Plus, she was hungry, and she'd really like to see Nathan and Abbey again before she left. On the other hand . . . Celeste realized there was no "other hand." Ugly sweater contests weren't one of the traditions she and her mother had shared, so it's not as if there was any danger she'd be overcome with fond memories.

And since there really wasn't any downside to going to the center, Celeste decided she'd better hurry and get ready—fortunately, she had just the thing to wear!

Chapter 9

WHEN CELESTE APPROACHED MAIN STREET AND NOTICED THE long line of vehicles, including two shuttle buses, parallel parked all the way down the road, she thought, *I must be the only person on the island not at the center yet.* It was an exaggeration, but not by much: drawing nearer, Celeste glimpsed into the large windows, and although the lights had been lowered, it was clear the place was packed. From the sidewalk she couldn't hear what was happening inside, but she could tell by the way everyone was turned in the same direction that they were listening to the master of ceremonies.

Hoping she wasn't too late, she breezed—literally; the wind was pushing her—toward the building. As soon as she stepped inside, the tantalizing aroma of clam chowder made her mouth water. The lobby was quiet and empty, except for Lee, who offered to hang up her jacket. When she removed it, he pointed to her shirt and whispered, "Great effort, but the Ugly Sweater Contest is over. Kanesha's just about to announce the winner."

Feigning ignorance, she whispered back, "There's an ugly sweater contest tonight?"

Lee momentarily appeared abashed. Then his face broke into a grin and he held the door open for her to enter the events room. When Abigail told her they were going to decorate it with paper snowflakes, Celeste never imagined this kind of transformation. There must have been more than a thousand flakes interwoven with hundreds of strings of lights, all of them cascading from the ceiling in varying lengths. Instead of snow, they looked like stars, a whole glittering galaxy's worth.

She stood motionless, mesmerized—until Lee let go of the door and it clicked shut loudly behind her, disrupting Kanesha's speech and causing everyone to twist in their seats and eye Celeste.

"S-sorry I'm late," she mumbled, utterly chagrined.

"No worries," Kanesha said into the microphone. "We're glad you came."

"Celeste, over here!" Abigail popped up and waved from a table near the podium, where Arthur was seated, too. As Celeste squeezed past the tables and chairs on her way to the front of the room, the tiny clinking of the bells on her sweater emphasized her every move.

"Uh-oh," Kanesha remarked. "If the judges hadn't already cast their votes, I think we might have had a serious contender for the prize."

Celeste scooted into the unoccupied chair between Abigail and Arthur. She felt so self-conscious for interrupting the ceremony she could hardly make eye contact with the other people seated at the table. However, she did briefly register Carol giving her a playful smirk. She also noticed Nathan was sporting a shirt covered in actual pine boughs, garland and ornaments. As she plunked into her seat, he did a double take. *Why does he look so surprised? My sweater might be tacky, but* he's *the one with a pine cone dangling from his armpit,* she thought.

That's when it struck her; no one else at their table was wearing an ugly sweater. It was possible Carol and Abigail hadn't had time to return home and change after they'd helped set up, but why was Arthur wearing the same vest he'd had on back at the inn? She stole a glance at the table beside her. Although the room was lit only by the ornamental lights overhead, it was bright enough for her to notice no one there was wearing an ugly sweater, either.

Nathan caught her eye and mouthed, "Sorry."

Sorry for what? Celeste wondered. She didn't quite get what was going on.

"As I was saying, this year we've decided there can only be one contest winner; no ties. So, without further ado, judges, may I have the envelope please?" Kanesha requested.

A woman whose name Celeste recalled was Sally whisked up to the podium and presented Kanesha with an envelope, which she opened with dramatic flair.

"And the winner is . . ." She paused and the younger members of the audience, including Abbey, drumrolled their tables. "Nathan White!"

Everyone burst into applause as Kanesha gestured for him to join her on the platform. He shook his head but got to his feet and pulled up the hood of his sweatshirt. Affixed to the pinnacle was a strobe-light star that flashed orange and blue and purple and pink and made the crowd go wild with laughter. Celeste clapped as hard as anyone when Nathan assumed a model's strut on his way up to the platform.

After the uproar died down, Kanesha said, "Congratulations, Nathan. You look fantastic. I know I speak for everyone here when I say I'm thrilled you won. Not only are you the most fashion forward person in this room, but you've done more for the community center in the past two and a half years than we could have ever imagined."

Her remark triggered more applause from the audience, but Nathan dipped his chin and held up his hand, as if refusing the compliment. Undaunted, Kanesha continued, "We've thrived under your leadership, commitment and ingenuity. And we're especially grateful that you've put up with all of us. We don't express our thanks often enough, so we wanted to be sure to say it now."

"Thank you, Nathan!" the islanders chorused, right on cue.

"It's been an honor and a privilege," he replied. Celeste wasn't sure if it was a trick of the twinkling lights, but for a second it looked like a tear shone on Nathan's cheek. If he was choked up, he recovered quickly, quipping, "What's my prize?"

Kanesha threw back her head and laughed. "That's another thing we love about you—your good humor. Lee, would you please tell this gentleman what he's won?"

"Certainly, Kanesha," Lee said over the loudspeaker. Imitating the voice of a game show announcer, he intoned, "Mr. White, you'll be able to show off your *en vogue* wardrobe when you and a guest use your gift card to experience fine Portuguese dining at Almeda's Restaurant, right here on Sea Spray Island."

There was more cheering and clapping. Kanesha handed Nathan an envelope tied in a big red bow and then gave him a hug. She must not have thought the mic would pick up on what she was saying—or maybe she did—because she stipulated, "Some restrictions apply. Your guest has to be a woman, and she can't be a relative. It's high time you start dating again."

This brought the biggest round of applause yet. Celeste may have been imagining it, but it seemed as if several people at surrounding tables glanced her way. As Nathan returned to his seat,

Kanesha explained that there would be a brief intermission before supper was served. "So feel free to get up and stretch or use the restrooms. But as my mother would say, 'Don't dillydally or you might end up leaving the table as hungry as you came.'"

As soon as the lights brightened and people started rising from their tables, Abigail asked, "Wasn't that a great prank, Dad?"

"Yeah, you got me good." Nathan laughed as he pushed his hood off. "You little stinker."

Abbey grinned and gave him a hug, obviously delighted with herself.

"You got *me* good, too," Celeste said, pretending to be upset. "I can't believe you didn't let me in on the prank, Abbey. And Carol. And you, too, Arthur! I wouldn't have shown up in an ugly sweater if I had known Nathan was supposed to be the only person wearing one."

"For the purpose of the contest, we defined ugly as anything we wouldn't want to be caught wearing in public," Carol explained. She pointed to a discoloration on her shirt a few inches beneath her chin. "See that? It's a coffee stain."

"There's something unsightly about my vest, too," Arthur claimed. That's when Celeste noticed it was misbuttoned.

"I told my dad we had to make our ugly sweaters instead of buying them this year. I didn't want to lie, so I made mine ugly by turning it inside out," Abigail explained. "And did you see Kanesha's? Her tag is showing."

Celeste stuck her chin in the air, still acting offended. "Those are mere technicalities. Other than Nathan, I'm the only one here wearing an *ugly*-ugly sweater. And *he* at least won a prize for his humiliation. What did I get? Nothing. Not even an honorable mention."

"She's right. You should share the prize with her, Nathan. Make a date to take her to Almeda's as your guest the next time she's on the island." This was Carol's most blatant attempt yet at pushing them together.

"Good idea," Arthur agreed.

Abbey was all for it, too, although her motive was different. "Yeah, you guys could order angel wings for dessert and bring me the leftovers."

Nathan looked as startled as a reindeer caught in headlights. "I'd-I'd love that," he stuttered. But was his reply more coerced than candid? Celeste didn't know.

Flustered, she reassured everyone she was just kidding, and she thought the whole thing was a terrific prank. Then she slipped out to use the restroom before supper was served.

In the hall, she took her place at the end of the line behind a woman whose sweater was pilled with fat fibers. A bald, cherubic-cheeked infant peeked over her shoulder. As the woman twisted from side to side in a rocking motion, Celeste recognized her profile.

"Hi, Patty," she greeted her. "This must be your grandbaby."

"Oh, it's good to see you, Celeste. Yes, this is Sasha, the one and only."

"Buh," said the infant, leaning toward Celeste with her arms out.

"Will you look at that? She must recognize your voice from the phone. Do you mind holding her for a sec while I go into the restroom?"

Patty shoved Sasha into her arms before Celeste could answer. The infant hadn't really wanted Celeste to hold her; she wanted to grab the shiny bells on her sweater. Because she didn't know how firmly they were attached, Celeste tried to keep Sasha turned forward, but the little girl writhed and screamed. So Celeste held her over her shoulder and bounced up and down. The sound of the bells jingling must have pacified her because by the time Patty emerged from the restroom, Sasha was cooing.

"You've got the magic touch—usually she fusses if anyone except her mommy or I hold her," Patty marveled. "Do you have nieces and nephews you babysit or are you just naturally good with children?"

"Neither," Celeste said, recalling that during school vacations, her mom would bring her with her to work when she was a nanny. "I had an amazing role model who taught me everything I know about caring for a baby."

"Well, you'll make a wonderful mother someday."

Even though the remark was incredibly presumptuous, Celeste recognized Patty intended it to be complimentary. "Thanks. I'm glad you think so," she said.

After she handed Sasha back to her grandmother, Celeste immediately noticed how empty her arms felt—which made sense, considering the little cutie was quite a butterball. But what she hadn't expected was for the feeling to travel up her shoulders and loop down deep into her chest, almost as if it was her heart that felt . . . not *empty* but as if something was missing.

Then Lee's voice came on the loudspeaker, urging everyone to return to their seats, and Celeste dismissed her fleeting emotion. *I travel too much to raise a child,* she reminded herself. *I probably even travel too much to give birth.* She could just picture the delivery: her labor would run long and she'd miss her flight to an assignment, so Philip would threaten to demote her.

As she stepped into the restroom, Celeste would have laughed at the thought, but it was a little too close to reality for her to find it funny.

NATHAN WAITED IN THE CORRIDOR FOR CELESTE TO RETURN from the restroom. Carol had told him about her flight delay, which came as no surprise, but he hadn't expected her to show up at the event. He wanted to be sure she felt welcome, especially since no one had forewarned her about the trick they were playing on him. He also hoped she didn't feel too awkward when his sister publicly suggested he take her out to dinner.

"I'm sorry no one filled you in on the prank," he apologized when she came out. "I've been told my daughter has been planning this for months. For her sake, I'm glad she pulled it off, but I hope you weren't too embarrassed."

"Embarrassed? No. Embittered? Yes."

"Embittered? Why?"

"Because obviously the contest was rigged. I understand how much your community appreciates you, but that shouldn't have affected the outcome of the competition," she teased. "I mean, seriously, just look at you!"

"What's wrong with me?" Nathan stuck his arms out to his sides. "I stand in verdant beauty."

"My point exactly, O Tannenbaum. This was an *ugly* sweater contest, not a beauty pageant," Celeste wisecracked. She narrowed her eyes. "Are those branches *stapled* on?"

"Hey, at least I don't have . . . What is that on your shoulder, anyway?"

Celeste laughed. He really liked those dimples. "Actually, I think it's baby drool."

"Classy."

"You should talk. Who tops a Christmas tree with a neon pink and orange star?"

"Someone who wants it to double as a disco ball." Nathan raised his hood and flipped the switch on. Tapping his foot, he pointed his index finger to the ceiling and then to the floor, '70s style, which caused Celeste to double over with laughter, just like she'd done when they were playing charades. He loved making her laugh, but he immediately lowered his arm when he saw movement in his peripheral vision.

"Don't stop on my account," Tim remarked to Nathan. Celeste straightened up, still clutching her sides. Flashing a smile at her, the pilot said, "I'm Tim, the pilot from the IslandSky flight you took from Boston. You're Celeste, right?"

"Yes. I'm impressed—I didn't think you knew my name since we didn't actually meet."

"To be honest, Patty told me. But I sure didn't forget your face."

What am I, invisible? I can't believe this guy just sauntered up and started flirting with her. It had been so long since Nathan had felt jealous that he hardly recognized the emotion in himself.

The pilot continued. "You've probably heard the wind's expected to die down overnight. The seas will take longer to settle, but the dock's supposed to reopen by noon. Apparently a freight ferry's coming in. Anyway, I'm scheduled to fly out at two-thirty—"

"That's fantastic!" Celeste exclaimed, clasping Tim's arm.

She's not just eager to leave Christmas Cove—she's ecstatic, Nathan thought. He understood why it was so important for her to get to the Caribbean, but did she have to practically hug the pilot?

"They're directing me to New York, though, not back to Boston," Tim clarified. "Patty said you're eager to get to the Caribbean. You might arrive there faster if you leave with me and catch a flight from NYC instead of hopping a ferry to the mainland and flying out of Beantown."

"Definitely. I'll let Patty know right away I want to book a flight. This is great!"

"Yeah. I can't wait to get back to the city. I've been going nuts. There's absolutely no nightlife here."

"What do you call all this?" Celeste made a sweeping motion.

Nathan couldn't be sure if she was joking or not, but Tim's snicker was decidedly derisive.

Rankled, he butted in, saying, "You won't find lobster bisque in Boston or in NYC that's on par with ours. And you'd never get it for free, so eat up and enjoy. I've got to get back to the program." Nathan turned on his heel to let the two of them finish their conversation, but a few seconds after he walked away, he heard Celeste's bells behind him. Realizing his behavior was borderline juvenile, he stopped and waited for her to catch up.

"Isn't it terrific that the airport is definitely going to be open tomorrow?"

Aware of how much it meant to her, Nathan couldn't begrudge her a smile even if he'd be sorry to see her go. He looked directly into her slate-blue eyes while he still could. "It's great. I know you've been worried about getting to the Caribbean in time for carnival."

"That's putting it mildly," she mumbled. "I'm relieved I won't miss my assignment, but I'm also happy I don't have to leave until two-thirty. Because that's, you know, *after* lunchtime."

"Yeah, it is," he acknowledged, wondering why she was so grateful for that. Carol must have promised she'd make something special. Then it dawned on him; she was hinting that he could take her out to Almeda's after all. Or was she? In case he was reading her wrong, he kept his invitation casual. "As it turns out, I just won a gift card to a fantastic restaurant in town. Since you sort of feel cheated, we could go to lunch together and split the prize, fair and square."

"Hmm. Yes, you're right. That might help me not to feel like I've been majorly defrauded." She stepped closer and adjusted the pine bough on his bicep. "It looks like you may have broken a limb—no pun intended."

Nathan chuckled and tried to think of a witty response, but his mind went blank. He felt heady from their banter. From her near-ness. Her fragrance . . .

"Nathan," someone called, and he lurched back. It was DeeDee Riley, a single mother Carol had set him up with once. She was a nice enough person, but they had little in common except their children; her son was Abigail's age. He introduced her to Celeste and then said, "We were headed back inside before the soup is gone."

"I won't keep you long," DeeDee replied. "I only want to find out if Bobby said anything that may have hurt Abbey's feelings yester-day at the Make-a-Flake event."

Nathan pulled his chin back. *If he did, she didn't mention it to me,* he thought. Before he could speak up, Celeste asked, "Are you referring to what he said when he saw her with her hair in braids? The comment about her ears?"

"That's the one." DeeDee put her palm to her cheek. Obviously, they both knew something Nathan didn't. "Ack. I couldn't figure out from what he told me, if he'd made the same remark directly to Abigail that he'd made to me. If he hadn't, I didn't want to make matters worse by bringing it up with her."

"Wait, what's this about?" Nathan asked.

DeeDee explained. "Bobby's been watching his favorite holiday movie for weeks. The main character's an elf and he totally loves the guy. So the other day he came home from the center all excited because Abbey wore her hair up. He'd never really noticed her ears before, and he said they were pointy, like the elf in the movie. He meant it as a huge compliment, although I doubt Abigail took it that way. His teachers and I have been working with him on developing empathy, but sometimes it takes a while for these things to sink in." DeeDee looked as if she was about to weep.

"That's true for us adults, as well as for children. Please don't give it another thought. There's no need for Bobby to apologize—I'll talk to Abigail myself," Nathan insisted. After DeeDee thanked him and continued down the hall toward the restroom, he softly told Celeste, "Ordinarily, I'd encourage the kids to work it out themselves with a little guidance. But Bobby struggles with some serious learning and emotional challenges. At this stage, it would crush him if he had to apologize to Abigail. But she'll understand once I explain to her how he intended his remark."

Celeste grimaced. "Umm . . . maybe it's better if you don't."

"Why not? Was she that upset about it?" Nathan was surprised she'd confided in Celeste about her feelings, since she was usually slow to express them. He appreciated her perspective, but Abigail was his daughter and he deserved to know if something was significantly troubling her. "Please tell me."

"Well . . ." Celeste made him promise he wouldn't mention that she was the one who told him what she was about to disclose. After he agreed, she said, "Abigail wasn't upset for herself. She was concerned that if you knew Bobby said she had ears like an elf, it would hurt *your* feelings because her ears are like her mom's. She didn't want you to feel angry or sad, especially not at Christmas."

That felt like a double punch to Nathan's gut. First, he was struck by his daughter's sensitivity to his feelings. Second, he was mortified that he had wrongly assumed Abbey had taken the braid out of her hair because Celeste had stood her up for the snowflake-making event.

He rubbed his jaw and reiterated, "I'll find a way to address it with Abigail without saying you told me anything. Thanks for letting me know."

"I'm just glad I have a bigger picture of what happened now. Because ever since I heard what Bobby said, I've wanted to take him aside and give him a real talking to about being kind. If

DeeDee hadn't come by, I might have been on the prowl for the poor boy tonight, like a mama lioness." Celeste chortled ruefully. Then she quickly stopped, adding, "Not that I'm equating myself with Abigail's mother. And I wouldn't have *really* scolded him. I only meant—"

"I know what you meant," Nathan interrupted her. "And I appreciate it that you felt so protective of my daughter. C'mon, if we're going to get anything to eat, we'd better hurry."

"Don't you mean we'd better *hustle*?"

"What?" Nathan didn't understand why she was editing his word choice. Was it an occupational hazard of being a writer?

"You're wearing a disco ball." She pointed to his head. "So instead of hurrying, we should *hustle*. You know, it's a '70s dance reference."

Nathan chuckled. He had completely forgotten the star was still blazing atop his noggin, and he supposed he should have felt foolish. Especially when Brent photographed him and Celeste entering the events room, and everyone broke out singing the stanza of "O Tannenbaum" that went: "'O Christmas tree, O Christmas tree, Your dress wants to teach me something.'" But all Nathan felt was elation because tomorrow he was going to lunch with the woman he hadn't been able to get out of his mind, no matter how hard he'd tried.

HOURS LATER, AS HE STOOD BESIDE ABBEY'S BED, SHE ASKED, "Do you know the only thing wrong with Souper Supper and the Ugly Sweater Contest tonight, Dad?"

I really can't think of a thing, he mused. "No, what?"

"They didn't serve soup. It was chowder. That's false advertising."

"Maybe that's because Samantha thought Souper Supper sounded catchier than chowder supper."

"Yeah, I thought of that, too. That's why I'm going to tell her she should call it a Chowder Chowdown next year."

Next year. The words hit him like a bucket of ice water, chilling him to the core. Because he'd been so exuberant about his lunch date with Celeste, Nathan had temporarily been able to squelch his anguish over the community center's future. But now he felt his eyes smart, just as they had when Kanesha expressed the islanders' appreciation of him during the event.

All day he'd been making calls to potential benefactors with no success. Nor did his exhaustive research uncover any more leads. He had two or three prospects left to contact, but after that, he was out of options. That was why he didn't feel inordinately guilty about leaving in the middle of the day to go out with Celeste. It wasn't as if a benefactor would materialize simply because he stayed in his office and wished for it to happen. He should know; he'd tried that, too.

Oblivious to her father's misery, Abbey chatted away. "I still haven't come up with a name for the bisque part of the title. Like, maybe it could be called, 'Chowder Chowdown and Bisque Bliss.'"

"That's very clever."

"Thanks. I'll try it out on Aunt Carol and Celeste at breakfast to see if they like it," she proposed. "It's too bad Celeste is leaving tomorrow before I get out of school. She could have been on my snow-sculpting team at the center."

Nathan felt a small compunction because he hadn't told her about their lunch at Almeda's. Although Abbey was clearly very fond of Celeste, he was still worried she might have reservations about Nathan dating her. He didn't want to trigger any anxiety for his daughter, especially not right before she went to sleep. He reached down and smoothed her hair behind her ear. "Ms. Riley mentioned to me tonight that Bobby made a comment about your ears yesterday."

Abigail wiggled her head deeper into the pillow. "Yeah, but it's okay. He wasn't being mean. He just says things like that. One time, in front of the whole class, he told the substitute teacher he wanted to give her a hug because her stomach looked soft and fat just like his grandma's," she said, as if she were trying to console Nathan instead of the other way around. "He meant it in a good way, it just came out bad. The teacher looked like she was going to cry, but that's only because she doesn't know Bobby very well."

Once again, he was moved by his daughter's insightfulness. "So his comment about your ears didn't make *you* feel like crying?"

"Nah." Abbey did a widemouthed yawn and then shut her eyes. "I'm fine with it."

"Good. Because I love your ears. They're like your mom's were," Nathan reminded her, even though she already knew that. He proceeded carefully, saying, "You know, when I think of your mom now, it doesn't make me as sad as it used to."

"Mm," Abbey murmured.

"But just because I'm not as sad doesn't mean I love her any less. A part of my heart will always be filled with love just for her. Nothing or no one will take that away. You understand that, right?" Nathan asked, but she was already asleep. He might as well have been talking to himself—and maybe he was.

Chapter 10

THURSDAY–DECEMBER 22

EVEN BEFORE SHE WAS FULLY AWAKE, CELESTE WAS HUMMING "six geese a-laying" along with the music from the clock on the town hall tower. When Patty had gotten home from the community center event yesterday evening, she'd put Sasha to bed and then very graciously logged on to the airline system and booked Celeste's flight to New York. It left at 2:38 P.M., which meant she had to be at the airport by 2:15 at the latest. She'd fly into another small airport outside New York City, catch a shuttle to JFK and take a nonstop flight to the Caribbean, arriving right around midnight, if everything went according to plan.

Since she hadn't wanted to take any chances that Philip would send someone else in her place, she'd texted him the details before she went to bed instead of waiting until the morning. She hadn't heard back from him by the time she'd fallen asleep. The thought passed through her mind that he may have been giving her the cold shoulder on purpose. When Philip was dissatisfied with a staff member, he'd frequently ignore the person before letting them back into his good graces. It was so rare for Celeste to fall out of favor with him that she couldn't remember how long his silent treatment usually lasted.

But as it turned out, when she lifted her phone from the nightstand, she saw she'd received a text from him. Let me know the minute you get there, he'd written.

Good—he's acting like his usual overbearing self. Will do, Celeste texted back.

Okay, that was settled. Now she could lie here a little longer and relax as she anticipated going to lunch with Nathan. Maybe her emotions were enhanced because she was so relieved the airport was reopening, but she hadn't felt this jubilant about a date since . . . since *never.*

She smiled, thinking about how goofy Nathan had looked all decked out in his greenery last night, especially when he'd started to dance. Yet his silliness was counterbalanced by how thoughtful he was. Not just about her feelings, either, but about Bobby's and DeeDee's and Abigail's. No wonder the islanders thought the world of him and had kept coming to the table to say hello or chat about his sweater. *He probably had to eat cold soup because they interrupted his meal—and our conversation—so many times.* That was partly why she was glad for the chance to get together with him over a nice, quiet lunch; she wanted the intimacy of a one-on-one conversation with him.

Oh, who was she kidding? She wanted the intimacy of a *date* with him.

It is a date, isn't it? Celeste asked herself. *Even if I essentially cornered him into inviting me to Almeda's, he had said he'd love to take me there.*

Regardless of who asked whom or what they called their time together this afternoon, it wasn't as if Celeste expected it to result in a long-distance relationship or anything even close to one. But if being in Nathan's company made an otherwise grueling month a little bit more bearable, who could blame her for drawing it out?

Picturing his soulful gaze and unruly locks and the small depression above his upper lip, she mused, *And if he wants to give me a kiss goodbye, I'd consider it a bonus.*

Now, the big dilemma: what was she going to wear? For pants, she'd put on the dress slacks she'd zipped into her carry-on before the flight. For a top, she had to choose between the green cable knit or the maroon sweater with elbow patches, since she couldn't wear the gray pullover again. She supposed she could ask Carol if she could borrow something else, but then Carol would know Celeste was going out with her brother *and* that she considered it a special occasion. She didn't want Nathan's sister to get her hopes up any higher than they already were, so she was going to tell Carol she was going into town to shop and she'd be back by two o'clock. It wasn't a lie; she wanted to buy her hostess a baby gift.

She put the two sweaters side by side on the bed. *Eeny, meeny, miny, moe,* she thought, alternately pointing at them. And then, *All righty, elbow patches it is.*

The maroon sweater was probably a good choice anyway, since it would fit better than the green one under the purple jacket Carol was still letting her use. Celeste and Nathan intended to meet at Almeda's, and after they ate, she'd walk back up the hill to the inn, where she'd change into her summer wear and collect her carry-on. From there, Carol would give her a ride to the airport. *Maybe Nathan will walk me back and that's when the goodbye kiss will happen,* she thought hopefully. *But I'm skipping ahead. First things first—like, breakfast.*

After showering and getting dressed, Celeste checked the weather online out of habit. Sure enough, it said the skies would be clear and the winds light. She took care of her personal online banking and then read for a while before heading downstairs at ten of eight. Pausing on the staircase, she listened for Abbey and Nathan's voices, but she didn't hear them in the kitchen. She detoured into the living room annex to see if Arthur was awake yet. Instead of reading in his usual chair, he was standing at the window, looking out.

"Good morning," she said gently, so she wouldn't startle him. "Beautiful day, isn't it?"

"Yes, it is," he answered, his back still turned. "I heard the airport is opening up again today—do you know if flights are arriving or just departing?"

"I can't say for sure if any planes are coming in. I only know mine leaves at 2:38."

Arthur twisted around to face her. In the bright sunlight, his face appeared pale and his smile weak, but he joked, "Does that mean Ebenezer is letting you keep your job?"

Celeste laughed. "For now, anyway."

"And well he should." Arthur sat down heavily in the arm chair, almost spilling his tea.

"Are you all right?" Celeste sat down, too. "You seem a little tired."

"That's because I was at a wild party last night," he jested. "It must have lasted at least until eight. Maybe eight-thirty."

"Hey—I was at that party, too!" Celeste grew serious. "And I'm really glad you encouraged me to go. Thank you, Arthur. It was exactly what I needed."

"As I said before, *we* needed you there, too."

Just then, Carol popped her head into the little room. "Good morning, Arthur and Celeste. Did I hear someone say they needed something? What can I get you?"

"Not a thing, except for breakfast," Arthur said, standing up. "Your accommodations are outstanding."

Celeste rose, too. "As someone who's spent the past seven years traveling around the world, I agree. You're the hostess with the mostess. There's something really special about your hospitality—and about the island."

"Aww, thank you. But you have to stop saying things like that, or I'll get all weepy," Carol warned, and Celeste understood what she meant because expressing how unique Christmas Cove was almost made her weepy, too.

ABIGAIL SNIFFED THE AIR. "WHAT'S THAT SMELL?"

"Does it smell like hazelnut?" Nathan held up his mug to indicate it might have been his coffee, even though he knew she'd been referring to his cologne, which he hadn't worn in so long he'd wondered if it had fermented.

"Are you going to Boston again?"

"No. Why?"

She slid her book bag off the table and shoved her lunch bag inside it. "Because you're wearing a nice sweater."

"I had to—all my ugly ones are in the clothes hamper," he joked, hoping to distract her from her line of questioning. Nathan hadn't realized it would be so obvious that he'd put extra effort into his appearance. *Does that mean I look especially good today, or that I look especially bad on other days?* he wondered, with all the insecurity of a fifteen-year-old boy. First dates did that to him; probably because he'd had so few of them.

"I can't believe we both overslept. I wanted to have breakfast at the inn."

"There wasn't enough time. Besides, I made waffles."

"The frozen kind. And you didn't heat the syrup like Aunt Carol does," Abbey carped. "But that's not why I wanted to go there—I wanted to say goodbye to Celeste."

"You said goodbye to her last evening." Nathan hadn't specifically asked Celeste not to tell Abigail they were going out for lunch, but fortunately, she hadn't let on. Before they'd parted ways last night in front of the inn, she'd given Abbey a hug "in case we miss each other in the morning." Then Celeste had turned to him and simply said, "Good night, Nathan."

"That was a really quick goodbye. You were in such a rush to get home."

"My pine needles were itching." Nathan wasn't kidding—he was surprised he didn't have a rash. "Tomorrow we'll eat breakfast at Aunt Carol's. I promise."

He hurried Abigail out the door and waited at the corner for her bus to arrive before he walked down the hill to the community center. Although a gentle breeze played with the ribbons of door wreaths, the sky shone blue and the sun was blindingly bright as it glittered across the powdery whiteness. Yesterday was the first day of winter, but Nathan was so euphoric, it could have been spring. He remembered this feeling, and it had nothing to do with the season.

When he got to the center, he said hello to Samantha and then popped in to thank Lee, Kanesha and the band of volunteers who were busy putting the events room back to its usual state in preparation for the day's programs. He'd barely hung his coat on the rack in his office when his desk phone rang.

"Hi, Nathan. It's Mark."

Nathan crumpled into his chair. *So long, euphoria. Hello, acetaminophen bottle.* "Hi, Mark. How are you feeling?"

"Like I got run over by a train—which is an improvement from yesterday. But eventually, I'll be fine," he said. "Anyway, sorry I've been out of touch. Our phone service had issues from the weather and I was, er, indisposed, as Donna mentioned. Since you didn't leave a message, I took that to mean we didn't get the grant?"

All this time Nathan had spent worrying about disappointing Mark, and Mark already knew? Nathan had planned to break it to him gently, but now he realized it was unnecessary—and impossible—to sugarcoat the outcome of the foundation's decision. Even so, it physically pained him to confirm, "No. Unfortunately we didn't." He took a deep breath and repeated what the foundation rep had told him about how the other organization had to sign off on the fine print before the decision was final. "But I have to be candid, Mark. I think it's over."

"Aarg," he groaned loudly. Hearing the disgust in Mark's tone made Nathan feel *so* incompetent, and he rubbed his temple, wincing. But then Mark said, "Excuse me. I'm moaning because I just shifted into a sitting position. As disappointed as I am in the foundation's decision, I feel even worse I haven't been available to support you. I understand and appreciate how much work you put into the application. However, just because it's over with the foundation doesn't mean it's over for the community center. I told Donna this morning I might be down, but I'm not out. I can still keep networking."

Encouraged, Nathan told him about the prospects he'd contacted and those he hadn't been able to reach. Mark added several more names and suggested the board could help grow the list, too. He promised to communicate to everyone immediately which directors were responsible for calling which prospects, depending on their professional and social connections. Nathan resisted the idea at first, since he didn't want to disappoint ten more people with the news about the grant right before the holidays.

"I appreciate your initiative, but you can't do all the work yourself, Nathan. Nor should you. The people who are on the board would be more disappointed if they found out we *didn't* ask for their help when we needed it," he said, and on second thought, Nathan realized he was right. Mark added, "Just remember, no man is an island—even if he lives on one."

"Uh, yeah, about that . . . I, uh, I was actually offered the job in Boston I mentioned to you," Nathan began. He explained he had no intention of accepting it unless it was definite that Sea Spray Island's center was shutting down. "However, they want my decision by the end of the day on December 26. I asked them to give me until December 31, since two weeks' time seems reasonable, but they couldn't honor my request. I hope you understand that if I didn't have to think about what's best for my daughter, I'd never—"

Mark interrupted, assuring him there was no need to explain. "Everyone understands you've got to take care of your family, so don't waste time feeling guilty. That said, I'm not anywhere close to giving up yet. Once the board members hear about this, they'll rally, too. And knowing that we've only got until December 26 will increase our sense of urgency."

By the time they ended their conversation, Nathan felt invigorated and he immediately began reaching out to the prospects they agreed he'd be responsible for contacting. Almost everyone he called was either out of the office until the new year or not interested in supporting the center. But one CEO said although his company wasn't interested, he and his wife might be willing to make a personal contribution. He promised he'd talk to her about it that evening and get back to Nathan by tomorrow. Motivated by even the slightest hint of success, Nathan dove into placing his other calls, and before he knew it, it was noon—time to meet Celeste at Almeda's Restaurant on the pier.

When he went downstairs, he noticed Ray, Vince, Alice and a few others gathered around Samantha's desk, captivated by whatever gossip she was sharing. Perfect; he could slip out without anyone asking where he was going or when he'd be back.

He exited through the side door and made his way toward Almeda's. Celeste was already waiting in front of the building. One hand holding a shopping bag, the other shielding her eyes, she gazed out over the cove. Her long, honey-colored hair cascaded past her shoulders in soft layers and her exquisite profile was illuminated by the reflection of sunlight on the snow. She must have heard him coming because she turned and smiled. "Takes your breath away, doesn't it?" she asked.

You read my mind. "Yes. It's beautiful," he agreed. "Am I late?"

"No. I'm early because I was already in the neighborhood, shopping. You're right on time." Just then, the town hall clock sang, "Twelve drummers drumming," and they both laughed.

Nathan suggested they go inside, where they could enjoy the gorgeous views without getting frostbitten. At the entrance, he reached to open the door for her but it wouldn't open. *Suave,* he thought and tugged the opposite door handle but that wouldn't budge, either. Then it dawned on him. "Oh, no! I totally forgot they don't serve lunch in the winter."

"Oh, no!" Celeste echoed, her expression crumbling.

Nathan's ears were flaming. He'd been so excited about taking Celeste out that he'd utterly forgotten the most important part of their date. He felt like a bumbling high schooler. "I'll call Angelo. He only lives a few miles south of here. He'll come over and open up. We'll have the whole restaurant to ourselves." *It will be romantic,* Nathan thought. Maybe he wasn't such a bumbler after all.

"You can't ask him to do that!" Celeste protested.

"Trust me, this is the kind of favor we do for each other here on the island. Since you probably won't get another chance to eat at his restaurant, he won't mind."

"*I* will. It's too much of an imposition. I'd feel selfish knowing he'd done it just for me."

"All right. There are plenty of other eateries right here on Main Street, as you must have noticed. There's also a French bistro a couple of miles from here, and a really popular seafood place on the opposite side of the island. We'd have to drive, but that's no problem. It all depends on what kind of food you like."

Celeste tapped her chin with her gloved hand. "Hm . . . I think it might be better if I don't eat a big lunch after all, since flying in a prop plane can make my stomach do cartwheels. I should probably stick to something simple. Like scrambled eggs."

"Really? Okay, well . . . There's a little hole-in-the-wall diner a few blocks from here that serves breakfast all day. It's good, but it's very plain." *And we'll have to sit on stools at a counter. We won't even be facing each other.* Talk about unromantic; Nathan might as well have been going to lunch with his brother-in-law Josh.

"I thought we'd eat at your place. Apparently, eggs are your specialty." Celeste gave him a saucy grin. "And this way, we won't be mobbed by your adoring fans who want to congratulate you on last night's big win."

She's saying she wants to be completely alone with me! This really is a date. Nathan had to swallow before he spoke. "I'd love to make you lunch. But I have to warn you, I'm not nearly as good of a chef as my sister is."

"I'll take my chances."

Nathan smiled and pointed to a side street. "Let's go up the hill this way, instead of back down Main."

"To throw the public off track?" Celeste teased as they began walking.

Nathan laughed. "It's not as if I'm a celebrity and they're the paparazzi."

"Maybe not, but it's pretty clear how highly everyone here thinks of you," Celeste said, which made Nathan cringe, since he was aware of how he was going to have to let them down. "What's wrong? Aren't you glad they hold you in high esteem?"

"I'm glad they appreciate my efforts—their support has been very encouraging to me," he acknowledged. "But I don't want to be on anyone's pedestal. It's a long fall if you don't live up to expectations."

"Even if you *do* live up to them, the pressure can be unbearable." Celeste seemed to understand exactly how he felt. But she changed the topic, asking, "Did you hear about the dock?"

"No." Since the tides in the marina were so extreme, the ferry dock was located on the other side of the island where the water was consistently deeper. He wondered if it had gotten washed over in the storm surge. "What happened?"

"The freight ferry sideswiped it. No one was injured, but the dock is damaged. They think they'll be able to repair and inspect it by late this evening or early tomorrow morning. No passenger ferries are coming in until they do. This one's going to anchor here, though, since it was delivering food and essential supplies. The stores are already running low from the—" Celeste cut herself off. "What's with the smirk?"

"Oh, I just find it humorous that you knew the scoop before I did. It's like you're a full-time islander," he teased. "Anyway, I'm glad no one got hurt and that you'd already decided to fly out instead of taking the ferry."

"Yeah, I really dodged a bullet." Celeste frowned, shaking her head.

Nathan knew what she meant, but he couldn't help needling

her. "Staying here for another day would have been that much of a hardship?"

"Not the staying here part," she clarified. "The part where I would have had to tell my boss I'd been delayed again, and he would have yelled at me."

"Why would he yell at you? *You're* not the captain who crashed into the dock. As my daughter would say, 'That is *way* unfair.'"

"I *way* agree. Unfortunately, though, Philip gets to make the rules, and the rest of us have to play by them if we want to get ahead. It is what it is."

Nathan took the hint she didn't want to talk about it any longer, so as they wove their way up the hill, he pointed out Kanesha's condo, as well as where DeeDee and Bobby lived. Within a few minutes, they'd reached his house. When they went inside, Nathan tried to usher Celeste past the crumbs on the kitchen counter and dirty dishes still in the sink, and into the living room. But she insisted on stacking the dishwasher and setting the table while he prepared their meal.

"At least let me hang up your coat for you," he said, and she allowed him to help her out of it. As she pulled her arms from the sleeves, he noticed her sweater had leather elbow patches. *I bought this sweater for Carol for her birthday four or five years ago,* he realized. He distinctly remembered that Holly had tried to talk him out of it. She'd said the color wasn't flattering and she didn't think his sister would like the elbow patches. Judging from the pristine condition of the garment, Holly had been right; it looked as if Carol had never worn it. Although this particular memory of his wife wasn't even remotely poignant, it made him feel maudlin.

Then Celeste turned to face him. "Thank you, Nathan," she said, and her warm, lovely smile melted away his momentary sadness.

"What would you like with your eggs?" he asked. "Bacon? Grapefruit? Yogurt?"

"How about toast?"

"Toast? That's it?"

"Yes. Can I have it the way you make it for Abigail?"

Nathan knew right away what she meant: sourdough bread topped with scrambled eggs and feta, and garnished with a sprinkle of fresh dill. "Ah, the house special. Or as I like to call it, the *Nathan White* House Special. It's fit for a president."

"So I've heard. Abbey said it's delicious."

"I'm surprised, considering only yesterday she was complaining about how often I make eggs for supper."

Celeste lowered her voice as if they weren't the only ones in the house. "I probably shouldn't repeat this, but she told me scrambled eggs were the one thing you make better than Carol does."

Nathan laughed. "Not the best compliment I've ever received, but considering my culinary skills, I'll take it."

They fell into easy conversation, and soon they were seated at the table. As they ate, Celeste mentioned again how much she'd enjoyed Souper Supper and the Ugly Sweater Contest.

"So did I, but I still regret that you were a hapless victim of the trick everyone played on me."

"Nah. I thought it was funny—although for a second I had a flashback to high school." Celeste took a sip of pomegranate juice before explaining, "My mom and I moved to a new town in autumn of my senior year. The very first week I went to school, I noticed posters all over the building reminding students to show their school spirit by dressing up that Friday. It was late October at the time, and I wasn't familiar with any of their traditions, so I assumed by 'dressing up,' they meant in costumes. But when I got to school that day, I found out that by 'dressing up,' what they'd really meant was wearing their best clothes. Suits and ties, skirts and dresses, even some formal wear."

"But you'd gone to school in a costume?" When she nodded, Nathan slapped his hand to his forehead and slunk down in his chair, imagining her embarrassment. "What did you go dressed as?"

"My favorite poet, Emily Dickinson. I wore her signature outfit— a blue, worsted shawl over a long, white dress with mother-of-pearl buttons."

"That's not so bad. At least you didn't go as a cat or a jack-o'-lantern or something like that."

"No, but I kind of wish I had. Because at least then my classmates would have realized I was in costume. Instead, they thought the clothes reflected my sense of fashion. I was so humiliated. I would have gone home and changed as soon as I realized my mistake, but I had a big test during second period, and I didn't want to miss it."

Nathan whistled. "Wow, that's dedication. You must have been one *very* serious student."

"It's true. I was obsessed with getting good grades. Except I was so flustered by my wardrobe mistake that I ended up completely blowing the test. And the subject was nineteenth-century American poets. How could a girl dressed as Emily Dickinson fail a test on nineteenth-century poets?" she asked, and they both cracked up.

Hearing Celeste share such a mortifying anecdote made it easy for Nathan to confide, "I bombed a lot of my tests in high school. And I didn't have an excuse like you did, other than that I was a slacker."

"Really? You seem like the type who has always been ultra-responsible."

Nathan made a scoffing sound. "*Pfbt.* No way. If I hadn't met Holly, I probably would have flunked out of college."

"Why? Did she help you study?"

"No. She threatened to break up with me if I didn't get my act together. I desperately wanted to keep seeing her, so I stopped skipping classes and started applying myself. To my surprise, I actually enjoyed academics." Nathan hadn't meant to share all of that. *Why am I telling Celeste how crazy I was about Holly? That's even worse than forgetting that Almeda's was closed for lunch,* he thought in the silence that followed.

But once she'd swallowed a bite of toast, Celeste said softly, "It sounds as if Holly brought out the best in you. I'm sure you brought out the best in her, too."

He nodded. She was right; their relationship *had* been like that. Nathan was relieved Celeste didn't seem uncomfortable hearing him talk about what he considered such a personal subject. However, he didn't want to dwell on the past when he only had another hour or so in the present to spend with Celeste. "What did you think of the eggs?" he asked lightly.

"Abigail was right—they were delicious."

"I don't have anything to serve for dessert, but we can swing by the bakery if you're up for a little walk."

"Sounds good. I've been wanting to try—" Celeste's response was interrupted by her cell phone ringing. She jumped up and fished it out of her jacket pocket. "It's Patty. Sorry, I've got to take this."

Even across the room, Nathan could hear Patty's voice coming from the receiver. "Hi, Celeste. I hope I'm not interrupting anything important?"

"No, not at all. It's fine. Why? What's up?" Celeste asked, disappearing down the hall.

Gee, good to know where I stand, Nathan thought. He felt stung. After sharing what he'd shared about Holly, he'd thought that he'd connected with Celeste on a deeper level. Come to find out, she was . . . What? Just killing time until her flight?

"You have got to be kidding me!" Nathan heard her exclaim. After a few minutes of similar utterances she returned, red-faced. "You won't believe this. Tim, the IslandSky pilot, suffered an allergic reaction to the lobster bisque last night, and he had to go to the ER. He's okay, but he's still getting IV fluids."

"That's too bad, but I'm kind of surprised that someone who's smart enough to become a pilot would do something so reckless as to eat a bowlful of food he was allergic to."

"I doubt he did it on purpose. Apparently, he's never tried lobster before. Or maybe he only developed the allergy recently, who knows." Celeste yanked her jacket from the coatrack, and as she was putting it on, she explained that Tim wouldn't be cleared to fly until the following day. Since two pilots were required on every plane, Gary couldn't fly Celeste to NYC alone. The next plane from Boston wasn't scheduled to arrive until five-thirty. That pilot and his first officer would switch planes and depart for New York at seven o'clock, with Celeste on board.

"This means I'm going to have to catch a late-night flight from JFK to the Caribbean. I'll have just enough time to get off the plane, check in to the resort and then go directly to *j'ouvert*." She picked up her shopping bag. "I have some urgent calls I need to make. I've got to go."

And out the door she went without so much as uttering goodbye—which was worse than unromantic; it was *rude*.

Chapter 11

CELESTE BARELY MADE IT TO THE END OF NATHAN'S DRIVEWAY before she had to stop. She felt as if she was on the verge of either hyperventilating or bawling. Maybe both. But at least she'd managed to get out of the house before Nathan could see how upset she was. *Nothing like blubbering on my way out the door to show him how much fun I had,* she thought.

Up until the moment Patty called, their luncheon had been nearly perfect; lots of laughing and flirting and meaningful conversation, including Nathan sharing a little bit about his relationship with Holly. It hadn't even mattered that Almeda's was closed because in a funny way, hanging out in Nathan's messy kitchen while he cooked eggs felt more intimate than fine seaside dining. More relaxed, too. Everything was going along so smoothly, and Celeste was crushed that it had come to such an abrupt end.

She closed her eyes, inhaling deeply. The air was as cold and sharp as icicles as it traveled through her nasal passages, down her throat and into her lungs. *How am I ever going to tell Philip my flight has been delayed even longer?* She exhaled. *And what's going to happen when I do?* Again she inhaled and then released her breath, repeating the process twice before continuing toward the inn.

Once inside, she hurried straight upstairs to call the airline in private. By now, she had the menu options memorized, and within seven minutes, she'd booked a different flight from New York to the Caribbean. Wishing the booking process had taken longer, she tapped Philip's name in her contacts list. With her finger poised over his number, she told herself, "I can do this. I can do this." But it turned out, she couldn't. Not yet.

Her legs felt rickety as she headed downstairs to ask Carol for a ride to the airport at six-fifteen instead of two o'clock. Just as she stepped off the landing, Arthur emerged from the living room, a folded newspaper tucked beneath his arm.

His smile faded when he caught her eye. "Celeste, my dear, what's wrong?"

That was all it took. The pressure had become too much and Celeste broke out in tears, like a burst dam. Arthur led her to the sofa by the fire. In between sobs, she told him about Tim and the lobster bisque and how much she dreaded calling her editor in chief to tell him what had happened.

When she was done explaining, Arthur commiserated. "I understand how frustrating it must be to experience another delay. But certainly Philip can't blame you for circumstances that are beyond your control."

"Oh, yes he can. And he will." Celeste sniffled. "Now I'll never get a promotion."

"Really?" Arthur narrowed his eyes. His skepticism was understandable—he didn't know Philip. "He'd pass you up for a promotion because you're late for *one* assignment?"

"Oh, I'm not going to be late," she clarified. "I'll get to my destination in the early morning, a couple of hours before *j'ouvert*."

"So, let me get this straight. Your delay isn't going to negatively affect the sponsor one whit? You're still going to cover the event in full and meet the publication deadline?"

"Yes. But that's not the issue for Philip as far as my professional performance is concerned."

"Then what is?"

"If I hadn't been busy changing in the restroom at the airport when I was paged, I wouldn't have gotten bumped from my initial flight and rerouted on a different plane to Sea Spray Island. Then it wouldn't have mattered whether there was a nor'easter or if the pilot got sick. Because I would have already been in the Caribbean by Monday evening, like I said I would."

"Aha, now I see the problem—it's that you're not perfect." Arthur stroked his beard with mock solemnity. "That is gravely, gravely disappointing."

Celeste hadn't realized how tightly she'd been clenching her jaw until Arthur's ridicule made her smile. "Believe me, I know how unreasonable Philip's expectations are, but—"

She stopped speaking because she heard a noise in the hall, and then Carol glided into the room, holding up her car keys. "You almost ready to go?"

"*I* am, but the pilot isn't." Celeste repeated Patty's account of what happened, and updated Carol about the change in her itinerary. "Could you take me to the airport around six o'clock or six-fifteen?"

"Of course, I will. I did just schedule a four-twenty appointment for a haircut, but I'm only getting a trim, so I should be back by five-thirty at the latest."

Celeste couldn't take any chances. She'd prefer to be dropped off now, if necessary. Better to be five hours too early than five minutes too late. "Are you sure?"

Carol twisted a curl around her finger, obviously reconsidering. "Mmm . . . Maybe to be on the safe side, I'll reschedule. I'd never forgive myself if I didn't make it back in time and you missed your flight."

Philip would never forgive you either, Celeste thought. *And he'd fire me.* But that wasn't Carol's problem, and she didn't want to inconvenience her hostess any more than she already had. Before she could ask if Carol could drop her off on her way to the salon, Arthur offered to take her to the airport if Carol's appointment ran late.

"As you know, I didn't bring my car to the island, so I'd have to use Josh's car, but I'll be very careful with it."

"I'm not even the tiniest bit worried about that," Carol said. "As I told you when you arrived, you're welcome to use it any time—if you don't mind driving the old beater."

Celeste questioned, "Are you sure I won't be interrupting your evening plans?"

"Not at all. We can arrive there extra early, if it puts your mind at ease."

"Thanks, Arthur. That would be *perfect.*" She emphasized the word so he'd know she'd taken their earlier conversation to heart.

But as soon as Celeste went upstairs and picked up her phone, the perspective she'd gained from talking to Arthur disappeared, along with her smile. She sat down on the bed and pressed Philip's number. Her only hope was that he wouldn't answer.

He didn't; a woman did.

"Hello. This is Philip's phone." The woman's voice sounded so unnatural that for one exultant moment, Celeste believed she had reached his voice mail. But then the woman repeated, "Hello?"

"Oh, sorry. Hi," Celeste uttered awkwardly. "This is Celeste Bell. I work with Philip. Is he available?"

"He will be in a sec. He had to dash into the wine cellar. Hold on," the woman replied, without introducing herself or explaining why she was answering Philip's phone.

I bet it's Mia, his girlfriend du jour, Celeste surmised. *He must have left the office early—or else he didn't go in at all.*

As an ironfisted micromanager, Philip only permitted his staff to work remotely if they were traveling on assignment. Otherwise, they were required to be in the office and at their desks five days a week, eight hours a day, minimum. Of course, the same mandates didn't apply to *him,* so it came as no surprise he was home with his girlfriend, apparently drinking wine in the middle of the afternoon.

Because her own mouth was so dry, Celeste was grateful Mia didn't attempt to make small talk. But the silence made the wait seem that much longer, and with every heartbeat, she grew more skittish. She was just about to say she'd call back later when she heard a loud click, followed by the *bing, bing, bing, bing* of a chime and then a door slamming. Were they in a *car?*

"Someone's on the phone for you," Mia said. Apparently she'd already forgotten Celeste's name.

"Who is it?" Philip asked.

I'm on speaker phone?! Celeste actually gulped, like in a cartoon. She couldn't bear to have this conversation in front of Philip's girl-friend.

"Who is it?" he repeated, and Celeste realized he'd been direct-ing the question to her, not to Mia.

"Hi, Philip. It's Celeste. It sounds like you're on the road, so I'll call you back later when I'm not interrupting." *And when your girl-friend won't be there to witness my humiliation.*

"Now is fine. Go ahead."

Celeste had planned to preface the bad news with the good, kind of like a police officer saying, *Your loved one is okay,* before adding, *but he was in an accident*. Except she intended to say, *I'm going to make it to the Caribbean before daybreak . . . but my flight has been delayed*.

However, she was so thrown off track by Mia's presence, she blurted out, "My pilot got sick from lobster bisque and he wound up in the hospital."

There was a quiet pause, as if he was expecting a punch line. When she didn't deliver one, he prompted, "You're joking."

Philip's tone was so flat that it was unrecognizable. For a second, Celeste wondered if Mia was doing an impersonation. Or if there was another man with them in the car. Then she realized what was going on: Philip *had* to control his temper because he didn't want to look bad in front of his girlfriend. *What a lucky break—this is even better than if I had reached his voice mail*, Celeste thought.

"Unfortunately, I'm serious. But there's another flight out this evening, and it will get me to the Caribbean a couple hours before *j'ouvert*. I'll have to hit the ground running, but that's no problem. I'll sleep on the plane so I'll be refreshed and ready to go," she said in her bubbliest voice, as if demonstrating how perky she'd be when covering the assignment. "I'll text you my travel itinerary."

"Good. I'll let the sponsor know you won't be checking in until the morning. Call me when you get there so I can follow up with you then."

Although Philip sounded almost cordial, Celeste wasn't fooled: she understood that "follow up" was code for "chew you out." But maybe once she'd actually arrived in the Caribbean, he'd relax a little and his bark would lose some of its bite.

Maybe, but probably not.

"Okay, I'll talk to you then." She was about to wish them a pleasant evening—especially Mia, her unwitting lifesaver—but Philip abruptly disconnected.

Relieved the call was over, Celeste leaned all the way back against her bed. Something crinkled beneath her so she sat up again. It was the bag of items she'd purchased earlier that morning. She hadn't planned to go on a buying spree when she'd started into town shortly before her lunch date. She was only going to pick up a gift for Carol's baby and then zip over to meet Nathan at the restaurant, all the while turning a blind eye to the yuletide decorations she feared would make her sentimental.

But as she was strolling down the hill, she'd caught sight of the cove. It was glimmering bright and blue, and sunshine was playing off the white, snowy dunes. Just looking at the wintry waterfront had made Celeste feel radiant by association. And suddenly she was overcome by an irresistible urge to go Christmas shopping— something she and her mother had always loved doing, despite their limited budget. Ironically, as she browsed the stores on Main Street, instead of feeling lonely, she felt closer to her mom.

Celeste could almost hear her quoting her favorite saying: "It's more blessed to give than to receive."

Which was how she'd come to have a large bagful of gifts on her bed now. Reaching into it, she pulled out the onesies she'd bought for Carol's baby. Because she hadn't been able to decide between the zebra, bumblebee or striped prints, she'd bought all three. The outfits wouldn't have been complete without matching booties and hats, so she'd bought three sets of those, too, as well as three bibs.

She laid them on the bed and reached into the bag again, removing the most *adorable* fleece teddy bear balaclava she'd bought for Sasha. Then the box of assorted organic teas for Arthur and hot cocoa for Samantha. After that, it was a sterling silver lobster-pendant necklace and a variety of hair accessories for Abigail. The only person she hadn't been able to find a gift for was Nathan.

Nathan. Celeste released all the air from her cheeks. She'd had such high hopes for their lunch date, and despite Almeda's being closed, it had started out so well. Just like the landscape, Nathan had appeared especially dazzling that morning. His baby blue V-neck cashmere sweater accentuated his chest and shoulder muscles and made the brown color of his eyes seem three shades deeper. The breeze had tousled his hair and tinged his freshly shaven cheeks. Admittedly, his cologne was slightly overpowering. But since she'd never smelled it on him before, Celeste figured the fact he'd worn it meant he considered their lunch to be a date, too. Or at least a special occasion.

And it *was* special. Eating alone at Nathan's house turned out to be a lot cozier than dining in a restaurant. Maybe it was because she ate out so often on her own, but Celeste relished spending the lunch hour doing something as homey as stacking the dishwasher while Nathan prepared their lunch. They'd joked and laughed the way they usually did, but this time they took their conversation to a deeper level. Nathan had even shared a little bit about his relationship with Holly. The date couldn't have gone better if Celeste had scripted it herself—until the moment Patty called.

I hardly remember what happened after she told me my flight was delayed again, Celeste lamented. She'd been so upset that she wasn't even sure whether she'd said goodbye to Nathan before she'd left his house. The only thing she knew for absolute certain was that their time alone together *hadn't* ended with a kiss.

Then again, she thought, as hope fluttered within her chest, *our time alone together isn't necessarily over yet . . .*

"HOW WAS YOUR LUNCH WITH CELESTE?" SAMANTHA ASKED when she wheeled into Nathan's office. It had been fifteen minutes since he'd slipped back inside the community center through the side entrance. He was actually surprised it had taken her that long to come looking for him. The mishap at the ferry dock must have distracted her from investigating the scuttlebutt about his personal life.

"It was fine," he answered brusquely. He would have asked how she knew he'd had lunch with Celeste, but he deduced that someone had seen the two of them trying to get into Almeda's and then jumped to conclusions. Conclusions which, in this case, were unusually accurate. "Did you come up here because you need something?"

"Just getting the spare key for the storage room. And checking to see if you made reservations for Lombardi's tomorrow," she replied, all smiles. When Nathan stared blankly at her, she hinted, "For our staff holiday party."

Every December on the last weekday before Christmas break, Nathan treated the staff to lunch at their favorite Italian restaurant. Since the holiday fell on Sunday, that meant their luncheon should have been scheduled for tomorrow, Friday. But until now, he'd totally forgotten about making the arrangements. He'd also forgotten that at the end of the meal, he'd intended to present the staff their year-end bonuses from the board of directors. Worst of all, he'd even forgotten where he'd stashed the checks.

"I'll make a reservation now. It's usually not too crowded during the off-season. Nicola should be able to fit us in."

"If not, we could get takeout. Or eat at your house. Or drive to the other side of the island and have a winter picnic in our cars. Which would you prefer?"

The question made him testy and he felt like saying, *I'd prefer you mind your own business.* Clearly Samantha was fishing for information so she could figure out which rumor she'd heard about him and Celeste was the most accurate. But Nathan wasn't biting. "Nicola will save us a table," he reiterated. "Thanks for reminding me to make the reservation. Please close the door on your way out."

After Samantha exited the room, Nathan ruminated. *The gossip must really be flying. I'd better talk to Abbey before someone tells her Celeste and I are dating and it makes her anxious.*

His daughter's feelings were one of several reasons Nathan regretted going to lunch with Celeste. He was still irked by her ungracious departure and resentful that she'd said she hadn't been doing anything important when Patty called. *She might not have considered it that significant, but I don't usually discuss Holly with anyone outside my family,* Nathan thought. Nor did he usually take such a long break away from the office in the middle of the day for social purposes. *It's not as if she was the one doing me any favors—she was the one who'd dropped the hint about going out to lunch together.*

He should have known better than to get involved with someone who was that consumed with her career in the first place. Not that he'd gotten *involved*, exactly. But he'd given her more thought and time than he should have. *It stops now,* he told himself, and this time, he really meant it.

He reached for his desk phone to make the reservation, but it rang in his hand before he could dial. The caller identified herself as Mark's daughter-in-law, Beth Rosen. She explained he'd mentioned he was soliciting funds for the center, so she'd told him about a new grant her uncle's corporation had established this year. Mark thought it sounded promising and asked Beth to discuss the opportunity directly with Nathan.

"I'll can run through the highlights now, and if you're interested, I'll send the application link." She told him that only nonprofits from Massachusetts were eligible to apply, which meant the applicant pool was significantly smaller than it had been for the other grant. Furthermore, the amount of the award was enough to cover the lease down payment and several months of operational expenses.

"It sounds great, but Mark mentioned we need the funding immediately, didn't he?"

"Yes. That's why this opportunity would be perfect for you."
Beth explained that applications were only accepted during the
month of December. They were reviewed on a rolling basis, and the
final deadline was midnight, December 24. To build suspense and
keep the entrants engaged, all of them—including the winner—
were notified of the results at nine o'clock on Monday, December 26.
And for tax purposes, the donation had to be completed by December 31. "The award has a long, official name. But guess what it's
called informally?"

"I don't know. What?"

"The St. Nick of Time Grant."

Nathan chuckled. That sounded like something Samantha
would have dubbed it. It also sounded too good to be true. "I wonder why I haven't heard of it before now."

"As I said, it's brand-new. There is a catch, however."

There always is, Nathan thought. "What's that?"

"Well, it's not a catch, exactly. But the application package can
be challenging to complete." Apparently, in addition to supplying
the usual mandatory pieces of information, applicants were required to submit a "creative narrative" about what made their organization so unique.

"You mean a case statement, right?" Nathan already had one of
these on file. A year ago, he'd consulted a freelance grant writer to
help him compose a summary about what the community center
did and how it would benefit from additional financial resources.
Nathan reused the document for all of his grant applications,
tweaking the details as necessary.

"Similar to a case statement, yes, but with an emphasis on "creative." They're looking for a really personal, out-of-the-box demon-

stration of what makes your nonprofit so unique." Beth suggested Nathan read through the application and let her know if he had any questions.

He already had one: *Can you put in a good word for us?*

Of course, he didn't ask her that. After thanking her and hanging up, Nathan immediately began perusing the application. As she'd indicated, much of it was standard. He could just cut and paste a lot of the information from past grant applications if he updated the data afterward.

Beth was also right about the strong emphasis on the creative narrative. Their current case statement, while powerful, wasn't original enough, and creativity wasn't Nathan's strong suit. So he decided he'd complete the factual parts of the application first and tackle the narrative after brainstorming it further. He was so absorbed in what he was doing that he didn't notice when Abbey opened the door and came into the room.

"Hi, Dad."

He flinched. "Hi, Abigail. You startled me."

"I knocked, but you didn't answer. I thought you were on the phone, so I tiptoed in." She came around to the other side of his desk to give him a hug. Her hair smelled like the outdoors, fresh and clean. "What are you working on?"

"Boring stuff," he equivocated, closing the lid to his laptop.

"Whenever I say that's what I did in school, you tell me it's not a good answer."

"I haven't heard you say that in ages," he replied, sidestepping her question a second time. "Why aren't you at the sculpture challenge?"

"Are you talking about the Snow-Slash-Sand Sculpture Challenge?"

"Is there any other kind?"

"No, but it's a tongue twister, and I want to hear if you can say it."

She sure is chatty today, Nathan thought. He really needed to get back to work, but he indulged her, slowly asking, "Why aren't you at the Snow-Slash-Sand Sculpture Challenge?"

"It doesn't start for, like, fifteen minutes and I need to warm up." In the afternoon, Abigail got off the bus right in front of the community center, with the other children enrolled in the afterschool program. The adult supervisor must have let them play outside for a few minutes today.

"Wouldn't you be warmer in front of the fire downstairs?" he hinted.

"Nah, this is fine." Abbey dropped her book bag on the floor and settled into the swivel chair across from him. "Can I go to Kaitlyn's house for supper? Her grandmother is making chicken soup with something called dumpings."

Nathan suppressed a chuckle. "Yes, you may, but I think you mean dumplings." He corrected her so she wouldn't inadvertently insult the senior Mrs. Knight's cooking. "They're like the matzo balls your Aunt Carol makes. Is Mrs. Knight picking you girls up here?"

"Yes. She's going to text you about it." Abbey twisted her chair from side to side. "Did you hear about the dock?"

"Mm-hm," he said as he nodded absentmindedly, raised the lid to his laptop and glanced at the application. There was an error in the budget section. He began to recalculate the figures, but he was distracted by Abbey spinning all the way around in her chair. "Quit that, Abigail."

She dragged her feet on the floor, slowing to a stop. "Why are you so grouchy?"

Believe me, sweetheart, you don't want to know. "I didn't mean to sound that way, but you were making me dizzy."

Someone rapped twice before opening the door. It was Kanesha. She greeted them both and handed Nathan a folder of papers to sign. "I tried to find you at lunchtime but you weren't here." She paused, clearly expecting Nathan to offer an explanation. He chose to outwait the silence.

Abbey, unfortunately, didn't. "Where did you go, Dad?"

"Back to the house," he fudged. This wasn't the time to tell her about his date—his *non*date—with Celeste. "Why were you looking for me, Kanesha?"

"To ask if you'd heard about anyone else getting sick after last night's supper? Brian felt terrible about the pilot," she said, referencing the owner of Salty's, the restaurant that had supplied the bisque and chowder for Souper Supper.

"You mean Captain Tim? I met him last night. What happened to him?" Abigail asked. Even though Nathan had taught her it was impolite to butt into other people's conversations, he understood why she'd consider herself to be included in this one.

"He had an allergic reaction to the lobster bisque. He became ill and had to go to the hospital." Nathan initialed a reimbursement request and began skimming the next document.

"Was it really an allergic reaction?" Kanesha questioned. "I heard it was food poisoning."

"He was poisoned?" Abigail sat straight up and grasped the arms of her chair. "Did he *die*?" she wailed dramatically.

"No, honey-girl," Kanesha said quickly to comfort her. She gave Nathan the evil eye, as if *he* were the one who'd brought up the topic in front of his daughter. "He's going to be fine. In fact, tomorrow he'll be back to flying a plane again."

Nathan could almost see the light bulb go off above Abigail's head. "Hey, that means Celeste couldn't leave Sea Spray Island today. You have her number in your phone, don't you, Dad? I can call her. She might want to come over here and be on my snow-sculpting team."

Needless to say, Nathan wasn't enamored of the proposition. He didn't want Celeste to think it was *his* idea to invite her to the center. Nor did he care to bump into her again. "I don't think she'll want to come. She's leaving on another plane a few hours from now."

"A few hours is *tons* of time," Abigail argued.

Aware that Kanesha was scrutinizing him—probably trying to figure out why he didn't want Celeste to come to the center—Nathan gave in. He reached into his pocket for his cell phone, but it wasn't there. Fantastic. He must have forgotten it at the house after lunch. Any other time, he'd just leave it there for the rest of the day, but he'd been giving his cell phone number, as well as the number for his office phone, to prospective donors. He couldn't risk missing those calls. "I left my phone at home. I'm going to have to run up there and get it."

"I'll come with you. We can stop at the inn, and if Celeste is there, I'll invite her in person."

"No," Nathan objected firmly. He was already pressed for time. Abigail would slow him down and there was no way he was stopping at the inn. "I'm not going right this second. I have to finish something I'm working on before I lose my concentration." *Too late for that.*

"Can I go by myself?"

"You already know the answer." As safe as Sea Spray Island was, Nathan had told Abigail a long time ago she wasn't allowed to walk between their house and the community center until her age was in the double digits. He considered it a rite of passage—for him, more than for her. A symbolic letting go of his daughter's hand.

"If I take a friend can I go?" Abbey clasped her hands beneath her chin.

"No. Don't ask me again, Abigail. I'll bring the phone to you when I get back."

"By then the challenge will have already started."

Nathan signed the last document and gathered the papers in a stack. "Kanesha will allow Celeste to join the fun whenever she arrives, won't you, Kanesha?"

"Of course." She took the folder from Nathan. "C'mon, Abbey, you can help me with the surprise. This year, I filled spray bottles with food coloring and water so everyone can paint their sculptures."

As Abigail got to her feet, Nathan said, "I'll stop by with the phone in a little while. Have fun."

"We will," Kanesha replied after a pause, even though it was obvious he'd been speaking to his daughter.

It was even more obvious that his daughter *wasn't* speaking to him.

As much as he regretted that there was tension between them, Nathan knew it would blow over once they had a heart-to-heart, father-to-daughter conversation tonight. Meanwhile, he had work to do.

Chapter 12

THE ROPE OF HANGING BRASS BELLS JANGLED BEHIND HER AS Celeste pulled the door shut and stepped onto the sidewalk. That was it, the last shop. For the past hour, she had searched and searched but she couldn't find a gift for Nathan. Oh, she'd seen plenty of items that would have been appropriate presents for a male acquaintance. But she didn't want to give him a generic gift just for the sake of it. She wanted to give him something meaningful. Something to show him how special she thought he was—and something for him to remember *her* by.

I guess I'll have to express myself in words instead, she thought. As she hurried toward the community center, she remembered the blank greeting card she'd bought that morning. It had a nighttime photo of Santa's Sailboat on the front. Celeste had intended to keep it as a memento of Sea Spray Island, but now she decided to inscribe a few lines in it and slip it to Nathan later this evening.

Before coming into town the second time today, she had offered to bring pizza and a salad with her to the inn when she returned.

That way, Carol wouldn't have to cook when she got home from her appointment, and Celeste would be able to eat a quick supper before her flight. Arthur and Carol had agreed it was a great idea.

"I'm dropping by the center after I go shopping so I can participate in the sculpting challenge. Should I invite Abigail and Nathan to join us?" Celeste had asked in a tone she'd hoped sounded impulsive.

"The more the merrier," Carol answered. "If they come, Nathan can give you a ride to the airport, since I asked Abbey to help me make a 'Welcome Home' sign for Josh the next time she came to the inn."

I knew I could count on Carol to contrive an excuse to push Nathan and me together, Celeste had thought. *That was almost too easy.* She was hopeful she'd get her goodbye kiss from Nathan after all.

But for now she was on her way to help Abigail's team in the snow-sculpting challenge. Judging from the rumpus coming from the opposite end of Main Street, the event had already started. Celeste picked up her pace as she headed toward the community center. There must have been more than forty kids clustered on the small, snowy front lawn, yet somehow Abigail spotted her before Celeste even reached the walkway.

"Hi, Celeste," she called, hopping toward her through the snow like a rabbit. "I'm so glad you couldn't leave. I mean, it's too bad Captain Tim got sick, but I'm glad you're still here."

"I am, too. Now I get to be on your team—although I have to warn you, except for making forts and snowmen, I've never done any snow sculpting. What are the rules for this challenge?"

Abigail explained that the students—including some teenagers not in the afterschool program—were divided into groups of four to six children each. Because Kanesha didn't want the older kids monopolizing the yard, she'd used bright ribbon to section it equally into smaller plots. The activity was meant to inspire teamwork, so each group was required to unanimously agree about what they wanted to sculpt before they began making it. When they were finished, they'd use spray bottles of water mixed with food coloring to "paint" their creations.

"Follow me and meet the team. But be careful not to step on anyone else's sculpture or Ms. Kanesha will send you inside early, and all you'll get for a snack is an icicle," Abbey warned, to Celeste's amusement.

After meeting Abigail's teammates—Kaitlyn, Ava, Zander and Malik—Celeste gestured to a boy lying spread-eagle on his stomach, holding his face up an inch above the snow. "I haven't met this boy yet."

"Bobby, get up," Abigail urged him. "I want you to meet Celeste. She's the writer I told you about."

And he's the boy she told me *about,* Celeste inferred.

"I can't. Malik and Zander will steal my snow." He stretched his arms out even farther, defending his territory.

"It's not *your* snow," Malik argued.

"Yes, it is. I called it."

"You can't call dibs on snow," lectured Ava. "Ms. Kanesha said we're a team, and we have to cooperate with each other."

"But she didn't say we have to *share.*"

Abigail quietly explained to Celeste that all of the kids in her group wanted to make a lobster, as a substitute for Sandy Claws. Except for Bobby, who wanted to make an elf. Since they were deadlocked, they couldn't start creating their sculpture yet.

"I see," Celeste replied thoughtfully, sneaking a glance across the yard at Kanesha. She was crouched in between two very young children who were crying. There were two other adult supervisors nearby, but they were busy breaking up a snowball fight between some older kids. *I guess it's up to me to find a solution.* Stalling, she suggested, "We'll have to compromise."

"Yes," Ava primly agreed. "To be fair to everybody, instead of making a lobster or an elf, we should make something completely different. Like a princess."

"No!" chorused all the other children, including Bobby.

Celeste tried negotiating for the best of both worlds. "We could make a lobster but give it pointy ears."

Everyone was in favor of that idea, except for Zander. "Lobsters don't have ears," he informed Celeste. "It wouldn't look real."

"Lobsters don't stand on their tail fins like Sandy Claws does, either," Kaitlyn pointed out. "It's called using your imagination, Zander."

He squeezed his eyes shut. "I'm imagining you aren't here." Then he opened them again. "Nope, imagination doesn't work."

"That's because you weren't imagining. You were making a wish," Malik corrected him. "If you want to imagine she's not here, ignore her when she talks."

"That's not being cooperative, like Ms. Kanesha said we had to be," scolded Ava.

Frustrated, Celeste's appreciation of Kanesha and the other activity supervisors was growing exponentially by the minute. How did they do this every day? She made the group her final offer. "We could sculpt a realistic lobster—without any ears—and paint it green, so he'd look a little like a lobster and a little like an elf."

"Yeah," Abigail piped up. "We could name him Elfish the Shellfish."

Bobby tossed handfuls of snow into the air like confetti as he jumped to his feet. "That's a *great* idea, Abbey! You are the smartest girl in the whole wide world after my mom and my two teachers and my grandma. And my other grandma, the one I call Nana. And my cousin Madison, because she's in college."

Abigail giggled. "Thanks, Bobby."

The rest of the children seized the opportunity to begin molding the snow into a lobster-shaped mound as Bobby turned toward Celeste. He extended his snow-encrusted, mittened hand so she could shake it. As if she had any doubt about who he was, he belatedly announced, "I'm Robert Riley, but you can call me Bobby."

Celeste grinned. "It's nice to meet you, Bobby. I'm Celeste Bell."

He let go of her hand. The lenses of his thick-rimmed glasses were clouded with steam, and he tipped his head so far back to peer at her, he almost toppled over. "Why do you have those dents in your face?"

At first, Celeste didn't understand what he meant. Then she smiled and pointed to her cheeks. "You mean these, right here?" When Bobby nodded, she explained, "They're called dimples, not dents."

"Why do you have those dimples in your face?" he persisted.

Biting her lip, Abigail shot Celeste an apologetic look, but Celeste winked at her to show she wasn't offended. "That's a good question. Doctors and scientists would say I have them because my dad had them. Kind of like you have the same color hair as your mom. When that happens, they call it heredity. But my mom used to tell me I got my dimples a different way."

"How?"

"Well, it's only a made-up story, and it's too long to tell you the whole tale. But the short version is that when I was five years old, I went outside on a really cold day. Because it was Christmas and it had snowed the night before, I was very happy so I stayed out for a long, long time. When I finally went back inside, I discovered my face had frozen in a big, joyful smile. After I drank a cup of hot cocoa and warmed up, it thawed out again. Except for these two spots, here and here." Celeste grinned and touched her face. "My mom said I've had these dimples ever since."

"Wow." Bobby's eyes were obscured by his steamy lenses, but

Celeste could hear in his voice how awestruck he was. "Do you think it's cold enough today for my face to freeze in a smile?"

She shrugged. "I'm not sure, but it's worth a try, isn't it?"

"I don't even *have* to try," Bobby said. "My mouth is already happy."

Abigail beamed. "So is mine."

Mine is, too, Celeste thought as the trio knelt down to help the others sculpt a lobster out of snow. *In fact, I don't think I could stop smiling if I tried.*

IT WAS ALMOST FOUR-THIRTY AND NATHAN STILL HADN'T COMpleted the institutional background section of the application—and that was one of the simplest sections. He kept getting calls from the board of directors. They either wanted to offer him encouragement or to update him on the status of their fund solicitations. In which case, *he* had to offer *them* encouragement, as they weren't having any more success than he'd had so far.

He'd also spoken at length about the creative narrative with Mark, who suggested Nathan call the grant writer they'd hired in the past to see if she had any suggestions. It took a while to track her down, and honestly, Nathan didn't think the ideas she came up with were any better than his. Meaning, they were fine, but he needed something extraordinary.

He tilted his chair back and was staring at the ceiling when someone knocked on his door. *Go away,* he thought. "Come in."

He sat upright to see Celeste standing on the opposite side of his desk. He was doubly dumbstruck by her presence. First, because she was *there*. And second, because her luminous smile and rosy skin were stunning. *Yeah, but those things don't make up for an unattractive temperament,* he reminded himself.

"Hi, Nathan."

"Hi, Dad." Abigail stepped out from behind her. His daughter was glowing, too; apparently, her sour mood had lifted. "We want you to come and see how our sculpture turned out," she buoyantly told him. "At first we couldn't agree about what to make, but then Celeste came and she helped us compromise. It's a good thing you called her."

Celeste furrowed her brow quizzically, so Nathan quickly explained, being careful to emphasize that it was his daughter's idea to invite Celeste to the center, not his. "When Abbey found out your flight had been delayed, she wanted to invite you to help her team, but I'd left my phone at the house, so I didn't have your number. I was supposed to go get it for her to use, but I forgot."

"You *did*?" Abigail sounded flabbergasted. "Seriously?"

Although his daughter's disappointment was understandable, her tone was a little too sassy for Nathan to tolerate. He opened his mouth to remind her to be respectful, but Celeste interposed.

"It all worked out, since I came, anyway. And I'm really glad I did, because I had such a great time." She smoothed the fringe on her scarf as she continued. "Also, I wanted to invite you both to eat supper with Carol, Arthur and me. I'm picking up pizza and salad on the way back to the inn."

"Aww." Abigail gently stamped her foot. "I can't. Kaitlyn already asked me to go to her house for supper. Her grandmother's making soup and dump-*lings*." She glanced smugly at Nathan as she stressed the *L* in the word, as if she was enunciating it for his benefit.

Where is she getting this attitude? he wondered.

"Oh, Abigail, that's too bad. I wish I'd asked you sooner, but I understand. Soup and dumplings are the best thing to eat after you've spent the afternoon outdoors. And you'll have fun with Kaitlyn." Celeste caught Nathan's eye. "Can *you* join us?"

"No, thanks. I've got a lot to do here. I probably won't leave until six-thirty or seven." *But I wouldn't join you even if I left at five.*

Celeste's crestfallen expression was so similar to Abbey's, they could have been twins separated by two decades. "You can't steal a few minutes away? A man's got to eat."

"A man's also got a deadline—you of all people should understand that." Nathan sounded snider than he'd intended, but he didn't understand why she was acting so let down. After her behavior this afternoon, did she really expect him to jump at the chance to entertain her until her next flight? No, thanks.

"Of course. Of course, I understand," she stammered. "I-I guess this is goodbye then."

"Yep. Guess so." Nathan stood up and stuck his hand out. "Good luck with your assignment."

For an instant, Celeste didn't move a muscle, except to blink repeatedly. Then she pulled off her glove and slipped her bare, smooth hand into his. He shook it briskly, but she didn't let go—it seemed she grasped his fingers even tighter. "I'm grateful I got to know you, Nathan. You made my layover on Sea Spray Island very special."

If she kept staring at him with those plaintive, dusty-blue eyes, he might have second thoughts about joining her for supper. He might have second thoughts about a lot of things. Like giving her a handshake instead of a hug. Instead of a *kiss.* He tugged his fingers away. "I hope your flight tonight is smoother than the one that brought you here." His knees felt weak, and he sat back down. "Take care."

Celeste stepped backward and twirled toward the door as Abbey grabbed her book bag off the floor where she'd left it earlier. "I have to go downstairs, too, Celeste. I'll be right there." She scowled at her father. "Do you know what time you're supposed to pick me up from Kaitlyn's house?"

Because Nathan hadn't been answering his cell phone, Kaitlyn's mother had called his office number to chat with him. It was one of the many other distractions—like this one—that had kept him from completing the technical sections of the grant application.

"Yes. At seven-fifteen."

Abbey adjusted her book bag on her shoulder and asked, "You're not going to forget to come because you're working on something important, are you?" This time, her tone was more forlorn than flippant, and it made Nathan shrink inside.

"No, honey. Of course not. Nothing—"

"Okay, just checking. I've got to go. See you later."

"I was going to say that nothing is more important to me than you are, Abigail," Nathan said softly, but she had already scampered out the door.

AS CELESTE SLUNK DOWN THE HALLWAY, HER CHEEKS SMART-ing with embarrassment, she realized she'd been wrong: she *could* stop smiling. Nathan's standoffish behavior hadn't merely thawed the grin from her face; it had liquefied it. Pausing on the balcony until Abbey caught up, she fought the impulse to cry. What in the world had happened in between their noontime rendezvous and now to make him act so distant? He seemed almost hostile, as if he was upset with Celeste for some reason. But why? Was it because she hadn't been able to go for a walk to the bakery after lunch? If so, that seemed unreasonable; he'd known it was urgent that she reschedule her flight and call Philip.

Maybe Nathan was pressured about his own work? He'd said he had a deadline, so maybe that was it. She'd also noticed tension between him and his daughter, which could have been affecting his mood. She would have thought of an excuse to send Abigail out of the room so she could ask Nathan in confidence what was troubling him, but he'd summarily dismissed Celeste first. *If that's how he wants to end our time together, it's fine with me,* she told herself, even though it was as far from fine as the North Pole was from the South. *At least I'll get to bid a fond farewell to Abigail.*

When the young girl reached her, they went downstairs, where Abbey was supposed to meet up with Kaitlyn and her mom. But Samantha informed her they'd gone to warm up the car and bring it around to the front of the building. So Celeste and Abbey trekked outside to wait for them among the snow sculptures.

"Elfish is looking a little green around the gills," Celeste joked to lighten the mood, but Abbey didn't get it. Or else she was distracted because the car had just pulled up, parallel to the sidewalk. Squatting down, Celeste embraced the young girl in a mama bear hug. "Thank you for including me in Christmas Countdown. You were right. It was awesome."

She intended to say more than that, but she didn't want to keep Kaitlyn and her mother waiting. Besides, the lump in her throat made it difficult to breathe, much less to speak. Abigail seemed teary, too, clinging to Celeste's torso and nestling her head against her shoulder.

"I don't want you to go." Her voice was muffled, and Celeste could feel the vibration of Abbey's words, right above her heart. "Can't you stay a little longer?"

If I cry, I'll make this more difficult for both of us, she warned herself. "I'm sorry, but I can't."

"Please?" Abigail pulled her head back and looked into Celeste's eyes. "Just through July?"

Celeste made a sound that was a cross between a sob and a snort of laughter. "July? That's seven months from now."

With her impeccable comedic timing, Abigail exclaimed, "Exactly. If you loved Christmas Countdown, you'll really love body-boarding. I can teach you how to do it."

Laughing, Celeste gave her another squeeze and then released her. "It's time to go enjoy supper with your friend."

"Okay. But if you change your mind about staying, it'll be worth it, I promise."

Abigail scuffed over to the car, and before she got in, she turned and waved. As Celeste lifted her arm to wave back, she noticed it again; an achy, hollow sensation running up to her shoulder, looping down into her chest and settling deep within her heart.

NATHAN SCRUNCHED HIS FACE INTO A SNARL, HOLDING THE tension in his muscles for the count of fifteen before releasing it. Nope, no better. He still felt as if his head was about to implode. Next, he massaged his temples. Then, his neck. When that failed, too, he reached for his acetaminophen bottle. Predictably, it was empty.

I probably had that coming, he thought. *I behaved like a dolt in front of my daughter.* Just because Celeste had been rude to him didn't mean he couldn't be more courteous to her. Especially since he needed to model polite manners for Abigail. He decided he could spare a few minutes to check out the sculpture they'd made and to give Celeste a more pleasant send-off.

Bypassing the elevator, he trotted down the staircase and into the lobby. It was deserted except for Sally and Vivian, who were knitting in front of the fire, and Samantha, who was simultaneously chatting on the phone and applying lipstick. *Looks like I missed Abbey and Celeste,* he thought. *As long as I'm down here, I might as well take a peek at the sculptures.*

Although it was already dark, the snowy lawn was readily visible beneath the powerful floodlights attached to the corners of the building. The students' creations included a fire truck, a castle, a dinosaur, two penguins and a motorcycle that was big enough to sit on. There was also a bodyboard, and next to it, a pair of very realistic legs were sticking up out of the snow, as if the bodyboarder had wiped out in the surf. At first, Nathan thought that was the sculpture Abigail's team had made. But then he noticed a man-sized lobster, and he knew without a doubt it was his daughter's team's handiwork.

Why is it green? he wondered. *Did the kids who made the fire truck use up all the red food coloring?*

Lee came out with a wide push broom and began sweeping stray streaks of snow off the walkway. "Hey, Nathan. Some of these aren't half bad, are they?"

"Half bad? They're masterpieces," Nathan replied. He pointed to a black, fist-sized bump in an otherwise undisturbed rectangle of snow. "Except that one. It looks like something the kindergartners started but didn't finish."

"Actually, a high school team did that. It's supposed to be a polar bear camouflaging itself on a glacier."

Nathan chortled. "They deserve an *A* for originality and an *F* for effort. Did anyone take photos of the sculptures?"

"Brent did—he recorded the kids making them, too. It's a good thing because they won't last much longer. A warm front is moving in tonight, and it's bringing rain." Lee stopped sweeping and leaned on the broom handle. "Next year Kanesha said she's scheduling the sculpting challenge for December 30 instead of December 22, so the kids' creations will have a better chance at longevity. I kind of doubt it will help, but you never know, a few days might make all the difference."

A few days might make all the difference. Lee's statement resonated in Nathan's mind as he thought of the unfinished St. Nick of Time Grant application upstairs. "Let's hope so," he said.

EVEN THOUGH SHE'D CALLED TO PLACE HER ORDER BEFORE leaving the community center, the food wasn't ready by the time Celeste walked over to the pizzeria. So she perched on a stool at the counter and double checked her phone for messages. Nothing from Philip, a good sign—or at least a sign that Mia was still nearby. But she had a text from Carol: My stylist is running really late. I'm not even in the chair yet. You and Arthur should eat without me. I still hope to be back in time to take you to the airport. I'm so sorry!!!

Grateful she had already thought of Plan B, Celeste quietly dictated her reply: We'll miss you, but please don't rush. The roads might be slippery. If you aren't here, Arthur has me covered.

A few minutes later, she was walking up the hill carrying a smaller pizza and salad than she'd originally envisioned when she'd planned on having five people for supper. *Nothing about this day turned out quite as I expected,* she thought. But at least she'd make it to the Caribbean on time, and that was what was most important. Kind of.

As she approached the inn, she glimpsed Arthur sitting in the armchair in the annex. She wanted to wave, but with her hands full, she could only manage a chin nod and smile. His changeless expression indicated he hadn't seen her through the reflection of the light on his side of the glass. At that moment, he happened to lean forward, rest his forearms against his thighs and drop his head. There was something so melancholy about his posture that Celeste felt intrusive observing him without his knowledge. She quickly walked under the trellis and up the steps into the inn.

Carol had already set the table before she left, so Arthur and

Celeste sat down to eat the pizza while it was still warm. As they dined, Celeste described the snow sculptures the students had made at the community center.

"A boy on our team named Zander told me that some lobsters can live to be one hundred years old. But I don't think Elfish will survive the week. It's supposed to rain tonight, so he'll probably be deteriorated, if not gone, by the morning. I just hope the rain doesn't keep up all day, or else the kids won't be able to go sledding."

Tomorrow was the Heading Sledding event, not Samantha's most memorable title. But as a writer, Celeste understood: everyone had a couple of clunkers in their body of work.

Arthur set his napkin beside his plate. Was he already done, after just one slice? Celeste knew why *she* could barely eat—the lump in her throat—but he usually had a bigger appetite. "Christmas Cove has really grown on you, hasn't it?" he asked.

Yes, especially the people, Celeste thought. But because she didn't want to have another breakdown in front of him, she kept her response light. "Yes, it has. But duty calls."

"Ah, duty." Arthur repeated the word, a faraway look in his eyes. He was quiet a moment before inquiring, "Do you mind if I ask a personal question?"

If it had been anyone else, Celeste would have been hesitant. But since it was Arthur, she nodded. *As long as answering it doesn't make me cry.*

"You've mentioned you want a promotion, and from what I've seen, you'll tolerate a lot of guff to get one. What I'm curious about is what's driving you. Is a senior writer position that much different from the one you have now?"

"Not really. But the salary's a lot better."

"Earning a living is definitely important," Arthur agreed, sighing. His features seemed to droop a little, as if he was disappointed.

Or maybe he was fatigued; he looked as wan as he'd appeared this morning. "Although I must say, you don't seem like the type of person who's motivated solely by money."

As it had before, Arthur's soft-spoken observation made it easy for Celeste to open up to him. "You're right. It's not really about having a higher income just for the sake of it." Celeste chuckled. "Actually, after I took my first creative writing course in college, I loved it so much that I told my professor I could be happy living in a shack on the beach and writing stories for the rest of my life . . . Of course, that wasn't realistic, which is why my career path eventually led me to *Peregrinate*. I started out in an entry-level role, but I've worked my way up, and I intend to keep going. See, my mother raised me by herself. As a single parent, she made a lot of sacrifices to give me opportunities that she never had. So . . ." Celeste ended her sentence with a shrug because her voice was perilously close to quavering. And quavering was only a breath away from crying.

Arthur filled in the blank, making the wrong assumption. "So she pushed you to excel?"

"No, no, not at all. She really wasn't like that. If anything, she used to tell me *I* was pushing *myself* too hard. Which I suppose I do sometimes, to show how much I appreciate all she did for me." Celeste paused before adding, "I mean, my mother was definitely happy for me when I succeeded. But that was only because she wanted me to have more career options than she had. She didn't want me to feel stuck."

"And do you?"

"Do I what?"

"Feel as if you have options at *Peregrinate*?"

He's referring to my situation with Philip because I told him Philip wasn't going to change, and I just have to grin and bear it, Celeste realized. Arthur's question unsettled her, and she didn't know quite how to answer. "If you're asking that because I can't do anything about the way my editor behaves, I don't think that's what my mother meant by not wanting me to feel stuck in a job."

"No? Isn't there more than one way to be stuck?" Arthur pushed his glasses farther up on his nose. "I think what most parents want is for their children to be happy in their chosen careers. The good ones do anyway—and it sounds to me as if your mom was a good one."

"Yes, she was," Celeste replied, reaching for her ringing phone.

It was Carol calling to tell her she'd wasn't going to be there in time to take her to the airport. "I'm only halfway finished. Asymmetrical cuts might be considered stylish, but right now, my head just looks lopsided."

"No worries. I'll wrap the pizza for you and put it in the fridge. I'm also leaving a couple little things beneath the tree." She'd wrapped the gifts earlier in the day, but she realized later that if Carol opened hers before she told Josh she was pregnant, she'd ruin the surprise. Speaking cryptically because Arthur was right across from her, Celeste said, "Don't open yours until . . . until after you've given Josh his gift."

"Okay, got it. That's so sweet of you to leave me a present. Even though I wish we could say goodbye in person, it might be better that we can't because I'd be blubbering like a baby. I've loved having you at the inn. I hope you'll come back soon."

"I've loved being here," Celeste replied, skirting the question of whether she'd return. "Thank you so much, Carol. You went above and beyond, with the wonderful meals and loaning me your—"

In the background, someone interrupted to ask Carol a question. She answered and then came back on the line. "My stylist says I have to put my phone down now. She's afraid she might accidentally snip my fingers." So the women were forced to end their call quickly.

While Arthur fetched the keys and went out to warm up the car, Celeste put the salad and pizza away and then dashed upstairs to her room to change. Although this time she also wore a pair of black leggings, she donned the same slate-blue swing dress, crochet cardigan and canvas sneakers she was wearing on Monday night.

Monday night. That seemed like ages ago. Celeste remembered Nathan telling her how quickly she'd feel as if she'd lived on Sea Spray Island all her life. *I don't feel as if I've lived here* all *of my life, but now I know what he meant,* she thought as she picked up her carry-on and the bag of gifts.

Downstairs, she slid the presents beneath the Christmas tree. Then she unhooked the starfish ornament from the bough in the back and rehung it in the front, where it had been when she arrived. Pausing to admire the fir's effulgent appearance, she brushed a single tear from her cheek.

"Have a merry Christmas, everyone," she said faintly and then walked out of the inn a final time.

Chapter 13

"WOULD YOU LIKE TO TRAVEL ALONG MAIN STREET OR SHOULD we take the other route?" Arthur asked after Celeste had settled into the car and buckled her seat belt.

"The other route. It's quicker." Celeste actually wasn't that concerned about the time. The airport was only a few miles away and security screening would simply be a matter of saying hello to Patty—and giving her the Christmas gift for Sasha. But Celeste wanted to avoid Main Street on the off chance she'd catch a glimpse of Nathan coming out of the community center. She still felt hurt and confused by his sudden indifference, and she didn't want a visual reminder of their goodbye kiss that wasn't.

Although they'd bypassed most of Main Street, their course still took them within view of Santa's Sailboat, which was anchored in the marina again, sparkling in all its kaleidoscopic splendor. Celeste involuntarily recalled how excited Nathan had been when they'd flown over it in the plane, and the memory made her sigh.

Arthur must have heard her because he quoted Shakespeare, inquiring, "'Parting is such sweet sorrow,' isn't it?"

In this instance, it's such bittersweet *sorrow,* Celeste thought. "Yes, it is."

"I'll feel that way when I have to leave, too," he remarked. They had driven beyond the illuminated residential neighborhoods and were passing through a long, uninhabited stretch of dunes and trees. Because of the absence of streetlights and the thickening cloud cover, it was too dark for Celeste to clearly see Arthur's face. But there was no mistaking the affliction in his voice when he added, "It hurts my heart."

From their mealtime discussions over the course of her stay, Celeste had learned that Arthur's wife had passed away almost thirty years ago. He'd never remarried, and apparently, he had only one child, the son he seemed reluctant to talk about. Arthur used to work in real estate, but he'd retired at seventy-eight, four years ago. So Celeste could understand why he'd be depressed about returning to his empty home after staying at the inn for a full month.

But it surprised her that he was so expressive about his loneliness; usually she was the one becoming emotional in front of him, not the other way around. Trying to think of something helpful to say, she glanced at him again and noticed he was pressing his fist against his breastbone.

"It hurts. My heart. Hurts," he panted.

Then the thunderbolt struck: his heart *physically* hurt. He was having chest pain.

"Pull over, Arthur. There's a wide shoulder, right up there," she directed him. Her calm manner belied the panicked thoughts stampeding through her brain. When he rolled to a stop and put the car in park, she got out, ran around to his side and yanked the door open. Beneath the dome light, he appeared pale and clammy, and when she took his pulse, it was racing.

"We need to get you to the hospital." Celeste was aware that most medical professionals would have advised she call an ambulance instead of trying to drive him to the ER on her own. However, the fire department was on the other end of town. The EMTs would have to drive all the way from Main Street and then double back to reach the hospital. It was twice as fast to bring Arthur directly there herself, so she helped him into the back seat and rapidly reversed their direction. Then she called 911 on speakerphone, explained the situation and asked if they could inform the hospital Arthur would be arriving soon.

After she hung up, he said, "When we get there—" Then he went quiet.

Celeste glanced in her rearview mirror; all she could see was that he was leaning back against the seat, and it appeared his eyes were closed. "Arthur!" she exclaimed frantically, fearing he'd passed out.

He let out a low, guttural moan, which was oddly reassuring. After a moment, the pain seemed to subside because he had the wherewithal to say, "When we get to the ER, you can drop me off at the door and then drive straight to the airport. Leave the keys with Patty. I'll arrange to pick the car up later."

Celeste was appalled at the idea of abandoning him on the hospital doorstep and then taking off for the airport. "Are you kidding me? What kind of person do you think I am?"

"A very lovely one. But the same can't be said for that boss of yours. I don't want you to miss your flight and get in trouble with him."

"I appreciate the thought, but that's not my priority at the moment—*you* are. Besides, even Philip would understand why I missed my flight under these circumstances," she assured him, although she half-doubted she was right. "Please stop talking and try to relax."

Arthur ignored her, insisting, "There's no need for you to miss your flight. The doctors will take good care of me whether you're at the hospital or not. The pain seems to be letting up. It might be indigestion."

"I hope that's the case. If you get a clean bill of health, I'll take you back to the inn and then I'll catch a ferry to Boston and fly to the Caribbean from there. But for now, you're stuck with me."

In response, Arthur groaned. And then he groaned again. *His pain isn't letting up—it's getting worse,* Celeste worried.

"Hang on, you're doing great. We're almost there." She'd accelerated until the hospital was within view. "Is there anyone you want me to inform you're going to the ER with chest pain? A sibling or your doctor from home?"

He didn't immediately answer. Celeste glanced in the rearview mirror. He was rubbing his breastbone with his knuckles again. "Yes," he replied. "Call Matt. My son."

He recited the phone number, but Celeste couldn't concentrate well enough to memorize it and he couldn't focus enough to enter it into her phone.

"Is he in your contacts list? I can call him from your phone—it's right here by the console."

"Don't do that. If he thinks it's me, he won't answer."

Arthur and his son are estranged? As they pulled into the hospital parking lot, Celeste assured him she'd look up Matt's number on his phone and then place the call on hers. She drove directly to the emergency room entrance, where two attendants were waiting with a gurney.

"Ah, the welcoming committee," Arthur said wryly.

When Celeste stopped, the men swiftly rolled the gurney over to the car and opened the door to help Arthur out.

"We'll need you to lie down here, sir," the attendant said, trying to shift him onto the gurney. But Arthur insisted he and Celeste needed to say their goodbyes first, "just in case."

Just in case what? she wondered, but she didn't want to know the answer. "I am *not* leaving," she reminded him.

Before he could say anything else, the attendants situated him on the gurney. As they rolled him away, Celeste went to park. Because the lot was mostly empty, she quicky pulled into an open space and turned the engine off. She scrolled through Arthur's contacts until she'd found Matt's number—he had a Boston area code—which she entered into her phone. It rang three times before he picked up.

"Hello?" He sounded exactly like his dad, but Celeste didn't want to make any assumptions and accidentally deliver the news to the wrong person.

"Hello. I'd like to speak to Matt Williams, please."

"Speaking. What is it?" he asked curtly. She didn't blame him; she probably sounded like a telemarketer. She was going to have to talk fast so he wouldn't hang up before she'd finished explaining.

"My name's Celeste Bell, and I'm a friend of your father's. He's okay, but I just took him to the ER on Sea Spray Island because he was experiencing chest pain. I don't know anything about his condition yet, but he wanted me to call and let you know he was going into the hospital."

There was a pause. It sounded as if there were children singing nearby and then a door closed. Matt asked in a low voice, "Is this another attempt to convince me to come to the island for Christmas?"

"What? No, of course not!" *Who would ever play a trick like that?*

"Okay. Well, thank you for letting me know. Goodbye." He hung up before she could ask if he wanted her to keep him updated on Arthur's condition, which he obviously didn't.

Or maybe he hung up quickly because he's so distraught. For all I know, he's already out the door and on his way to catch a ferry here, Celeste supposed, trying to give him the benefit of the doubt. But it seemed unlikely, considering Arthur had said Matt wouldn't answer if he knew it was his father calling.

I can't imagine Arthur doing anything to alienate his son, Celeste thought. On the contrary, it seemed he'd been reaching out to him. Hadn't Matt asked if her call was *another* attempt to convince him to come to the island for Christmas?

Celeste remembered Arthur telling her one of the reasons he enjoyed sitting in the annex was that it allowed him to people-watch. But in reality, there were few passersby on that street, since most of the residents were summer homeowners who weren't on the island during the off-season. *Has he been waiting there every day in the hope of seeing his son come up the hill?* Celeste's eyes filled at the thought. It made her twice as determined to stay with Arthur now, even though he'd said it wasn't necessary.

Before getting out of the car, she deliberated for a moment about whether to inform Philip she'd missed another flight. Technically, he'd told her to call when she arrived, not when she was—or wasn't—on her way. Celeste knew there was a direct flight from Boston to the Caribbean right before midnight. If everything checked out with Arthur, she could still catch a ferry to the mainland and board the plane on time. It would be close, but it was doable. *If I miss that flight, I'll have to call him. But I'm not calling him now,* she decided, which made her feel as if she'd given herself an early Christmas present.

For the past few minutes, the sky had been intermittently spitting hard, icy drops of rain, but they were coming faster now. So when Celeste got out of the car, she sprinted toward the hospital. Inside the entrance, she quickly wiped her sneakers on the mat and then approached the registration desk.

A woman who looked familiar slid the glass window sideways. "Hello," she said in a chipper voice that seemed more appropriate for an amusement park than an emergency room. "Are you here for yourself or to see someone else?"

"Someone else. His name is Arthur Williams. He just arrived a few minutes ago."

As the woman scanned her computer screen, Celeste noticed her name tag—Stephanie. That's right; she was a friend of Samantha's. Celeste had met her at Souper Supper. "The docs are evaluating him now."

"Can't I go in and see him?"

"Sorry. Not until they're done with the eval, and only if he gives consent. But don't worry, the docs here are great—and I'm not saying that just because I'm married to one of them." She pointed to a row of plastic chairs that looked exactly like the ones in the airport. "Have a seat and someone will be out to update you soon."

Since the waiting room was completely empty, and she was too fidgety to sit, Celeste unzipped her purple jacket and paced the perimeter, silently praying, *Please, please, please let Arthur be okay.*

On her fourth time around, she felt dizzy so she dropped into a chair. *Arthur was well enough to talk and joke and stand, so that must mean his condition isn't serious,* she tried to console herself, even though she knew that wasn't necessarily true.

She wished she could call someone to help calm her nerves, but because of Carol's pregnancy, she didn't want to cause her unnecessary alarm. Celeste would contact her later, when she had a better sense of what was going on. *I could call Nathan.* She rejected the thought as soon as it popped into her head. Even if he hadn't be-haved so apathetically toward her, he'd left his cell phone at home and he was probably picking up Abigail right around now.

Her phone buzzed in her pocket, jarring her from her thoughts. Celeste had never been so happy to see Patty's number and hear her friendly voice.

"Hello, sunshine," Patty said. "Are you running a little late? I told the pilot to hold his horses, but he's antsy to take off before the weather gets worse."

"The flight hasn't departed yet?" It was past seven o'clock.

"Nope, Roger's idling on the runway. I told him you'd be here any minute, but I don't know how much longer I can stall him."

She's actually holding up the flight for me? Celeste marveled. *This kind of thing only happens on Sea Spray Island—or for celebrities.* She told Patty to signal the pilot it was okay to leave, since she wouldn't be boarding after all.

"Ack!" Patty squawked. "You could have called me earlier to let me know."

She'd been so frantic, the thought never even crossed her mind. "You're right—and I'm so sorry I didn't. Thank you for asking the pilot to wait and please extend my apologies. I really appreciate your thoughtfulness."

"You're welcome. After all the delays *you've* experienced, I fig-ured we could wait an extra fifteen minutes for you. Hang on a sec." Patty must have left to give Captain Roger or air traffic control the all clear. She came back onto the line a moment later. "So, you decided to stay on Sea Spray Island. Does this have anything to do with your lunch with Nathan this afternoon?"

Oh, brother. Celeste had to think of a way to disavow Patty of that notion without lying or disclosing any information about Ar-thur's ER visit. "No, absolutely not. I-I had to turn around because of a . . . malfunction," she said, meaning Arthur's heart wasn't working as well as it should have been.

Patty chuckled. "Is that how people from the city say they had car trouble?"

"No, I think it's because I'm a writer," Celeste responded vaguely. "I'm sorry, but I've got to run now. I appreciate how helpful you've been with all of my flight arrangements, Patty." Before hanging up, she mentioned she'd gotten a gift for Sasha, which she figured Carol would hand off to her.

"That's so nice of you. I wish I weren't at work. I could put my grandbaby on the line so she could thank you for herself. Oh, well. Have a merry Christmas, Celeste."

"Merry Christmas," she echoed.

A few minutes later a red-haired woman in a white medical coat stepped through a door near the registration office. "Is there a Celeste here?" she asked, as if Celeste weren't the only person in the room.

"Yes. I'm Celeste." Celeste wanted to stand, but she didn't know if her legs would support her. *Please, please, please tell me Arthur's going to be fine.*

As the woman approached, her heels clicking against the tile, it seemed as if she were moving in slow motion. When she reached Celeste, she introduced herself as Dr. Moran, glanced down at her clipboard and asked her to confirm who she was there to see.

"Arthur Williams." Celeste's mouth was so parched that her answer was barely audible.

"I'm sorry. Can you repeat that?"

Why is she being so officious? Something terrible must have happened. Celeste's eyes welled. "Arthur Williams."

"Thank you for confirming. On an island this size, it's important for us to be extra-vigilant about patient privacy laws," the woman explained, lifting a page on her clipboard. She scribbled something and then dropped her arm to the side. "So, it's good news. Arthur didn't experience a cardiac event—he had a gallbladder attack. He has several large gallstones, and we've recommended surgery to remove his gallbladder. However, he's opted to wait until the new year, when he's back home and under the care of his physician. With dietary restrictions, we're hopeful he'll be able to avoid another attack until then."

Celeste wasn't aware she'd been holding her breath until she exhaled it all at once in a loud puff. "That's wonderful," she exclaimed. "Thank you."

"In a few minutes, someone will bring you to his room so you can say goodbye. Your grandfather tells us you've got a ferry to catch."

Celeste was about to correct her mistake, but she changed her mind. After all, in the past week, Arthur had been more of a grandfather to her than her own grandfathers had ever been, so in a way, Dr. Moran was more right than wrong.

"I HOPE THIS WEATHER DOESN'T RUIN THE SNOW SCULPTURES," Nathan said to Abigail as they drove home from Kaitlyn's house. Icy pellets were bouncing off the windshield and pattering on top of the car. "I think I know which one you made—the lobster, right?"

"Yeah. Elfish," Abigail mumbled.

"Elvish Presley? I get it—he's a *rock* lobster, right?" Nathan was quite proud of that pun—Celeste would have laughed, but Abigail was silent. "You know, because a rock lobster is a kind of lobster, and Elvish Presley because he was called the king of rock 'n' roll."

"It's not El*vish*—it's El*fish*. Elfish the Shellfish."

"Aha, now I get it. Elfish because he's green. That was going to be my next question."

Nathan rolled into the driveway extra slowly—the pavement was *slick*. As soon as he parked, Abigail darted into the house ahead of him. Before he'd even hung up his coat, she asked, "What happened to all the dishes that were in the sink this morning?"

"They're in the dishwasher." Nathan had wanted to ease into the subject of his lunch with Celeste, but he noticed their place settings were on the table still. Abbey would spot them in another millisecond, too; she didn't miss a thing. "Come into the living room, there's something I want to talk to you about."

He settled on the sofa and patted the cushion beside him. But Abigail dropped into the recliner. Balanced on the edge of the seat, she ducked her head and combed her hair around her face like a tent. It bothered Nathan that he couldn't see her eyes when they talked, but he had to pick his battles.

"How long is this going to take?" she asked. "I want to go to bed."

"Yes, I noticed you seemed kind of tired today," he suggested. "Or is there something else going on? Something you want to discuss with me?"

"No. *You're* the one who said you wanted to talk."

"I do, but I want to give you a chance to tell me if anything is on your mind first."

"Why? Am I in trouble?"

"No." Recognizing their conversation would keep circling unless he changed course, Nathan admitted, "I just thought I'd mention to you that I invited Celeste over for lunch today. We were going to go to Almeda's since I won the gift card, and she wanted to try the salt cod fritters, but I forgot they don't serve lunch in the winter. So we came here and I made eggs, and she rinsed the dirty breakfast dishes and put them in the dishwasher."

"Was it a date?" Abigail asked, point-blank.

"Why? Is that what someone told you?"

"No. But you were acting kind of weird this morning, like you were hiding something." Without lifting her head or pushing her hair from her eyes, she somehow pointed directly at his chest. "And you've never worn that sweater to work."

She's always been highly perceptive, Nathan thought. Because he didn't want his daughter to grow up second-guessing herself—or him, for that matter—he replied as honestly as he thought appropriate, considering Abbey's age. "You're right, I only wear this sweater for special occasions, and I considered going to Almeda's with Celeste to be special. It was a chance for us to spend time with each other one-on-one before she left. I think she has a lot of great qualities—like being so fond of *you*—and I'm glad I got to know her while she was here. But that's all there was to it."

"Are you going to call her or visit her in Boston?"

"No, honey. Absolutely not."

"Are you sure you're not going to change your mind?"

"I'm positive."

"Because your heart belongs to Mom?"

Nathan didn't quite know what to say. Yes, he'd told Abigail that Holly would always have a special place in his heart, but that wasn't quite the same as saying his heart still *belonged* to her. Sensing what his daughter was actually concerned about was that he'd forget her mother, he replied, "Something like that, yes." *And it's also because Celeste considers her career to be more important than her relationships.*

Abbey shook her hair from her eyes and lifted her head. "Can I go to bed now?"

"Sure. I'll be there in a few minutes to say good night."

After she'd shuffled from the room, Nathan leaned back against the cushion and closed his eyes. Whew, what a day. And it wasn't over yet—he still had to put in a couple of hours wrapping up the technical sections of the application so he could move on to the creative narrative. He had a little more than forty-eight hours until the deadline. Tomorrow, the community center would be hopping, but Kanesha and the other aides were taking the students sledding on the golf course. They were walking there, which meant the event would take longer than usual, so he wouldn't have to worry about Abbey hanging out in his office and getting bored.

On Saturday, the center would be open until twelve. If Nathan didn't finish the application by the time it closed, he'd ask Carol if Abigail could spend the afternoon at the inn, so he could work on it without distractions. Then he'd meet up with them for supper and participate in the candle lighting and singing on the town green.

His plan settled, Nathan pulled himself to his feet and went to say good night to Abigail, but her room was dark. In the light from the hallway, he could barely see the wetness on her cheek. Had she been crying? Her posture was too rigid for her to be asleep—she was faking. Whatever was troubling her, she still didn't want to talk about it. Tomorrow, he'd try again. He kissed her forehead before whispering, "I love you," into her ear.

When he returned to the kitchen for his laptop, Nathan noticed the dirty dishes on the table again. Seeing them reminded him of Celeste's story about going to school dressed as Emily Dickinson, and he chuckled. But the anecdote was quickly replaced by the memory of how quickly she'd taken off after lunch. Despite what she'd said about being grateful she'd gotten to know him, her actions had told a different story. Nathan would be kidding himself to think they'd see each other in the future—not that he wanted to, anyway. He quickly stacked the dishes in the dishwasher and turned it on, as if to rinse the last traces of Celeste from his house—as well as from his mind.

EVEN THOUGH ARTHUR'S PAIN HAD DIMINISHED SIGNIFICANTLY, the doctors preferred for it to subside completely before he was discharged. Meanwhile, he was receiving IV fluids for dehydration. So after Celeste booked her flight from Boston to the Caribbean, he insisted she drive the car to the ferry terminal right away instead of waiting for him to be released.

"You can leave the keys beneath the floor mat—actually, on this island, you could leave them in the ignition and it wouldn't be a problem," he said. "I'll retrieve the car tomorrow."

"But how will you get home tonight?"

"Once I receive my discharge papers, I'll call Carol to pick me up. There's no sense in her sitting around here waiting for me, either. That reminds me, do you have my phone?"

Celeste set it on the tray table beside his bed. "I hope it's okay that I added your number to my contacts list."

"Of course. I'd welcome a call from you anytime. By the way, did you reach Matt?"

She hesitated, not wanting to be the bearer of bad news. "I spoke to him briefly, yes."

"What did he say?"

"He, um, basically just thanked me for calling."

"Ah, well, at least he didn't hang up on you." Arthur took a sip of ice water through a straw. "You must wonder what happened to cause such a rift between us."

Celeste jiggled her head back and forth. "It's none of my business. And I won't mention anything about him to anyone else."

"I know. I trust you. I'd tell you more, but it's time for you to go or you'll miss your ferry."

Celeste knew he was right, so she gave him a hug. As when she'd bid goodbye to Abigail, there was so much she wanted to say, but it all came down to, "Thank you, Arthur."

"Thank *you*, Celeste." He released her. Then he made a shooing motion with his hands. "Go on, skedaddle."

When she exited the building, Celeste noticed there was a thin sheen of moisture on the pavement and the precipitation sounded more like sleet than rain as it landed. *I hope the temperature doesn't drop any lower. If this turns to ice, I wouldn't want Carol driving in it,* she thought.

Despite being short on time when she reached the car, she waited for the defroster to clear the windows completely before she inched out of the parking lot. Although she'd barely touched the gas pedal as she pulled onto the main road, the back of the car squiggled before it straightened out again.

"I don't like this," she said aloud. "Not one bit."

She continued at a crawl along the dark, unfamiliar lane, grateful that she didn't pass any vehicles coming in the opposite direction. Within minutes, her shoulders were hunched and sore from gripping the steering wheel so tightly and the squeaking windshield wipers had pushed her to the brink of a headache. *Three miles to go,* she encouraged herself.

Half a mile later, she spotted a red, blinking traffic light in the distance. Even though she'd been traveling under 15 mph, she took her foot completely off the gas pedal, planning to coast to a stop at the intersection. But the road unexpectedly dipped, causing the car to gain momentum, so she had to tap the brakes. It could have been that she applied too much pressure—or that the hill was steeper than she'd thought—but instead of stopping, Celeste hydroplaned.

And then she overcorrected.

And then the car spun in a complete circle.

And in a slower half circle after that.

And then it skidded sideways, drifting to a stop less than a foot from the snowbank at the edge of the road. The vehicle may have been stationary, but it took another two full minutes for Celeste's mind to stop reeling and her pulse to deaccelerate.

When she'd gotten her bearings again, she realized she was facing in the opposite direction she'd been heading. It was as if the decision had been made for her: she wasn't going to the ferry; she was going back to the hospital. *I'd rather drive myself there now than arrive in an ambulance in half an hour,* she thought.

Her fingers trembling, she lifted her phone off the passenger seat and pressed Arthur's number. After recounting what had happened as calmly as she could, she told him she was coming back and she'd take him to the inn in the morning, when it was safer to travel.

"I think that's a wise decision, but I regret I've caused you to miss your assignment. I hope you don't get in trouble with your editor."

"No assignment is worth risking my life," Celeste replied. "So who cares how Philip reacts?"

But she did care, at least a little. Not enough to change her mind but enough that her stomach did backflips all the way to the hospital. When she arrived in the lot, she parked but left the car running since she kept shivering. *I might as well get this over with now,* she thought, and pressed Philip's number in her phone. Unfortunately, he answered.

"You'd better be calling to tell me you're within shouting distance of a palm tree," he said by way of greeting.

Nervous, Celeste quipped, "That depends on how loudly you can shout."

Philip seemed to take that as an invitation to demonstrate his volume. He let loose a stream of invectives that was as long as it was loud.

Where's my buffer, Mia, when I need her? Celeste wondered, holding the phone away from her ear.

"So what's your excuse this time?" Philip jeered. "The pilot had another medical emergency?"

"Kind of. I mean, it wasn't the pilot, but there was a medical emergency." Celeste was so wound up it sounded as if she couldn't get her story straight. "The man taking me to the airport was having chest pains, so I had to bring him to the emergency room."

"Your driver had a heart attack?"

"He's not my *driver*—he's my friend." It may not have been the best moment to split hairs, but the distinction was important to Celeste. "And yes, I thought he was having a heart attack."

"You *thought*? So he wasn't?"

"No. It was gallstones. But we didn't know—"

"Whatever. Not interested," Philip interrupted. "Just act like the responsible professional I used to think you were and tell me when the next flight leaves the island."

Used to? Okay, that one hurt. Celeste had a feeling Philip's insults were only going to get worse. "That was the last one departing tonight."

"The next sentence out of your mouth had better be that you're calling me from the ferry."

"I tried to catch one, but on the way to the dock, I spun out on black ice. I read online that it's only raining in Boston, but it's colder here and the roads are essentially impassable."

There was absolute silence on the other end of the line. Had he hung up? No such luck. "You know, Celeste, lately I think you've been *trying* to get fired."

Fired? She had thought he might threaten to demote her, not terminate her employment at the magazine completely. Celeste immediately started bargaining, "I-I-I could leave early tomorrow morn—"

"And miss *j'ouvert?* That's a major highlight of carnival!" Philip shouted. "The sponsor would never accept those terms. They wanted the whole three days or nothing."

"There's a midnight flight from Boston. Is there anyone who can go in my place?"

"Not anymore there isn't. Two days ago when you promised you'd make it to the Caribbean in time, I was gullible enough to take you at your word. Now all the qualified writers are out of town, celebrating with their families. And if you think *I'm* changing *my* Christmas plans to clean up *your* mess—"

"I don't." *Not because you* shouldn't, *but because it's unthinkable that you'd ever be that helpful or generous.* "In the past, when someone has ended up missing an assignment, we've refunded the sponsor and offered free advertising in the magazine. Could we do that now?"

"Ingenious. I've only been the editor in chief for fourteen years, so thank you for reminding me of our customer retention policies," Philip said sardonically. "Since you're so full of advice, what exactly do you propose we do for the Christmas blog? Post selfies and stories about what we received in our Christmas stockings?"

You *wouldn't even get a lump of coal if I were Santa Claus,* Celeste thought. Her mind leaped to Sandy Claws, which made her think of Abigail suggesting she write a feature about Christmas Cove. "I can write about Sea Spray Island," she proposed.

"Ooh, that's real cutting edge," Philip ridiculed. "Coastal New England at Christmastime. No magazine has ever done *that* before."

"Trust me, this island is different."

He snorted. "I doubt that, but it's all we've got. I'll smooth things over with the sponsor, but when you send me your post for editing, cc Ed and Colton. And be sure to add a profuse apology for screwing up on the Caribbean assignment."

Edmund Grayson and Colton Browne were the CEO and president of *Peregrinate*. Philip had never asked Celeste to cc them on any correspondence. He preferred to nitpick every last jot and tittle of his staff's work before the execs saw it, since their writing reflected on him, too. *It's almost as if he's distancing himself from my post,* she thought. *He's hanging me out to dry.*

But she genially agreed, adding, "The post will be excellent—I promise you won't be disappointed."

"Too late for that," he replied and hung up on her.

Chapter 14

FRIDAY—DECEMBER 23

EVEN THOUGH HE HADN'T GONE TO SLEEP UNTIL AFTER ONE o'clock, Nathan woke before six. His phone alarm wasn't set to go off until six thirty, and he was unusually cold, so he pulled the comforter over his head, closed his eyes and mentally planned his day.

Since he'd finally finished the informational sections of the application last night, he could devote himself to writing the creative narrative today. One of the suggestions the grant writer had made was to interview the islanders about what the community center meant to them.

"Compile a selection of testimonials in the residents' own words," she'd advised.

The problem with that idea was that it would require disclosing *why* he was interviewing them. In which case, knowing how fast the news would spread, he might as well make an announcement on the PA system. Nathan considered offering a phony reason for why he needed their testimonials, but that went against his conscience. It was one thing for him to keep the bad news about the center's funding a secret until after Christmas, but it was an entirely different matter to ask people to share their personal experiences under false pretenses.

Back to square one, he thought. He stuck his hand out from beneath the comforter and felt around on the nightstand until he'd grasped his phone. It was 6:18. Why hadn't he heard the clock on the town hall tower singing "six geese a-laying" yet?

Oh, no—we must have lost power! He hopped to his feet and raced to the window. It wasn't quite first light yet, but it was bright enough to see that the tree boughs were weighted down, the power lines were sagging and there was a shiny crust of ice atop the snowy yard.

The community center was used for public shelter during weather emergencies, so in the event of power outages, Nathan was required to keep the building open from 7:00 A.M. to 9:00 P.M. And staff were expected to be on-site the entire time. Which meant he had a little more than a half hour to get there. He quickly dressed and brushed his teeth. Then he checked his e-mail for an announcement from the superintendent; unsurprisingly, school was canceled. *Abigail will have to stay with Carol today,* he thought, striding down the hall to her room.

"Abbey." He wiggled her shoulder. "Abbey, wake up."

"Mmm," she murmured. "I'm cold."

"That's because we lost electricity. Come on, I need to go to work. School's been canceled, so you can spend the day with your aunt Carol. Bring your toothbrush and pajamas in case I'm late coming home, and you decide to sleep over at the inn."

Abigail rolled over. "If school is canceled, why can't I go with you?"

"Because I've got too much to do today."

"That's okay. I'll be hanging out with my friends."

"They might not be there. You know the rules—people who've lost power have first priority. No one else is supposed to come to the center. The outage might not be affecting your friends' houses, so they'll stay home."

"But *we* lost power, so don't *I* have first priority?"

"Not when your aunt owns an inn with four fireplaces, you don't. Besides, you said you wanted to eat breakfast at Aunt Carol's this morning. So, let's go. Up and at 'em."

But Abigail dawdled, and they didn't get out the door until 6:47. Halfway down the street, Nathan realized he'd left his laptop and phone in his room, so he had to jog back and get them. Abbey kept walking and reached the inn before he did.

"The door's still locked," she announced from the front steps. "If we ring the bell, we'll wake up Mr. Williams. I should just come with you to the center instead."

"No dice." Nathan phoned his sister.

"Nathan?" She sounded groggy when she answered. "Is everything okay?"

"Yes, but you must still be in bed—otherwise you'd know we've had a power outage. I need to get to the center ASAP. Can Abigail spend the day with you?"

"Absolutely." Carol yawned like a lion into the phone. "Hey, I have to tell you what happened when Arthur was taking Celeste to the air—"

The last thing Nathan had time for this morning was a story that involved Celeste's trip to the airport. He cut his sister off. "Sorry, but I've got three minutes to get down to Main Street. Abigail and I are standing on your doorstep. Can you just come and unlock the front door?"

"Can *you* just keep your thermal britches on?" Carol growled. "I need to find my slippers—these hardwood floors are freezing."

"Okay, bye." Nathan turned to Abbey and told her Carol would be right out. "I've got to go, but I'll try to call you later."

As he hurried down the walkway, he heard the door open and Carol saying good morning to Abbey, who asked, "Did you get your hair cut? It looks nice."

Nathan turned to wave, but the pair had already gone inside and shut the door. *One small problem solved; one giant problem to go.*

"DID YOU GET ANY SLEEP LAST NIGHT?" ARTHUR ASKED Celeste. She was drinking coffee while he ate the low-fat, "gallbladder-friendly" breakfast a staff member had delivered to him on a tray. Even though he should have been discharged the evening before, because of the ice storm, the hospital staff had found a bureaucratic loophole to allow him to stay in his bed overnight. Celeste, however, had been relegated to the waiting room.

But when Stephanie, the receptionist, had found out Celeste was going to have to try to sleep sitting on one of the hard, blue plastic chairs, she'd brought her to a waiting lounge in the cardiac care unit. "The recliners here are more comfortable than my bed at home," she'd told her. "When I'm on break, I come up here for a nap. It's a slow night in this wing, so you should have the lounge all to yourself. As long as you're quiet and respectful, none of the nurses will kick you out."

The recliner was downright luxurious, and Celeste had covered up with two freshly laundered blankets she'd found labeled and wrapped in plastic in the closet. Yet she'd lain awake for hours, trying to imagine how best to capture Christmas Cove's uniqueness for the blog. Whatever she wrote would be accompanied by photos, of course. However, as gorgeous as the land and seascapes were, it was really the people living there who made the island so special.

All except one—Nathan, she'd thought begrudgingly. But she hadn't *truly* felt that way. How he'd acted in his office was inconsistent with his behavior toward her the rest of the time she'd been in Christmas Cove. She had to believe there was some kind of misunderstanding that caused his abrupt change in attitude. And now that she was staying on the island through Christmas, she intended to find out what it was.

"Did you have a good night's rest?" Arthur repeated the question, and Celeste realized she'd been lost in thought and hadn't answered.

"Mm. You wouldn't believe how comfortable the recliners are upstairs." She didn't want to make Arthur feel worse by admitting she'd been awake most of the night. He already felt bad enough that she'd missed her flight and the ferry. For that same reason, she'd downplayed Philip's angry reaction the night before when Arthur had inquired about her phone conversation. All she'd said was that he was initially upset, but then they agreed she'd write about Sea Spray Island for the blog. Now, she volleyed Arthur's question back to him. "How was *your* sleep?"

"Let's put it this way—the mattresses at the inn are much higher quality." He poked at a chunk of hard, unripe melon with his fork. "And so is the food. But I'm grateful to this hospital. The doctors and nurses have taken excellent care of me, just as they did for my son, when he was here."

Celeste widened her eyes. "Your son was hospitalized on Sea Spray Island?"

"Yes. He spent the summer here fifteen years ago. He had a sort of . . . crisis, you might call it. He'd devoted his entire career to working for a miserable man—a tyrant, really. Which is why it gets my hackles up to hear about your editor. Not that I'm equating Philip with my son's manager—his was far worse. Anyway, years and years of too much stress eventually took its toll, and he wound up spending three weeks in this hospital."

Celeste didn't ask whether Matt's health crisis was physical or mental; if his father had wanted her to know, he would have said. Whatever his son had suffered, it was distressing enough to shadow Arthur's face with sadness all these years later. "I'm sorry to hear that. Is he doing better now?"

"Yes, thanks to this island—and by that I mean the hospital staff, the community and the setting. The summer he spent here marked a pivotal point in his life. After he recovered, he quit his job and never looked back. He's passionate about his new career, but his first priority is his family. He married a lovely woman, and I'm told they have three children. Two girls, one boy."

Arthur's never met his grandchildren, Celeste realized. She couldn't help but be curious about his falling-out with Matt. But she was moved that Arthur confided in her, and she had no intention of asking prying questions.

Besides, an aide came into the room and told them she'd heard the roads were drivable again. "The temperature is nearly forty degrees, and the sun's out in full force. There are still a lot of limbs on wires, so most of the island is without electricity. If the inn doesn't have power, you're welcome to hang out in the lobby, but I'm afraid your time at Sea Spray Island's Hospital Hotel is up, Mr. Williams."

"No late checkout?" he teased.

"No mint on your pillow, either," she riposted. "But we'll let you take home your slippers, along with this handy list of dietary restrictions. Oops. I mean dietary *suggestions.*"

"You had it right the first time," he grumbled, but he was smiling.

When Celeste and Arthur stepped outside a few minutes later, they both squinted and shielded their eyes. Sunlight reflected off the black, wet pavement. The snow was glistening, and the electrical wires and tree limbs were coated with dripping ice. The beautiful brilliance was a welcome contrast to the ominous gloom of the previous evening, and it filled Celeste with optimism about writing her blog post.

As they journeyed back to the inn, she realized she'd only traveled on that road during the evening hours; once last night and once when Carol had given her a ride from the airport. Until this morning, she hadn't been able to see the rolling dunes and high bluffs, or the water just beyond them. So when she caught sight of the royal, undulating ocean, since no one was behind them, she coasted to a stop, speechlessly staring at it.

They'd crested the hill and were idling at the same spot where Carol had stopped to point out the marina in the distance below. In the daylight, Celeste not only glimpsed the marina, Santa's Sailboat and the shops on Main Street; she also had an unobstructed view of Sea Spray Island's neighborhoods, hills, woods and coastline. And surrounding all of it, the majestic waters, as far as her eyes could see.

"That's amazing," she exclaimed, just as she'd remarked the first time she'd stopped here.

"It is. And we wouldn't be enjoying it today if my son hadn't deliberately sabotaged his employer's scheme to develop this land. There'd be a monstrously large village of condos right along that dune there. And that one, too." Arthur pointed at a snowbank in the distance. "As you can imagine, the developer could have made a fortune in profits. But the structures would have ruined the aesthetics—as well as stressed the water supply—for the rest of the islanders. Matt had seen his employer destroy one community after another with his so-called development. He'd finally had enough. He tipped off some conservationists before the deal went through. There were legal battles and negative publicity, and so much contention that Matt wound up in the hospital here. But as I said, he's

doing much better now. As for the island . . . Well, you can see for
yourself how it all turned out."

Celeste's initial opinion of Arthur's son was starting to shift.
"Good for Matt!"

"Right. But not so good for his employer."

Celeste smirked. "Yeah. He must have been livid."

Arthur turned and met her eyes. "I was."

"You?" Celeste was stunned. When Arthur said he'd worked in
real estate, she'd thought he meant he'd sold individual houses, not
anything on the scale he'd just described. Now she was getting a
better picture of what had led to his estrangement with his son. But
what didn't make sense was how Arthur had described himself; as
a miserable, angry man. A bully. "But you don't seem like—" She
stopped herself from saying it.

"Like what? A merciless, money-grubbing tyrant who would put
his greed and ambition above the good of an entire community?
Above the well-being of *his own son*?" Arthur broke eye contact and
faced the marina again. "That's exactly who I was."

Celeste vehemently shook her head. "Maybe that's who you
were, but I don't think you're like that now."

"Yes, well, having a quadruple bypass can change a person." He
sighed. "Unfortunately, it can't change the past."

"No, but there's the possibility of forgiveness in the present, isn't
there?"

"That's why I came to Sea Spray Island. I know how special this
place was to Matt, and I thought he'd agree to meet me here this
December. I wanted to show him how sorry I am for what I put him
and this community through. I figured there was no better time for
reconciliation than at Christmas, but obviously, he's not interested."

"You never know, Arthur. He might show up. There's still time."

"Coming from someone who missed a plane *and* a ferry last

night, that's not resounding assurance." He chuckled and Celeste did, too. Then someone gave a friendly tap of their car horn behind them, so they continued down the hill toward Christmas Cove.

When they opened the door to the inn, Carol and Abbey were right there to greet them both with such big hugs, it was as if they'd just returned from a three-year Antarctic expedition. Which actually was kind of what the past sixteen hours had felt like to Celeste. There was a large "Welcome Home" sign hanging above the living room doorframe.

"It was going to say 'Welcome Home, Uncle Josh,'" Abbey explained. Her cheeks were splotchy and her eyelids were swollen, as if she'd been crying, but her voice was animated. "Then Aunt Carol told me you were in the hospital, Mr. Williams, and that you were coming back, Celeste. So Uncle Josh's name got axed—but don't tell him that, or he won't feel special."

"Your secret's safe with us," Arthur assured her.

"Go sit by the fire," Carol directed them. "I'll make tea. The power just came on a few minutes ago. It's going to take a while for the house to warm up again, so you might need to keep your coats on until it does."

But Celeste wanted to change into warmer clothes. Since Carol still hadn't touched anything in her room, she put on the borrowed running pants and sweatshirt from the lost-and-found bin that she'd left folded on the bed with the other borrowed items.

Then she joined the others for tea, and the four of them chatted about everything from Carol's haircut and Arthur's special diet to the cancellation of the Heading Sledding event and Celeste's new blog assignment.

"Does this mean you're going to be here for Christmas?" Abigail asked, clearly overjoyed she'd get to spend more time with Celeste. The feeling was mutual.

"Yes, it does. I'll be working, but I don't have to catch a ferry until Monday afternoon or evening," she said. "And since you inspired my idea, I wondered if you could help me today? I need to walk through town and over to the cove to take photos."

"Definitely. I can't wait until our island is famous!"

Celeste cautioned Abigail not to tell anyone she was writing about Christmas Cove. Otherwise, if Philip didn't use her post for some reason, the islanders would be disappointed.

"What should I say if someone asks us what we're doing?"

"Tell them the truth—we're taking photographs because Christmas Cove is so special that I want something to remember it by."

IF NATHAN THOUGHT HE WAS GOING TO GET TWO SECONDS of peace to work on the grant application this morning, he was dreaming. During weather emergencies, the center's regularly scheduled programs were canceled to accommodate the ages and interests of the individuals and families whose homes had lost power. Since it was difficult to predict who would show up, Kanesha often had to create specialized activities at the last minute. The regular volunteers usually had to stay home with their school-age children, so Nathan, Lee and Samantha pitched in however they could.

Today, Lee refereed a game of dodgeball. Samantha made popcorn and converted a classroom into a cinema. And Nathan read stories to a group of preschoolers who were supposed to be settling down for a nap. When they didn't, he abandoned the activity and helped them make tents with their blankets and mats instead. Kanesha, meanwhile, juggled the other activities, including a computer class for senior residents, a group soap-making lesson and a junior high pool tournament. At noon, the staff also prepared and

served snacks and hot beverages, as well as jam or cheese sandwiches for those people who hadn't brought lunches from home.

Sometime in the middle of all this, Nathan was called on to
mediate an argument between Sally Archer and Samantha. According to Sally, it was impossible to conduct her yoga class because
Samantha was leading children in singing Christmas carols on the
other side of the adjoining wall. Since all the other rooms were being used, Sally suggested the children try lip-synching. Needless to
say, Samantha thought the idea was absurd.

Because there were only two participants in Sally's class, Nathan offered to let them use his office. "I'm on lunch clean-up duty
for the next half hour, anyway."

After her class was over, she stopped him in the hall to complain. "Your phone rang so many times, we would have been better
off staying next door to the singers. I finally answered it just to
make it stop."

She said Gerald Kerley—the promising major donor Nathan
had spoken to the day before—had called to say he was sorry, but
his wife wanted to award their year-end donation to the local children's museum instead of to the community center.

Sally made a clucking noise. "You know, I told him that was a
real shame because I would have loved to order more yoga blocks
this winter. So guess what? He's sending us a check for $200!"

Nathan rubbed his forehead, disgraced that Sally had wheedled
a $200 donation from a multimillionaire. *That's what I get for letting
her use my office. No good deed goes unpunished,* he thought as he
rounded the corner into the lobby, where Lee was showing two high
school boys how to use a mop and wringer. There was a small pool
and a smattering of bright-red droplets on the floor in front of Sandy
Claws.

Nathan panicked. "Did someone get hurt?"

"No. It's food coloring," Lee assured him, pointing upward.

Apparently, the teenagers had duct-taped a cardboard cutout of Santa Claus in Sandy's claw. Then they'd used the spray bottles of food coloring from yesterday's event to make it look as if Santa was dripping blood.

"That is really *not* funny, guys," Nathan admonished, knowing how much the inflatable decoration meant to the younger students.

But Lee spoke over him. "I've got it covered, boss. I'm making them mop it up before it traumatizes the littler kiddies."

To Nathan, that didn't seem like a strong enough consequence, so he told the boys, "Since there's a power outage, I'm not kicking you out today, but starting tomorrow, you're banned for a week because of your vandalism."

"But we'll miss the rest of Christmas Countdown," the shorter one complained.

"You should have thought about that before you defaced the lobster. If your parents have any questions about my decision, they can call me."

As he climbed the stairs, one of them muttered, "Bah humbug," and Nathan couldn't be sure it wasn't Lee.

In his office, he listened to a half dozen voice mail messages— all left by board members who hadn't had any success with their solicitations. *Don't waste time calling to tell me that. Call when you actually have good news to share,* Nathan thought.

He was playing a message from Mark when Samantha wheeled into his office. What could possibly be so important that she had to follow him up here to tell him in person? "What is it now?" he barked.

"Vince Motta bought coffee for the staff. The bakery has a generator, so he stopped there on his way over here. He said he figured by now we could use a shot of the good stuff. He got us each a biscotti, too." She set a covered paper cup and a white paper bag on his desk.

"That's nice. Thanks."

"Don't thank *me,* it's from Ray." She circled toward the door, but then she paused to remark, "By the way, you were so busy this morning I thought I'd help you out by calling Nicola to tell her we couldn't make it there for lunch. I suspected the restaurant would be closed because of the power outage, but I didn't want to assume. You know how she gets when people reserve a table and then don't show."

"Ugh. I completely forgot to make a reservation in the first place," Nathan admitted, as if Samantha hadn't already discovered that during her conversation with Nicola. "Thanks for calling to cancel it all the same."

"No problem." She pointedly added, "Sometimes it's the little things we do that show our coworkers how much we care about them."

As she rolled from the room, Nathan thought, *If she's peeved at me for forgetting to make a lunch reservation, how's she going to feel when she finds out I forgot where I put the staff's Christmas bonuses?*

Chapter 15

BY THE TIME CELESTE AND ABIGAIL RETURNED FROM THEIR
photography quest, it was one thirty and they were famished. Carol
mentioned that Arthur had gone upstairs to take a nap after eating
a bland lunch, but she'd made chicken curry and rice for the three
of them.

"It smells *so* yummy, Aunt Carol," Abigail said as they sat down
together. "This is another reason I'm glad Dad won't let me go to the
center today. My friends who went there probably only got jam
sandwiches and graham crackers."

"Your dad doesn't want you to go to the center today?" Celeste
questioned.

Carol quickly clarified that it wasn't that he didn't *want* Abigail
there. But as a courtesy, most people who hadn't lost power avoided the
community center. Otherwise, it became too crowded and chaotic.

"Oh. I was going to go over and snap a few photos, but I don't
want to add to anyone's stress."

"No, that's fine. They just want to avoid everyone from every household showing up at the same time. You definitely should go," Carol urged. "I'll send curry for Nathan. He'll be surprised to see you, since I didn't get a chance this morning to tell him you were still here."

"I'll go, too. There's safety in numbers—my dad can't kick us both out." Abigail was so straight-faced that it was difficult to tell whether she was serious or joking.

When they arrived at the center, Celeste and Abbey stopped on the front lawn to mourn the eroded condition of the snow sculptures. Most of them were either half-melted or pockmarked from the sleet and rain and their colors were faded.

As soon as they went inside, Zander ran up to them and asked, "Did you see Elfish?"

"Yeah, all of his green melted off. He looks terrible," Abbey answered.

"No, he doesn't," the boy protested. "He looks like he's molting!"

Celeste grinned. "Now *that's* using your imagination, Zander."

He dashed off, and Celeste and Abbey went to hang up their coats and scarves. They passed Kanesha bustling through the lobby. A silver whistle dangled from a cord around her neck, and she was carrying a clipboard.

"Are you here to participate in the relay races, Abbey?"

"I-I can't," she faltered. "I've got to help Celeste do something important."

Celeste seized her chance to say hello to Nathan in private. She anticipated he'd be too busy for a deep discussion, but she hoped to set up a time to talk to him later. "Go ahead, Abbey. I'll bring this curry to your dad, and then I'll come back to watch you compete and to take a few photos. Kanesha might need my help timing the races, right, Kanesha?"

"There's no *might* about it—I definitely will. So don't dillydally."

When Celeste reached Nathan's office, she found the door partially ajar, but she knocked and waited until he said to come in. He was standing sideways, rifling through a filing cabinet perpendicular to the outer wall. Papers were strewn across his desk, and a tall stack of folders was balanced precariously in one corner. For some reason, a wastebasket occupied his swivel chair.

"Hi, Nathan. Did you lose something?"

"Yeah—my patience," he muttered absently, before glancing up to see who had entered. When his eyes met hers, he didn't do a double take; he did a quadruple. Followed by a scowl. "Why aren't you in the Caribbean, like you're supposed to be?"

He sounded so annoyed that if Celeste had closed her eyes, she would have sworn it was Philip speaking.

"I missed my flight. And then I missed my ferry. It's a long story, but—" She was going to say that she knew he was busy now, but she hoped they could meet to talk in private later.

He didn't give her the chance. "Sorry I asked—I don't have time to hear it."

Celeste was so stunned, her mouth fell open. For a second all she could do was stare at him as he resumed combing through the hanging file folders. Then she regained her composure enough to reply, "Right, I understand. Carol asked me to drop this off." She set the thermal bag on his desk and fled the room.

Halfway down the hall, she whirled around. This time, she barged into his office without warning. "Actually, Nathan, I *don't* understand," she blurted out. "I mean, I get it that you're busy. But I don't get why you're being so rude about it."

He raked his hand through his hair, shook his head. "That's rich coming from *you*."

"What do you mean by *that*?"

"I'd spell it out, but it would take too long." Nathan shoved the top filing cabinet drawer shut and yanked open the middle one.

"Are you angry because I had to cut our lunch date short yesterday? Because if that's what you're upset about then I'm sorry, but you know how important it was for me to go book a new flight and call my editor."

"Yes, Celeste, you've made it abundantly clear how important your career is to you." He pivoted to face her, his eyes flashing. "But guess what? I might not be as ambitious as you are, but *my* career is important to *me*, too. I have a family to support and an entire community depending on me. I don't expect you to understand what that's like, because you only have to look out for yourself. But take my word for it—it's a lot of responsibility, a lot of pressure and a lot of work. So as I've already said, I'm busy. I don't have time to stand here arguing about which one of us is rude." He turned toward the filing cabinet again, adding, "And, just to be clear, I wouldn't call yesterday's lunch a *date*."

"Neither would I." Celeste leaned forward to emphasize how much she meant it. "I'd call it a *mistake*."

And as she left, she jerked the door shut with such force that she thought she heard the pile of folders topple from Nathan's desk onto the floor.

BY SEVEN THIRTY, THE UTILITY COMPANY HAD RESTORED power to all of its customers on the island. And by eight o'clock, the last stragglers had cleared out of the community center, which meant the staff wasn't required to remain on-site until nine after all.

"I've got some paperwork to finish, so I'm going to stick around a little longer. I'll lock up behind you," Nathan told Kanesha and Samantha. They were waiting in the lobby for Lee to finish checking that the lights were off in all the classrooms.

"Look at what Celeste gave me, Kanesha," Samantha said, displaying the contents of the gift bag on her lap. From the way she was ignoring Nathan's presence, it was obvious she was still ticked off at him. "Purple cocoa mix and lavender marshmallows to match my hair. She got it at the Treasure Chest. I didn't even know they carried stuff like this. She is *so* sweet."

Yes, she can be, as long as she's got nothing better to do, Nathan silently retorted.

"She's inventive, too. My indoor relay races this afternoon were a flop, so she suggested sock-skating Olympics. She got the idea because she nearly wiped out on the floor in classroom A. It was that day she fell in the cove and was walking around here without any shoes on. Anyway, the kids were having such a great time, I wanted to try it myself," Kanesha raved. "You should have seen your daughter, Nathan. She might be small, but that girl is *fast.*"

Abigail was here? Nathan was surprised. Why hadn't she popped into his office to say hi? He was going to ask whether Carol had come to the center, too, but then Lee came ambling toward them, so Nathan walked everyone to the door.

After locking up, he returned to his office. It was finally quiet enough for him to work on the creative narrative without any distractions, but he still couldn't focus. His thoughts kept drifting to his interaction with Celeste that afternoon. It astounded him that she'd shown up at his workplace unannounced on the busiest day of the year and accused *him* of being rude, just because he didn't have time to listen to her complain about missing her flight.

And yet he also kept picturing the injured expression on her face when he'd pointed out that she didn't know what it was like to be responsible for anyone but herself. *I refuse to feel guilty about that remark,* he thought. *It was the truth, and sometimes the truth hurts.*

He rubbed his eyes and stared at the blank page in his online document. It was no use. He was beat. After a hot meal and a shower, he'd try again, but first, he wanted to see his daughter. However, when he got to the inn, neither Carol nor Abigail were in the living or dining room. Not in the kitchen, either. He walked down the hall and rapped on the door to Carol and Josh's private quarters.

Carol was sitting on the bed, tying a gold ribbon around a large box.

"Hi, Carol. Where's Abbey?"

"Room 3."

Nathan was caught off-guard by his sister's curtness. Usually she was chattier. Had Abbey given her a hard time about something? "Is she asleep already?"

"Maybe. She and Celeste were discussing the project they're working on together."

"Celeste! You mean she *still* hasn't left the island?" He'd assumed she'd caught a flight sometime after her visit to his office.

"No. Didn't she tell you? She's staying until the twenty-sixth. Since she didn't get to the Caribbean in time to cover *j'ouvert*, she's writing a post on Sea Spray Island. I've invited her to join us for our Christmas festivities, of course."

Carol appeared to be studying his response, so Nathan fought to keep his expression neutral even though the idea of spending Christmas with Celeste had as much appeal as last year's fruitcake. "I didn't talk to her very long. She just dropped some food off and left."

"You're welcome for that, by the way." There it was again: Carol was being uncharacteristically snarky.

"Thank you . . . Did everything go all right with Abigail today?"

Carol got up and closed the door. Her voice low, she said, "You know I'd never repeat something she told me in confidence unless there was a really good reason. But I think you should know she spent her first hour here in tears."

"She did?" Nathan was alarmed. "Why?"

"Well, for starters she said you're always correcting the way she talks . . ."

Nathan briefly squeezed his eyes shut and pinched his nose, recalling some of their recent conversations. "Ack. I didn't mean to hurt her feelings—I was trying to be instructive."

"I know you were. But that's not the real issue, anyway. It's that she feels like you've been angry at her a lot lately."

"That's not true!"

"And that you make promises you don't keep—"

"What promises?"

"You didn't help her with the Make-a-Flake project like you said you would. Or bring her your phone so she could call Celeste. Things like that. She thinks you don't like her very much. That you're always trying to get away from her. And I've got to tell you, Nathan, given the way you dumped her on my doorstep this morning, I can see how she got that impression."

Nathan dropped into an armchair. "I-I have a lot going on at work."

"I know you do," Carol said, even though she didn't know the half of it. "And I completely understand why you can't always take Abigail into the office with you or stop what you're doing to participate in the activities with her. But you might want to find another way to communicate how special she is to you."

Nathan leaned his elbows against his thighs and buried his face in his hands, devastated that he'd hurt his daughter's feelings. That she believed he didn't like her very much, when in fact he *loved* her with every fiber of his being.

"I'm a terrible father," he said, choking back a sob.

Carol came over to him and placed her hand on his shoulder. "No, you're not. You're just a human one."

"You have no idea how important it was to me that Abigail enjoyed Christmas Countdown this year. Instead, I've ruined it for her."

"Are you kidding? Abbey's had so much fun sharing Christmas Countdown with Arthur and Celeste that *I* almost feel as if *I've* been cast aside," Carol joked. Then she added, "Seriously, I'm sorry Arthur had a gallbladder attack, but I'm glad it prevented Celeste from leaving, for Abbey's sake. She is *thrilled* she gets to help her with the blog post."

Nathan had no idea what his sister was talking about, so she launched into an account of how Celeste had missed both a flight and a ferry off the island the evening before because she'd taken Arthur to the hospital. "It's strange, but Arthur told me she would have been able to make it to the ferry terminal in plenty of time before the roads iced up. But Celeste insisted on staying at the hospital until she was sure he was okay. I'm surprised she took that risk, considering what her boss is like, but it sure meant a lot to Arthur."

Everything I thought and said about Celeste was true of me, Nathan realized as his sister was speaking. *I was the one who was being rude and self-centered. The one who cared more about his career than about other people's feelings. I am the world's biggest clod.*

"Nathan, are you okay?" Carol asked. "You look like you're in pain."

If I am, it's because the truth hurts, he thought. "I need to go say good night to Abbey. I hope she'll forgive me." He hoped Celeste would, too.

Upstairs, Nathan crept down the hall so he wouldn't disturb Arthur. When he reached Room 3, he paused. The door was closed, but the room was dark and he could hear Celeste talking in a subdued voice. Was she reading? No, the light was off; she must have been telling Abigail a story. Hesitant to interrupt, Nathan listened.

The story was about a little girl who went outside to play in the snow on Christmas Day. The weather was so cold that when she came in, she discovered her smile had frozen on her face. As Celeste regaled his daughter with the sweet tale, Nathan was so enchanted he didn't move a muscle until it ended. Then he backed away from the threshold just as Celeste slid sideways through the door. She caught her breath when she saw him.

"I didn't mean to startle you. Is Abbey sleeping?"

"Yes." Celeste took a step toward her room, but Nathan stopped her.

"Can I talk to you? Please? It's important." She nodded, so he asked her to wait there a minute. He tiptoed into the room and kissed his daughter's forehead. "I love you," he whispered into her ear. And then he whispered it into her other ear, too.

When he came out, he motioned toward the stairs. Celeste frowned, but she followed him down to the living room. She walked as far as the sofa, but she didn't sit when he did, so he jumped up again.

Crossing her arms, she gazed toward the fireplace. "Go ahead, talk."

Nathan needed a moment to compose his apology, but he was worried if he didn't speak quickly, she'd leave. He stammered, "I, um, I overheard that story you told Abigail. You really have a way with words. I thought you were reading it from a book."

"Is that the important thing you wanted to tell me?" Celeste looked ready to bolt.

"No. Well, it *is* important, and I *do* mean it. But what I really wanted to talk to you about is the things I said to you today in my office that I *didn't* mean. Things that aren't true at all. I was wrong to imply you were self-centered and only concerned about your career. I've seen and heard about all the things you've been doing for other people on the island, especially for my daughter." Nathan paused, hoping for some acknowledgment that he was getting through to her, but her profile was inscrutable. He nervously shifted his stance. "I was having an extremely stressful day, but that's no excuse for lashing out at you. The bottom line is that *I* was the one who was being selfish and self-important and rude—not you. I'm very sorry, Celeste, and I hope you'll forgive me."

His mouth too dry to say anything else, he held his breath and waited for her response.

CELESTE HESITATED. EVEN WITHOUT LOOKING INTO NATHAN'S eyes, she knew how earnest his apology was. She could hear it in his voice; he was practically pleading. But there was something else she needed to address before they could reconcile. "I understand I caught you at a bad time this afternoon, but that doesn't explain why you acted the way you did yesterday. When I came to say goodbye, you totally blew me off. It seemed like I'd done something to offend you. But the only thing I can think of is that I left before we could take a walk to the bakery. Was that what you were upset about?"

"Sort of, but not exactly. I mean, I understood why you had to leave so quickly." Nathan squirmed, pushing his hair off his forehead. "It, uh, it seems petty now, but I was kind of irked that you left without saying . . . I don't know. Something like, 'I had a good time.' Or even goodbye. And to be honest, I think my ego was bruised because I overheard you telling Patty she wasn't interrupting anything important."

Celeste was mortified. "I am so sorry, Nathan. The only reason I said that to Patty was because I didn't want her to ask me a bunch of intrusive questions. I just wanted her to say why she called as quickly as possible so I could get off the phone, and then you and I could walk to the bakery." She shook her head. "And I definitely should have said goodbye, and told you I had a terrific afternoon— because I did. But I was so upset about our lunch being cut short and my flight being delayed that all I could think about was getting out of the house before I had a complete meltdown in front of you."

"It's okay. I shouldn't have taken it to heart. You were preoccupied. And stressed."

"Yeah, but still . . ." After being vexed with him for the better part of the day, Celeste was suddenly drained. She sat down on the sofa. "No wonder you thought I was rude."

Nathan sat, too. "I'm not exactly the poster boy for good manners. Today I abandoned my daughter on Carol's doorstep without giving her a backward glance. I also hollered at Samantha when she was bringing me coffee. *And* I banned two high school kids from the community center for a week."

"Really? What for?"

"Defacing the inflatable lobster."

Celeste giggled. "Technically, I don't think lobsters have faces to deface."

"Yes, they do—they have eyes, anyway."

"No kidding. Zander told me they pee out of them."

Nathan grimaced. "You are aware you just ruined my all-time favorite summer meal forever, aren't you?" Celeste giggled, but he turned serious. "I really am sorry for my behavior and the hurtful, unfair things I said to you."

"I forgive you, Nathan. But not everything you said was unfair."

"What wasn't?"

"You were right when you said I don't understand what it's like to have a family and an entire community depending on me . . . But what *you* don't understand is what it's like not to have anyone to depend *on*."

"No, I don't." Nathan's voice was gentle and so was the look in his eyes. "But I'd *like* to understand."

So Celeste confided about her father leaving them, growing up poor and watching her mother work so hard to give her daughter a better life and more options than what she'd had. Nathan was such a rapt, empathic listener that she felt as comfortable talking to him as she had when she'd confided some of the same things to Arthur.

When she finished, he thanked her for sharing her story. "This might not mean much coming from a former slacker, but I'm impressed by your ambition to make the most of your opportunities. I hope Philip promotes you really soon."

"I appreciate the thought, but I'll be fortunate if I still have a job—*any* job—when I get back to the office." Celeste told Nathan about her new blog assignment, and what Philip had said during their last phone conversation. "So the pressure's on to come up with a really unique way to present Christmas Cove. Have you got any suggestions?"

"Ha!" Nathan uttered. "If I did, maybe I could save both our jobs."

Celeste was shocked when he proceeded to tell her that the community center had lost its funding and was on the brink of shutting down. If that happened, not only would all the staff lose their jobs but Nathan and Abbey would have to move off-island. He had even lined up a position in Boston just in case. His last hope was that he'd win a grant, but he only had until midnight tomorrow to compose a creative narrative.

"Oh, Nathan, that's awful," Celeste sympathized. "You've been carrying such an incredible weight on your shoulders. I had no idea."

"No one else does, either—except the board members. I didn't want to spoil anyone's Christmas. And I hate letting people down." He pressed his palms against his eyes and kept them there for so long, Celeste wondered if he'd fallen asleep. Then it occurred to her he might be tearing up but didn't want her to notice. She scooted closer and tugged his sleeve.

"Hey," she said. When she repeated it a second time, he dropped his hands but didn't meet her gaze. "There's still time. We'll put our heads together and come up with something phenomenal. Something that we can tailor for both our purposes. A one-for-all. Or a two-for-one, whichever. We can do this."

"You really think so?"

"If we can't, then I don't deserve to call myself a writer. I'll go get my laptop." Celeste rose and so did Nathan.

"I left mine in Carol's quarters. I'll be right back."

"While you're there, will you ask her if she has any snacks? It's going to be a long night. We'll need sustenance."

Nathan followed Celeste into the hall. "Sure. But I hope she doesn't want to join us."

"Just ban her from the living room. I've heard you're good at banning people," Celeste joked.

"Or *you* could slam the door on her. *You're* good at slamming doors."

She laughed at the reference. "Did that giant stack of folders slide off your desk?"

"Like an avalanche."

"An avalanche? Wow. I hope no one was injured."

"One guy was." Nathan gave her ponytail a playful tug. "But he recovered completely."

"Good." She twisted her head to grin over her shoulder. "Now, go get your laptop. As Kanesha would say, no dillydallying. We've got jobs to save."

Chapter 16

SATURDAY—DECEMBER 24

EVEN THOUGH SHE'D ONLY GOTTEN A FEW HOURS OF SLEEP, Celeste hopped out of bed and into the shower the minute she opened her eyes. She frequently experienced an adrenaline rush when she was up against a deadline, but that wasn't the only reason she was so wound up this morning. It wasn't even the main reason—*Nathan* was.

Maybe it was because last night they'd both been so vulnerable about their worries. Or because they were partnering in a secret project. It could have been because of the lighthearted way they'd bantered. Or that they were sitting so close. Maybe it was that dip above his lip, the cleft in his chin or the way his voice went throaty when he said her name. Maybe it was all those things. But whatever the reason, Celeste was so eager to see him again that she felt like . . . well, like a kid on Christmas morning.

When she jounced downstairs for breakfast thirty minutes later, she found Arthur and Carol in the dining room, drinking tea and juice, respectively. The table was set—for five—but their plates were clean and the only food in view was a heaping bowl of fruit salad.

"Nathan and Abbey are serving us this morning," Carol explained. "It should only be another minute."

"They're using your kitchen? I thought you never allowed anyone in there."

"I don't. They're bringing egg tarts from the Portuguese bakery."

"And whole wheat *papo secos* for me." Arthur patted his stomach. "Gallbladder attacks have their advantages."

"Is this a December twenty-fourth morning tradition in your family?" Celeste asked Carol.

"No. Nathan popped by early so he could spend a little father-and-daughter time with Abbey before work."

The sentence was barely out of Carol's mouth when the pair came sweeping into the dining room, their arms stacked with cardboard boxes.

"Merry Christmas Eve Day." Abigail's cheeks were ruddy, just like her dad's, but his smile was even wider than hers.

"Merry Christmas Eve Day," Arthur, Carol and Celeste chorused in unison, as if they'd been rehearsing it.

"Is all of that for us?" Carol asked.

"These boxes are. The others are for Kanesha, Samantha and Lee." As everyone was helping themselves to the breakfast goodies, Nathan explained that he was supposed to take his staff to Lombardi's for lunch yesterday, but they couldn't go because of the power outage. "I'll take them next week. But I'm bringing pastries because this morning I have to tell them I misplaced their Christmas bonuses."

"Oh, brother, you didn't." Carol groaned, holding her hand against her forehead. "I don't think pastries are going to make up for that."

"Neither do I, but their mouths might be too full to yell at me." Nathan rubbed the back of his neck. "It's going to be embarrassing asking the board to issue new checks. But I've looked everywhere, and I just can't find them."

"I'll vouch for that—you should have seen his office yesterday." Celeste snitched. "It looked like the place had been ransacked by a flock of seagulls."

"Did you check your attach-egg case, Dad?" Abigail asked.

Nathan paused, holding a tart halfway to his open mouth, as if he hadn't understood she'd meant attaché case. *If you're going to correct her pronunciation, please do it gently so you don't spoil this special meal,* Celeste silently begged.

But Nathan just questioned, "The one I carry my laptop in?"

"No. The leather one you only use on special occasions. It's hanging on the back of the door in your office, beneath your scarf. You told me to remind you that you were putting something important in it for Christmas. I thought it was my present, so I didn't look." Abigail pushed a napkin across her lips. "But I was super tempted."

Nathan pumped both of his fists, egg tart and all, toward the ceiling. "Whoo-hoo! Abigail, you're a genius!" Everyone gave her a raucous round of applause, which made her blush from one darling, unfurled ear tip to the other.

When they quieted down, Arthur asked if Celeste and Nathan had made any progress on Celeste's project the evening before. *How did he know about that?* Celeste wondered. *Carol must have mentioned it to him before I came downstairs for breakfast.*

"We made some progress, yes, but I don't think the article is quite there yet."

"You want me to take a look at it and tell you what I think?" Abigail offered, with all the nonchalant collegiality of a thirty-five-year-old.

Celeste bit back a smile. "Sure. I'd appreciate that."

Since Abbey planned to leave with Nathan so she could help Lee and Kanesha set up for the Eats & Treats Party for Kids Only, Celeste went and got her laptop and brought it to the table.

"Hmm," Abigail murmured when she'd finished reading it. "My teacher would say it has a lot of good descriptive words. I really like the photo of the pier. And the close-up of the shell wreath on the door of the Treasure Chest."

"Thanks, Abbey." Because she'd told the young girl that writers needed to be able to accept criticism, Celeste asked, "Is there something you think I need to change?"

"Well . . ."

"It's okay, give it to me straight." *After seven years of working for Philip, I can take almost anything.*

"It's kind of boring."

"Abbey." Nathan shook his head.

"That's okay. I want her honest opinion. Go ahead, Abbey."

"It's not, like, cozy enough. And it isn't funny at all. You didn't even mention the Ugly Sweater Contest."

"Honey, Celeste is writing this article for adults, not for kids," Nathan gently interceded.

"But it still needs to be engaging," Celeste acknowledged. *Our jobs are riding on it.* "Thanks for your feedback, Abigail. I'll take it into consideration."

"MAYBE ABBEY AND I COULD HELP YOU REVISE IT AFTER THE center closes at noon," Nathan offered. Last night he and Celeste had stayed up past midnight discussing possible angles and putting their ideas into words for both her article and his narrative. He suspected she'd stayed up another hour or more after he left, revising what they'd come up with so far. It didn't seem fair that she was going to bear the brunt of the work again today.

"Uh, sorry guys, but I can only help until three o'clock," Abigail informed them. "Remember, Dad? I got invited to Bobby's. His mom is going to teach us how to make tree ornaments and then she's taking us out for Chinese food."

Nathan hadn't remembered until now. "That's right. Ms. Riley is bringing you to the bonfire and caroling on the town green afterward, isn't she?"

"Yup. I'll meet you there, in our usual spot. But since the ground is covered in snow, Samantha said she's changing the event title to Fired Up for Caroling on the Town *White* instead of the town *green*."

Nathan smiled. By this point, he thought Samantha's puns and rhymes was wearing a little thin, but he loved that his daughter appreciated them. "I'm still available for help if you want to bounce any ideas off me," he said to Celeste.

He hoped she understood he meant he definitely *would* help her after lunch, but he had to be careful how he phrased it in front of the others. He didn't want them finding out that he and Celeste were also working on the grant application. Nor did he want Abigail in particular to think he was overly eager to spend time alone with Celeste—even though he was.

Was he *ever*. Especially if it meant this afternoon would be anything like last evening.

Once they'd resolved the conflict between them, Nathan had felt even closer to Celeste than before they'd argued. He was moved that she'd confided in him about what her life had been like when she was young, and he'd gained more insight into her aspirations and fears. In turn, it had been a relief to share his burden about the center's funding. Not just because she'd offered to help him with the creative narrative, but because she'd offered him understanding about the pressure he'd been under.

After their initial personal conversation, they'd mostly just discussed their work projects. But that hadn't diminished how romantic it felt to sit with Celeste beside the fire, his eyes fixed on her eyes. On her face. Her lips. Admittedly, a few times when she'd been talking, he'd been watching her mouth move, but he hadn't been thinking at all about her words . . .

If it hadn't been for the clock ticking on the application deadline, last night could have been a truly incredible evening. Scratch that. If it hadn't been for the clock ticking on *Celeste's departure*, it could have been a truly incredible evening.

Regardless, it had been wonderful enough to make Nathan wish he hadn't promised his daughter he didn't have any interest in dating Celeste. *Technically, what I really said was that I wouldn't call her or try to get together with her once she left the island,* he reminded himself. *I didn't give Abbey any guarantee that I wouldn't flirt with Celeste while she was here. And I never said a single word about whether or not I'd kiss her . . .*

"Are you still with us, Nathan?" His sister's question cut into his thoughts. "Arthur wanted to know if there were any events for adults at the center today or if the kids got to have all the fun."

"There's a gift-wrapping activity at ten. Then a cookie and coffee hour from eleven until we close at noon. And the bonfire and caroling at seven this evening is open to everyone."

"I might stop in for cookies after my morning walk," Arthur mentioned as he rose to leave the table.

"You should drop by, too, Celeste and Carol," Nathan suggested.

"Not me. I've got to go grocery shopping. I hope everyone likes beef bourguignonne. I'm making it for supper—it's one of Josh's favorite meals."

Nathan had the good sense not to tell his sister he'd completely forgotten Josh was flying in this afternoon. *That's another example of how overly preoccupied I've been with this funding situation,* he realized. *I wonder what else I've missed around here.*

On their way to the center, Abigail and Nathan stopped at the bakery so he could buy the staff's favorite coffees. Then while Abbey went into the events room to begin placing the folding chairs around the tables for the kids' party, he dashed upstairs to get the bonus checks and cards, which were right where his daughter had said they'd be. He arranged the pastries on a tray in the kitchen and brought it to the reception area just as Kanesha and Samantha entered the building, with Lee a few paces behind them.

"What's all this?" Kanesha asked.

Nathan greeted them with his daughter's phrase, "Merry Christmas Eve Day!" Presenting each of them with a card, he added, "These are from the board. I wanted to give them to you during our lunch at Lombardi's yesterday. But as you know, the weather didn't cooperate. And to be perfectly honest, we might not have been able to go there anyway because I forgot to—"

"That's okay, you can take us next week." Samantha interrupted his confession, winking to show all was forgiven. "The important thing is that you remembered to give us our bonuses. Now some of us can finish our shopping in time for Christmas."

Nathan so appreciated that for once Samantha was actually keeping a secret, he could have hugged her. And then he *did* hug her. He hugged Kanesha and Lee, too, saying how much he appreciated their diligence, teamwork and flexibility. "I hope you know I think the world of each of you."

"Thanks, boss, but can you save the speech for Lombardi's?" Lee cracked. "We've got fifty kids coming here in less than an hour, and I want to enjoy this coffee in peace while I still can."

"Absolutely," Nathan said. "You three go sit by the fireplace, and I'll help Abigail with the chairs."

When he was done, Nathan went upstairs to call the two high schoolers he'd banished yesterday to tell them they were welcome back at the center, provided they agreed not to wreak havoc with any of the decorations again.

After ending his call with the second boy, he checked his e-mail. He had several messages from board members telling him they'd tried their best, but the biggest donation any of them had received was for ten thousand dollars, to be paid over the course of the following year. The final message he checked was from a name he recognized but couldn't immediately place. When he opened it, he realized who'd sent it; the foundation rep from Boston.

He wasn't surprised to read the grant had officially been awarded to the other finalist. What caught him off guard was that he didn't feel shattered by it. He didn't even feel all that disheartened. Probably because he'd known it was coming and, on some level, he'd already accepted it. Also, because he'd transferred his hopes to the St. Nick of Time Grant.

Picking up his phone, he called the board president. Mark took it well, too. "It's unfortunate, but I think it's to our credit we made it as far as we did," he said. "So how's the creative narrative coming along?"

"Slowly . . . and not that surely," Nathan admitted. "But the good news is I have an extremely talented writer helping me."

"Do you mean the freelancer?"

"No, a volunteer. Her name's Celeste. She was actually supposed to be on a writing assignment in the Caribbean, but her flight was diverted to the island. She's had several weather delays, so she's here through Christmas."

"*Hmpf.* Sorry to hear she missed her trip to the tropics. But for your sake—and for the center's—I'm glad she's been stranded and is willing to help you out," Mark commented. "I haven't heard you sound so upbeat in a long time."

"That's because I know if anyone can come up with a winning narrative, Celeste can," Nathan told him, which was true, but it wasn't the only reason he sounded so buoyant again.

CELESTE READ HER REVISED ARTICLE FOR THE THIRD TIME. SHE knew it was good enough to post, but that didn't mean it was good enough for Philip. *Even if I wrote something worthy of a Pulitzer Prize in literature, he still might fire me,* she thought. Ordinarily, the possibility would have made her nearly sick with anxiety, but this morning she only felt sick of being intimidated by him.

He can fire me from Peregrinate, *but it's not as if he can ruin my entire future as a writer,* she told herself. *I don't even need him as a reference—I have an impressive portfolio of work that speaks for itself. I could freelance if I had to.*

It was the first time since she'd started working at the magazine that Celeste seriously had to consider what it would be like working as an independent contractor. Philip had often warned his staff the pay and travel perks wouldn't come anywhere close to matching what they received from *Peregrinate.* Not to mention the benefits package.

But if I were freelancing, I wouldn't have to come into an office every day when I'm not on assignment, like Philip requires us to do, she realized. *And that means I could cut back on my expenses by moving out of Boston. I could live anywhere—even on Sea Spray Island.*

Celeste chuckled when the rogue thought popped into her head. While it was empowering to remember that even if she lost her job, she'd be okay in the long run, she had no intention of getting fired. She'd struggled too hard to become a senior writer for Philip to snatch her dream away from her now. *I'll just keep revising the article as many times as it takes to make it absolutely stellar,* she decided.

She carried her laptop downstairs and into the annex, hoping Arthur might offer his perspective on her post. Now that she knew he wasn't simply reading the paper or watching passersby, there was something poignant about seeing him in his usual chair. She sat down beside him and asked, "Mind if I join you?"

"Please do. I just returned from my daily walk, but I'm not quite ready for tea and cookies yet. I'm resting before I head over to the community center."

"Resting and . . . watching?"

"For Matt, yes." He'd answered the part of her question she hadn't wanted to voice. "I haven't given up hope. I have a good feeling about today."

His optimism was encouraging to Celeste. "Then I won't give up hope about getting my blog post right, either. Would you mind reading it and telling me what you think? I've revised it, but it feels like it's missing something."

"I'm honored you'd want my opinion." After he'd finished it, Arthur commented, "You're an extremely gifted writer, Celeste. Your prose is vivid and elegant, and describes the beauty of Christmas Cove perfectly."

"Thank you . . . Do I hear a *but* at the end of that sentence?"

"But I understand what Abigail meant when she said your article wasn't cozy. It's a little dry, a little removed. Sea Spray Island is a friendly, quirky community."

"I tried to write about that here." Celeste pointed out a paragraph.

"Yes, you wrote *about* it but from a distance." He handed her laptop back to her. "I understand *Peregrinate* requires you to assume a certain tone that's consistent with its brand. But I think if you were to share your experience at Sea Spray Island, as told in your own voice with your own words, the result would be more engaging. Especially if you let go and have a little fun with it. Pretend it's an assignment for the college writing courses you enjoyed so much."

"Yeah, I could tell the story about how I fell in a tidal pool during a nor'easter and afterward the islanders gave me newly knitted socks and discarded workout clothes so I wouldn't freeze on my way back to the inn."

"Now *that's* a truer reflection of what makes Christmas Cove . . . Christmas Cove."

"I was just kidding. Philip would never publish an article like that."

"You said he wanted something original," Arthur argued. "Couldn't you submit two posts and let him choose which one he prefers? The traditional one you've written here *and* something unexpected? Even if he rejects the latter, he might appreciate it that you've put in extra effort."

The wheels started turning in Celeste's brain. Arthur's suggestion about telling her personal story just might work both for her project and for Nathan's. He'd mentioned he'd considered interviewing islanders about what the center meant to them, but he'd decided against it because he didn't want them to find out about the financial crisis. But what if Celeste created a *traveler's* testimonial about what the center meant to *her*? It wouldn't even have to be a written piece; she could narrate a video and customize it for each of their projects.

"Arthur, that's brilliant!"

He adjusted his glasses, looking pleased. "Why, thank you."

"I'm going to run over to the community center to talk to Nathan about how to get in touch with Brent, the guy who's always taking photos at the community center. He might allow us to use a few of them. You want to come with me?"

"Not yet, thanks. I'm still on watch." He gestured toward the window.

Celeste saluted him. "Okay. I'll see you later."

She supposed she could have called or texted Nathan to get Brent's number, but then she wouldn't have been able to see the look on his face when she told him about what Arthur had suggested. And she wouldn't have been able to stand right in front of him—close enough to smell a hint of his shaving cream and to see the flecks of gold in his eyes—when she did.

"It'll be great," she said, ideas flicking on like light bulbs in her mind, even as she was speaking. "I'll include a photo of you and me in the clothes we wore from the lost-and-found bin and caption it, 'Christmas Cove is the kind of place where people will give you the shirts off their backs and the socks off their knitting needles.' Or something along those lines."

"Yeah. And you could mention the dress code is casual here, and show that photo of us in our ugly sweaters," Nathan recommended, laughing. "We'll have to find a way to include Sandy Claws and Elfish the Shellfish, too."

Celeste snapped her fingers. "Oh, I know! We can say that on Sea Spray Island, visitors have two choices of lobster—jumbo or frozen."

"That's good, really good."

"You don't think it's too corny?"

"That's part of its appeal. But for the sake of the grant application, we can add details about how many free meals the center hosts each year. For every joke, we'll intersperse factual information about the essential services the community center provides the islanders."

"Smart thinking." Celeste tapped her chin. "You know what I

wish I had? A photo of me toppling into the tidal pool. I'd use it to begin my post. I'd write that I wanted to go to the Caribbean, but I ended up falling hard for Christmas Cove instead."

"Brace yourself." Nathan put his hands on her shoulders. "We don't have a photo of that—but we have a *video*."

Celeste pushed against his chest with her palms, just a little nudge. "You're kidding."

"I'm not. Brent recorded it from the balcony window upstairs."

"That's perfect!" In her excitement, she impulsively flung her arms around him.

"It is, isn't it?!" He hugged her, too. It was just a friendly, spontaneous embrace, an expression of their shared excitement.

At first.

Yet after they stopped laughing, Nathan loosened his grasp, but he didn't release her. And Celeste kept her cheek pressed against his breastbone, her head tucked beneath his chin as he whispered, "I thought you'd be upset, so I didn't want to tell you."

Does he mean he didn't want to tell me about the video or about this—about how he feels? Celeste wondered. Either way, her answer was the same. "I'm not upset. I think it's wonderful. I—"

The doorknob rattled and Nathan sprang back. At the same time, Celeste reared her head, like a spooked horse, right into his chin. She heard his bottom and top teeth knock together, just before Abbey came in.

"Hi, Celeste. Hi, Dad. Did you bite your tongue?" she asked because Nathan was rubbing his jaw. But she was too hyper or too sugared-up to wait for his response. She chattered, "I hate it when I do that. We had so much fun at the party! I'd tell you what we did, but I can't, because it was kids-only. Did you revise your article, Celeste?"

"Not yet, but I've got some great ideas, thanks to Arthur and your dad." So she filled Abigail in while Nathan called Brent, who said he was happy to share his photos. He preferred to show Celeste and Nathan his online galleries in person and agreed to meet with them at three thirty.

By the time Nathan got off the phone, it was past noon and the center was closed, so the three of them walked up the hill for lunch.

"Look, there must be another guest at the inn." Abigail pointed to a car in the driveway.

It can't be who I think it is, can it? Celeste wondered, tamping down her hope. Yet as they were hanging their jackets and scarves on the coatrack, Arthur emerged from the living room. His eyes were dancing, his skin was flushed and he looked twenty years younger than he'd looked an hour earlier. Celeste immediately intuited what he was about to announce.

"There's someone I'd like you to meet in the annex—my son, Matt."

Matt was the spitting image of his dad, except with hair and without glasses. He politely shook their hands, but his posture was rigid and his smile seemed strained, which Celeste supposed was understandable, given that it had been years since he'd spoken to his father.

After making introductions, Arthur explained, "Carol's packing us a lunch to eat on the ferry. Matt's had a sudden change of plans, so he's bringing me home to spend the holidays with his family."

No, Celeste thought. *Matt's had a sudden change of* heart— *which is even better.*

"You're leaving already?" Abigail whined, but Nathan put his hands on her shoulders from behind, signaling her not to complain.

"We'll miss not having you with us for Christmas," he remarked diplomatically, without pressing Arthur for more information.

"I'll miss all of you, too," Arthur said. "I'm sorry about my hasty departure. But it's supposed to start snowing soon, and we don't want to travel in bad weather."

"Believe me, I know how unpredictable that can be," Celeste commented, as Carol entered the room carrying two large tote bags.

"This one contains your lunch," she told Arthur and Matt. "And this one has a few gifts."

"Wait, I have something to add to that." Celeste retrieved the present she'd bought for Arthur from beneath the tree and slid it into the second bag.

They helped carry his luggage and escorted him and his son to the driveway. Because Matt wanted to make the one o'clock ferry, they had to make their goodbyes quick, which was just as well; Celeste easily could have started crying. Partly because she didn't want to say goodbye to Arthur again. But mostly because she was overjoyed that he'd received the gift she knew *he'd* wanted more than anything else for Christmas.

He hugged each of them, and Celeste overheard him quietly tell Abbey, "Maybe next year I'll bring my grandchildren here for Christmas Countdown."

"You don't have to wait that long—you could bring them in July. I'll show them all the best beaches," she softly replied. Celeste couldn't have been prouder of her graciousness if she were her own mother.

Everyone wished the two men merry Christmas a final time. Right before Matt ducked into the car, he caught Celeste's eye and mouthed, "Thank you."

She nodded. "Safe travels."

The four of them huddled together in the driveway and waved until Arthur and his son drove down the hill and out of view.

Chapter 17

AS THEY WENT INSIDE THE HOUSE, ABIGAIL LAMENTED, "I WISH Mr. Williams could have stayed until Christmas."

"So do I, Abigail," Celeste said, as they walked into the house. "But sometimes we have to let go of the people we care about. Especially when they're doing something they really want to do. Mr. Williams loved being here, but I think he'll *really* love being with his grandkids, and they'll love being with him, too."

"I know," she grumbled. "But it was just, like, his son showed up and now all of a sudden he's gone. If I *knew* he wasn't staying for Christmas, I would have felt sad, but I could have, you know, gotten used to it before it happened."

Nathan winced. He thought he'd been protecting his daughter by waiting until he was sure the center was going to shut down before he told her they'd have to move. But now he wondered if he should have started preparing her for that possibility already. *Maybe I should have started preparing the entire community, too— including Carol,* he worried. Picturing her and Josh standing alone in their driveway, waving as Abbey and Nathan pulled away in a moving truck motivated him to get back to work on the narrative.

Of course, he was also inspired by the fact that working on it meant he got to spend more time in close proximity to Celeste. Whatever had transpired between them in his office when they'd hugged had made every nerve in his body hum—in a good way. Well, except the part when she'd clipped his jaw with her head. That had just plain hurt. He was pretty sure the attraction was mutual, but was that all it was—attraction? Nathan hoped he'd get a chance to discuss it with her this afternoon. Maybe a long-distance relationship with Celeste wasn't so far-fetched after all, provided Abigail could come to accept it.

While Celeste went upstairs to stash her laptop and Abbey was washing her hands for lunch, Carol handed him a sprig of mistle-toe. "Could you hang this for me, please?"

"Gee, Carol, could you be any more obvious?" he asked scorn-fully. "I refuse to put this up."

She stuck her hands on her hips. "Why not?"

"Because I don't want Celeste to think I need to use a clichéd Christmas prop as an excuse to kiss her."

Carol huffed loudly. "For your information, I want you to hang it on the bottom of Josh's 'Welcome Home' sign so *I* can kiss *him* when he gets home. Which, by the way, I think he'll find flirty and romantic, not clichéd."

"Oh, sorry." Nathan's mistake set his cheeks and ears ablaze. He reached up to hook the sprig to the sign.

"It's interesting to hear you say you don't need an excuse to kiss Celeste," Carol mused. "Meaning . . . what? That you *could* kiss her just because you want to? Did something happen between you two you want to tell me about?"

"No. Shh. She might be coming," Nathan warned. "C'mon, Carol. Knock it off."

"Or what? You'll tell Mom I'm teasing you about your girlfriend?" She gave him a wicked smirk, just like she used to when she was holding something over his head in high school.

Fortunately, she didn't say anything about the mistletoe in front of Celeste, but Nathan's ears continued to burn throughout lunch. *How old am I, anyway?* he asked himself, disgusted. Yet at the same time, he reveled in the adolescent feeling of having a crush again. Even though he'd dated someone last summer, he'd never felt like *this* around her. He'd never felt like this around anyone, except Holly.

When they were done eating, he told Celeste, "Brent is supposed to meet us at my house at three thirty, but if you'd prefer to work in the living room here, I can text him and let him know."

"You want to invite Brent to the inn later?" Carol asked.

"Yes. Is that a problem?"

"Not usually, but . . ." Carol shook her head. "Never mind. It's fine."

"No, let's go to your house, Nathan," Celeste broke in. "Abbey can show me her room. I'd like to see where she hangs out."

"No you wouldn't. It's a mess," Abigail countered. "The inn is a lot neater than our house."

"Then let's work at the community center."

"Lee turned the heat down for the holiday since the building is closed until Tuesday. It'll be too cold. Besides, Carol's making beef bourguignonne for supper. I love the way that smells when it's simmering."

Celeste and Carol exchanged cranky frowns. Had they had a disagreement and wanted a little distance from each other?

Then Celeste hinted, "Since Abigail is eating at Bobby's house and Arthur obviously won't be here for supper, maybe you and I could get takeout or something." She gave him such a penetrating look that he took it to mean she wanted him to ask her out for supper. But then she empathically added, "This way, your sister can have a nice, quiet meal alone with her husband on his first evening home after being gone for over two weeks."

Ohhh. Nathan finally caught on. "Yeah, yeah, you're right, let's go." He jumped up and rushed toward the doorway as if the house were on fire, which sent Celeste and Carol into peals of laughter.

"I don't get it," Abbey said, pushing her chair back. "What's so funny?"

"Just holiday cheer. Have fun making ornaments with Bobby and your other friends," her aunt replied, kissing the top of her head as she cleared her plate from the table. Then she said to her brother and Celeste, "Good luck with your writing project. I know you won't steer her toward any clichés, Nathan."

He rolled his eyes and waited in the hallway for Celeste to gather the things she needed from her room, including a gift bag.

"Do you suppose you could take me to the airport before we start revising?" she asked when they got outside. "I want to give this gift to Patty and snap some photos of the lounge. I'd also like to get a few shots of the bay from the crest of that really high hill on our way home. You know the one, right?"

"Sure," Nathan agreed, secretly delighted she'd said, "on our way home" instead of "on our way back." It may have only been a slip of the tongue, but even so, it was a far cry from what she'd said five days ago about not wanting to be "stuck" in Christmas Cove.

In addition to taking her to the places she'd mentioned, Nathan and Abbey also showed her the oceanside beaches where Abigail went bodyboarding in the summer. As well as the main harbor and a few other touristy sites that were closed for the season, such as the 1692 windmill, the miniature golf course Carol liked and the clam shack shaped like an actual clam.

Fortunately, the sun was bright when they started out, so Celeste had been able to get decent photos of the overlook near the bay. But during the final leg of their tour, the sky began to turn gray. "Looks like those are the snow clouds Arthur mentioned were on the horizon," Nathan commented conversationally.

"Mm, looks that way," Celeste agreed. "You know, carnival in the Caribbean would have been fantastic, but I'm really glad I get to have a white Christmas after all."

"Do you mean you're glad about the snow or you're glad you're with the White family for Christmas?" he teased.

She gave him a sidelong glance beneath her lashes. "Which do *you* think I mean, Nathan White?"

If his daughter hadn't been in the back seat, Nathan would have stopped the car right then and there and kissed Celeste until he got a ticket for blocking traffic. Instead, he accelerated.

From behind him, Abbey gripped his headrest. "Dad, why are you driving so fast?"

"Because it's almost three o'clock—I don't want you to be late for Bobby's ornament-making party." *And because I want a few minutes alone with Celeste before Brent comes over.*

HURRY UP AND ANSWER THE DOOR, CELESTE THOUGHT ONCE she and Nathan had accompanied Abbey to the front steps of the Rileys' house. *If we get back quickly, Nathan and I can have a few minutes to ourselves.*

Finally, DeeDee appeared. Holding the storm door open, she invited Abbey to join the other kids in the kitchen. Then she told Celeste, "Bobby has been trying nonstop to make his face freeze into dimples. I don't know where you heard that story, but I'm grateful you told it to him. He hasn't spent so much time outside since last summer. The fresh air calms him down and wears him out—he's been sleeping through the night again."

"Aw, thanks for letting me know." Celeste was tickled her story had positively affected him.

As they walked back to the car, Nathan asked, "Have you ever thought of publishing that story?"

"Not recently. But when I was taking creative writing classes in college, I used to dream of becoming a children's book author."

"You still could, you know. Like I've said, you really have a way with words."

The smile he put on her lips lasted the rest of the way up the hill—and then she spotted Brent pacing the sidewalk in front of Nathan's house, a half hour early. Not that Celeste would have complained. Brent had a wealth of photos and videos to choose from, he offered her technical pointers and his clip of her falling into the cove was utterly sidesplitting. Even better, he'd zoomed in close enough so viewers could tell what was happening but not so close that her face was recognizable. For his part, Brent was thrilled to discover he'd be handsomely compensated if Philip accepted the post for publication.

But the man talked. So. Much. He had an opinion on *everything*, including what they should order for takeout—he recommended buffalo wings, extra spicy—and then he invited himself to stay for supper.

"Since I'm going caroling after this, I might as well stick around in case you need different photos or help with anything else," he said.

All Celeste really needed was a quiet place to work. She slipped into Nathan's office while he ate wings and listened to Brent's discourse about which Christmas tree light bulbs were most energy efficient. Celeste had really hoped she'd finish Nathan's project in time for him to send it before they went downtown. But she needed about ten more minutes to give it a final polish, and she didn't want to make them late for caroling. Besides, if she asked Nathan to review it, Brent probably would have tried to stand over his shoulder, since he believed she'd been working solely on her post for *Peregrinate*.

At least this gives me a good excuse to come back here tonight, she realized as she walked into the kitchen.

"You all done?" Nathan asked.

"Not quite, but I can see the finish line. How long does caroling last?"

"Strictly an hour and ten minutes—we only sing two songs after eight o'clock."

"Oh, that's fine then. Where's Brent?"

"He left to photograph the bonfire in case you need extra images."

"I'm glad he thought of doing that." *For more than one reason.*

When Nathan held her jacket up so she could slip it on, she smelled the minty toothpaste on his breath and was tempted to lean back into his arms and say, "Forget caroling. Let's stay here, just you and me." But she couldn't do that to Abbey.

And as soon as they reached the sidewalk, she was glad the temptation had passed because she wouldn't have wanted to miss this scenery for anything. Big fat flakes of snow were drifting through the air like feathers and were enhanced by the shimmering lights wound around the trees and shrubbery, and looped along the picket fences.

As they walked through the neighborhood, Celeste gushed, "I feel like I'm inside a snow globe."

"Me, too—the kind that plays music."

They paused to listen to the singing already rising up the hill toward them. Celeste could barely make out the words: "'Silent night, holy night. All is calm, all is bright.'"

"We should go," Nathan said after the last stanza. He offered her his arm. "The pavement might be slippery."

She held on until the road was flat again and they continued with the other residents down Main Street to the town green. Abbey ran up to them right away. She was carrying a paper bag, which she quietly asked Nathan to hold but not to peek into. Then she led them to where everyone was encircling the bonfire. For some reason, gold ribbons divided the area into sections, which were numbered from one to twelve. Nathan, Abbey and Celeste eased into the zone marked "five," just as the other islanders finished singing "Little Drummer Boy."

Each song was introduced without fanfare; Alice Wright simply announced the title and then she started everyone off with a few bars. There were no musical instruments, just the harmony of the townspeople's voices filling the wintry night air. Their faces were illuminated by the bonfire, and as Celeste scanned the crowd for Carol and her husband, she realized she knew more people here by name than she knew in her neighborhood in Boston. There was Samantha and Stephanie. Kanesha, Patty and Sasha. Lee and Brent. Jerome. DeeDee and Bobby and Kaitlyn and Zander and Malik. Ray and Vince and Vivian. Dr. Moran. And look—Captain Tim. Was he back again or hadn't he ever left? *I wonder if he's learning to appreciate the "nightlife" here,* Celeste thought.

Just when she'd concluded Nathan's sister had decided not to come, she spotted movement out of the corner of her eye. Two sections over, Carol was lifting her hand in a small wave. A tall, stocky, square-jawed man was standing behind her, resting his chin on her shoulder, his arms wrapped around her stomach. Just as Celeste had sensed that Matt had arrived by Arthur's expression, she knew with one glance at Josh that Carol hadn't waited until Christmas Day to tell him she was pregnant. The sight of the blissful couple was so touching it made Celeste shiver.

Then everyone began singing "Joy to the World," her mother's favorite Christmas song. But instead of feeling joyful, Celeste was ambushed by such a deep, longing ache for her mom she felt as if she might crumple to the ground. The faces of the people opposite her went blurry in the disarray of falling flakes and rising embers. She tried to blink back her tears but that just pushed them down her cheeks. Hoping no one had noticed, she quickly wicked them away with her glove. But when she dropped her hand to her side, Nathan inched closer and discreetly interlaced his fingers with hers.

"You need to leave?" he asked softly out of the corner of his mouth.

Without looking at him, Celeste mumbled, "It'll pass." And it did, before the song had even ended, largely because of Nathan's sympathetic, supportive gesture.

She let go of his hand right before Abigail turned and whispered, "This is my favorite part."

There was a moment of silence before the town hall clock tower sang out the single line, "eight maids a-milking," at the stroke of the hour.

Then Alice took the song from the top, crooning, "'On the first day of Christmas . . .'" *Now* Celeste understood why the crowd was divided into twelve sections. Taking turns, each group was supposed to sing what their true love gave to them at the appropriate time in the song, while the other groups were silent. It was so much fun participating that Celeste nearly forgot she'd just been on the cusp of breaking down.

At the end, everyone applauded but there was one more song to go. "This is my other favorite part," Abigail told her as Alice broke out with "We Wish You a Merry Christmas." Apparently, the tradition was for the islanders to sing the song all the way back to their vehicles or, if they were walking, all the way back to their homes.

After Josh had met Celeste and greeted Nathan and Abigail, the five of them started up the hill, serenading and being serenaded by the people they passed. But halfway to their destination, Carol conked out. "I'm too winded to sing *and* walk."

She suggested everyone come in for snacks and eggnog. But Abbey said her stomach was too full, and Celeste mentioned she had to get her laptop from Nathan's house and do a little more work.

"On Christmas Eve?" Carol protested.

"Better to get most of it done on Christmas Eve than to leave it for Christmas Day."

"My stomach really hurts, Dad," Abigail complained after they'd said good night to her aunt and uncle on the sidewalk by the inn. "I think I ate too many sweets today."

"How many is too many?"

"Don't ask. I can't talk about it."

When the three of them entered the kitchen, Nathan flicked on the light. Abigail must have been nauseated by the sight or smell of chicken bones still piled on a plate on the table because she lurched toward the trash bin and threw up in it. "Don't look at me," she cried when she finished.

Recalling how she always used to feel embarrassed when she was sick as a girl, too, Celeste offered to go draw her a bath, leaving Nathan alone to care for her. After running the water, she set a clean towel and pajamas for Abbey on the vanity, and returned to the girl's room to plump the pillows and turn down the bed. Then she retreated to Nathan's office and put the finishing touches on his video-narrative.

While Abigail was bathing, he came in and sat down next to Celeste. He reported that Abbey didn't have a fever and was feeling better, but he wasn't convinced she was done vomiting. "I feel guilty you've been doing the lion's share of the work—"

"It's okay. Just take a look at this quickly before your daughter needs you again," she told him. "Let me know if there's anything you want to change."

Nathan watched the video, nodding and chuckling at the appropriate places. But Celeste could tell he was distracted because of Abigail, and she didn't blame him. "It's fantastic, Celeste," he said after watching it a second time. "Better than I could have hoped. I don't know how I'll ever thank you."

"Don't. Not until you've won the grant."

"I'll thank you then, too, because I know it's going to win." His fingers hovered over the keyboard. "There's not a thing I'd change, so can I press 'send'?"

"Hit it."

He did. Four seconds later, he received an automated confirmation of receipt via e-mail.

"Congratulations," Celeste said, even though the moment felt anticlimactic. She began gathering her things. "It's all over now except the waiting."

"You're leaving already? But I-I can still help you with your project."

"Maybe tomorrow. Tonight you're on barf duty."

And with those words, Celeste relinquished any hope she'd had that Christmas Eve would end on a romantic note.

Chapter 18

SUNDAY—DECEMBER 25

CELESTE RAISED THE SHADE AND PEERED INTO THE FRONT yard. It must have continued flurrying overnight because the snow that was already on the ground was coated with a pristine dusting that scintillated in the morning sun. Farther in the distance, fluffy clouds were lifting from the horizon, and throughout the cove's sapphire waters, whitecaps rose and fell like snowdrifts.

Philip can flout it all he wants, but there's a good reason coastal New England Christmases are pictured on magazine covers, she thought.

There was also a good reason why people loved this particular island so much. *Many* good reasons. Thinking about how much she was going to miss it there, Celeste lingered at the window, savoring the scenery before reluctantly tearing herself away to take a shower.

When she was done showering and drying her hair, she opened the dresser drawer and said aloud, "Looks like I've only got one choice left." She'd wear the green cable-knit fishermen's sweater with her slacks. She wished she had something a little more stylish, but at least the sweater would be warm, and it was an appropriate color for the holiday.

However, when she tried to put it on, she discovered its cuffs were very snug—she had to bend her thumbs beneath her palms in order to fit her hands through the ends of the sleeves. It was just as difficult trying to push her head through the collar. The knit was so tight she could barely pull it over her crown and even then it wouldn't go any farther down than her nose. She blindly kept tugging until it stretched enough so that she was able to poke her head out like a turtle.

By then her hair was a mess, so she curled it into loose spirals, swept a coat of mascara over her eyelashes and applied lipstick. She hurried downstairs, donned the wool coat Carol had left hanging for her on the rack, instead of the usual purple jacket, and slipped out the front door.

Last evening after returning to the inn, Celeste had spent an hour visiting with Carol and Josh. They'd invited her to go with them to an early church service and then the Caring & Sharing Gift Basket Distribution at the hospital on Christmas morning. Because Abigail had been sick and would probably need extra sleep, they'd assumed neither she nor Nathan would join them. The plan was for the family to gather at the inn at ten o'clock to open their gifts. Then Carol would prepare brunch.

Although Celeste had said she'd love to eat with them, she'd declined the rest of the invitation, as she wanted to go to a later morning church service.

"It's something my mother and I always did together. We never drove or took the bus—we always walked," she'd explained. And since the service she wanted to attend was being held in Christmas Cove's historic meetinghouse, she figured while she was there she'd snap a few final photos of the building for her article.

Now, as she meandered down to Main Street, the frosty air stung the inside of her nose each time she breathed in. The weather was *definitely* cold enough to freeze a smile on her face. She chuckled to herself, recalling her mother's story, based on real life, about how Celeste had gotten her dimples. *Mom always thought the reason I was so happy that day was because it had snowed or because I was so fond of Christmas.*

Those things were part of it, but mostly Celeste had been smiling because her mother had been given three consecutive days off from work. In contrast with almost every other morning of the year, when they'd have to rush off to work and daycare or school, they'd spent three quiet, leisurely mornings just being in each other's presence.

That's sort of how I feel now, she mused. Obviously, her mother wasn't there in person, but she was present in Celeste's thoughts. Going forward, she decided she'd never try to escape during the holidays again. Instead, she'd start a new Christmas morning tradition: as she walked to church, she'd deliberately and gratefully reflect on as many favorite memories of her mother as she could recall.

NATHAN UNDERSTOOD WHY CELESTE WANTED TO SPEND Christmas morning honoring a practice she'd once shared with her mother, but he was also eager to see her again. He peeked out the window so often even Josh noticed.

"Don't worry. Celeste said she'd be back in time to eat with us," he remarked. They had already opened their gifts, and the two men were gathering discarded wrapping paper in the living room while Abigail set the table and Carol began preparing brunch.

"I'm not worried. I'm just . . . impatient. My stomach's growling, and the sooner Celeste gets here, the sooner Carol will let us eat breakfast."

"You seriously expect me to believe that?" Josh ribbed him. "How gullible do you think I am?"

"Apparently you're gullible enough to believe whatever stories my sister's been telling you."

"Carol didn't have to tell me anything—how you feel about Celeste is written all over your face."

Nathan had been bending over to pick up a length of ribbon, but he jerked his head upward. "Really? Do you think Abbey noticed?"

"So what if she did? It seems like she's wild about Celeste."

"She is. But that doesn't mean she's okay if *I'm* wild about her, too." Since Nathan knew Josh was already onto him, and he could trust his brother-in-law to keep his confidence, he replied candidly. "Besides, I promised Abigail I wouldn't try to get in touch with Celeste once she leaves the island."

"Why would you promise her that?"

"You remember what happened when I dated that woman last summer. It stressed Abbey out."

"Probably because your daughter was smart enough to recognize *that woman,* as you call her, wasn't right for you. She wasn't right for Abbey, either."

It helped Nathan to be able to bounce his reservations off his brother-in-law. "You might be right. But even if Celeste feels the same way about me as I feel about her, I have my doubts about whether it would be logistically feasible for us to date. She lives in Boston and travels *all* the time."

"You could find a way to make it work if you really wanted it to."

"But don't you think, you know, if things got serious between Celeste and me, Abigail might feel like I'm being disloyal to Holly or something?"

"*Abigail* might feel that way, or *you* might feel that way?"

"I may have had a couple passing thoughts about it, but I've worked through them. I'm concerned it's going to take longer for Abbey to be ready. When I promised her I wouldn't try to get in touch with Celeste, she seemed really worried I'd change my mind."

"Or she was worried you *wouldn't* change your mind," Josh

stated with the kind of confidence that implied he had inside knowledge. Had Carol told him something Abigail had told *her*? Reflecting on the conversation he'd had with his daughter about Celeste, Nathan could see how he might have misinterpreted Abigail's comments.

"I like to think I'm doing what's best for my child, but sometimes I realize I haven't got a clue," he admitted with a sigh. "This parenting stuff is *hard*."

"So I've heard—but I'm still looking forward to it next summer."

The meaning of what Josh said didn't sink in right away, but when it did, Nathan pushed his shoulder in disbelief. "Carol's *pregnant*?"

Josh grinned. "Yup. I'm going to be a dad."

"Whoo-hoo!" Nathan whooped and clapped him on the back.

Abbey ran into the room, followed closely by Carol, who asked, "Is something wrong? What's all the shouting about?"

"You're pregnant!" Nathan told her, as if she didn't know.

Uncharacteristically bashful, Carol blushed. "That's right, I am."

As he gave his sister a congratulatory hug, Nathan told Abigail, "You're going to have a baby cousin pretty soon, Abbey."

"I know. Aunt Carol let it slip the other morning. I was sworn to secrecy. She didn't want the entire island finding out before Uncle Josh came home. But it makes sense I'd be the first to know so I can get ready to do a lot of babysitting."

Nathan's laughter belied his apprehension. In the past month, he'd frequently found himself wondering how he'd manage to raise Abigail in Boston without Carol's help. But now he was worried about how his sister would raise a baby without him and Abbey around to give her a hand when Josh was traveling. *We won't have to move if we win the grant*, he reminded himself. *And the video-narrative Celeste made is fantastic*.

Just as he was thinking about her, she appeared in the living room doorway. "Merry Christmas, everyone!" she greeted them. Her long, flaxen hair was curled in wide coils, her cheeks were as pink as her lips, or vice versa, and her sterling-blue eyes glinted like the ocean. Whatever she'd done this morning had agreed with her; Nathan had never seen her look so striking.

"Merry Christmas," they all repeated.

Then Carol prodded Nathan's shoulder. "Don't just stand there—take Celeste's coat so she can come in and sit by the fire."

"Oh, right. Right," he bumbled. He stood behind her as she wiggled her arms from her sleeves.

Just as she turned to hand him the coat, Abigail shouted, "You two are under the mistletoe! You have to kiss each other!"

"Abbey, remember your manners," Nathan cautioned.

"It's a Christmas custom, Dad. It would be bad manners *not* to kiss each other because that's like saying someone has bad breath or cooties." She folded her arms across her chest and tapped her foot.

Josh shot him a look that he interpreted to mean, *I told you that your daughter wouldn't mind if you got involved with Celeste.* And Carol gave him a self-complacent smirk; later Nathan undoubtedly was going to have to listen to her extol the value of mistletoe as a kissing prompter.

For as many times as he'd imagined kissing Celeste, Nathan never pictured himself doing it in front of an audience, especially not his family. She, however, looked as amused as the rest of them, which he found strangely attractive.

"What are you waiting for?" she taunted, pushing her hair back and offering him her cheek. So he bent down and grazed his lips across the skin just above her left dimple.

He half expected someone to shout, "You call *that* a kiss?" Not that he would have minded a do-over, but it would have been humiliating to be called out on his technique. Or lack thereof.

But Carol only said, "That was sweet."

Then Abigail asked, "Celeste, you want to see the new body-board and fins my dad gave me?"

As his daughter showed her the gifts, Nathan took Celeste's coat into the hall, where he stayed until his ears quit burning.

CELESTE HEARD HERSELF OOHING AND AHHING OVER ABIGAIL'S Christmas presents, but her mind was topsy-turvy from the quick peck on the cheek Nathan had just given her. Her light-headedness was completely out of proportion—she'd received a more passionate kiss than that the very first time she'd played spin the bottle as a preteen.

But it wasn't the kiss itself that was making her giddy. It was that everyone else seemed in favor of it happening in the first place. She would have expected as much from Carol, but it meant a lot to have Abigail's approval. And it was icing on the cake that Josh had been smiling, too. It was almost as if they were all suggesting that Nathan and Celeste would make a good couple.

On the other hand, maybe she was reading *way* too much into the situation.

It's not as if we could really date each other, anyway. Even if Nathan and Abbey moved to Boston, I travel too often to sustain a serious relationship. The only way it could work out is if I lost my job and Nathan moved. And both of those scenarios were unthinkable. But that didn't mean Celeste was giving up on getting a *real* kiss from Nathan before she left.

After Abbey had shown Celeste everything she'd received for Christmas, she went to the dining room to finish setting the table. And Carol told Josh that as her "sous chef" for the day, she needed his help in the kitchen. So Nathan and Celeste sat on the sofa together in front of the fire.

"Abigail seems to be feeling a lot better," Celeste remarked.

"Her stomach has settled down, but she's running on pure excitement. She was up half the night, so when the lack of sleep catches up to her, she's going to crash hard. How about you? Did you stay up late finishing the project?"

"I stayed up late, but I didn't quite finish the project. I've got until noon to turn it in, and I'm almost done. As soon as I've warmed up, I'm going to go add one brief paragraph and a couple of photos to the traditional version. Then I'll submit them both."

"When will Philip decide which one he wants to use for the blog?"

"He's got to post one of them by three o'clock today. But I've decided I'm not going to log on to the site to see which one he chose until tomorrow. I'm not going to check e-mail or phone messages or texts, either," she asserted. "It's Christmas, and I figure I deserve a break. If he hates what I wrote and wants to fire me, I won't find out about it until tomorrow after 9:00 A.M."

"That's the spirit!" Nathan slapped his thighs. "I mean, I don't think he'll fire you, but I agree you deserve a break. Nine o'clock is when I'm supposed to hear about the grant, too, so if you want, we can check our e-mail together."

"For moral support?"

"I was thinking more like so we could celebrate. But either way, no fair peeking ahead of time. Deal?" They shook hands on it and then he said, "And, uh, if you don't have other plans, maybe at some point today the two of us could go for a walk to the cove or for a drive, so we could have time alone to talk or something."

"Sure, I'd like that."

She'd *love* it, actually, but she wasn't going to hold her breath. Because getting time alone with Nathan was proving to be as challenging as getting off Sea Spray Island during a nor'easter.

———

AFTER THEY'D EATEN BRUNCH, NATHAN LED THE OTHERS IN clamoring for a sneak preview of Celeste's video. They loved it, of course, especially Abigail.

"My dad told me not to tease you that day you fell in the cove, Celeste. But you have to admit, this is hilarious."

Josh laughed harder than Abbey, even after watching it three times. They also enjoyed the parts about the Ugly Sweater Contest and the snow sculptures. Carol, however, was so moved by the non-humorous references—including Celeste's description of her as "the generous, sisterly and effervescent innkeeper"—that she teared up.

Impressed by the entire video, Nathan boasted on Celeste's behalf, "She's portrayed our island and family in such a positive light, once it's posted you'll never have another vacancy, Josh and Carol."

"That's fine with me—I could resign from my consultant position and work full time at the inn," Josh said.

Carol agreed. "And then *I* could resign from my position at the inn and work full time taking care of our baby."

Nathan winked at Celeste, hoping all this talk of resigning didn't make her worry about her own job security. But she just smiled and said how pleased she was that they liked her video. They watched it a fourth time and then Josh mentioned the game was about to start. Usually on Christmas Day, he and Nathan caught a couple afternoon basketball games on the TV in the den. During commercials, they'd help Carol and Abbey piece together a maddeningly difficult thousand-piece jigsaw puzzle of a white rabbit in a field of snow.

However, this was no usual Christmas Day. Celeste was only going to be here until tomorrow evening, since she had to be back in the office on Tuesday. And now that Nathan knew—or at least strongly suspected—his daughter would be okay with them dating, he was dying to try to get a better sense of how Celeste felt about the possibility of a long-distance relationship.

But he couldn't do that until they had some privacy. So instead of enjoying the game or the puzzle or even Celeste's presence among his family, he grew more and more agitated as he tried to contrive some excuse for why they needed to go off alone. Carol and Josh would have understood if he'd told them that he and Celeste were going for a walk and they weren't invited, but he couldn't imagine telling Abbey that.

Ironically, around half past three, Abigail said *she* wanted some alone time and went upstairs to read her book about wolves. Nathan assumed she probably needed a nap but didn't want to admit it. He figured he'd wait a minute until after his daughter had left the room before asking Celeste to take a walk with him, but Carol pounced first.

"Would you mind helping me finish making dinner, Celeste?" she asked.

"I'd be honored—even though I know you're only asking me because your sous chef is too busy watching basketball to help."

"No, that's not why. It's because I fired him after he dumped my leftover potato water into the sink."

Without taking his eyes off the TV, Josh remarked, "I was trying to help by washing out the pot. How was I supposed to know you were going to use that water for making gravy?"

The three of them laughed, but Nathan was so exasperated he could have plucked his beard out. Fortunately, he didn't have a beard to pluck. But he felt like he could have grown one in the amount of time it subsequently took for them to eat dinner. And then dessert. And then to clear the table and hand wash and dry the china that Carol wouldn't allow anyone to put into the dishwasher.

Granted, Nathan loved good food as much as the next guy. And he appreciated that after spending so much time—so, *so* much time—preparing the meal, his sister didn't want everyone to devour it in twelve minutes. But the entire process just felt *interminably* long.

Finally, around seven o'clock, Carol asked who wanted to join her and Josh for a stroll through the neighborhood to view the lights.

"I do," Abigail exclaimed. "Wait until you see the Weavers' display this year, Uncle Josh."

"How about you, Celeste? Nathan?"

"I think I'll pass, thanks," she answered. "I had a nice long walk to church and back this morning."

"I'll pass, too—I've seen the Weavers' display already." By the look on Josh's face, Nathan knew how lame his excuse sounded, but he didn't care. He would have claimed he'd broken his leg if that's what it would have taken to be able to stay behind with Celeste.

But once he was finally alone with her, he had no idea how to say what he wanted to say. Absolutely. No. Idea. For the first several minutes, the silence was punctuated only by the crackling of the burning logs, which could have been romantic if they'd had more time. To add to the pressure, Celeste kept fiddling with the fabric on her sweater, as if she was getting bored or restless.

She abruptly sat up straight and exclaimed, "I forgot—Carol and Abigail haven't opened their gifts from me yet, have they?"

"No. They saw them under the tree though."

"They'll have to open them when they get back from their walk." She relaxed her posture again. "I'm sorry I didn't get *you* a gift. I wanted to, but I couldn't find anything meaningful enough."

"What could be more meaningful than helping me with the creative narrative?" Nathan had the perfect opening to discuss how much Celeste meant to him and suggest maybe they could see each other again in the future. But for some unintelligible reason, he found himself asking, "So, where will you be spending New Year's Eve?"

"Well, that depends. If I'm fired, I'll be staying in Boston." Celeste fidgeted, causing Nathan to regret bringing up an uncomfortable sub-ject. "And if I'm *not* fired, I'll still be staying in Boston. It's one of those rare occasions when I don't have to travel for a holiday assignment."

"That's nice. It probably gives you a chance to catch up with your friends?" *Now* he was moving in the right direction.

Celeste's lips turned down and she squirmed. "Unfortunately, I've let a lot of my friendships slide. Or else my friends have been the ones to drop me, it's hard to say. But I understand why—most people don't want to be in a relationship with someone they rarely see."

"*Most* people but not all." Nathan turned sideways so he could look at her directly when he asked his next question. Noticing she had a silver speck of glitter that was dangerously close to the outer edge of her eye, he reached to brush it from her skin. "You're sparkling—" he started to say.

"Sorry, but I can't do this!" Celeste jumped up, trampling Na-than's ego to dust.

She can't do this? I haven't even told her how I feel yet!

"I can't focus on anything you're saying because I'm sweltering in this stupid sweater. I've got a T-shirt underneath, so just give me a second." She lifted the bottom hem up over her torso and shoulders. Nathan laughed from sheer relief. However, Celeste couldn't seem to get the sweater over her head, and she clearly thought he was laughing at her expense. Standing in front of him with her arms in the air and her face obscured by the fabric, she wailed, "It's not funny. This collar is so tight I feel like it's strangling me. Help me get it off!"

Nathan rose and tried to pull the collar up higher, but he couldn't get it over her chin. "Stop wiggling."

"I can't help it. I'm hot, and it's making me claustrophobic," she griped. "I know I shouldn't look a gift horse in the mouth, but this sweater is even more uncomfortable than that ugly rust-colored one your sister let me borrow."

"The one with the elbow patches?" Nathan had managed to free her chin but now he couldn't get the material past her nostrils.

"Yes," she answered from inside the sweater. "That thing made me itch like crazy."

He was amazed; Celeste's reaction to the sweater was the same as Holly's had been. "For your information, *I* bought that for Carol, and it's maroon, not rust-colored. I thought it would be warm since it was made of wool."

"Yeah—*steel* wool. I swear I had paper cuts by the time I took that thing off."

Nathan started laughing, which made his hands shake, and he accidentally poked Celeste in the eye as he continued tugging at the collar. However, his efforts paid off—her head popped free of the fabric. But she wasn't completely in the clear yet. She had pulled the sweater over her head and down the lengths of her arms, but she couldn't get her hands out of the cuffs. The body of the sweater dangled, inside out, to the floor. Nathan picked it up and pulled.

"Stop walking backward—you're stretching the sleeves," Celeste cautioned.

"How can they stretch lengthwise but not widthwise?"

"Nathan, stop! I don't want Carol getting mad at me."

But he refused to forfeit their sweater tug-of-war, even after he heard the front door open and everyone came into the room.

"WHAT ARE YOU TWO DOING?" ABIGAIL ASKED. THEN SHE GIGgled and pointed. "You've got static electricity, Celeste. Your hair is sticking out everywhere."

"I was trying to take this sweater off, but the cuffs are so tight I can't get my hands out," she explained. "I feel like someone should be reading me my Miranda rights."

"Let me try," Carol offered, tugging on one of the cuffs while Nathan tugged the other one. When she had no success, she said, "I'll go get a pair of scissors."

"You're going to cut it? *I* gave you that sweater two Christmases ago." Josh was genuinely pouting.

Bad taste in clothing runs in this family, Celeste realized. *I should try to influence Abigail's fashion sense while there's still time.*

"It's either I use scissors or we call in the jaws of life."

"You could use butter," Abbey suggested. "That's what people do when their rings get stuck on their fingers."

"You want to slather *butter* on the sweater I gave my wife?"

"No, not on the sweater, Uncle Josh. Just on Celeste's wrists," Abigail assured him. "And her fingers. And maybe a little on her arms in case we need to back the sleeves up and get a running start."

The notion made Celeste laugh so hard she started hiccupping. "That's—hic—that's okay," she managed to say. "I'm—*stop* pulling, Nathan!—I'm not hot any—hic—more. I'll just keep the sweater on after all."

"You're going to wear it indefinitely?" Josh questioned. "Carol's never getting her sweater back?"

"Oh, settle down," Carol scolded him. She convinced her husband that if she made two neat snips in the cuffs, Vivian Liu or one of the other knitters at the community center could repair it for her, no problem. But while Carol was looking for a pair of fabric shears, Celeste managed to scrunch her fingers closely together enough so that the sleeves finally slid off and the cuffs survived intact. Which was more than she could say for her mascara and her curls.

She went upstairs to wash her face and brush her hair, and when she returned she suggested Carol and Abigail unwrap their presents from her. Abbey had enough self-restraint to allow Carol to open her gift first.

"It's indirectly for both of you," Celeste told Josh, hoping to appease his indignation about the pullover.

As Carol squealed over the tiny outfits, Nathan grumbled about being the last person there to learn she was pregnant. "Aw, poor boy," she teased. "You're so left out."

"That's not what I'm saying," he objected. "It's just that if I had known, I would have gotten the baby a Christmas gift, too. Your loss, sis."

Josh broke in. "If you two are done with your sibling rivalry, Abbey's been waiting patiently to open her gift."

Abbey put the lobster-pendant necklace on as soon as she removed it from its box. When she saw the hair accessories, she asked if Celeste would use them to style her hair in a couple of minutes. "First, we have to give you something." She handed Celeste a gift bag. "It's from all of us, but I picked it out."

"Aw, that's so thoughtful." Celeste reached in and removed a teal-blue hoodie that read "I ♥ Sea Spray Island" in small letters on the front, upper left-hand side.

"It might seem touristy, but the material's so soft I bought one for myself, even though I'm an islander," Carol told her.

"The color's perfect," Celeste raved. "And it's true—I *do* heart Sea Spray Island."

Abigail handed Celeste a smaller box. "This one is just from me."

Celeste untied the gold bow and lifted the lid. Inside were two handmade Christmas tree ornaments. One was an intricate snowflake, delicately composed of white, silver and aqua-colored beads. The other was an icicle created out of aluminum foil, glue and lots and lots of blue glitter. Holding them up, Celeste complimented her, saying, "They're beautiful, Abbey. And they're twice as special because you made them."

"I wanted to give you something that reminded you of spending Christmas with us."

I could never forget it, Celeste thought as Abigail went to get a hairbrush.

When she returned, she appeared to be dragging, and as Celeste combed the girl's locks from her forehead with her fingers, she noticed it seemed hot to the touch. She waited until she was done braiding Abbey's hair before remarking, "You look very pretty, but how are you feeling? I noticed your skin seems warm."

"I'm okay," she insisted, but Nathan came over and felt her forehead and then her cheeks.

"You've got a fever, Abigail. I'm afraid we need to go home now."

The fact that her eyes immediately welled indicated Abbey wasn't quite herself. "But, Dad, it's only eight o'clock."

"I understand, sweetheart, but it's important that Aunt Carol doesn't catch whatever you have. You want her and the baby to stay strong and healthy, don't you?"

"Yes." She sniffled. "I just don't want Christmas to be over yet. We were having so much fun."

I know exactly what she meant, Celeste thought an hour later when she retreated to her room. Balanced on the edge of the large claw-foot tub as she waited for it to fill, she reflected on the day. It had been much lovelier and more enjoyable than she ever could have hoped to experience—even if she hadn't received the kind of kiss she'd wished Nathan would have given her.

Chapter 19

MONDAY—DECEMBER 26

CELESTE TEXTED NATHAN AS SOON AS SHE AWOKE AT SIX thirty: How's Abbey?

Her phone rang immediately. "Good morning," Nathan greeted her. "Abigail's okay. She's sleeping now, but it was a rough night. She had some, um, GI issues, and she's pretty achy. Bobby's mom texted me because he got hit with it on Christmas Eve. I guess Ava had it, too, and she's already feeling a lot better, so at least it's short-lived. I feel terrible I dismissed it too quickly. I thought she'd just eaten too much and was overly excited about Christmas."

"That's understandable, especially because she didn't have a fever until last night."

"Yeah, but now Carol's been exposed to whatever bug she has."

"She said she felt great last night. And you and I haven't had any symptoms, either, so I think we're safe."

"Actually . . ."

"You're sick, too? Oh, Nathan! It's wretched trying to take care of someone when you're . . . retching. What can I do to help?"

"Nothing. I don't want you to catch this, too," he insisted. "Seriously, you can't come anywhere near us."

If Nathan wouldn't allow her anywhere near him, then that sealed it: Celeste had to kiss her goodbye-kiss goodbye.

I'd rather get the flu, she thought, thoroughly dejected.

"Are you still there?" Nathan asked after a long, silent spell.

"Yes . . . Can I bring you anything and leave it on the doorstep? Crackers? Ginger ale?"

"I, er, can't talk about food at the moment. Can I get back to you on that later?"

"Sure. So I guess this means we can't check our e-mail together. Are you up to checking it over a video call?"

"Trust me, it's better if I remain invisible. How about if we check it while we're on the phone instead?" Celeste agreed, and Nathan said he had to go catch a few more Zs and he'd call her a couple of minutes before nine o'clock.

Celeste could scarcely accept that she was going to have to leave Christmas Cove without a kiss from Nathan, but it was altogether inconceivable that she wouldn't get to say goodbye to him—and to Abbey—in person. *Maybe by late afternoon, if I wear a scarf around my nose and mouth and stand across the room from them, I can at least stop by one last time,* she schemed and went to take a shower.

Afterward she put on her new Sea Spray Island hoodie and a double pair of leggings. Since it wasn't yet time for breakfast, she stood in front of the window, staring at the cove. Its flat surf and the drab color mirrored her mood. At the moment, Celeste's one and only consolation was that Philip hadn't called or texted yet. That had to be a good sign, didn't it?

———————

AS SOON AS NATHAN WOKE UP THE SECOND TIME, HE WENT TO check on Abbey. Although it was temporary and relatively minor, his child's suffering last night had been a perspective changer. A reminder of what mattered most. Whatever anxiety he'd had about the outcome of the grant was negligible compared to how much he worried about his daughter when she was ill. But right now she was sleeping so soundly that she didn't stir when he placed a hand on her forehead. And if she still had a fever, it was a low-grade one.

Relieved, he carried his laptop and phone into the living room and dropped into the recliner, altogether drained. He had hoped he'd at least get to say hello—or goodbye—to Celeste from the doorway if she came by later. But considering the way he felt right now, he'd be fortunate to get out of the chair again before tomorrow morning.

I should have been quicker to express myself yesterday before that whole fiasco with her sweater. But maybe I'll be less nervous talking to her about it on the phone in a couple of days when I'm feeling better, he tried to convince himself.

Deep down, he feared the opposite; that the distance between them would put distance between them. And that it would become even *more* difficult to communicate over the phone how much he cared about her. *If that's how I feel now, how will I ever maintain a long-distance relationship long-term?*

He couldn't dwell on that at the moment—Celeste was probably waiting for his call, so he pressed her number. She asked how he and Abbey were feeling and then she told him that Carol, Josh and she had all taken their temperatures before breakfast and they were all normal. "Your sister said to tell you she's going to bring S-O-U-P to you this afternoon."

"Soup? That's nice, but why are you spelling it out?"

"Because I don't want to make you queasy by talking about F-O-O-D," she said with all sincerity.

Nathan didn't know any other woman who could make him smile the way Celeste did, especially not when he felt so crummy. The clock sang, "nine ladies dancing," so he said, "I think that's our cue. Do you want to check your e-mail first, or do you want me to check mine?"

"You should—yours was due first."

"Okay. But no matter what happens, I want you to know how much it meant to me that you helped—"

"Yes, you appreciate it, I know. And you're welcome. Now open it. The suspense is killing me."

He clicked on the e-mail message that had the grant's official name in the subject line. "'Dear Nathan,'" he read aloud. "'Thank you for applying to receive the St. Nick of Time Grant this year. Your video captured our attention immediately, and the judges viewed it several times. It was outstanding in a pool of other exceptional submissions.'"

"Yes!" Celeste hurrahed.

Nathan's mouth continued reading before his brain could absorb the words. "'However, we found another organization's mission to be more compelling . . .'"

"No *way*! No, no, no, no, no!" Celeste objected. "That doesn't make any sense. What could be more compelling than a place that not only helps a stranger feel included at Christmas when she's still grieving, but it actually helps her feel *joyful*?"

She continued ranting, listing other examples of how the center provided for the community. "The center's not only for recreation—you provide nutrition and education and literally a warm place for people to gather. Or a cool place, in the summer. And it gives your volunteers a sense of purpose and-and-and—"

She was so upset on his behalf that it diffused much of Nathan's own disappointment. "It's okay, Celeste. Really."

"No, it's not okay. It's terrible. Now the center is going to close and the staff will lose their jobs, and you and Abbey are going to have to move off-island." At the end of her sentence, Nathan could hear her blowing her nose.

"It's a huge, disheartening blow, yes. And there are going to be major challenges and adjustments," he acknowledged. "But the community will find a way to band together. The board will do its best to tide the staff over financially until they find other employment. And I can accept the job offer in Boston, which isn't all that far from the island, so Abbey and I will get to see Carol and Josh and the baby on the weekends. It's not the end of the world." It wasn't, but it was certainly no picnic, either. Still, what could Nathan do except resign himself to the reality and begin to help everyone get through the upcoming transitions?

"Maybe I made the video too jokey—"

"Stop it, Celeste. If it weren't for you, the judges wouldn't have taken a second look at my application. It's not your fault. It's not the board's fault, and it's not mine, either. We did absolutely everything we could to save the community center." Nathan took a modicum of comfort in the truth of his own words. "It's time to accept the outcome and begin to move on from here."

It took some arguing, but he eventually convinced Celeste to check her e-mail, too. After a couple of clicks, she said, "Hmm, strange. I don't have any e-mail messages from Philip."

"That's good, isn't it?"

"Not necessarily. He uses the silent treatment as a weapon. Wawait. I have a meeting invitation . . . from Colton Browne. He's the president. The one Philip required me to cc on my submission."

Uh-oh. "What's the meeting subject?"

"It just says, '*Peregrinate* video.'" She groaned. "They must have hated it or thought it was a joke. They're going to fire me, I just know it."

"Don't jump to that conclusion. Even if the video wasn't a good fit, it's not as if you left them high and dry, without anything to post at all."

"Yeah, unless Philip also hated the other piece I wrote and told them it wasn't unique enough. Let me check the blog." There was tapping in the background. Celeste exhaled heavily. "Phew. They used the one that was in the traditional format. Maybe— Hey, wait a second. They added the video at the end."

Celeste was making a funny sound. Was she *choking*? "Celeste? Are you okay?"

She was laughing. Or crying. Or both. "You're not going to believe this, Nathan. You should see all the likes and shares and comments it got. Subscribers *loved* it."

Nathan was as happy for her about her success as she'd been sad for him about his disappointment. Summoning the last of his energy, he cheered so loudly he was surprised he didn't wake up Abbey. Celeste gave him the passcode so he could log on to the subscribers-only blog, too, and they reviewed the first twenty-some comments together.

"The president's going to offer you a promotion," Nathan told her. "I bet anything that's why they scheduled a meeting with you. When is it?"

"Oh, terrific," she muttered. "Philip must not have told them I'm still out of town. I wouldn't put it past him to try to make it look as if I'm not really interested in the president's feedback. He scheduled the meeting for today."

"What time?"

"One o'clock."

Nathan swallowed. *That soon?* "You can make it. Ask Carol or Josh to drive you to the ten-ten ferry. You can schedule a driver to meet you on the other side of the water. You'd better hurry."

"But—but I was going to drop by your house. Even if I had to stay outside on the doorstep, I really wanted to say goodbye to you and Abbey in person."

I wanted that, too. "Nah. There's no time. This is important." He forced a laugh. "You've been wanting to get off this island for an entire week, so get going already."

Celeste hesitated. "Okay . . . Will you explain to Abigail, and tell her I'll call her later?"

"You'd better because I want to hear what your new job title is."

After they hung up, Nathan pulled the lever on the recliner and leaned back. He knew he should call Mark and then he should phone the community center in Boston. It might have been the flu talking, but he was wholly exhausted from turning himself inside out over the funding crisis, and he couldn't bring himself to do it yet. Not physically, not emotionally. He closed his eyes, and he'd just nodded off when his phone buzzed. It was a text from Celeste: "If you're awake, look outside."

Curious, he slowly boosted himself to his feet and went to open the front door. Celeste must have thought he wasn't coming because she was at the end of his walkway, headed in the opposite direction. He called her name and she twirled around. She was grinning so broadly he could see her dimples all the way from there.

"Make sure Abigail sees it." She pointed to where she'd made a snow angel on the front lawn and inscribed "Bye, Abbey!" in an arc above it.

Nathan shivered, thinking of Celeste lying down in the snow. "You must be freezing—but that was nice of you to come over. Abigail will be pleased."

"It was worth it. Besides, I wanted to see your face again."

Nathan chuckled, touching the thick stubble on his chin. "That's a nice parting image."

Josh, who was idling his car in the street, rolled down the window. "You'd better hurry or you'll miss your ferry."

"Been there, done that," Celeste joked, but then she waved. "Bye, Nathan."

Maybe we'll get together in Boston sometime. The words flitted through his mind to the tip of his tongue, but he didn't express them. He was still too let down to accept his pending job offer, much less make plans for his social life after he moved to Boston. "Goodbye, Celeste."

He watched as she walked out into the street toward the car. Just before she got in, she scooped a handful of snow off the roof and turned around. Her palm flat, she blew on it, sending Nathan a snowy kiss. It rose in a puff, and within a blink of his eye it vanished, and so did Celeste.

THE FIRST THING CELESTE DID WHEN SHE GOT OUT OF THE office was to call Nathan and Abigail from her car. Abbey answered, sounding hoarse but happy. She said she was tired, but her stomach was better. Her aunt had dropped off *papo secos* from the bakery and homemade turkey soup, which her father was reheating for her for supper.

"He let me read the comments people wrote about your video. Didn't I tell you it was a good idea to use photos from the Ugly Sweater Contest?"

"Yes, you did. I'm glad you gave me your honest opinion." They chatted a little longer, with Abbey describing the upcoming events at the community center.

"Samantha sent out an e-mail saying Heading Sledding has been rescheduled for Wednesday, the same day as Save the Date to Skate. I hope I can go. I'll definitely be completely better by then, but I don't know if my dad will be. He was in the bathroom so many times—"

Abigail was cut off by her father. "Excuse me. May I use the phone now? Your soup is ready."

Abigail and Celeste said goodbye, and Nathan came on the line. "How did the meeting go? I've been wondering all day."

Because he'd received such crushing news that morning, Celeste tried not to sound *too* enthusiastic about the opportunity she'd discussed with the publishing president. She told him that Colton had said he was impressed by her fresh and humorous yet poignant perspective on Christmas Cove. He and the CEO, Edmund Grayson, had long been discussing supplementing *Peregrinate*'s online subscriptions with an additional blog, one that focused on culture and community rather than on vacationing and sightseeing.

Philip had resisted the idea, arguing that they should stick with what was working. But when Colton saw how popular Celeste's video was, he recommended pushing forward with the new business venture. Edmund, however, wasn't completely sold.

"So basically I've got until January second to put together a presentation to convince Edmund that this could be a profitable endeavor. Which means I've got to do a lot of market research and come up with an editorial schedule, destination suggestions, budget estimates—that kind of stuff."

"Why is all that your responsibility?"

"Because if they decide to follow through with it, Colton wants to make me the editor. Actually, I'd be the only staff member working full time on it at first. We'd start small and hire more writers if this thing takes off. Eventually, there might even be a separate print issue."

"That's great, Celeste!"

"Yeah, and what's even better is that I wouldn't have to report to Philip any longer. He'd edit my copy, but that's it."

Nathan whistled. "Nice."

"*I* think so, but Philip's incensed. After Colton left the building,

Philip called me into his office and accused me of being an opportunist and going behind his back to undermine his editorial authority. Which is inane, since *he* was the one who ordered me to cc the CEO and president on my submission."

"That guy's a piece of work."

"Yeah, unfortunately, he's still my boss though. There's no guarantee that Edmund's going to approve this new blog, so I can't afford to tick Philip off any more than I already have. As it is, he's getting revenge by making me travel on New Year's Eve after all."

"You're kidding—where's he sending you?"

"Times Square. He actually was supposed to go there himself. Ordinarily, he wouldn't stoop to write a post for the domestic blog, but his girlfriend has never been to the city, so it would have been a way to impress her without paying for the trip himself. They must have broken up already, though, because he suddenly has no interest in going."

"But once the new blog is approved, he won't have any influence over when or where you travel?"

"Nope. Not if I accept the promotion."

"*If?*" Nathan sounded incredulous. "You have qualms? This opportunity sounds tailor-made for you."

"In a lot of ways it is. I'd have more creative freedom, a better salary and I wouldn't have to travel as frequently, which would be a welcome change," she said. "But because the emphasis would be on submerging myself in community life, I'd be gone for longer stretches of time."

"And that's a drawback because you'd prefer to hang out in Boston more often?" Nathan questioned.

I might, now that you and Abbey are moving here. Celeste knew better than to give voice to that thought. For one thing, because she'd just departed Christmas Cove, she was overly sentimental. For another, it wasn't as if Nathan had ever expressed an interest in continuing to develop a relationship with her. She certainly couldn't make a career decision based on an attraction that had only lasted a week.

Hoping to get a better sense of where he stood in regard to his feelings about her, she replied, "I don't know . . . Do *you* think I should take the job if it's offered to me?"

WHAT NATHAN THOUGHT CELESTE SHOULD DO AND WHAT HE wished she'd do were two different things. But then he remembered what she'd said to Abbey when Arthur left: *Sometimes, we have to let go of the people we care about. Especially when it's better for them.*

He cleared his throat. "You've been working your entire career toward an opportunity like this. So unless you have some serious reservation, I think you should go for it."

"You're right," she agreed, but a little too quickly. "But enough about me. Did you talk to the board president yet?"

"Yeah . . . Just a sec, okay?" A door closed in the background. "Sorry, I need to be extra careful that Abigail doesn't hear."

"Oh, no. That bad?"

"No. That *good.* You're not going to believe it, but this afternoon we received an anonymous donation that will secure our lease and cover our operational expenses for the next eight to ten years."

"Wh-what? You're joking!"

Nathan may have been laughing, but he definitely wasn't joking. "I promise it's the truth."

"That's *fabulous,* Nathan. I don't even know what to say. You should see me right now—my jaw is on the floor," she prattled. "Do you have any idea who the donor was? Could it have been the foundation in Boston? Or maybe the St. Nick of Time Grant people gave a second award?"

"No. It definitely wasn't a corporation or a foundation. Believe me, they'd want to get as much publicity as they could. This bene-factor insisted on absolute anonymity, so I'm assuming it was an individual. My theory is that the person died a while ago and be-queathed a percentage of their estate to us, because usually it takes a while to hammer out all the legalities. But we already received a deposit in our account this afternoon."

"That's what I call perfect timing!"

"It sure is. And the size of the donation is unbelievable, espe-cially considering they anonymously gave the same amount to the hospital and the island's conservation organization. At least, those are the rumors I've read online." Nathan chuckled. "Not that I put much stock in local gossip."

"Well, you know I won't let on that I know anything about it, even though I'm so thrilled for you I wish I could shout it from the rooftop."

"Thanks. I was dying to tell you. I mean, Mark was happy, too, but it's not the same—" He stopped talking. "Uh-oh, Abbey's call-ing me. She needs my guest password so she can check the latest comments on your video. She's been monitoring it all day."

"Aww, that girl is one of my biggest fans."

"I am, too." *In so many ways . . . You have no idea.*

"The same goes for me about your big win. Congratulations, Nathan."

"Congratulations to *you*. And good luck." *Why does that feel like goodbye?*

"Thanks. Stay in touch, okay?"

That's the kind of thing only people who aren't *going to stay in touch say—people who* are *going to make contact don't need to re-mind each other.* "I will. Bye."

Chapter 20

FRIDAY AND SATURDAY,
DECEMBER 30–DECEMBER 31

ON FRIDAY EVENING, CELESTE BOUGHT TAKEOUT FROM HER FA-vorite Chinese restaurant and ate it in the dark, staring out her apartment window. The large, blinking blue star on the side of the building opposite hers reminded her of the one Nathan had worn on the hood of his ugly sweatshirt. She also thought about how much she missed the view from her room at the inn. And the claw-foot tub. And Carol's cooking. She turned on the light and set the container of shrimp and broccoli in the fridge. She wasn't hungry.

All week she'd worked on the presentation with such fervor that the days flew by without her noticing. Suddenly, she'd look up and her colleagues were putting on their coats, leaving for the night. She'd stay a couple hours later and was usually so sapped that she'd collapse into bed as soon as she got home.

What else was there to do, anyway? The first two evenings she'd watched the Christmas Cove video a dozen times, but it had made her painfully nostalgic, so she'd had to stop. On a couple of occasions she'd been tempted to call Nathan, particularly after Abigail had texted a clip of the two of them sledding. But Celeste's brain was so wrapped up in work that in some ways it seemed like her trip to the island belonged to another lifetime. Besides, Nathan hadn't called *her*.

"It's probably better that he doesn't keep in touch," she said aloud to herself as she went into her bedroom and began packing for her trip to New York the following morning. She'd never forget her time on Sea Spray Island, but it was literally a diversion from her real life. Her real profession. Nathan and Abbey were staying where they were, and she was moving on. It was time to put Christmas Cove behind her and look forward to beginning a new year.

She removed the ornaments Abbey had given her from where she'd hung them in her windows. Then she dragged a plastic storage bin, which held her other Christmas decorations, from the back of her closet. When she opened the lid she immediately noticed a small, square wrapped box sitting atop the others. She had forgotten all about it.

Last year, instead of following the tradition of presenting Celeste with a new ornament when they had decorated the tree together, her mother had given it to her the day after Thanksgiving. Aware that her mom suspected she wasn't going to live through December, Celeste wouldn't open the gift. It was as if she believed her refusal would somehow prevent her mother from dying before Christmas. Of course, her mother had died anyway, and afterward Celeste had been too grieved to unwrap the box.

"I'm stronger now," she said as she untied the ribbon, opened the lid and lifted the ceramic ornament from its nest of tissue paper. Celeste gasped when she saw it was a square-shaped yellow cottage that looked exactly like the one they used to stay at on the Cape, right down to the lilac tree next to the door and the flower boxes beneath the front windows.

Mom must have had this custom made, just for me, she realized. Her fingers trembling, she slid the accompanying note card from its envelope.

Home is where your heart is, it read in her mother's elegant, flowing cursive.

As it turned out, Celeste wasn't as strong as she'd thought; she couldn't stop the tears from slipping down her cheeks. Then she remembered Arthur saying loneliness wasn't something a person should suffer alone, and Nathan holding her hand when she'd become weepy at the bonfire. It made her feel twice as lonely, and she lay down and cried herself to sleep.

When she woke the next morning, her nose was stuffy, her eyes were swollen and she only had fourteen minutes before the driver arrived to take her to Logan. Because she'd been so concerned she'd miss her flight again, she had scheduled her ride an hour early. It was a decision she rued as she sat in the boarding area, cornered by an extraordinarily gabby cosmetician from Framingham, who suggested several products Celeste could use to brighten her under-eye circles.

When Celeste's phone rang, she was so relieved for the excuse to get away from the woman that she would have gladly spoken to Philip, if it came to that. To her delight, it was Arthur, wishing her belated congratulations on her video. He said he'd purchased an online subscription just so he could see which format Philip chose. "I'm pleased—although surprised—he decided to include the video."

"Actually, he didn't—the CEO did." Celeste explained the situation and told him about her new potential promotion.

"That's wonderful." Arthur's reply was followed by a characteristically thoughtful comment that was part question, part statement. "Although you don't sound entirely happy about it."

Celeste should have known his power of observation wasn't

diminished simply because they were speaking on the phone instead of in person. "I don't sound happy?" she repeated back to him.

"Not nearly as happy as when you described the snow lobster you'd sculpted with the children at the community center."

"That's because that was so much fun," she replied, chuckling at the memory. "But this is . . ."

"Duty?"

"I was going to say *work*. And as work goes, it really is an ideal arrangement." She felt as if she was trying too hard to convince him. Or maybe *she* was the one who needed convincing. "It's what I've spent my career striving toward. In fact, it's even better than becoming a senior writer."

"So it's your dream come true?"

"I suppose it is, yes."

"In that case, I wish you all the best with it."

Arthur's response reminded her of when she'd told her mother she was going to become a senior writer, and her mother had replied, "If that's your dream, I'm behind you all the way."

Back then, she hadn't heard the *if* as distinctly as it struck her in hindsight. *Did Mom have doubts I really wanted to be a senior writer?* she wondered. *Or was she emphasizing she'd be behind me no matter what I did, as long as it was my dream?*

An overhead page disrupted Celeste's train of thought. She asked Arthur, "How was Christmas with your son and his family?"

"We've had our ups and downs, but we're working through them," he answered frankly. "Mostly it's been marvelous though. I can't tell you how overjoyed I've been to get to know my grandchildren. To think, if it hadn't been for Christmas Cove taking such good care of Matt—taking him in, really—all those years ago . . . Well, let's just say I'll always be indebted."

"I'm grateful I got to be a part of their community when I needed it, too," she quietly acknowledged.

"They helped me a lot, as well—and by *them,* I'm including *you,* Celeste. Thank you for being my confidante."

"It was my privilege."

After wishing each other a happy new year and disconnecting the call, Celeste reflected on what Arthur had said about feeling indebted to the Sea Spray Island community. Out of nowhere, it dawned on her: Arthur was the benefactor! He was the one who made those huge donations. It *had* to be him, didn't it? It was perfectly logical that he would have donated to the hospital out of his sense of gratitude. And to the conservation organization out of a sense of guilt. Or at least with the intention of wanting to help preserve what he'd once almost destroyed.

But why would he have donated to the community center? It hadn't even been in existence when Matt was on the island. And Arthur couldn't have been aware of the dire straits it was in because Nathan and the board had kept the financial crisis a secret. Unless . . .

Was Arthur in the annex the evening Nathan told me *about the center possibly shutting down? Did he overhear our conversation—or part of it until we left to get our laptops?* Celeste couldn't be absolutely sure one way or the other. Regardless, she decided she'd never mention her theory to anyone, not even to Nathan. Because if she *was* right, then Arthur clearly wanted to protect his anonymity, and as his trusted confidante, Celeste was committed to protecting it, too.

Her phone vibrated in her hand with a text from Philip: Checking to be sure you're at the airport.

She texted back: Yes.

Meaning you're on your way, or you're actually there?

I'm here. Waiting to board.

In the women's room or in the boarding area?

Was he really going to badger her like this until she started her new job? It was excessive, even for him. Celeste was dithering about whether she'd respond at all when she received another text: Wouldn't want you to miss another flight, right before your big presentation. Edmund might think you're not capable of handling additional responsibility.

What a weasel. As angry as Celeste was, she had the self-control to choose her words carefully, knowing he could show her text to the CEO and president. She pressed the mic icon and dictated: Thanks so much for your concern, Philip. You're absolutely right. It's important to demonstrate I know how to handle responsibility and that includes prioritizing. My time is better spent putting the finishing touches on my presentation than going on an assignment. Especially one that you originally accepted and then changed your mind about because your girlfriend didn't want to go with you. So you'll have to find someone else to replace you. I'm not going.

She hit "send." Then, in case Philip tried to threaten he'd report her to the president or CEO, she preemptively informed him, I'll let Colton know about the change in plans. I'm sure he'll agree my presentation takes priority.

Five seconds after she sent the text, her phone rang, but she turned it off and strode toward the ticket counter. She was going to Sea Spray Island, even if she had to take a prop plane to get there.

NATHAN HAD A LONG LIST OF REASONS HE SHOULD HAVE BEEN on cloud nine: the community center was fully funded. He and his daughter wouldn't have to move off their beloved island. His staff would keep their jobs. His sister and brother-in-law would soon be parents. And Celeste had gotten a promotion that was even better than she'd expected. He *was* grateful, but that didn't necessarily mean he was *glad*.

Frankly, after Celeste left, he felt as if his heart was a concrete slab.

No. It was worse than that.

He felt as if his heart was a concrete slab, and he'd fallen overboard into the cove. As hard as he was trying to make it back to shore, he could barely keep his head above water.

Carol must have noticed he was struggling because on Saturday, while Josh and Abbey were watching TV, she took Nathan aside and asked, "Are you sick again or are you moping? Because if you're sick, I shouldn't be around you. And if you're moping, you shouldn't be around me. You're trying my patience, and I'm not above using my fluctuating hormones as an excuse for really letting you have it."

Nathan's response? He sighed—a dangerous thing to do, considering his sister's mood.

"Oh, grow up," she yapped. "If you miss Celeste and want to develop your relationship, call her. Tell her how you feel."

Nathan didn't bother denying Celeste's absence was the reason he was glum. "I can't. She's got a great opportunity. I don't want to interfere with her career."

"Who said anything about interfering with her career? I'm just saying you should tell her how you feel. Start there and see what happens." Carol steepled her hands below her chin and pleaded, "Listen, my dear brother. You do so much for everyone else—for Abigail and for me and for this entire community. You never hesitate to go above and beyond for any of us. Now, do this one thing for *you*. You owe yourself that much. You owe *her* that much. Abigail can stay with Josh and me. Go talk to Celeste. Take her out to dinner. Kiss each other beneath the fireworks—unless that's too cliché for you." She playfully nudged his shoulder.

It wouldn't have been a bad idea if she'd suggested it twenty-four hours ago. "I can't. She's on an assignment in Times Square."

"Duh! Then meet her in New York." The second nudge his sister gave him bordered on a shove. "What could be more romantic?"

Just like that, Nathan's heart went from concrete slab to helium balloon. "You're right. I'll do it."

He hadn't moved so fast since he'd been a member of his college's track team. He sprinted home to pack a bag and book a flight to New York. He considered calling Celeste, but her phone would likely be in airplane mode; besides, a gesture like this required an element of surprise. He'd call when he got there.

"Where are you going?" Abigail asked when he returned to the inn with carry-on bag in hand.

"I-I want to spend New Year's Eve with Celeste, honey."

She wrinkled her nose. "Is this a date?"

"I guess it is, if she agrees. I know I said I wouldn't date her, but I've changed my mind. Is that okay with you?" *Please don't say no*.

"Of course it is, Dad. Except you shouldn't wear that hazelnut cologne you wore last time. It smells bad."

Nathan laughed and kissed his daughter goodbye. Then Josh drove him to the airport and dropped him off an hour early because he and Carol were concerned Nathan might change his mind. They couldn't have been more wrong, but he was secretly relieved because he intended to use the solitude to figure out how to express himself to Celeste.

Unfortunately, his plan had a hole in it. Namely, Patty—chatty Patty—was on duty. "The plane hasn't even arrived from Boston yet and there's a forty-minute layover before it continues to New York," she informed him. "You must be awfully eager to get to the city. Is everything okay?"

"Yes, everything's fine. I'm, uh, I'm going to see the ball drop in Times Square."

"You're missing the Festivity Finale Fireworks in Christmas Cove to go to *New York City*?" Patty sounded so aghast that Nathan was slightly worried she wouldn't let him board the plane. "By *yourself*?"

"No, I'm, uh, I'm meeting a friend there." He moved toward the door. "Excuse me, Patty. I'm going to step back outside for some fresh air before I get on the plane."

Nathan paced around the parking lot, trying to think of what he wanted to say to Celeste, but everything that came to mind sounded like a greeting card. Even after he heard the droning of the incoming plane as it descended, he took a couple more laps. The stroll didn't inspire him any, but at least it kept him from getting the third degree from Patty.

Finally, he decided he'd have to hope the words came to him en route to New York, and he headed toward the airport entrance. Just as he opened the door, a blond woman stepped out. He was so startled he almost let it swing closed on the small suitcase trailing behind her.

"Celeste?!"

"Nathan?!"

"What are you doing *here*?" he asked.

At the same time she questioned, "Where are you going?"

"Please, you talk first," Nathan insisted.

"I'm here for Polar Bear Plunge." She repeated her question to him. "Where are you going?"

"To—to Times Square. To find you. To tell you I like you. A lot," he blurted out. *Good grief. I'm not even speaking in full sentences.*

This is the best speech I could come up with to win her over? She's a writer!

And if he didn't feel dopey enough already, Patty tapped on the window pane right behind Celeste and yelled, "Your plane's here, Nathan!" as if she was his mom, telling him supper was on the table.

"It's okay. I'm not going," he hollered back, equally uncouth. But Celeste seemed unfazed. She was grinning at him . . . Or was she laughing? No, he knew what that look meant now; it wasn't condescension. It was fondness, with a little bit of amusement mixed in.

Nathan just needed a moment to get his head together, and he'd find another way to express himself. He motioned for Celeste to follow him. As they wheeled their carry-on bags farther down the sidewalk, he said, "I'm really glad to see you, but won't Philip be angry if you don't cover the assignment?"

"Philip will be angry no matter what. That's just how Philip is," she said. "But I'm done putting up with it." She told him that she'd decided if Edmund approved the blog, she was going to offer to work on it on a part-time schedule. If he and Colton turned her down, she'd start an independent writing and editing business, but she was resigning from her position as a travel writer reporting to Philip.

"I don't need a lucrative position to be content. I need to feel free—or at least not to feel as if I'm at someone else's mercy. I realized that's what my mother wanted for me. It's what she meant when she said she wanted me to have options," she explained. "I've always dreamed of living near the ocean and writing a children's book, so that's what I'm going to do."

Nathan's mind couldn't take in what his ears were hearing. "You're moving to Christmas Cove?"

"Yes. This is where my heart is now. It's what you'd said would happen—I love it here so much, I never want to leave. Not permanently, anyway. If I work on the blog, I'll still travel. And obviously I'll also have to go back to Boston to pack up my apartment."

"But you came here this weekend so you could participate in Polar Bear Plunge?"

"To be honest, I'd forgotten all about the plunge until Patty asked me if that's why I returned," Celeste confessed. "I actually came back this weekend because I thought I'd left something here that I really wanted. But while I was on the plane I realized I was wrong."

"What was it you thought you'd left behind?"

"A goodbye kiss from you."

Somehow he summoned the courage to ask, "But you don't want one anymore?"

"No." She smiled slyly, tilting her chin upward. "I want a kiss *hello*."

When Nathan shivered, it wasn't from the cold.

He stepped closer and slid his fingers into Celeste's hair. Cupping her face with his palms, he held her gaze for a long moment before he moved his mouth over hers, silently expressing all the things he'd wanted to tell her.

He might have bungled his speech, but the kiss was absolutely eloquent.

After they finally separated, he said, "Hello, Celeste. Welcome back to Christmas Cove."

She laughed. He loved those dimples. Those eyes. Those lips. "Hello, Nathan," she answered. "It's great to be home."

Acknowledgments

There aren't enough words to thank my family for being a constant source of support, encouragement and inspiration. I'm very grateful to Pam Hopkins for believing in this book. Also, a huge thank-you to my editor, Anne Sowards, for her insightfulness and enthusiasm. Thanks to RCD for naming the island. Last but certainly not least, thank you to my lovely readers.

Carrie Jansen earned an MFA in creative writing and published many poems and short stories before becoming a novelist. An avid bodyboarder and beach walker, she spends as much of the year as she can on Cape Cod, where she draws inspiration for her contemporary romances. She also writes Amish romance novels under her pseudonym, Carrie Lighte.

CONNECT ONLINE

CarrieJansen.com